All my adult life I
in trouble, and th
being one…

Frank sat on the edge of his desk. "Holy shit." He looked at his shoes for a moment. "Did they say no cops?"

That surprised me. "Yes, apparently they did. How did you know?"

"You're here. Is it just the money, or is it personal?" he asked.

"What the hell—yeah, how did you know that?"

"Makes sense. This isn't about the cash. They want to make the family suffer. The cash is just dessert."

I shrugged. "So, what do we do?"

He raised an eyebrow. "We, paleface? Not we. Me. You are a cop, last I heard. When they said 'no cops' did they say 'no cops except for a friendly Detective Inspector'?"

"All right, what can you do, then?"

He went behind his desk again. He stood still, considering something. "I could use your help, you know, but not with the badge. You lose that badge, you can help. Otherwise, piss off."

"Fine. I'll lose the badge. What can I do?"

"I'll get some friends together, then I'll contact you. When are they going to contact Walsh for the money?"

"I don't know. He gave me his private number, and I told him I'd call him as soon as I had an answer. What should I tell him?"

Frank grew firmer in expression, determined. "Call him and say that three men will be at his office at…" He looked at his watch. "One this afternoon. He knows me, and I'll introduce the others to him. Tell him that if we're successful, the others will submit a bill. I won't."

I nodded. "I'll tell him. Can I meet you there then?"

"Not if you're still a cop. This is not going to be a 'by the book,' do you understand?"

"I understand."

Terror grips the city…

In a series of brutal murders, three young women have been killed on the subway, and panic spreads through the transit system. To make matters worse, one of the investigating detectives is considered a suspect. Detective Inspector Ian McBriar and his team need to track down the real killer before more lives are lost. The one thread that links the deaths together is a thin one, and the only thing the murders have in common is something that makes no sense. This may be Ian's last case: ghosts from his past, and a chance for a better future, could change his life.

Death Never Lets Go is the fourth exciting installment in the *Ian McBriar Murder Mystery* series, set in Toronto in 1978, the story of a Metis police detective who conquered bigotry, prejudice, and his own personal tragedies to succeed.

KUDOS for *Death Never Lets Go*

In *Death Never Lets Go* by Mauro Azzano, Ian McBriar is now a detective inspector with the Toronto Police Department and it's 1978. This time Ian is investigating the brutal murders of three young women, which seem to have no motive, or at least not one that makes any sense. Ian also has some personal issues to work out, from some jerk of a kid and his father who are neighborhood bullies, to one of his best friends getting into serious trouble. Ian's loyalties are tested, and he wonders if he can do his job and still be a good friend when he needs to be. And will this be Ian's last case? Things are happening in his life that make his future uncertain. As always, Azzano has crafted a tight, fast-paced mystery, with plenty of twists and turns—sure to hold your interest from beginning to end. ~ *Taylor Jones, The Review Team of Taylor Jones & Regan Murphy*

Death Never Lets Go by Mauro Azzano is the fourth book in his *Ian McBriar Murder Mystery* series. This time we are reunited with Ian, Patrick, and the gang at the Toronto Police Department, as well as Frank who is now retired from the department and working in the private sector. Ian is now a detective inspector and in charge of his investigations. This time three young woman are murdered on the transit system, and clues are slim to non-existent. The only thing the murders seem to have in common is that they all took place on the transit system or nearby. One victim is found still on the train when it gets to the end of the line, one was pushed from the platform in front of a train, and the third was tossed over a bridge into the path of an oncoming train. While Ian tries to gather clues on the murders, outside forces are conspiring to put him in an untenable position. When a close friend gets into trouble, Ian has to make a decision—continue to be a cop or help his friend. How can he choose, and what will happen to his investigation if he leaves the force? *Death Never Lets Go* is a worthy addition to the series, fast paced and hard hitting—a page turner from beginning to end. ~ *Regan Murphy, The Review Team of Taylor Jones & Regan Murphy*

Death Never Lets Go

Mauro Azzano

A Black Opal Books Publication

GENRE: CRIME THRILLER/PARANORMAL THRILLER MYSTERY/ SUSPENSE

DEATH NEVER LETS GO

Cover Design by Mauro Azzano

Print ISBN: 978-1-626946-55-2

First Publication: APRIL 2017

Published by Black Opal Books **http://www.blackopalbooks.com**

DEDICATION

To Alison, for pushing me to keep writing.

To Jennifer, Aaron, and the rest of my family. Their support and pride has helped me immensely.

A special thanks to Michael for his story idea that became the basis for this book.

Prologue

It's a summer night. The occasional sound of crickets from the field nearby, crystal clear in the hot June air, punctuates the stillness of the evening, the silence between chirps making the quiet evening seem even more hushed. A woman gets out of her truck and walks across the street, toward home. She clutches her mail—letters and bills—to be read tomorrow.

A red pickup turns the corner and drives her way. The pickup accelerates, heading straight for her now, weaving side to side in the narrow road. She holds her arm in front of her eyes, trying to see the driver over the glare of the headlights. The truck closes the distance to her now, and she hurries to get out of the way, but too late. She screams, and the truck hits her.

ↂↂ

I woke up. I sat up, rubbed my face, and looked over at Karen, on the other side of the bed.

"Bad dream?" she whispered.

"Yeah, the same one for a few nights now," I said softly. "Must be thinking about the trip back home, doing it to me." I slid back under the covers. "Get some sleep, hon."

She sighed and fell asleep. I closed my eyes, hoping to get back to sleep too. The phone rang.

"Christ, now what?" I muttered. I sat up, picked up the phone on the second ring, whispered "Hello?" and listened to the voice at the other end. "All right, come and pick me up in the morning," I said.

"Everything all right?" Karen asked.

"Just work stuff," I muttered and went back to sleep.

CHAPTER 1

"Okay, it's eight-fifteen, last chance. Who wants these scrambled eggs?" I called.

"Just toast, thanks. I've got a lunch meeting," Karen yelled from upstairs.

I turned to Ethan. "How about you, champ? Do you want eggs? They're hot."

Ethan shook his head. "I don't want eggs, Dad. Can I get Cheerio's?"

I sighed, frustrated. "Nobody wants the eggs? I hate to throw them out."

Ethan put his arms on the counter and rested his head on his wrists. "Cheerio's," he repeated.

"Man, tough crowd," I grumbled.

Behind Ethan, a small girl in pink pyjamas made her way down the staircase, stepping gingerly sideways, step by step, holding onto the railing above her for support as she went.

I grinned. "Hi, Charley, good morning."

The little girl ran up to me and grinned. "Hi, Dad."

"So, would you like scrambled eggs?" I asked, hopefully.

She stared up at me. "No. Don't want rambled eggs."

"What would you like for breakfast, then?" I asked, exasperated.

"Toast," she stated.

"Fine." I sighed. I scraped the eggs into the garbage can and closed the lid.

I turned to rinse the plate. A chime in the distance told me that there was someone at the front door. The fact that he rang the bell three times told me who it was.

"Come!" I yelled.

The front door opened. A tall, slim, man in a blue-black suit sauntered through to the kitchen counter and sat at a barstool.

He smiled at the little girl. "Good morning, pretty Charlotte," he cooed.

She giggled and smiled back. "Hi, Uncle Pat."

"Hey, Patrick, have you had breakfast?" I asked.

"No, boss, I haven't, actually," he said cheerily. "I don't suppose I could get scrambled eggs?"

I glanced at the garbage can and sighed. "Coming right up." I studied him. "I assume you're not here for a social visit?"

He glanced at Charley and Ethan. "Sorry, no, I just came to drive you to work."

"Ah," I said softly.

I beat two eggs, poured them into a frying pan, put bread in the toaster, then passed the meal to Patrick.

He nodded thanks and ate heartily. I poured him a coffee. He grunted and kept eating.

Charley watched all this, fascinated. "Dad?" she asked.

"Yes, sweetheart?"

"I want rambled eggs," she said.

Karen came downstairs, clipping on an earring, and smiled at Walsh. She smoothed her skirt and tugged at her blouse sleeves, preparing for a day at her office. "Good morning, Patrick. What brings you out this early?"

He gave her a soft smile in return. "I just wanted to bring Ian up to speed on a situation."

Karen glanced at me then back at Walsh. "Is everything all right?" she asked, worried.

He nodded his head, reassuringly. “Just doing some cleanup work, nothing serious,” he said.

Karen smiled again and nodded, not quite relaxed. “Be careful, both of you,” she said.

Chapter 2

An hour later, Patrick Walsh drove south on Yonge Street, turned right at a side road, left into the buses only entrance at the Davisville subway station, then slowed, looking for a place to park.

A man in overalls, with *Toronto Transit Commission* embroidered on the breast pocket, waved to get our attention then shooed us with both arms, pointing back at the exit. Walsh picked up the placard on his dashboard that said *Police Business* and held it high. The man read it and nodded. He pointed to a back corner of the lot. Walsh stopped at the spot the man had indicated and got out.

"So, what do we have to go on so far?" I asked.

"It looks like it could be a suicide, but something's not quite right," Walsh said.

I sighed. "Okay, where's our customer?"

Walsh spoke to the man in the coveralls, and the man led us down a back stairway, to a set of spur tracks on the far side of the subway platform. There, parked apart from the other trains, was a subway car, all on its own.

A dozen uniformed police officers, forensics men in lab coats, and subway workers in overalls wandered around the subway car, talking to each other and writing in notepads.

I pulled out my badge and held it up as I walked to the subway train, stepping gingerly over the tracks, being careful not to trip on the rocks between the rails.

One of the uniforms saw me, nodded at the badge, and yelled into the open door of the train. "Inspector's here," he called to someone inside. He waved me over. "Morning, Ian. Got a cold one for you."

"Hey, Perry." I nodded. "Have you been here long?"

He glanced at his watch. "Hour and a half or so. You got this from here, boss?"

"Yeah. Go get yourself breakfast. We got it from here," I said.

He smiled gratefully and made his way to the exit stairs, weaving between commuters waiting for the trains, and disappeared into the crowd.

The subway car had all eight doors open: three on each side, one at either end. I unbuttoned my jacket, grabbed the long bar at the end door, and swung my leg up to get on board. To my left was the tiny enclosed cubicle where the driver sat. To my right was the window seat my kids always wanted to sit at on the train, the one with a bird's eye view of the track. Down in the main part of the train car, just around the corner from the driver's booth, was a short bench. On the bench was a young woman, wearing a light tan raincoat, with a matching leather handbag and shoes. Her head was resting against the nearest window, her eyes closed, her lips slightly parted. There was pallor to her skin that could have been nothing, but the one thing that I kept staring at was a small trickle of blood coming out of one nostril.

I squatted down to face her and said a silent prayer for her soul. Walsh squatted beside me and touched her hand, softly.

"It's a shame that she had to die so young. Too young to suicide," he said, quietly.

It seemed he was trying to not disturb her. I nodded and looked at my watch: nine-fifteen.

"What makes you think it's a suicide?" I asked.

Walsh pointed. "Notice the blood stain on her nose—poison? Still, it could mean anything."

“Do we have a time of death?” I asked.

Walsh pulled out his notebook. “She was on board as the train stopped for the night. She had a bus transfer in her pocket from High Park Station, stamped last night at nine forty-three. She got on at High Park, picked up a transfer to catch a bus when she got off the subway, then supposedly killed herself? I don’t buy it.”

I smiled slightly. Walsh was good at thinking around corners. “You mean, why bother getting dressed up and getting a transfer if you don’t intend to get off the train?” I asked.

Walsh nodded. “Also, she has a sandwich in her purse. Nobody gets ready for the evening, makes a snack, then says ‘You know what? I think I’ll kill myself instead.’”

“Do we know where she was going?” I asked.

“Not yet. When the train stopped for the night, the conductor saw her, thought she was asleep, and figured he’d wake her up in a few minutes. He got busy and forgot about her, then this car was moved here for routine maintenance. The night crew found her around three—thirty.”

I huffed acknowledgement. A grunting sound behind us made us both look: a middle-aged man in a tweed jacket—the coroner—heaved himself up onto the subway, his Gladstone bag clanging against the chrome handrail as he got aboard.

He stood up straight and tugged his coat lapels, then walked right over to the dead woman.

“Morning, Ian. Patrick,” he said. Walsh nodded.

The coroner squatted, stared at the woman’s eyes for a good thirty seconds, then slipped on a pair of surgical gloves and turned her hands over. He examined her palms, rubbing them with his thumbs, and gingerly placed them back in her lap.

“So, any idea what caused her death?” I asked.

The coroner shook his head. “I’m thinking it could be poison, but I’d have to wait till the autopsy is finished to be sure. I can let you know this afternoon, around five.”

"Are you calling it now?" I asked.

He stood up. "Yes, she's officially dead."

He turned and nodded at the door of the subway. Two thin, sad-faced young men were struggling to lift an aluminum gurney onto the train. They rolled it up to the woman, unzipped a heavy black plastic bag and placed her into it. They zipped the bag closed, gathered her purse, shoes and a collapsible umbrella and put the items into a paper grocery bag, then stored the bag under the woman on the gurney.

We watched them roll the gurney to the door, lift it expertly down and carry it over the rocky track bed to the subway platform. They heaved the gurney up, subway passengers giving them a wide berth, and wheeled it to a service elevator at the end of the station.

The coroner turned back to Walsh and me.

"She isn't out of rigor yet," he said. "If I had to guess, I'd say she was killed a little after nine at night, but before two in the morning. Close enough?"

"Thanks. Poison, you said?" I asked.

"That's a preliminary. The blood out the nose could be a sign of poison, but as I say, we'll see."

He hopped off the train, then headed off to join the two men with the gurney. I pulled my Moleskine notebook out of my pocket and opened it at the first blank page.

I wrote *Thursday, June 8, 1978* then I noted the details of the day—the time, weather, subway car location, car number, and the names of all the people on the train. It occurred to me that I didn't know the name of our victim.

"Patrick, do we know who she was?" I asked.

He pulled out his Moleskine notebook. "Ah, yeah, sorry, boss." He flipped to a page and read. "Her name was Brenda Grant. We found a driver's license in her purse, along with a business card and about forty dollars. She lived on Bloor Street, across from High Park. That explains why she got on the subway there."

"So it probably wasn't robbery," I said.

"Right. Not a lot of cash on her, but some money, so it was not a robbery."

"Did she have anything else with her?" I asked.

Walsh flipped the page. "Yeah, keys. It looks like a house key, a mailbox key, and a Datsun key."

"So, she has a car. Why would she take the subway if she has a car?" I asked.

He wrinkled his nose. "I wondered that too. Maybe it's in the shop or something? Or she was going to drink and didn't want to drive? We'll check it out this morning."

I nodded. "Okay, keep me posted. I'll get a ride home to get my car—I'll meet you at the shop."

I climbed down onto the tracks, picked my way back and climbed the maintenance ladder to the platform. The cluster of commuters stared at me, as though I'd just landed from Mars. I smiled and nodded hello to them, then found a uniform and asked for a ride home.

Twenty minutes later, I was back at my house. Karen was on the phone in the den, talking to a client. Charley was playing with a pair of three-year-old twins, all chasing each other around the living room as the twins' mother tried to keep them from breaking furniture.

I walked into the living room, dodging children. "Morning, Helen," I said.

The woman nodded. "Hi, Ian. How's it going?"

"The usual mayhem," I answered. I bent down and looked at her children. "Theo, Melina, how about a big hug for uncle Ian?"

They raced over and quickly hugged my leg, then peeled off and went back to chasing Charley.

Their mother shrugged. "They're feeling lively this morning, I guess."

I nodded. "So, what's on your agenda today?"

Karen hung up the phone and smiled at me. "Hey, you. We just got the contract we were after—we're going to lease out a small apartment building. It means we're getting noticed. If we do well here, the developer will give us other buildings as they're ready to occupy. It could be a very big deal for us."

"Wow. Does that mean I can retire and have you support me?" I asked.

She smirked. "Sure. Of course, you'll have to earn your keep, you realize."

"But I thought—didn't you say you were going to the office today?" I asked.

"I have a couple of meetings I can't reschedule," Helen answered. "Karen's taking the kids while I go in. She'll go in this afternoon."

Karen and Helen had found a niche, leasing out new apartment complexes. They were very good at it, and developers saw them as well worth their commission. One watched the younger children while the other worked, and that way both were able to work. The arrangement seemed to benefit both women.

"Ah," I said, remembering something. "Frank was going to drop over on Saturday, but I promised to hold a barbecue for the department. I assume you don't mind a crowd?"

Helen chuckled. "I'm sure he'll enjoy catching up with his old buddies. We'll be here."

"Great. Meanwhile, I have to get to the shop," I said. I wrapped an arm around Karen and kissed her passionately. "See you later, sweetheart." Kneeling down I put my hand on the back of Charley's head. "Bye, Charlotte. See you tonight."

She giggled. "Bye, dad."

I slid into my Caprice, pulled out of my garage, made my way onto Keele Street, then headed north toward the Fifty-two Division police station. I turned on the radio, picked up the microphone and waited for a pause in the chatter.

"Dispatch, Fifty-two zero six," I said.

"Go, zero six," said a voice.

"Morning, Nadine. Any messages?" I asked.

"Good morning, Ian. No messages."

"Thanks, dispatch. Zero six out."

I parked at Fifty-two Division, behind the painted plaque on the concrete curb which read "DI McBriar."

There was a stack of manila file folders on the seat beside me—the tedious, but inevitable, paperwork that came with the job. I got out of the car, walked around to the passenger side, scooped the papers up in both arms, and managed to straighten them so that they wouldn't scatter onto the roadway, then carried them to the front door.

As I wondered how to open the door without dumping everything, a familiar reflection in the glass came up toward me.

I turned to look at him. "Hi, Terry, can you get this door for me?" I asked.

"Sure thing." Terry Parker said cheerily. He held the door open wide and let me in first.

I thanked him and went past the front desk, through the doorway to the detectives' room at the back of the building. I dropped the paperwork on the corner of my desk and sat down. I had only three weeks to sort through them—personnel reports, overtime authorizations, expense claims and the like, before month end. Then I was taking some time off. There was a glass paperweight on my desk, a souvenir of my honeymoon in Venice, and there were six or seven pink telephone message slips under it. I flipped through them, deciding which to answer first.

One of the secretaries walked up to me and automatically placed a mug of coffee on my desk. "Good morning, Ian," she said. "Anything for me in this stack?"

"Good morning. Yep," I answered. I took the top two manila folders and handed them to her. "These are done. The rest should be done by next Friday. Enjoy."

She nodded. "Thanks. They aren't due till early July, though."

"I know. I'm going to be off then, though," I said.

"Are you going on vacation somewhere?" she asked cheerily.

I shook my head. "Memorial service, in Saskatchewan."

"Ah, right. I forgot. Sorry." She winced and left.

ᘛᘚᘛᘚ

I worked at my desk for the next two hours, answering phone calls, requisitioning office supplies and following up leads on old cases. By now it was after eleven in the morning. The sun had moved high overhead, and the pavement outside was hot. Every time somebody opened the front door, a whiff of asphalt came into the detectives' room. I needed to take a breather. I stretched and rolled my head, then shook my arms loosely and stood up.

Another puff of hot asphalt-tinged air washed in from the parking lot, and I looked up to see who had opened the door. Patrick Walsh, my Sergeant, was talking to a pretty woman in an olive green pants suit and low heels. They spoke briefly and walked over to me.

"Hey, Patrick, any news?" I asked.

He nodded to his new detective constable. "Why don't you tell him, Alex?"

She nodded. "Yes, boss. The dead lady, Brenda Grant, lived in an apartment building across from High Park. We interviewed her landlord. She lived alone, no complaints, no boyfriends, no trouble, and she'd just started a new job. She was very excited about it, he says. I agree with what Sergeant Walsh said—it doesn't sound like suicide."

I sighed. "Okay. Any word from our coroner yet? I don't suppose he has anything solid yet, but I'm curious if he has any ideas."

Reynolds pulled out a flip-up notebook. "I spoke to him, and they just got the body washed and prepped, but he seems confident he'll be able to tell us by later today. Anything else?"

I shook my head. "Nope. Keep up the good work, Alex. Anything from your end, Patrick?"

Walsh shook his head. “Early days, Ian. We’ll keep you posted.”

I smiled at the constable. “So, Alex, how do you like plain clothes?”

She gave me a wide grin. “It’s even better than I had hoped. I like this job, Inspector.”

I frowned. “There is one problem, though. I’m not happy with an aspect of your work.”

Her face fell. “Sorry?” She looked at Walsh. His face was stony.

I reached into my drawer and pulled out a new Moleskine book. I handed it to her ceremoniously, with both hands. “You are not in uniform any more, Detective Constable Alexandra Katherine Reynolds. Here—this is what my detectives use to write down their notes.”

A small group of men in the room started whooping and clapping. Reynolds turned beet red and covered her face with the Moleskine. She looked at it, then at Walsh, who was grinning at the initiation rite, then at me. “Thank you, sir. Thank you very much.”

I smiled. “Good. Now that we’ve settled that, get to work, both of you.”

Reynolds tucked the book under her arm and walked to her desk, taking congratulatory handshakes and good wishes from the other detectives in the room.

I nodded her way. “How’s she doing?” I asked Walsh.

“Fearless—she doesn’t hesitate to ask questions or knock on doors. She’s very direct, but also very tactful. I’m not sure I could have gotten the same information she did today. Maybe it’s just that men are more likely to talk to a pretty woman, but she can be very driven, very focused when she needs to be.”

I brought up something I needed to ask. “Still, you are keeping it platonic with her, then?”

Walsh shrugged. “Yes. Absolutely. Can you think of a faster way to derail my career?”

"You do know I had to ask you, Patrick. Thanks for the reassurance, though."

Walsh smiled. "No problem, boss. Ah, by the way, Miss Grant's car key in her purse, remember? She had a 1973 Datsun 610. It started right up, and I drove it around the block. Nothing wrong with it I could find, so she must have left it home because she was going to drink or stay out late or something."

"But why make a sandwich?" I asked. "If I was going out for the evening, that's not the kind of snack I'd bring. That doesn't make any sense."

Walsh nodded and went to his desk. "Sounded odd to me, too. Let me think about that one."

I turned back to sit down again, but a hand across the room waved at me. I walked toward it.

Captain Van Hoeke, his slicked back hair thinning and gray in streaks, waited for me to follow him to his office then sat at his desk.

I followed and sat across from him. He pointed a pencil at the door, and I closed it.

He leaned back, cradled his head in his linked hands, and nodded. "So, what do we have on the board today?"

"The dead woman on the subway—we're trying to figure out if it was suicide. It could be, but it seems unlikely. Something's out of place."

"'If it walks like a duck, and quacks like a duck?'" Van Hoeke said.

"Right. 'If you're suspicious, then it's a suspicious death,'" I quoted.

Van Hoeke nodded slowly. "Good, keep me posted. How's Patrick doing with our newest detective?"

"He likes her. So do I. She's smart, and she's energetic. I think she'll do well," I said.

"No roving eye in her direction?" Van Hoeke asked.

"Nope. Patrick sees her as forbidden fruit. I saw that from day one, and he reiterated it this morning."

Van Hoeke reached behind him and picked up a sheet of

paper. "Good. Now, you're off as of…the twenty sixth, coming back in three weeks, right?"

"Right."

He put down the paper and glanced up at me. "You're sure you only need three weeks, Ian?"

"Yes, boss. That'll be fine."

"All right. Next important topic, what are you cooking on Saturday?"

"It's a surprise. Nobody knows but me."

Van Hoeke smirked. "Yes, Rebecca tried to wheedle it out of Karen, but she couldn't find out anything either. It's quite a feat to stump my wife."

"She'll find out Saturday, then." I grinned. "I've got to get back to work, Captain."

I went back to my desk.

By mid-afternoon, I had done about half of the paperwork in the stack. I called the coroner, and he suggested I pick up the preliminary autopsy report.

I drove to the morgue, a brand new facility on College Street, and waited in the reception area for the coroner. He had changed out of his surgical garb and was wearing the same suit he had on in the morning. He walked out through a thick door, solid metal except for a small wired-glass window, and waved a couple of sheets of paper in his hand.

"Hello, Ian," he said genially. "Well, we know what killed her now. Care to guess?"

He handed me the papers.

I shook my head. "No, that's your job. I bring you the what, you tell me the how."

I glanced at the papers. There was the standard medical language, notes from the autopsy and a page with the outline of a body, an X in red ink over the left breast.

"What am I looking at?" I asked.

"She was stabbed. A sharp knife, possibly a stiletto or something similar."

"How would she have been stabbed, then?" I asked. "And where?"

"I found a puncture mark, through the skin and into the heart. It's what made me suspect a stiletto in the first place."

"No chance that the wound was from a previous injury, I'm guessing?" I asked.

"No. it was a fresh wound. It went directly through her clothes, into her left ventricle. She would have been dead in seconds."

"A puncture. So, what—someone walked up to her with a knife and just stabbed her?"

The coroner nodded.

"That doesn't make sense though, does it?" I mumbled. "I mean, she looked calm, peaceful, not like she'd been fighting off someone jabbing a knife into her. Why would she let someone do that to her—walk up and stab her with a blade?"

The coroner shrugged. "I did my job. The 'how' is my job. The 'why' is your job. You go do it."

I thought for a moment. "It could have been a woman that did it, then, right? Not just a man?"

"Sure. It doesn't take much effort to stab someone."

"Are you finished with the autopsy, then?" I asked.

"Not totally, but I had a feeling you'd want this to go on. We'll have the final results by tonight."

I nodded. "All right, good. Thanks, doc. Talk to you later." I turned to leave.

"Hey!" he called after me. "Are we still on for Saturday?"

I smiled. "Sure. Bring your wife."

He grinned. "What are you making this time?"

"It's a secret. You'll find out Saturday," I said. I drove back to my office.

I spent the rest of the day sifting through information about the dead woman. There wasn't much there, but one detail stuck in my mind.

She had recently started a new job, Walsh had told me. Where was she working? Where did she work before that?

Just before five, Walsh and Reynolds came back and

dropped off some paperwork. I waved at them to come closer.

They sat across from me. I handed the coroner's sheets of paper to Walsh, and he read them before passing them to Reynolds.

"Stabbed, huh? Not much blood for a stabbing, though," he said.

Reynolds nodded. "Yeah, you'd expect a pool of blood, right?"

I shook my head. "That's in the movies. Depending on where and how someone is stabbed it can be relatively clean. Any more information about her?"

Reynolds pulled her Moleskine out of her jacket pocket and opened it. "She started working at this new job about three weeks ago, her landlord says. She was giving him post-dated checks for the rent, because she had changed banks recently, so she gave him new ones as of June first."

"Where did she work?" I asked.

"She was a receptionist for a law office downtown, at University and Dundas."

Reynolds flipped pages as she spoke. "They say she applied for the job in April, and started there in May."

"How was she doing there?" I asked.

Reynolds nodded. "I talked to one of the clerks about her. She was very competent, very personable, and was reorganizing their paperwork to boot. I also asked about office romance, and they told me that she had been asked out by a couple of the lawyers, but she was firm about no hanky-panky at work."

Walsh smirked. "Hanky-panky? Who's your mom—Doris Day?"

I chuckled. "All right, then. Tomorrow, I want you to—" The phone rang. "Ian McBriar," I said. I listened to the man on the phone and grunted understanding. I made a scribbled note, thanked him, and put the phone down. "Well, that certainly changes things," I said. "Apparently, she was also pregnant."

Reynolds turned to a page in her Moleskine. "She went to church." She flipped pages back and forth, looking for something. "Jarvis Street Baptist Church. I spoke to the pastor there, and he says that she'd been going regularly for six years. It could be even longer, but he's only been there since 1972. Do you think that she might have been involved with someone at her church?"

"How did you know she went there?" I asked.

"She had their phone number in her address book. That's why I called their pastor."

Walsh stared at her. "When did you call him?"

"At lunch today."

He shook his head. "Is there only one of you, or do you have a superhuman twin?"

Reynolds frowned, puzzled.

"He's complimenting your enthusiasm." I smiled. "Good work, Alex."

Chapter 3

At five-thirty, I pulled into my driveway and parked behind Karen's car. Helen's car was parked on the street, and from inside the house as I opened the door, I could hear the squealing of three small children.

"I'm home!" I called.

Karen's voice came back. "In the kitchen!"

I dropped my car keys on the hallstand and wandered through to the kitchen. Karen and Helen, as they often did, were talking over each other and finishing each other's sentences.

I wrapped an arm around Karen and squeezed her, then gave her a passionate kiss.

"Hey, hon. How was your day?" I asked.

Helen gave me a mock frown. "No kiss for me?"

I shook my head. "Frank would kill me. So, what did you two ladies get up to today?"

"Well," Helen said. "We signed a contract for a new high-rise in Etobicoke. A hundred and fifty-eight units, all for us. That one was mine. Karen got a lead on another one for this August, on Lawrence Avenue. It's fewer units, but it's commercial, so the fees are higher."

"Nice." I smiled. "So, can I retire and buy that Porsche after all?"

"Only if we don't eat," Karen said.

Helen smirked. "Speaking of which, what's going on

with the barbecue Saturday? Rebecca Van Hoeke has been pestering me, but I keep telling her I'm in the dark about it. What are you making, Ian?"

I shrugged. "You'll find out Saturday. It's a secret. Nobody but me knows."

Karen nodded agreement. "He's kept it a secret from me too. Whatever—I don't mind."

Helen looked at her watch. "Anyway, I should get home. Frank will be wondering where we are. Are all the application forms filled out, Karen?"

Karen handed her a stack of paper. "Yeah, the ones turned upside down look like they're going to be rejected, but the rest should go through all right. Do you want to sort them tonight or tomorrow?"

Helen scooped up the stack and stuck it under her arm. "No, I'll go through them tonight. We'll get a fresh start on the new applicants tomorrow. Talk to you later. Come on, kids."

She gently herded Theo and Melina ahead of her and they went out to her car.

I watched them go and turned to face Karen. "So, what's for dinner?"

She smirked. "It's a surprise, unless you tell me what's on the menu Saturday."

I grinned. "A surprise it is, then."

Karen huffed in mild irritation. "You won't even tell your wife what you're making, then?"

"Sure," I said. "On Saturday."

ଓଓ

Friday morning. At seven-thirty, I was eating toast and reading the newspaper, savouring a leisurely breakfast and mentally winding down for the weekend. I heard Karen's slippers, scuffing the carpet as she came down the stairs, and automatically poured a coffee for her.

She wandered into the kitchen, grunted a 'morning' and took the mug from me. She took a large sip, letting the coffee warm her as it slid down her throat, then she let out a satisfied sigh.

"Ah. Good morning, sweetheart," she said. She stretched back and tucked her elbows behind her head, her breasts flattening slightly against her tank top, and a strip of skin showing above her pajama pants.

I leaned forward and playfully kissed her navel. The unexpected touch made her stand up straight. She glared at me for a second, then grinned widely.

"What are you—fourteen?" she asked.

I smiled. "In my mind, yes. Always will be."

She took another sip of coffee. "So, do you need me to buy anything for tomorrow? Anything at all?"

"Nope, thanks."

"Nothing you need to set up, or defrost, or whatever?" she probed.

I took a sip of my coffee. "I've got it covered, thanks."

She popped bread into the toaster and turned to face me, wrinkling her nose as she decided how to ask what she was thinking. "Are we going to have something unusual? Like a regional delicacy or something?"

I shrugged. "Depends on your point of view, I guess."

She shook her head, defeated. "Better be damn good, that's all I can say," she muttered.

She leaned forward to get jam from a lower shelf, and her top bowed open, showing skin down to her navel. I hooked a finger into the neck of her shirt and pulled it out.

"Enjoying the view?" she asked.

"Uh huh," I said. "Always have."

She leaned close to me and rubbed her breasts against my chest. "So, what would I have to do to make you tell me what you're cooking?"

I smiled. "You'd have to wait till tomorrow." She frowned and leaned back then poked her tongue out at me. I kissed the outstretched tongue. She withdrew it and smiled sheepishly. "Wow, that was exciting," I teased. "Stick it out again."

She chuckled. "Later. I have to work today, by the way. I'm dropping Charlotte at Helen's, and I should be in the Kipling Avenue office till four, if you need me."

"All right." I nodded. I turned to make a note on the family calendar, stuck to the side of the fridge. The phone on the wall rang, and I turned around to answer it.

"Hello?" I said.

Walsh's voice came through, not quite panicky, but urgent. "Hey, Ian, got a situation here. Can you come meet us?"

I picked up a scribble pad and pen. "Go," I said.

"Dufferin subway station, northwest corner of Dufferin and Bloor," he said.

"Ok, what do we have?" I asked.

"Another body. I'd like your perspective on this one, boss."

I looked at my watch. "I'll be there in fifteen minutes."

I grabbed my gun and badge and tossed my jacket over my arm. Karen sat up from her toast and stared at me.

"Is anything wrong?" she asked.

"Yeah, I think Patrick wants some help on this one. I'll call you this afternoon."

She frowned. "Be careful, all right? Be careful. Ian, are you listening to me?"

I nodded. "Not to worry, hon. I'm just there to give an opinion. See you later." I put my hand behind her head and gave her a long kiss. "Bye," I said.

Chapter 4

It took me less than ten minutes to get to the subway station—down Rogers Road, right on Dufferin, then straight south till I got to the subway stop. I put my gumball on the roof and only used the siren to blip slower drivers out of the way.

When I arrived, there was a fire truck, an ambulance, two yellow cruisers and Walsh's plain beige LTD already clustered around the entrance to the subway. A man in a navy jacket with 'TTC Supervisor' embroidered on it paced the sidewalk, puffing on a cigarette stub. I got out of my car and walked toward the man. He waved a clipboard at me and shook his head.

"Sorry, the station's closed. Please go to the bus stop on the other side of the street," he said.

I held up my badge. "I'm here to meet my sergeant," I said. "You have a dead body?"

The man looked over his shoulder then back at me. "Hell, yeah. Second one in two days. We usually only get a couple bodies a year. This does not look good for the Transit Commission."

"Right," I said. "Where am I going?"

"Down the stairs, go right and follow the Eastbound train line signs. We got that track blocked off, but the Westbound trains are still coming through, so it's kind of busy down there."

I walked down the steps, a rush of cool air blowing up toward me as a train approached the station. There was the whistle of brakes as the train stopped, and a sshhh sound as the doors opened. Before I could turn the corner and move out of the way, a cluster of people, some with their head down and some looking straight at me, stomped up the stairs past me. The sudden rush of commuters made my claustrophobia come back, a mild case of the shivers that passed as soon as they went by. Around the corner from me, the subway's doors went sshhh again and I heard a soft whine as the train left, sucking air back down the stairs as it went.

I turned right as instructed, down the steps the commuters had just come up, to a set of sawhorses and yellow tape across a different stairway. I stepped over the tape and made my way down those steps. A uniform with a grim expression glared at me, so I held up my badge. His face softened, he nodded and waved me around the corner.

At the subway platform, two ambulance attendants were unfolding a gurney off to one side, while a transit worker waited, pacing, beside them. In the pit below, where the trains usually ran, I could see the top of Walsh's head gesturing and calling orders to a handful of uniforms.

His suit, a gray silk, reflected the red traffic signals in the subway tunnel when the angle was right, and flashed pale from the overhead lights when he looked up. He saw me, nodded without missing a breath, and kept talking to the uniforms. They nodded and scattered to follow his orders.

I walked over to where the ambulance attendants were waiting and looked over the edge of the platform. In the pit, sprawled across two train tracks, was a woman, in her early thirties, it seemed, wearing a tailored jacket and a black skirt, face up, her eyes open in panic. She could have just been lying there scared, but for the frozen expression in her eyes. She was dead.

I said a quick prayer for her soul then leaned a little closer. I hadn't noticed it before, but the train had cut off her right arm just below the elbow, and her right foot at the ankle. Two pools of blood, oozing into the concrete, made a garish red figure eight beside her. As my eyes became accustomed to the dim light in the pit, I saw that the train had hit her face too, peeling her right ear and cheek completely off the scalp, and crushing her skull on that side.

I stood up and looked around. At the other end of the platform was Reynolds, talking to a train conductor. He seemed ready to either throw up or pass out any moment, but she smiled softly, touching his arm and nodding as she spoke, calming him down. She saw me, blinked slowly to acknowledge me, and spoke to the conductor for another minute. She led him by the forearm to a bench and got him sitting, said something to him that made him smile weakly, then she came over to me.

"Hello, Alex. So, are you still glad you took this job?" I asked.

"Morning, boss. Yes, very much so, sir, despite the messy stuff." Her expression went suddenly hard. "We got a call—this woman was on the platform, waiting for the train, when all of a sudden, according to witnesses, she jumped in front of it. No explanation, no scream, nothing."

"You think she jumped, or was she pushed?" I asked.

"I'm not sure," Reynolds said, furrowing her brow. "She had a transfer in her hand. Why grab a transfer if you're going to jump? That sounds like the one from yesterday, though, doesn't it?"

I frowned. "Yeah. Murder makes more sense. Did our witnesses see anybody push her?"

Reynolds shook her head. "No luck. Everyone was looking down the tunnel at the oncoming train, and she was at the end of the row of people. Ironically, if she'd been fifty feet further down the track, it would have slowed to a crawl by then, and she might have survived the hit."

I shook my head. "Why does this not seem logical? Why would someone do it that way?"

Reynolds nodded. "Exactly. I was thinking about that. If

I wanted to push somebody in front of a train. I'd look for her at the end of a line of people and wait till they're all looking away, then I'd push her in front of the train."

"There you go." I nodded. "Pass that idea on to Sergeant Walsh."

She grinned and headed over to the edge of the platform. She squatted down, motioning at me with her pen as she explained her theory to Walsh. He glanced my way, smiled, and nodded.

Walsh spoke to a uniform in the pit, climbed up a metal stairway and came over to join me. "Hey, Ian. How are we this fine morning?"

"Good. Seems you have everything in hand. How's Alex doing?"

He glanced over his shoulder at her. "She's going to be a sergeant by next year at this rate. I'm glad to have her on my team."

We both looked at the platform. Reynolds was making expansive gestures, waving at one stairwell as she spoke to the uniforms, nodding at them and getting agreement for something, then she stood up and joined us.

"All right," she said. "The coroner is here, and he's transporting the body to the morgue now. Do you have anything else for me to do, Sergeant?"

Walsh looked over his shoulder. A uniform was gingerly lifting a plastic bag with a foot and a hand in it, placing it with the body on the gurney.

"Carry on, Alex. Keep me posted," Walsh said.

"Ah," I said, remembering. "I suppose both of you are coming over tomorrow?"

Reynolds nodded. "Wouldn't miss it for the world, boss."

Walsh grinned. "Yeah, like I'd pass up a free meal at your place."

"Are you bringing a date, Patrick?" I asked.

"Yes, I'm bringing someone," Walsh said, cautiously. "See you there."

I made my way up the stairs and back to my car. The man with the embroidered jacket and the clipboard was pacing out front, sucking on a palmed cigarette and waving his clipboard at commuters, directing them toward a bus across the street. He sighed, his shoulders sagged, and he tapped his watch.

"Look, do you know how long your people are going to be here?" he grunted. "We got to get the trains running again. My supervisors are getting really pissed at me."

"I understand." I nodded. "Do you want to come down to the tracks and help pick up the severed body parts? That should speed things up."

The man glared at me for a few seconds. "Very funny. Just snap it up, all right?"

"We'll be done today, that's all I can promise," I said.

I went back to my car and drove to the station.

I read through the autopsy report on the first woman, looking for something I'd missed, something that would let me know where to look. There was nothing. She was just riding on the subway, and someone stabbed her. Why? Also, did they just rush up and do it when she wasn't looking? Did they threaten her, coerce her, then stab her? I didn't see that on her face, though. When I saw her, her face was calm, at ease, as though she was expecting the blade, welcoming it, not afraid of it.

By four fifty-five, I was exhausted. I'd read, signed, approved and forwarded forms all afternoon, and I just needed to go home. There were a dozen or so men in the detectives' room, wrapping up for the week, like me. I stood at one corner of the room and waited till their talking subsided to a low rumble.

"Can I get your attention?" I called out. The sound stopped and they all looked at me.

"All right. Now, you all know that we found a second body today, right?"

They all nodded and grunted agreement.

"She was apparently pushed in front of a subway train, at

Dufferin station. We're interviewing witnesses, but it doesn't look like anybody saw what happened. Okay. Now, anybody needs more information, the folder is on my desk. Read through it, and don't hesitate to pass on any ideas. We're really stumped right now, so no idea is a bad idea. All right?"

One man's hand came up from the middle of the room. "What about tomorrow?" he called.

"Right, the barbecue. How many of you are coming?" I asked. All the hands went up. "So, at least four?" I joked.

The men laughed. I nodded. "Good, bring a date. Nobody will be allowed on my property before twelve-thirty. But if you arrive after two, I can't guarantee you any food."

The men laughed again. The same hand went back up. "What are you making, boss?"

"You'll find out tomorrow," I answered. "But dress western—cowboy duds. See you all then."

I threw my jacket over my arm and headed out to my car. I called dispatch and let them know I was off duty till Monday, then drove the ten minutes down Keele Street toward home.

I pulled into the driveway, opened the garage door and parked on the far left side, giving enough room for Karen to park when she got home. I went up the stairs to the kitchen, looked around and listened. Not a sound.

I poked my head up the base of the stairs. "Hi!" I called. Again, silence.

I shrugged and opened the fridge door. There was a wedge of cheesecake in there, and it was all mine. I munched on forkfuls of it and sipped a glass of milk, sitting at the table and listening to jazz on the radio. Grover Washington oozed through the house, a mellow sax that slowed my pulse and got me calmed down just listening to it. I flipped quickly through the morning paper, reading parts I hadn't had a chance to read earlier.

A sound from the front door made me look up. The door opened and Karen shooed Charley in ahead of her, then trailed Ethan behind her. She shuffled, trying not to trip over the little girl, and glanced up at me. She smiled. "Hey, you. Have you been home long?" she asked.

"Hi, hon. No, just a few minutes," I said. "Whose cheesecake is this?" I pointed my fork at the few remaining crumbs.

"Helen brought it over. She got it from a bakery uptown," Karen said. "How is it?"

I nodded, munching. "Not bad. Pretty good."

"Good. I'll let her know. Are you making dinner tonight?" she asked.

"Yep. Then I have some prep work to do in the basement," I said.

I put the empty glass and plate in the sink and walked around to meet Karen.

"Hey, you," I said. I gave her a warm hug and kiss. "How was your day, hon?"

"Good. We got most of a floor rented today, I think, unless a ton of credit applications are bad. Still, we'll probably be in that building till late July, by the looks of it. How about you?"

I winced. "A bad one, on the subway. We'll see—Patrick and Alex are on it. They're there now."

I bent down and playfully pinched Charley's nose between my fingers. "How about you, sweetheart? Did you have fun today?"

Charley grinned, her cheeks dimpling like Shirley Temple. "Hi, Dad. I made a s'prise."

I gasped. "Wow. A surprise? For me?"

Charley held out a sheet of paper with popsicle sticks and pasta glued to it. I took it from her and smiled.

"That is so lovely, thank you," I said. I clutched it to my chest. "Thank you, sweetheart." I gave her a big kiss on the forehead. She wiped her head with the back of her hand and giggled.

"All right, everyone relax—dinner will be in a half hour," I said.

I stuck Charley's work of art on the fridge and pulled out food. I sliced up chicken, vegetables and salad stuff, and had Ethan set the table. Karen finished up some paperwork as I grilled the chicken, tossed peppers and sprouts in soy sauce and fried them up. Charley watched me, fascinated. She was mesmerized as the food flipped up out of the pan, turning an arc in the air and falling back down into the pan again.

I called everyone for dinner and set the food out. Charley struggled up to her high chair, Ethan held the side of it steady, and I made sure everyone was seated and eating.

Karen wolfed down the first few bites of her chicken and vegetables, then slowed down and sighed.

"Gosh, it's been a long week, you know?" she said. "I'm really looking forward to tomorrow."

I nodded. "Good, glad to hear it."

"So, what are we having?" Karen asked, casually.

I grinned. "You'll find out in eighteen hours."

After dinner, Ethan played with a new toy in his room, Karen got Charley into pajamas, then she sat down with me in the living room. I read some progress reports while Karen stacked rental brochures, and soon we'd both put work away and watched something mindless on TV.

Karen stroked my hair, looking over at me, examining me.

"What?" I asked.

She frowned, the way she always did when she was going to say something silly, and pursed her lips. "Have you ever thought of shaving off your moustache?" she asked.

"Why? It took me years to grow it," I said, puzzled.

She held up two fingers in front of my mouth and squinted. "I dunno. It might make you look younger."

I shrugged. "Why? Does it tickle your navel when we.. you know…"

She laughed out loud and backhanded my arm playfully. "You idiot. No, that's not what I mean. I just think it makes you seem…more mature, that's all."

"Older," I said.

"Yes."

"'Old gray fart' older, or just 'I could be golfing on weekends' older?"

She leaned back, plopped her feet into my lap and closed her eyes. "Rub my ankles, Ian."

"Yes, Miss Scarlett," I said, in a Southern accent.

ꕤ

By ten-thirty, both children were fast asleep, and we were in bed, reading. The night was warm, with summer just around the corner, and we were near the longest day of the year. Even at nine, when the kids were already in bed, there was a soft blue glow in the western horizon. A scent of mown lawn and pine wafted up from the open window, reminding me that the barbecue would fill the yard with people. Karen was in a tank top and briefs. I was in boxers.

She sat cross-legged on top of the sheets, flipping through a copy of *Cosmopolitan*, as I skimmed a cookbook for final tips on my upcoming event.

Karen leaned toward me and poked my arm. "Listen to this," she said. "'After the age of thirty-five, men often lose interest in sex with their wife and are likely to cheat.' What do you think?"

"Hmm?" I asked.

"Do you think you'll lose interest in sex with me and want to cheat?" she asked.

"I dunno, maybe," I joked.

She reached under the sheets and slipped her hand into my boxers. She caressed the inside of my thigh, still reading her magazine. "So wives are supposed to find a way to keep their husbands interested in them. What do you think?"

I put the book down and leaned back. "I think I should buy you a subscription to this magazine."

Karen giggled and got up onto her knees. She peeled off

her top and threw one leg over my chest. "So, are you bored with me, then?"

I rubbed my hands up and down her back, then slid them into the back of her briefs.

"Ask me in an hour," I purred.

I flipped her onto her back and climbed on top of her. I fumbled with my boxers, finally using my toes to peel them off and toss them onto the floor. I pulled her briefs down and threw them on the floor too. I held her wrists up, over her head, and kissed her from the inside of the elbow on her left arm, across to her breasts, then out to the inside of her right elbow.

Karen squirmed beneath me, sighing with delight and anticipation. She had a smile on her face, waiting for me to lean down and kiss her. I bent down and kissed her navel, then moved up and kissed the valley between her breasts, the underside of her neck, and finally her lips. I moved my arms to hold onto her hips, and she wrapped her arms around my neck. We made love.

Even after five years together, every time I felt her skin against mine, every time I felt her leg muscles throbbing as we made love, it felt like the first time. Only better. We finished with Karen on top of me, collapsing onto me, stroking my calf with her ankle.

I threw my hands out to my sides. "Wow," I said. "You got all that from a magazine?"

"You helped. The magazine didn't do all of it," Karen said.

I sighed. "I'm definitely going to get you a subscription."

She folded her hands, one on top of the other on my chest and rested her chin on them. "Still not going to tell me what's on the menu?" she teased.

"I'll tell you in the morning," I said. "Want some ginger ale?"

She nodded.

"Be right back," I said. I put my boxers back on and tiptoed down the hall.

I passed Ethan's room, listening to hear him sleep. He was lying on his back, his mouth open, the covers scrunched down at his ankles. I pulled his sheets up and he grunted something, then rolled onto his side, still asleep. I opened the door to Charley's room and checked on her. She was curled up in a ball, her stuffed doll held tight against her stomach. I went downstairs and poured two glasses of ginger ale, then came back up and gave one to Karen.

"So, the question I asked an hour ago. You're still not tired of me?" she asked, mischievously.

I grinned. "How could I possibly be tired of you?"

She sat up, the light from a half-moon out the window outlining her bosom. She took a sip of ginger ale and put her glass on the night table beside her.

"Right answer, you smooth talker, you." She tugged at the waistband of my boxers and pulled me close. She leaned forward and nibbled at the skin around my navel, then wrapped her hands around my backside and softly kissed above and below the navel.

She pulled out the waistband again and looked in. "Boy, I still have the touch, don't I?"

CHAPTER 5

At six-thirty in the morning, I got up and made coffee. I set up frypans for eggs and French toast, mentally taking note of what I still had to do. By seven-thirty, everyone was awake and downstairs, munching happily on breakfast. I scooped dirty plates into the dishwasher as soon as they were empty, and looked down at my watch. Five hours till the barbecue. Just enough time.

I went down to the basement, hauled out a pair of large metal drum halves, cut the long way so they formed big troughs when set down, and carried them up to the backyard.

I arranged cinder blocks to rest them on, then I brought up bags of charcoal and metal grills to rest over the drums. I got the charcoal burning in both, then laid the grills over them.

I went back downstairs and brought up a small portable gas barbecue, some tools, and a couple of heavy picnic coolers. The coolers held what had been filling the downstairs fridge a few moments before—pounds of beef ribs, sausages, pork chops, and gallons of homemade chili.

By ten in the morning, I'd set up an assembly line for my barbecue. The ribs were on a low heat, warming the bones without searing the meat yet. The chili was on the gas at a simmer, and the rest of the food, condiments, thick bread, buns and utensils were on a long side table. Two other tables sat off to one side, draped in gingham cloth and covered with paper plates and plastic cutlery, waiting patiently for people to show up.

I knew that some people could not wait till twelve thirty to show up. I quietly bet myself that the first guest would show up just after noon. I quickly checked the food, confident that I could leave it alone for a few minutes, and went inside to change. I put on my red plaid shirt, my skinny cowboy jeans, and pulled my riding boots out of the closet. I got out a square cardboard box and retrieved my Stetson hat, the oxblood red felt adorned with images of buffalo and horses in intricate beadwork. This barbecue would be an homage to Saskatchewan, and I wanted to get everybody in the western mood.

From the den, I pulled out another, larger cardboard box, and brought it up to the backyard. It contained a stack of straw cowboy hats, purchased for this barbecue.

Charley was dressed in jeans and a plaid tee shirt, and Ethan had been given clothes like mine to wear for today. I told them that when a guest arrived, he or Charley should give them a hat and say "howdy."

I saw him whispering to his sister, conspiring with her about something. I leaned down and smiled at Charley.

"Okay, sweetheart, so when people come over, what do you say to them?"

"Daddy."

"No, not Daddy. 'Howdy.' Can you say that?"

She giggled. "Daddy."

I huffed, in mock irritation. "No, you say 'howdy.' Can you say 'howdy'?"

"Daddy." She giggled and squealed at the joke.

I rolled my eyes and feigned frustration. In fact, her sense of humor was keen, and that made me very proud.

I thought of something. "Okay, Charlotte, what's my name?"

"Howdy," she said.

She and Ethan roared with laughter. I grinned to myself,

took a large straw hat out of the box and placed it on Charley's head. It went over her ears and rested on her shoulders. She lifted it up, pouted for a second, then put it down again, laughing with glee.

Eleven-thirty. I had stirred, seasoned and tasted the vat of chili, then basted the ribs with a homemade sauce. I had marinated the pork chops till they were soft enough to cut with the side of a fork. Now I just had to wait for the first wave of people to arrive.

I could have predicted who would be the first person to come. I could have also predicted almost word-for-word what he would say. I would have been right on both counts. My old partner, Frank Burghezian, now working at a security think-tank downtown, sauntered down the side path and into my back yard, a couple of minutes before noon.

"Hey, Ian," he said, casually, looking around. "Just figured I'd come over early in case you, um, needed any help." His eyes scanned the food sizzling over the metal drums.

"Hey, Frank." I smiled. "I'm glad you're here. I need someone to test the chili and tell me if it's okay."

He looked at me the way a starving man looks at a steak. "Sure, no problem. You bet."

I leaned down and picked a straw hat from the box beside me. "Well, first, you have to dress the part. It's a western barbecue." I handed him the hat. He grinned and put it on his head.

He spread his arms wide. "Does this hat make my ass look big?"

"It's not the hat, Frank," I joked. I scooped a ladle of chili from the cauldron and doled it into a bowl for him. I put the bowl on a large plate, with a fat spoon and a thick slab of toast.

"There you go," I said, handing it to him.

He took a spoonful in his mouth and chewed it, tasting the flavor.

"So, does it pass muster?" I asked.

He looked down at the bowl. "Can I get this intravenously? Really, Ian, you've topped yourself with this stuff."

He went back to the chili, scooping it feverishly into his mouth. "Mm. Yeah, real good, man."

Karen sauntered out in one of my old denim shirts, jeans and tennis shoes. She adjusted the straw hat on her head and stuck her hands in her back pockets, making the breast buttons on the shirt bulge.

"Hey, can I help, hon?" she asked. Charley stood beside her, still giggling at her private joke.

I shook my spatula at Charley and closed one eye in mock anger. "Yes, you can teach your daughter to say 'howdy' to the guests."

Charley squealed with delight. Karen squatted and placed a hand on Charley's shoulder.

"Sweetheart, what do we say to people when they arrive?"

"Daddy," Charley said.

"No, 'howdy,'" Karen corrected.

Charley chortled and covered her mouth. "Daddy."

Karen rolled her eyes and patted Charley's head. "She gets this from you, you know."

I wrinkled my nose and poked my tongue out at Charley. She laughed out loud again.

In groups of one and two, people showed up. By early afternoon, the long tables were full of men and women eating, laughing, drinking beer, and singing along with the music from my little tape player. Forty or fifty people with straw hats, dancing to music by Stomping Tom Connors, Bev Munro, Waylon Jennings and Johnny Cash.

I doled out a plate of ribs to Frank, his second or third, I think, and watched his expression as Martin Van Hoeke bumped his arm playfully to jockey for position. They traded good-natured barbs, laughing as they did.

From the corner of my eye, I noticed two more people coming into the yard. I didn't pay much attention to them, but Van Hoeke and Frank stopped talking and froze, so I turned to see what had caught their attention. Walsh came first, in jeans and a crisp navy shirt, the tailored sleeves rolled up to his elbows, an ivory silk lining showing on the inside of the cuffs. He took the hat Charley proffered and tickled her nose, prompting a giggle from the little girl.

Walsh accepted another hat from Charley and handed it to the woman with him. Martin and Frank were still staring at her. She was in her forties, by the looks of it, with shapely slim hips wrapped in a pair of corduroy pants, and a sleeveless sweater that clung to her body like chrome on a bumper. As she raised her arms to place the hat on her short strawberry blonde hair, the sweater rode up, exposing two inches of smooth firm skin.

Walsh waved at us, smiled, then took the woman by the arm to join us.

"Hi, all." He grinned. "I don't think you've met my mom, have you?"

The woman smiled the same beguiling smile Walsh usually did, and stuck out a hand. "You must be Ian," she said, her voice alone raising my temperature. "It's lovely to finally meet you. I've heard so much about you from Patrick."

I took her hand. It was soft, cool, almost electric. "Um, hi. Yeah. Hi," I muttered.

She smiled. "I'm Elizabeth. You can call me Lizzy. Everybody does."

I repeated her name and said something, all vowels and muttering, as I remember.

Walsh introduced Frank and Van Hoeke, then he and his mother got food and wandered around, talking to other guests and shaking more hands.

Van Hoeke shook his head, finally, and leaned toward Frank. "See, I told you there was a god. There's your proof."

Frank gnawed at the rib in his hand and grunted. "I tell you, Marty, that's worth going to the divorce lawyer for, there. I never thought I'd get hot and bothered over someone's mom."

Walsh's mother and Karen talked for a minute or two,

laughing and nodding together, then Karen wandered my way.

"Hey, how are you doing?" she asked, looking at the food.

"So far, so good. We may have some leftovers after all," I said.

"She's very pretty," Karen said, casually.

"Who?" I asked.

She glared at me. "Lizzy. Patrick's mother."

"Ah, right. Her."

Karen shook her head. "Yes, I know you noticed her. All the guys did."

"Remarkable looking woman," I admitted.

Karen shrugged. "She's very personable, very easy to talk to."

Helen wandered up and nodded. "You're not drooling over her with the rest of the guys, Ian?"

I shrugged. "It's a flash in the pan. After a while, they'll all be back to normal."

Helen wrinkled her nose and faced Karen. "So, she runs a charity, sits on a bunch of boards, jets all over the world, plus she's had three kids and *still* looks like that?"

Karen nodded. "Yeah, too bad she's so damn nice, it makes it a lot harder to hate her."

For the next hour, we all stood around, chatting, eating and laughing. The feeding frenzy around Walsh's mother passed, and people again clustered in their natural groups.

A little after two, Walsh walked up to me, a look of urgency on his face. He glanced at his pager.

"Boss, can I use your phone?" he asked.

"Sure. Help yourself." I pointed my spatula at the back door to the kitchen. Walsh unclipped the pager from his hip and read the display.

He disappeared into the house. I organized the food that was left, condensed it so it could fit on one grill, and called to see who wanted any more. A few people wandered up and filled their plates, chatting pleasantly and eyeing the remaining ribs and chili, mostly just hanging around.

Walsh's mother came over to me, an empty plate in her hand. Her sweater seemed thinner than it had an hour before. "Hi, can I get one of those pork chops?" she asked.

I glanced over at her and smiled. "Coming right up," I said, trying not to stare at her. I slid the pork onto her plate, along with cornbread and salsa. She nodded appreciation and leaned in close.

"I want to thank you for what you did before," she said, softly.

"Pardon?" I muttered. I was still thinking about her sweater.

"You promoted Patrick to sergeant. It means the world to him, you know. I just wanted to thank you for that."

I shrugged. "He got it on merit. He earned those stripes."

She smiled. Her sweater rode up slightly and showed navel again. "Yes, his father and I are both very proud of that. Again, I wanted to thank you for putting him up for promotion."

"Sure. But if he ever outranks me, I quit."

She laughed a hearty laugh and leaned back. A broad band of skin above and below her belly button showed. That image would stay in my mind for weeks.

Walsh came back out, holding a piece of paper in his hand. "Sorry, Mom," he said, turning to look at me. "Got a call, boss. Mom, can you get a ride, or do you want me to drop you home?"

She smiled, a smile that was both proud and worried. "No, you go. I'll get Sam to pick me up."

Walsh nodded, wrapped an arm around her waist and gave her a peck on the cheek. "OK, bye mom. Boss, see you Monday morning."

He went out the side gate, his straw hat still in his hand. His mother and I watched him leave. Reynolds walked up to me, standing at the spot where Walsh had been.

"Something wrong?" she asked.

"Patrick got a call," I said.

She handed me her straw hat. “Sorry, boss. Wonderful party, amazing food. Got to catch him.”

She walked briskly out after Walsh, accelerating to almost a run.

“And so it goes,” I said.

Walsh’s mother watched her leave. “Does it ever get to you?” she asked.

“What—the pace, the stress?” I asked.

“Yes, but also the sadness, the violence. Doesn’t that ever get to you?”

I shrugged. “I speak for the dead. They need to be heard, and so I feel I speak for them. As long as I think of it in those terms, I can do my job. If I were to think only about the lives lost and the crimes committed, then I couldn’t do my job. I’d go mad.”

She smiled sadly. “Patrick has often talked about you—you care about these people, he said. You work very hard to get justice for the victims.”

“That is what I do, after all.”

She nodded. “As I say, I appreciate you taking care of him. May I use your telephone?”

I pointed at the kitchen door. She smiled thanks and went in. She came out a moment later.

“Thanks very much. You have a lovely house, by the way.”

I shrugged. “It’s modest, but we call it home.”

She rested one elbow against a chair back, and her other hand on her hip, making a slinky S shape with her body. That image stayed in my mind for a long time, too. In the afternoon sun, the shadow cast by the brim of her hat fell in a zigzag shape across her shoulders.

“Great party, it’s a good crowd.” She smiled. “I should send our caterers over here for lessons.”

“You’re too kind.” I chuckled. “But thanks anyway.”

I sighed and looked over at the crowd of people in my yard. As the food disappeared, I changed the music to a mellower sound—Ian Tyson, Gordon Lightfoot—and the crowd lazed, slouching in lawn chairs or lying on the grass, watching the shade from my neighbor's trees creep up my back wall.

A few couples danced to the slower songs, then sat back, laughing and relaxing in the warm sun. Others merely stretched out in chairs and lazed. A couple of the detectives fell asleep, which I saw as a huge compliment.

Thirty minutes later, a figure came through the side gate, very tall, very burly, in khaki slacks and a windbreaker. I watched him walk silently over to Walsh's mother.

"Mrs. Walsh, you called for me, ma'am?" he said, with a voice like a tuba.

She nodded. "Thanks, Sam. You know Inspector McBriar, don't you?"

He kept his hands at his sides and blinked at me. "Hello," he said. His eyes scanned the food.

I grinned. "Nice to see you again, Sam. Would you like some chili or ribs?"

He looked at Walsh's mother for permission. She smiled and patted his arm. "Go ahead, I'd like to talk to some people here before we go."

He looked back at me. "Sure. Thanks. Thank you very much."

I handed him a big plate and he loaded up on food, piling stacks of ribs and pork chops on it, then he sat at the end of one table, introduced himself and started eating.

Ten minutes later he dumped the few meager scraps into a trash can, deposited the plate on a table and stood patiently as Walsh's mother said goodbye to some people.

She nodded to him and walked toward me.

She held a hand out. "Thank you so much. This was a real treat, so very different from the boring things I usually have to do."

I took her hand and smiled. "Please come and visit us any time. It was a pleasure to meet you."

She headed for the side exit. The big man leaned down close to my ear and placed a massive hand on my shoulder.

"Awesome food, thanks, man," he mumbled, and followed her out. In the kitchen window, looking through the house to the front street, I could see them heading to a Mercedes sedan.

Sam held the back door open for her, looked around for anyone suspicious, then he closed the door and they drove off.

As the sun went down, the guests went with it. I handed out doggie bags and food wrapped in foil, leaving me with just a few things to pack up once the metal drums cooled down.

By early evening, our home was back to normal. Ethan watched TV in the basement, while Frank and Helen's twins slept in Charlotte's room, scattered over her bed.

We four adults gathered around the kitchen table, enjoying coffee with ice cream. We talked and laughed, discussed politics and argued about the best places to get fresh produce.

Frank and Helen eventually carried their sleeping children to their car and drove home. Ethan went to his room and fell asleep, and Karen and I went to bed.

She snuggled in beside me, threw an arm over my ribs and sighed.

"Happy about how the party went?" she asked.

"Yeah, I think everybody enjoyed themselves. That's it done for another year, anyway."

"Are you looking forward to seeing your dad?" she said, yawning.

"Of course. He said he's looking forward to see you and the kids, too."

"Good. Us too," she muttered. She sighed deeply and got very heavy.

CHAPTER 6

At six in the morning, I got out of bed before everyone woke up.

I put on a light gray suit and pale silver tie, then I drove to Immaculate Conception Church.

The early service was sparsely attended on most days, and on this warm Sunday morning it was even less busy than usual. I had the entire pew to myself, so I stretched my legs to one side and opened my prayer book. It happened to fall open at the prayer of Saint Gregory of Nazianzus, the "prayer at dawn." I read the first line, a passage I knew well, as though for the first time.

"I rise and pledge myself, Lord, that this day I shall do no evil deed, but offer every moment as a sacrifice to you." Thinking of Walsh's mother at the barbecue, I felt somewhat guilty. Then again, Catholics aren't perfect, just forgiven, as an old religion professor once told me.

I sat through the Mass, managing to keep my mind on the service, and only thought about work when I stepped out of the cool church and into the bright light of the morning outside. I squinted, held up my hand to shield my face from the sun, and looked out to find my car.

Walsh was leaning on the front fender, nervously smoking a cigarette. This was not good.

"Patrick, nice to see you. I suspect you're not here for the Mass, though?"

He shook his head and dropped the cigarette on the ground, then dragged his foot backward to crush it.

"Yeah, sorry, boss. Inspector Coogan is on duty today, but she's up to her eyeballs with her own work, so I figured I'd touch base with you."

"Fair enough. What's up?" I asked.

"The second body, on the tracks at Dufferin Station. We got an ID on her."

"We have her name?" I asked.

He nodded. "Gwendolyn Morgan. Who calls a kid Gwendolyn?" he said. "Anyway, she lived alone, just like our other woman, and she worked at Bell Telephone on Dufferin, just a two-minute walk from the subway."

I thought about that for a moment. "But she was on the platform to get on the train, early in the morning. Why was she getting on then? Wouldn't she be getting off the train then, in the morning, to go to work?"

Walsh smiled. "That occurred to me too. She was a long-distance telephone operator. She worked the night shift. She was on her way home when she died."

"Where did she live?"

He flipped back a page and read something. "She lived on Gothic Avenue, just off Bloor Street."

I frowned. "Across from High Park?"

"Yeah, about a block from where our first victim lived. We're going to check today if they knew each other. That could be a common link, I'm guessing. But something Alex mentioned bothered me."

"What's that?" I asked.

"If she was going home, why was she on the Eastbound platform? She'd be heading Westbound, going home. Why was she going the wrong way?"

"Good question. Let me know what you find out," I said. I looked at my watch. "I'm expected at home for breakfast. Did you want to come along?"

Walsh grinned. "Sorry, I promised my father I'd come for breakfast too. See you tomorrow."

He reached into his jacket pocket, pulled out a flat gold case, and extracted a cigarette. It had a silver filter on the end with 'PW' embossed on it. He reached into another pocket and came up with a slim gold cigarette lighter. It also had 'PW' engraved on it. He lit the cigarette, a blue butane flame turning the hot tobacco orange.

He turned to leave then stopped himself and turned back. "Ah, I almost forgot. Tomorrow night I have a charity thing to do, so I'll be off duty after six, just wanted to let you know."

"Sure. Some special event?" I asked.

"Not a clue. All I know is we're donating a bunch of money for this group that's building houses somewhere. You could come too, if you like. There's free champagne. Bring Karen with you."

I shook my head sadly. "That's not exactly my scene, but thanks anyway."

"You're sure? I can lend you a spare tuxedo."

I chuckled. "In that case, absolutely not. Thanks anyway, Patrick."

He gave a movie star smile and nodded. "Enjoy your breakfast, boss." He walked away.

ꕥ

I drove home, walked into my house and dropped my keys on the front hall table. There was no sound from anywhere—it was totally quiet.

"Hello?" I called. I heard a faint snickering from behind the doorway to the kitchen.

"Hello? Anybody home?" I said. The snickering again, this time followed by a "Shhh."

I played dumb and walked into the kitchen. Ethan and Charley jumped out from behind a counter, yelling "surprise." Karen sat on a stool and watched them, amused by the antics.

I squatted down and gave them both a hug. "Good surprise, guys, thank you both very much."

Karen hugged me. "Hey, you," she said, and kissed me passionately.

"All right, what's for breakfast?" I asked. Everybody looked at each other.

I gasped and put my hands on my cheeks. "You didn't make me breakfast?"

Ethan tugged at my sleeve. "We're taking you out for breakfast, Dad."

"Cool. Where are we going?" I asked.

Karen smiled. "We're ganging up on you guys. Helen and the kids are taking Frank out for breakfast. We're going to join them there."

"All right, let me change out of my suit, and we'll go," I said.

I sat in the right seat of Karen's Valiant and watched the kids settle into the back. Karen turned the ignition key and the starter motor groaned, but the engine didn't catch. I smirked, amused. She waited for a few seconds, sighed and turned the key again. This time she pumped the gas pedal. The engine started, ran for a moment, then stopped. Karen pursed her lips.

"Son of a bitch," she muttered under her breath. She turned the key again, glaring at the dashboard. She hit the steering wheel with the butt of her hand and grunted. The engine caught, sputtered to life, and Karen smiled, pleased with herself.

She put the car into gear and we drove to meet Frank and Helen. Helen's car was in the driveway of a restaurant, a rather upscale eatery at a golf course off Eglinton Avenue.

Frank was on the sidewalk outside the restaurant, holding Theo's hand, telling him what he knew about golf, and explaining why people played it.

Helen was beside him, tugging at Melina's skirt, smoothing the wrinkles from the car ride.

I lifted Charley out of the back seat and onto the driveway, then took her hand as we walked to join Frank's family. Ethan and Karen walked to my other side, and we all went in.

The restaurant was nice, all white linen tablecloths over thick oak, the smell of polished leather and lavender in the air, and waiters in black slacks with burgundy aprons, smoothly refilling glasses of water and cups of coffee.

Helen sat everyone at the table, three booster seats appeared, and we settled in to eat. Frank sat beside me, digging in to devour his pancakes and eggs without a word, then sneaking a sausage from Helen's plate when she pretended to not notice.

We all talked, laughed, explained to the smaller children what a country club was, and relaxed for a while. I looked out at the first tee, just beyond the patio, watching a quartet of business types argue over wind direction. One of them took a swing.

The ball bounced about three feet and stopped. The others laughed, loud enough that I could hear them through the glass.

The simple cruelty of their reaction struck me. Would they feel the same way about the dead women we had found if they'd come across them? Would they still have laughed?

I felt a poke in my ribs. I turned around to look. "Hmm?" I asked.

Karen leaned forward. "Frank has a question for you," she said, pointing at him.

"Yeah?" I asked.

"How's work going?" he asked. It did not sound like a casual question.

"Fine. Why?"

"You look preoccupied."

I nodded. "Patrick buttonholed me at church this morning. It has not been a fun week."

"Word is you've got some gruesome scenes, and no clues. That so?"

I nodded. "We have no clues yet, but we found that the

two women lived close to each other. That's something to work with, anyway."

He nodded. "Let me know if you need any help, of course. I'm just kind of lounging right now, not much at work to do."

"Sure. I appreciate it," I said. I hoped it sounded sincere.

He looked at me for a moment, reading me. "Just cause, you know, you're not too keen on the gruesome stuff."

"It's all right, Frank. It goes with the badge—you know that."

He shrugged. "Okay. You know where to find me." He went back to his pancakes.

I felt bad cutting him off like that, and decided to let him believe he could help.

"Actually, you could give me some ideas about the cases, if you like," I said.

"Hmm?" he asked, patting his mouth dry.

"Both women were found with subway transfers, even though neither probably needed a transfer. We can't figure out why."

"Why does that bother you? A lot of people grab transfers—they have a time stamp on them. If you don't have a watch, it's a quick way to tell what time it is," he said.

"It's just coincidental that both would die in the subway, and with transfers in their pockets?"

He nodded. "How were the killings done?"

I glanced over to make sure the children were not listening. They were busily rolling napkin rings along the tabletop, oblivious to us.

"The first one was stabbed with a sharp blade, the second was pushed in front of a train. No connection between them we can find," I said. "Ah, except that the women lived a block apart."

"Why the subway, though?" Helen asked.

"How do you mean?" I said.

"The subway has to mean something to the killer. He chose the places where he's going to do these things. He could hurt the women in parking lots, in movie theatres, on the street, yet he has chosen the subway both times. Does he work for the transit system, or was he frightened by trains as a child, what?"

I rubbed my face. "Do you realize you've just given me more ideas in the last ten minutes than we've had in the last four days?"

Helen grinned. "My pleasure."

Frank nodded. "Does that mean you can pick up the tab and expense breakfast?"

CHAPTER 7

Monday morning, I got in my car and started the engine. I picked up the microphone and closed my eyes for a second, then called in.

"Fifty-two zero six to dispatch."

"Go, zero six," said a woman's the voice.

"Zero six, any messages?"

I worried about what I might be told.

"Zero six, no messages," said the woman.

I sighed, relieved. "Thanks, Nadine, zero six out."

I drove to the station. I placed my file folders on the corner of my desk and grabbed a coffee from the kitchen, then started reading through telephone messages.

About ten minutes later, the phone rang. "Detective Inspector McBriar," I said mechanically.

Karen sighed. "Hey you, it's me. I'm really frustrated. The car won't start, again."

"Ah, crap. It's really a rough time for this to happen," I said. "Can Helen give you a ride today?"

"Yeah, but can you call one of your mechanic friends? This is getting to be a real pain."

"All right. Leave the car keys in the mailbox, and I'll get back to you right away," I said.

I called an acquaintance, a mechanic with a shop a few blocks from my home, and explained the problem to him.

He said he'd tow the car over right away, but might not be able to look at it till later in the week.

Given that, I called the local Hertz and reserved a car for Karen to drive while her Valiant was in the shop. Then I called Karen back and told her where she could pick up the rental car. The entire process took maybe twenty minutes.

At that point the morning went on autopilot. Van Hoeke called everyone to order and held the regular Monday morning meeting. The major topic, of course, was our two dead women. Walsh and Reynolds described the scenes, gave details and asked for information. Van Hoeke let them finish, then gave his customary 'get out there and do good work' line.

The room became a moving mass of white shirts and brown jackets, zigzagging around each other to get to their cars. I watched them leave, and the office suddenly got very quiet.

For a moment, I didn't notice Van Hoeke sitting on the desk beside mine. He waited till I looked up, then touched my arm.

"Walk with me, Ian. I want to buy you a Danish," he said.

"Sure," I answered. This was unfamiliar territory. He never went out for coffee.

"By the way," he said. "Rebecca thanks you for the lovely time at the barbecue. She also appreciated the kosher dogs and chicken strips."

"Not at all, Martin. It's always a pleasure to see you and Becky at our place. You know that."

We stood outside, waiting for the coffee truck to show up, not speaking, just staring at the driveway as if we could will the truck to appear.

Finally, a silver box on wheels careened into the lot, tooting its horn and squealing tires as it lurched to a stop. A shortish, rotund man with a permanent smile, like he'd just heard a good joke, jumped down from the driver's seat and ran around to open the side panel.

A few of the office staff let Van Hoeke go first, silently showing respect for his rank.

He bought a pair of pastries and we walked back into the building, still silent. We grabbed coffees and sat in his office. He stood, reached past me and softly closed the door. "Well, Ian, how's the job going?" he asked, casually.

"As far as I know, pretty good, sir," I said, cautiously. "Do you know something I don't?"

He took a bite of his danish and chuckled. "This is not a meeting to reprimand, son."

He put the pastry down and patted his mouth. "Do you know how long I've been doing this job?"

"What, you mean, Captain?" I asked.

He shook his head. "I mean, how long I've been with the police department?" He leaned back and cradled his head in his hands. "I met Rebecca during the war. She was in the CWAC, the Canadian Women's Auxiliary Corps, posted to Croydon, and my family lived just down the street from her billet. It was love at first sight. She was going home to Toronto after the war, so when the RAF demobbed me I took my savings and bought a ticket here. Sometimes, decisions are just so obvious you never question them. That's why I came to Canada. And that's why I called you in here."

"All right," I said. "I'll bite. Why am I here?"

"How would you like to sit in my seat?" he said simply.

I could feel myself blush. I leaned forward. "From where I was sitting four years ago, I'd have to skip about five pay grades to take your spot. Why would you want me to do that?"

"Very soon, I'm going to retire," he said softly. "You only live once. I want to take a long cruise, spend time in England with my few surviving relatives, travel to Israel, paint watercolors of beaches. The kids are out on their own, and they don't need us anymore. It's our time now."

"You still haven't said why you want me in the position. There are several other men who could do the job just as well."

"Yes, but you have an advantage over all of them. We've been told to give preference to minorities when promoting officers, and technically, you count as a minority, Ian."

"You mean because I'm a Metis?" I asked, irritated.

"You're considered a full Indian, in the system. If I choose you, I'd fulfill the affirmative action mandate, and still promote someone I think would be perfect for the job. What do you say?"

I sighed. "Let me think about it, boss. Can I take a couple of weeks to mull it over?"

He smiled and held out his hand. "Fair enough. Let me know then."

"Meanwhile, this stays between us?" I asked.

"Between us," he echoed.

I took his hand. "You realize that last time you promoted me, Karen got pregnant."

He laughed. "You can't blame me for that—I just sign the forms, that's all."

ଓଓ

I went back to my desk to finish my danish. Walsh and Reynolds were standing there, waiting patiently for me. Walsh smiled a disarming smile.

"Everything all right, boss?" he asked, glancing back at Van Hoeke's office.

"Yeah, fine," I said. "What's up?"

Reynolds leaned forward. "We think we found a link between the dead women."

Walsh smiled. "What she means is, she found the link. Take the credit when it's due, Alex."

Reynolds grinned, a dimple-faced teenager sort of grin. "Okay," she said. "It turns out that Gwen Morgan was a client of the law office where Brenda Grant was working. According to the staff, Gwen suggested Brenda apply for the job there."

"Gwen lived near Brenda, right?" I asked.

"Yeah, boss," Reynolds said. "We spoke to the other staff at that office, and they said that Gwen used those lawyers because Brenda was an old school friend, and recommended them. Otherwise, Gwen might not have gone to that office, and who knows, she might not have been killed."

I scratched my cheek, thinking. "So, as far as we know, the only point where both women came together was the law office. Have we talked to the lawyers in that practice yet? See if any of them sets off any bells for us?"

Walsh shook his head. "We spoke to everyone in the office. Nobody stands out. Then again, Brenda was pregnant, so I have to believe that her condition enters into it somehow."

"Why the sandwich, though?" I asked. I frowned. "Why on earth would she get on the subway with a stupid sandwich in her purse?"

Reynolds smiled. "We found out about that, too. She was on her way to a movie theatre, the Willow on Yonge and Norton. Apparently she went to the movies a couple of times a week. You'd have liked her—she was an old movie buff. Anyway, there is this old guy who runs a newspaper stand at Yonge and Sheppard. He recognized her photo, and he told us that whenever she went to the movies, she used to make a sandwich to give him. He doesn't remember how it started, but he appreciated it. I guess she was just a nice person, that's all."

"So what else did the old guy say?" I asked.

Reynolds flipped to another page of the Moleskine. "Right. He said she always went to the movies alone, always bought a copy of *Life Magazine* from him, always gave him a sandwich. She would take the subway to Sheppard then take the bus to Norton. That explains the bus transfer in her pocket, and the sandwich in her purse. So it wasn't suicide. It was certainly murder."

"All right, carry on, you two," I said. "Keep me posted."

They turned to leave, then Walsh stopped and came

back. "You remember I have this family thing to do tonight, right?"

"Yeah, don't worry, Patrick. It's fine."

He nodded. "Good stuff. Thanks, boss. See you tomorrow."

I had a brief image of Walsh's mother in a slinky evening gown. I put it out of my mind.

ↂↂ

The medical examiner sent me a thick envelope. Inside was a report on the two dead women, along with photographs.

One was a photo of Gwen Morgan, lying on a cement slab in the morgue. Her face was turned to one side, showing where the gravel under the train had peeled the skin away from her skull.

Another photo showed her arm bone, the jagged end of the ulna, poking out beyond torn flesh. She had died of blood loss, according to the post-mortem, bleeding to death in the subway tunnel before the paramedics could get to her. It would have been painful, not very quick, and not a merciful way to go.

Why did he do it? Did he know her, or did he pick her at random? But then, she had a connection to the other victim. It couldn't have been a coincidence. She wasn't chosen at random, it had to be that the killer was after her specifically. But why, that was the question.

I spent the rest of the day completing the reports on my desk, feeling good that at least that I'd gotten that accomplished. Around five o clock, Van Hoeke turned out the lights in his office, locked the door and walked over to my desk.

"So, Ian, any more news on the investigation?" he asked.

I shrugged. "We think there's another link between the two women. Alex found it. Apparently, they went to the same law office. That is, one was a client, and one worked there.

Beyond that, they look different, they're not both blonde, or brunette, they had different jobs, and there were no other common links we could find. We're still looking."

He nodded, considering the information. "How's Alex doing with young Patrick?"

"He seems happy with her work. I think she's got real potential, boss. She's very sharp."

"She reminds me of you, you know. She is very by-the-book, just like you. She doesn't take shortcuts either, just like you. I like that about her."

"I'm flattered. But I do like that about her too." I got up and grabbed my coat from the rack behind me.

"C'mon, Martin. I'll walk you out."

We strolled out together, enjoying the warm afternoon air. Van Hoeke lifted his hand, placed a tweed cap on his head, and got into an antique burgundy MG convertible.

"You're still driving the old MG?" I asked.

"Only on nice days. You still have your Fiat too, right?"

"Yes. Again, it's only for nice days. Charlotte loves riding in it, and Ethan wants to drive it when he's older, he says. Time will tell if I still have it running."

He turned the key and the MG's engine rumbled, a cloud of blue smoke puffing out behind.

"See you tomorrow, Ian. Good night." He drove out onto Keele Street and headed home.

I smiled to myself. I imagined myself in his position, getting into my little Fiat at the end of the day, telling a new Detective Inspector to have a good night, letting him, or her, do the heavy work while I shuffled papers.

I had been with the police department for less than a decade. Most men weren't offered the Chief's job until they'd been in the force twice that long. It was a tempting offer. The extra pay was certainly tempting, and the prestige, the status, and the 'one-upmanship' of being a Native supervising a room full of white men was tantalizing.

I drove home. Karen was arranging papers in piles, stacked high on the dining room table. She glanced up at me. “Hi,” she said, and went back to her work.

“Hey,” I answered. “What’s for dinner?”

“No idea. What do you feel like making?” she said, without looking up.

“Chinese. I’ll call them,” I said.

There was a menu from The Golden Dragon on the side of the fridge. I picked up the phone, ordered a mix of favourite items, and hung up. I joined Karen in the dining room and sat down.

She looked up and smiled. “Hey again, you. So, how was your day?”

“All right. No more victims, anyway, so that’s good. Where are the kids?” I asked.

She pointed at the ceiling. “Ethan set up that train set Frank gave him, and he’s showing Charlotte how to run it. They’re having fun.”

“Fine. So, how was your day, hon?” I asked.

She placed a sheet of paper on a particular pile and sat back. “Good—very good. We leased a big chunk of the floor, and it means we should be out of that project early. That would mean a nice bonus for us, by the way.”

“That’s good. Dinner should be here in twenty minutes or so,” I said.

She stood up and smoothed the front of her skirt. She leaned back slightly, stuck out her elbows and ran her fingers through her hair. Even all these years later, it still gave me a thrill to watch her do that. I wrapped an arm around her waist and pulled her close.

I kissed her, firmly, for a long while, then stepped back. “Wow, still exciting after all this time.”

She grinned. “I’m glad I still pass muster. By the way, Charlotte has been asking a bunch of questions about our trip. I said you’d answer them when you got home.”

“Right. I’m going to change. Be right down.”

I jogged up the stairs, past Charley’s room to Ethan’s.

Both children were sitting cross-legged on the floor. Ethan had set up a large oval train track on the floor, running a short set of cars along it, letting Charley work the controller. She made the train lurch forward, stop quickly then back up, trying to get used to the sensitive knob. I watched them from the doorway for a minute, then I left them to their play.

I changed to jeans and a sweatshirt, put my gun away, hung up my suit and dumped my shirt in the laundry. I now felt I was off work, finally.

A few minutes later, a knock at the door signalled the arrival of food. I paid the young man and brought in a cluster of white paper boxes. We all chose our favourite foods, Charley getting suggestions from Karen, and started to eat.

After dinner, we watched TV till around eight. Charley fell asleep in Karen's arms. She had asked me questions about Saskatchewan, why grandpa John lived there, and could we drive there in my Fiat. I explained that we would fly there in a plane. She said she wanted to fly it. Ethan drew pictures of horses and cactus, even though I told him there were no cacti in Saskatchewan. By ten o clock he was asleep too.

I made a cup of tea for Karen, hot chocolate for myself, and turned off most of the lights in the house. We sat in the darkened living room, relaxing, sipping our drinks before bed.

I finished my hot chocolate, washed my cup and turned to head up the stairs, looking forward to reading for an hour in bed. There was a knock at the door.

It was soft, tentative. It was followed shortly after by another knock, louder, insistent. Before I could get to the door, there was the sound of fists pounding on the door.

That worried me. I stopped at the fireplace and picked up a heavy poker, then went to the door. I opened it, the poker behind my back.

Reynolds was on my front step, pacing back and forth. On the sidewalk behind her was a uniform, looking uneasy.

"Sorry, sir, I had to speak to you right away," she said apologetically.

"Sure, what's up?" I asked.

She turned to the uniform. "Thanks, Kelsey. I'm all right from here."

He grunted "Okay," walked to his cruiser and left.

"Come inside," I said.

She followed me into the kitchen and sat at the counter, facing me. She was clearly trying to decide how to say something.

"What's up, Alex?" I asked. "What's wrong?"

"We have another body," she said softly. "Another woman."

"Crap," I muttered. I rubbed my face and sighed. "Where was this one?"

"On the beach, at the Canadian National Exhibition grounds."

I shook my head. "Damn, I hoped he'd stop till we could catch him. Why choose the CNE for a dump site? There's no subway anywhere near there."

She shrugged. "I know. Do you know where I can find Sergeant Walsh, sir?"

"He's at a charity event at the O'Keefe Centre," I said.

"No, they said he'd left already. He's not answering his pager, either. That's not like him."

"Maybe he got lucky?" I offered. "You know Patrick."

"Maybe. Look, I hate to ask, but could I talk to you about this one? I need your advice."

"All right. For what it's worth, I think you're doing fine so far."

"There's more, Inspector," she said, sadly.

She reached into her jacket pocket and pulled out a plastic bag. It was sealed and signed by her, dated today. Inside the bag was a slim gold cigarette lighter, engraved with the initials *PW*.

"That's Patrick's lighter," I said.

"Yeah, it certainly looks a lot like his lighter, sir," she

said carefully. She put the bag on the counter. "It was found under this woman's body. Do you think it's possible that Sergeant Walsh had something to do with this?"

"What do you think?"

She shrugged. "You've worked with him way longer than I have, but I don't believe he would be capable of anything like this, do you?"

I looked at the lighter. It was tempting to pick it up, hold it in my hands, feel it for myself, but I felt that I shouldn't touch it. "What exactly happened to her?"

"She was strangled. A wino found the victim and her purse in the grass, beside a park bench."

She leaned forward, resting her elbow on the counter. "The body was found about two miles from the O'Keefe Centre. Sergeant Walsh was there for a charity event this evening. If it's remotely possible that he was involved, then we have to question him."

I sighed. "You know Patrick. You work with him. Come on, Alex, that's not remotely like him. You know that."

"No, sir, I agree. But I have a piece of hard evidence here, and I have to take it in. I just wanted to let you know about it first, that's all." Her voice sounded sad, pleading.

"Do we have a name for this woman?"

She nodded. "Her name is Phyllis Adams. One of the officers on scene recognized her. He said she's a prostitute, high class, very exclusive, not your typical street walker."

"That's even less likely, then. I could never imagine Patrick picking up a prostitute."

She threw her hands in the air. "Look, Inspector, you and Patrick are friends, I know. But it's my responsibility to log this evidence. I can't just ignore that we found it."

I sat back and sighed. "Detective Constable Reynolds, you go ahead and do your job. Take the lighter in. Log it as evidence, by the book. I'm going to get to the bottom of this. Wait here."

I went upstairs, told Karen that something had come up, and I needed to talk to Patrick, then I put my suit back on and drove Reynolds to her car at the crime scene. It took under ten minutes to get from there to the O'Keefe Centre.

It was almost midnight, but a steady stream of men in tuxedoes, and women in evening dress, moved in and out to waiting limousines and private cars. I felt underdressed in my plain suit.

I showed my badge at the door and was directed to a side corridor, where I asked a doorman in a tuxedo where I could find Walsh. He politely told me it was a private event, but when I pulled out my badge he ushered me to a meeting room. There was another man inside this door, holding a clipboard and scanning the crowd. I asked him if he'd seen Walsh.

"Mister Patrick? Yes, sir, but he left some time ago." He glanced at my off-the-rack suit and smiled, a smile that said "please go away."

"Did he leave all by himself?" I asked.

He frowned. "I'm sorry, sir, but our guests are very protective of their privacy. Thank you."

I held up my badge. "I am his superior officer. He may be in trouble. Now, was he alone?"

The man looked around nervously. "Look, we all know Patrick, and we know he likes the ladies. A lot—I mean, a *lot*. It's not my business if he gets lucky, you know."

"So he didn't leave alone?"

The man slowly shook his head.

"All right. Can you describe the woman he left with?"

The man rolled his eyes. "Yeah. On a scale of ten, she's a twelve. Like, five nine, legs up to her armpits, dark green eyes, a face to make you melt, you know the type?"

"Yeah, that sounds like Patrick's type. Did he say anything to you, like where he was going?"

The man shrugged. "He just looked happy, like he was going to have a really good time. All I can tell you is what I overheard."

That got my attention. "What did you hear?"

"She said her car was parked at the beach, and she asked

if he could take her there. It sounded like she was going to be very grateful, if you get my meaning."

"Yeah, I get your meaning." I sighed. "Did you get her name at all?"

"No, but he called her 'Phyllis.'"

"Wasn't she on the guest list?"

He squirmed. "She got into the gala by smiling. She in some kind of trouble?" he asked.

"She very well might be. Thanks for your help." I pulled out a business card. "Listen, if you hear from Patrick, can you give me a call?"

"Sure, you bet." He read the card. "Hey, you're that cop, the one that got shot way back?"

"Yes, that was me. Back in seventy-three. Anything else you can remember?"

"They left with some good champagne."

I frowned. "How so?"

He poked a thumb over his shoulder. "Mr. Patrick Walsh bid on a charity bottle of Dom Perignon, the good stuff. Three hundred dollars, as I recall. He took it with them."

"Three hundred dollars for a bottle of wine?" I asked, incredulous.

"Yeah, go figure. Wine all tastes the same to me. The rich buggers in here say they can taste the difference. I don't believe it."

"Did you hear any more of what they said?" I asked.

He nodded. "Yeah. She said 'so, can you take me back to my car?' And he said 'sure, anything else I can do for you?' So she whispered something to him, and he says 'sure, let's go.' So they went."

"All right, thanks. Look, again, let me know if you hear anything or remember anything, all right?"

He nodded and I left. I got into my car and clicked the microphone.

"Fifty-two zero six to fifty-two forty-four."

A minute later, Reynolds' voice came on. "Go, zero six."

"Alex, did we find a bottle of wine with that body?"

There was a pause, then, “Yes. Dom Perignon, the bottle says…I think.”

“All right. See you at the office in the morning.”

“Roger, four-four out.”

I went back into the O’Keefe Centre and found the man with the clipboard again.

“Hey, is Mister Walsh senior here? Kieran Walsh?”

He frowned. “He just left, sir.”

“Did his driver look like a real big guy?” I asked.

“You mean Sam? He didn’t wait for his driver, he hailed a cab.”

“What cab company?” I asked.

“Sunshine Cabs—I remember the logo.”

“Good, thanks.”

I walked out to the main entrance, on Front Street, and looked down the row of waiting taxis, searching for a Sunshine Cab. There was only one in the line of taxis.

I walked over and leaned in to talk to the driver. I pulled out my badge. “Hey, can you radio your dispatcher? I need to find out which one of your drivers just picked up a fare here.”

“Yeah, that was me. I took that fare.” The man grinned.

“Where did you take him?”

“Them. It was some older guy and his wife. Man, she was something, you know.”

“Where did they go?”

“Seven blocks away. Colborne Street, behind the King Eddy Hotel.”

I pulled a five-dollar bill out of my pocket. “Good. Thanks. If they call for a cab in the next ten minutes, tell your dispatcher you’ve got it, but don’t go, all right?”

He smiled at the money. “Sure, you bet.”

I drove to a nondescript building on Colborne, marked with a simple plaque that said *A.D. MCMXXV*. There was a buzzer by the door, almost invisible. I pushed the button and waited.

A moment later, a voice came through a tiny speaker. A man's voice, deep and growly.

"Yes?" he said.

"Sam, it's Ian McBriar."

There was a long pause. "Can I help you, Inspector?"

"I don't have time to play games. Let me in, Sam."

There was another pause, then a buzzer sounded and the door popped out about two inches. I pulled it open and walked into a wide lobby.

I had been here once before, during the day. The lobby was polished marble, all potted ferns and fragrant flowers then. Now, late at night, it was only a dim space with a pair of weak red lights leading to the elevator.

I got into the elevator and pressed the button for the floor I had visited before. The elevator stopped, the door opened, and I took a step out. Immediately, a huge hand pressed against my chest and stopped me.

Sam glared down at me. "I'm sorry, I will have to search you for weapons, Inspector," he said. His usual demeanor, understated strength and power, was gone. He glared at me, looking ready to tear me in half if I pissed him off. I leaned to one side and looked around him. Kieran Walsh was standing beside a desk, staring at a telephone. His wife, Lizzy, was in a pale pink gown, her pearl bracelet the same shade of pink as the dress, a glittering diamond necklace on her neck, cascading to her cleavage, highlighting the freckles on her skin.

Kieran looked at me and smiled a warm smile, but mechanical. "Ian, what brings you out here so late? I thought we were the only people who worked at this hour."

I shook my head. "Mister Walsh, what's going on?"

His smile faded somewhat. "I'm not sure I understand, Ian."

"Where's Patrick?" I barked.

His wife glanced at him, a look of panic in her face, for just a split second. She looked back at me and tried to smile. "Why, he's a very busy young man, you know that. I'm sure he's doing whatever young men do." She widened the smile, not very effectively.

"We found his cigarette lighter under a dead prostitute. Can you explain that?" I asked.

Sam put his hand on my shoulder and pulled me back slightly. "Time to go. Get out of here," he grunted.

I shook free and glared at him. "You don't want to screw with me right now, Sam. I know you're just doing your job, but I'm doing mine, too. Do not screw with me."

He opened his mouth to protest, closed it again, and looked to Kieran for advice.

Kieran blinked very softly. Sam walked to the elevator and sat in a chair by the door. Kieran turned to a small cabinet, a deep red rosewood bar that creaked as he swung open the door.

He took out a bottle and three glasses. "Would you like a drink, Ian?"

He read the label on the bottle. "Can I offer you some single malt? It's Glen Garioch."

"No, thank you," I said.

"You're sure? It's twenty-five years old, quite good."

"No."

He shrugged and poured a small glass for himself and one for his wife. "Bottoms up," he said and took a sip. He closed his eyes, seeming to appreciate the whiskey, then put the glass down.

"Now, then, where were we?" he asked, as if nothing had happened.

"Where's Patrick?" I asked firmly.

He smiled softly. "Believe me, Ian, I have absolutely no idea."

His wife took a small sip of her scotch and grimaced. "Key, tell him."

"Tell me what?" I asked.

She looked at me, pleading. "We don't know where Patrick is."

"Your husband said that already."

"I'm afraid something terrible has happened to him. Can you help us?" she asked.

Kieran glared at her. I had never seen him angry. "Liz, stop it. We'll do this on our own."

"Do what?" I asked. "What will you do?"

He stared at me, unable to hide a look of disgust. "This is a private family matter. Please do us the courtesy of leaving my family alone. Thanks for your concern, but Sam will see you out."

"No, it is not a private family matter. Patrick is at the very best a material witness to a murder. At worst, he's in a world of trouble. I expect to see him at his desk tomorrow morning, to tell me his side of the story. What assurance can you give me that he will be there?"

Kieran thought for a moment. "Ian, I'm sorry, I have been very rude to you. I'm sure you have his best interests at heart, and I know that he thinks of you as a very close friend. Believe me, as soon as we hear from him, we will tell him to contact you." He smiled, but his shoulders sagged. That told me he was hiding something painful.

I shook my head. "What the hell is going on?" I said. "I will find out eventually, you know."

Kieran nodded at Sam, and the big man got up. Kieran looked at me, determined. "It's very late. Good night, Ian."

Sam grabbed my arm and steered me into the elevator. We rode down wordlessly, then he led me through the lobby, opened the front door and ushered me out. He pulled the door closed behind him and I heard a deadbolt clunk.

"Son of a bitch," I grumbled.

I got in my car and grabbed the microphone. "Fifty-two zero six to Fifty-two four-four."

A half minute later, Reynolds' voice came on. "Yeah, boss?"

"Where are you, Alex?"

"Just getting ready to leave the scene."

"Can you meet me for a quick coffee?" I asked.

"Sure. King, just west of Simcoe, in ten?"

"Roger. Zero six out." I hung up the microphone.

I drove to the only open coffee shop on that block of King Street. There was a yellow cruiser out front, a pair of uniforms in the window seat, munching sandwiches on their dinner break. I walked in and nodded to one I recognized. He smiled and offered me a seat, but I politely told him I had to talk to someone.

He understood my need for privacy. The two men went back to eating.

Three minutes later, Reynolds came in, rubbing her eyes in fatigue. She sat across from me and looked around. I opened my mouth to speak, but a waitress, a small round woman in a pale blue uniform, came over and handed us menus.

"You want coffee?" she asked, a slight European accent in her voice.

I nodded. "Yes, please, and pie. Apple pie, no ice cream. Alex, what would you like?"

"A burger, with fries. Everything on it," she said. The waitress left, Reynolds leaned forward. "You *know* something," she said quietly.

"Maybe, but I'm not sure exactly what I know," I whispered. "Patrick is AWOL. His parents are worried shitless, and they won't tell me why."

Reynolds looked around. The two uniforms were still eating, discussing the past weekend. "Something else, boss. Patrick's still not answering his pager. He always answers his pages."

I sighed. "Okay, so what are the options, Alex? He killed her, and he's hiding out? Or he saw what happened, and he's checking it out on his own?"

"He'd still answer his pager in any case, though, wouldn't he?" she said simply.

"Yeah, you're right. He'd answer his pager."

The waitress brought out Reynolds's burger and my pie. She leaned forward and smiled. "Them two officers already got the tab for this. They said 'you're welcome.'"

I looked up as the uniforms were leaving. The man I recognized smiled, waved and walked out.

I managed to catch his eye and waved thanks to him as he left.

Reynolds ate quickly, stuffing food into her mouth and swilling coffee. I watched her, curious.

"Miss a meal, did we?" I asked.

She nodded and patted her mouth. "Didn't have breakfast, didn't stop for lunch. I should know better—it always makes me a little punchy."

I took a bite of pie and sipped my coffee. A beige sedan rolled slowly past, and for a brief moment I thought it was Patrick's car. I was wrong—his car was a Ford, this was a Dodge.

I sat back. "Alright, so let's say you're Patrick. Let's say you found out something about this murder, maybe about the others, too. What would you do?"

"Call it in, first thing. I'd get the forensics guys on the scene as soon as I could. Or, if it wasn't solid evidence, I'd let someone else know, just in case."

"Right, that's basic police procedure, basic by-the-book investigation. Patrick would always do it that way. Sorry, but I can't understand why he's gone missing," I said.

"His parents don't know where he is?" she reiterated, puzzled.

"No, I don't think so. They seemed pretty upset, so I don't think they're hiding him or anything."

She rubbed her eyes. "Look, let's say he shows up for work tomorrow morning with a really good explanation for what happened. How dumb would we feel running around all night?"

I nodded. "Yeah, okay, you're right. Get some sleep, Alex. I'll see you in the morning."

I got home after two in the morning. The house was dark, except for a soft glow from the street, and the only sound I heard was the clock in the kitchen, ticking loudly in the dim light.

I crept up the stairs, not wanting to wake anybody. I went past Charley's room, then Ethan's. I turned the corner and entered our room. The reading lamp was on at Karen's side of the bed, but Karen was fast asleep, a magazine in her lap.

I took off my clothes, slid into bed, and reached over to turn the light off. Karen opened her eyes, ever so little. "Hey, you," she said. "Everything all right?"

I kissed her softly. "Everything's fine. Go to sleep."

She closed her eyes again, and her breathing became deeper. I closed my eyes and tried to sleep.

I dreamt of Walsh, sitting on a park bench with the prostitute, talking to her, smiling at her, then turning toward her and choking her to death. It didn't seem right. It didn't seem like anything Patrick could do.

I woke up and rolled over. My clock said it was three forty-five in the morning. Go back to sleep. This time, I dreamt of Patrick and the woman talking, but a smoky, vague figure shows up and hits Patrick with something, then it chokes the woman. She screams, tries to run away, but the figure has hands around her neck, squeezing tighter and tighter, till she stops screaming. I woke up again for a while, then I fell back to sleep.

CHAPTER 8

I was awake for good at five-thirty. I showered, dressed, and made coffee. By six-thirty, Karen was downstairs, saying little. She shuffled into the kitchen, wrapping her robe tight around her.

She took a cup from the cupboard and poured herself coffee. "Want to talk about it?"

I shook my head. "I don't know what's going on," I said. "As soon as I know, I'll tell you."

"This sounds serious," she said. "What does Patrick have to say about it?"

"I have no idea." I sighed. "We can't find him. He's gone missing."

By seven-thirty I was dressed and in my car, headed for Fifty-two Division. I parked at my usual spot and went to my desk. Reynolds was already there.

"Hey, Alex, been here long?" I asked.

"Just a few minutes." She shrugged. "No sign of Sergeant Walsh, sir. Have you heard anything?"

I shook my head. "Nope. I'm giving it till nine this morning, then we call out the dogs."

I went through the overnight reports. No unusual traffic accidents, no unmarked police cars found abandoned, no indication of where he could have gone, no sign of Patrick.

I hesitated to ask the squad room to look for him. If he turned up, it would be embarrassing for both of us. If he was somehow involved with this woman's death, unlikely as it seemed, then I didn't want anybody else but me getting to him first.

Maybe the dead girl could tell us something? I called the pathologist. He would have looked at her body, at least, even if he hadn't performed an autopsy yet, and he might have something he could give me. The phone rang twice then he picked up.

"Yes?" he barked.

"Hey, Doc, I have some questions for you," I said.

"You don't waste much time, do you, Ian?" he said.

"No time for that. This is very important. What can you tell me?"

"Every case is very important to you. Why don't you just let me do my job?"

"No. this is different. I can't explain right now, but I need to know what you know."

He sighed. I heard paper rustle. "All right. She died around ten last night, based on internal body temperature and where she was discovered. She had alcohol in her system, and she was choked to death by a very strong pair of hands."

"What else?" I asked.

"She had one of your detectives' business cards in her purse. Your men should be more careful with crime scenes."

"Whose card?" I asked.

"Our young Mister Walsh. Why did he leave a card with a victim?"

I rubbed my forehead. "Doc, can you hold off on that piece of information, just for the day? As a personal favor."

I heard silence at the other end for a moment. "All right. But tomorrow I release it, agreed?"

"Thanks, doc. I hope I can explain soon."

I looked at my watch. Nine thirty. No sign of Walsh. I had waited long enough—time to get to the bottom of this.

I drove downtown, to the building on Colborne Street, and pressed the buzzer on the door.

A minute later, a female voice, older, raspy, said "We're closed for business today."

The crackling of the intercom went dead before I could say anything.

I pressed the button again. The voice returned. "What?" she barked.

"This is Ian McBriar. Let me in."

A minute later, the voice returned. "I'm sorry, but we can't help you. Please come back later."

"Wrong answer. Let me in now, or I come back with a dozen men," I growled.

Another long minute later, the door buzzed and popped open slightly. I walked in.

The lobby was exactly like it had been last night, but it seemed that there was disorder, things out of place, a mess on a desk that was out of keeping with the neat décor.

I walked directly to the reception desk at the end of the lobby. A woman with ash gray hair, in a tailored jacket and satin blouse, glared at me.

"I want to know where Patrick is.," I said.

She shrank back slightly and glanced off to one side. The big man, Sam, appeared from nowhere and walked up to me. He was in the same jacket and pants he'd been in the night before, and his eyes were red and bleary. He glared down at me.

"Mister Ian, please leave, sir," he said, his voice creaky with fatigue.

"No. Where's Patrick?" I asked. "If I have to tear this building down brick by brick, I will do it. Believe me, I will find out what happened to him."

The woman looked back and forth between Sam and me. She seemed to be waiting for something to happen. Her phone rang. She jumped, and looked at me, worried. It rang again, and she placed her hand on the receiver, deciding something.

"Durham and Walsh," she said, professionally.

Her eyes widened. "Yes," she said simply. She pressed an intercom button and leaned forward.

"It's him," she mumbled. She transferred the call to somewhere, and hung up.

"That was Patrick, wasn't it?" I barked. "Don't lie to me, it was him, wasn't it?"

She shook her head, her mouth open. "No, it wasn't. Honestly. No."

I leaned back and ran my fingers through my hair. This was getting me nowhere. The elevator door behind her opened, and Kieran Walsh walked out. He was in the same tuxedo shirt he'd worn last night. His hair was disheveled, his face showed a growth of stubble. He hadn't been to bed. He looked at the woman, slumped his shoulders and turned to face me.

He smiled slightly and stuck his hand out. "Hello, Ian. Sorry about being so curt with you last night. Unfortunately, we had a small crisis. Business doesn't run on a nine-to-five schedule."

I didn't shake his hand. "That doesn't cut it, Mr. Walsh. We're still looking for Patrick."

He glanced at the woman and back at me. She shook her head. She thought I didn't see it.

"No, she didn't tell me," I said. "All right, so where is he?"

Kieran pursed his lips and took my arm. "Come with me."

We rode the elevator to the fourth floor, Sam shadowing us, and we walked to the back of the building, where I had never been before, an open area with several metal desks.

Kieran took me to his office. It had walls of dark red-brown wood, polished and burnished, with a wall of legal volumes opposite two wing chairs. He motioned to a chair across from a massive oak desk, and I sat down. Before I could speak, Lizzy Walsh came in. She was also in the same clothes as the night before, but her makeup had been washed off, and her hair was sticking out at all angles. She sat in a chair beside me.

"First, I need your promise that you will keep everything we say here in the strictest confidence," Kieran said. "It's vital that I can count on you, otherwise this conversation ends right now."

"Yes. You can trust me to keep a confidence, unless you've committed a crime," I said.

"Ah. No, not me," he said.

"Patrick? What did he do?"

He shook his head. "No, never. Patrick is absolutely honest—you must know that."

"Then where is he?" I asked.

He sighed. "I had a call last night. They said they want money in exchange for Patrick's release."

I sneered. "You're telling me he's been kidnapped? When? By who?"

Kieran fidgeted with a piece of paper on his desk. "We did well with our investments in Chile. You saw our little celebratory purchase."

"Your boat, the *Santiago*," I said. "Very nice."

He nodded. "Not everyone did so well after we left that market. One party in particular thought we left without warning, before they had the chance to liquidate their holdings, and they lost a large sum, large for them, in any case. I think some of those parties might want compensation. I think they decided that this is how they want to get back at us for that."

"How much do they want?" I asked.

"Five million dollars." He said it simply, almost casually.

"But, it would be impossible for you to raise that kind of money, right?" I guessed.

"Not at all. We could draw that from current funds." He shrugged. "But, two things: first, I'm not convinced that paying them would guarantee that we'd get Patrick back safely. Second, this sets a terrible precedent for our community. If it became known that our families were so vulnerable, then it would be open season on all of us. We can't have that."

I sat back for a moment, digesting what he'd said. "How soon do they want it?"

"I told him that we would have to draw it from a number of different institutions, and that it might take several days. He said if I don't give them the money in seventy-two hours, they'll start sending pieces of him in the mail." His voice trembled and finally broke as he said it.

He shook his head. "Please, Ian, I beg you, they said that if I called the police, they would kill him right away. Please, I'm begging you, just stay out of this, for Patrick's sake."

I stood up. "I owe Patrick a lot. He kept my family safe last year, and he is a true friend to me. I can't just abandon him."

Kieran ran his fingers through his hair and leaned back. "What can I do, Ian? I'd gladly trade places with him, you must realize that, but I don't know where to go for help, and I can't let you be involved. They said no police. I promised them, no police."

I thought about that for a moment. "You're right, no police. Look, give me two hours. I want you to stay right here, all right?"

"What can you do? You can't do anything for me, you know that."

I shook my head. "I have an idea. Can I call you here? As I say, give me two hours."

He pulled out a card and wrote down a number. "This is my private line. Nobody knows this number. Whatever you do, I beg you, don't do anything to place him in any more danger."

He handed me the card. I nodded and got up. The big man, Sam, stood up as I did and waited by the elevator door, watching me. I walked into the elevator, with Sam right behind me. We said nothing for the length of the ride down.

As the door opened, he put his arm across the opening.

He leaned close to me. “You better not do anything to hurt mister Patrick, you hear?”

I smiled weakly. “Believe me, Sam, that’s the last thing I want to do.”

He pulled his arm away and I left.

CHAPTER 9

University Avenue is home to a number of law firms, company head offices, and a cluster of businesses that seem to do nothing more than deal with other businesses. One such building, a large glass box, was where Frank Burghezian worked. I'd only been there a few times, but I knew the building.

I parked out front and put my 'Police Business' sign on the dash. Then I thought about it, took the sign off, and paid for parking at the meter.

I sprinted up the steps to the front door, crossed the lobby to a long desk with three women sitting behind it, and waited for one of them to notice me. She looked up at me and raised an eyebrow.

"May I help you?" she asked.

"Ian McBriar to see Frank Burghezian," I stated.

"Is he expecting you, Mr. McBriar?"

"No."

She shook her head. "I'm afraid he is very busy. Perhaps if you could make an appointment—"

"No. Tell him I'm here. It's important."

She pursed her lips, picked up a phone, and dialed a number. A few seconds later, she looked up at me. "Hello, it's Beryl in reception. There's a Mr. McBriar here, and he says it's—"

She listened for a moment. "Oh, I see. Sorry, all right."

She hung up the phone. “I’m so sorry, Detective Inspector. Please go up to the..”

“I know where he is, thanks very much, Beryl.”

I walked past the women to the bank of elevators, pressed the button for the fifteenth floor, and went up. At the end of a green marble hall, a side door with a brass plaque read *F. Burghezian.* I went in.

Frank stood and looked me up and down. “Hey, kid, what’s up?” he asked, smiling.

“Patrick is in trouble. We need your help.”

His smiled evaporated. “How bad?”

“He’s being held for ransom. We have seventy-two hours, or he comes back in pieces.”

Frank sat on the edge of his desk. “Holy shit.” He looked at his shoes for a moment. “Did they say no cops?”

That surprised me. “Yes, apparently they did. How did you know?”

“You’re here. Is it just the money, or is it personal?” he asked.

“What the hell—yeah, how did you know that?”

“Makes sense. This isn’t about the cash. They want to make the family suffer. The cash is just dessert.”

I shrugged. “So, what do we do?”

He raised an eyebrow. “We, paleface? Not we. Me. You are a cop, last I heard. When they said ‘no cops’ did they say ‘no cops except for a friendly Detective Inspector’?”

“All right, what can you do, then?”

He went behind his desk again. He stood still, considering something. “I could use your help, you know, but not with the badge. You lose that badge, you can help. Otherwise, piss off.”

“Fine. I’ll lose the badge. What can I do?”

“I’ll get some friends together, then I’ll contact you. When are they going to contact Walsh for the money?”

“I don’t know. He gave me his private number, and I told him I’d call him as soon as I had an answer. What should I tell him?”

Frank grew firmer in expression, determined. "Call him and say that three men will be at his office at…" He looked at his watch. "One this afternoon. He knows me, and I'll introduce the others to him. Tell him that if we're successful, the others will submit a bill. I won't."

I nodded. "I'll tell him. Can I meet you there then?"

"Not if you're still a cop. This is not going to be a 'by the book,' do you understand?"

"I understand."

I went back downstairs and stopped at the desk again. "Beryl, is there a private room where I can make a quick phone call?"

The woman nodded. "Follow me, please, Inspector," she said.

She led me around the corner, unlocked a small office and pointed to a desk. "Here you are. Please lock the door once you're finished, sir."

I sat down and took Kieran Walsh's card out of my pocket. I dialed his number and waited.

One ring later, the phone picked up. Walsh's voice said "Yes?"

"It's Ian. I have a contact that will assist you with the situation. There will be three men at your office, at one this afternoon. One of them is Frank Burghezian."

There was relief in his voice. "I know Frank. I understand he's very…resourceful."

"He asked me to tell you that, when they are successful, the other two men will require payment, but Frank will not. Is that agreeable?"

"God, yes, anything." He sighed. "Thank you, Ian, thank you."

There was a pause, then he said, "I'm putting all my trust in you, you know."

"I understand, sir. See you this afternoon."

ଔଔ

I drove quickly to Fifty-two Division. I still had a job to do, and two dead women to investigate, plus the dead prostitute. That said, I didn't feel I could do it and help Patrick, too. I had a decision to make.

I rushed into the detectives' room and looked around. Reynolds was at her desk, talking to Terry Parker and reading a report. She looked up, glad to see me.

"Hey, Alex., I said. "Be with you in a minute."

I walked past her into Van Hoeke's office and closed the door. I sat down, and Van Hoeke leaned back, watching me. He put down his pen.

"What can I do for you, Ian?"

"I have to have a leave of absence, or I'll have to quit the force," I said.

"Really?" he asked, mildly amused. "Why is that?"

"Sorry, Martin. There is something I need to do, something very important, and I can't do it as a police officer, so I have to take a leave or I'll have to quit the force." As I spoke, my resolve weakened. Inside, I knew that the decision was the right one, the only one, but something inside me withered when I said those words.

Van Hoeke examined me, his head tilted. "I see. How's Frank doing?"

"Fine."

"And young Patrick, how is he?" he continued.

"I haven't spoken to him today," I said truthfully.

"He's a busy man. I'm sure he's tied up with whatever is going on for him," Van Hoeke said.

My eyes widened. He knew. Or he had guessed, somehow.

He frowned. "Ian, I'm fed up with your insubordination. I am going to suspend you from the department for five days. Will that be enough time for you to…reflect on your behavior?"

I grinned. "Yes, thanks. I'm sure I will be able to reflect on my actions in the time I'm off."

I unhooked my gun and left it on his desk, along with my badge. He put them in a drawer.

He pointed to his door. "Instruct the troops, then get the hell out of here, Ian." As I stood to leave, he added, "By the way, Rebecca would like Karen to call her later."

I nodded. He could say in all honesty that he knew nothing about this crisis, and Rebecca would fill him in on the details as the affair progressed.

I sat, facing Reynolds and Parker. "Listen," I started. "For the next while, I will not be in. I will not, repeat not, be available. Do not contact me. Terry, you'll be the acting sergeant on the dead women case, and Alex will be your DC. Alex, get him up to speed on everything. Anything new about our victims?"

She shook her head. "She had some money in her purse, about two hundred and fifty dollars. There was no ID in there though, no keys, nothing. The purse had lipstick, a compact, a hair brush and stuff, so it's not like they dumped it out or anything, but there was nothing in there to identify her. We'll keep on it."

"All right. See you guys in a few days. I'll tell you then what's going on, all right?"

They nodded, puzzled, and I left.

I decided that I couldn't use my car while I was suspended. If I did, I would still be acting as a cop. I dropped off the Caprice at the motor pool, called a cab and went home.

Karen was in the dining room, working on some papers. She heard the door open and called out. "Hello? Hi?" she said.

"Hi, it's just me," I called and went in to join her.

"Hey, are you home for lunch, or what?"

"No, I've been suspended from the force. I can't explain why right now."

She gasped. "Suspended? Why? What's wrong? Why have you been suspended, Ian?"

I shook my head. "It's pro forma. Look, honestly, I can't explain right now. When I can, I'll tell you everything."

She sat back, her mouth open. “What’s going on, Ian? Are you in some kind of trouble?”

“No, hon, not me. Listen, I really don’t have time to explain. Can I take your car?”

“Yeah, sure,” she muttered. She rummaged through her purse and handed me a plastic tag with a pair of keys on a ring. “Here,” she said. “Exactly what is going on, Ian?”

I looked at the key tag. “You got a Pinto?” I asked.

She shrugged “That’s the only car they had. Sorry.”

I sighed. “All right. Look, I’ll be home later. I really can’t talk now. I’ll talk to you then.”

She stared at me, reading my face. “Look, whatever you’re doing, be careful, all right?”

“Yup,” I answered.

I drove back downtown, parked on Colborne Street, and rummaged for parking change. I plugged some nickels into the meter and pressed the buzzer on the door frame. This time, the door opened without anyone asking me who I was. I went into the lobby and headed for the elevator.

At the reception desk, the woman in the jacket looked up at me with a pleading expression. “Please go up.”

I nodded and took the elevator to the fourth floor. As the door opened, I heard a familiar voice.

“So we’re tied in here,” Frank said, “and we have the recorder set up there.” He looked up as he saw me. “Hey, Ian. Good to see you. I’ll bring you up to speed.”

There were two men beside him, both in their late thirties, early forties, both were serious and firm-muscled, both were compact, both looked like they could hold their own in a fight.

Frank waved at one, a man with curly red hair and a freckled face. “This is Tom Bagley.” He pointed to the other man. “And Harry Pogue. They’re here to help us to get Patrick back.”

I stuck out a hand. “Hi, Mr. Bagley. Or do you prefer Tom?”

He smiled a warm, inviting smile. "Hi. Call me Teabag. All my friends do. Do I call you Ian?"

I nodded, shook his hand, and faced Pogue, the other man. "Harry. Good to meet you."

He was about five feet eight, the same as Frank, with a sad face, like his dog had just died. He shook my hand. The grip surprised me. It was solid, hard, and it seemed effortless.

"Hi, Ian. Let's get this show started," he said, pointing at a box under a telephone on Kieran's desk. It had wires and cables coming out of it, and was plugged into a wall socket.

"What are we doing?" I asked.

Pogue waved his hand. "We've piggybacked the phone, so when they call we can record the conversation. Teabag's got a contact at Bell that will help us trace the calls, and I'll be your spokesman with the perps."

"You've done this kind of thing before?" I asked. He just looked at me and said nothing.

"You don't want to tell me?" I prodded. He turned away and adjusted something on the box under the phone.

He looked at Kieran. "It's a little after one thirty. I figure they won't want to wait too long before they call with the details. Right about now, Patrick has asked for food, or a toilet break, or something, so they're thinking that the sooner they get him gone, the better."

"What do we do until they call?" Kieran asked. The strain in his voice was painful to hear.

"Read a book, take a nap. Don't get nervous, or you'll make mistakes. I know it's hard, but just stay loose." Pogue's voice was calm, measured. He sat beside the phone and closed his eyes.

I sat across from Pogue, wondering what he had planned. I tried to sit still, but I was jittery, nervous. How he seemed to be so calm was beyond me.

Pogue seemed to be fast asleep. We sat there for almost thirty minutes, saying nothing, then the phone rang. We all jumped. Pogue slowly opened his eyes and stood up. He looked around at us. "No matter what, nobody makes a sound, all right?" The phone rang again. He put his hand on the receiver. On the third ring, he picked it up. "Hello?" he said. A speaker on the side of his box let us hear what the other person was saying, at a low volume.

"Kieran Walsh?" the voice said, gruffly. It was a man, not old, not very young. There was a twang I couldn't place in the voice, an accent.

"No, I work with him," Pogue said. "I'm doing the negotiating for him."

There was a pause. "No cops, no tricks, no bullshit. You got that, right?"

"Right," Pogue said. "We need to know he's alive, that he's fine, though. We want a photo of him, a Polaroid holding today's newspaper."

"You don't make the rules. We make the rules," the voice said.

"We don't get a photo, you don't get money, simple as that," Pogue said. "Then we'll pay you."

There was another pause. "You'll get your photo. We'll call later and tell you where to find it."

"Fine. Then the deal is what?" Pogue answered.

"You know the deal," the voice came back. "Five million in cash. We'll tell you where and when."

"I understand," Pogue said. "It's six million dollars now. I understand."

We all looked at each other, but we said nothing.

There was a pause at the other end. "We said five. Five million. What kind of game are you playing?" The voice was definitely accented, now, stressing vowels.

"No problem. We can get the six million for you by tomorrow night. Just don't hurt Patrick at all, all right?" Pogue said convincingly.

"You screwing with me?" the man said. He paused for a moment and laughed. "Oh, I get it. You're skimming from the boss. You want some of that cash, too."

"Yes, that's right," Pogue said, calmly. "We just want him back, safe and sound, that's all."

Another pause. "I keep half your money. You get five hundred thousand, take it or leave it."

Pogue covered the mouthpiece with his hand and nodded at Kieran, who looked ready to faint.

"Got him" Pogue whispered. He spoke into the phone again. "All right, listen, I can hear street noise in the background. You must be at a pay phone, because you know that they can't trace a call from a pay phone. Six million it is. Where can I contact you when we have your money?"

The man sighed. "No. I will call you, at exactly eight tomorrow morning. You better have good news for me." He hung up.

Pogue hung up the phone and looked at his watch. "Eight am tomorrow morning. Very good."

Kieran Walsh got up and walked over to him. He was shaking, trembling with fear. "What were you doing? Why did you say six million? What were you doing?" he wheezed.

Pogue grinned. "He thinks I'm on the take. He thinks I'm out to shaft you, that I'm crooked. He'll think he can trust me a lot more now, because he believes I'm as crooked as he is."

I shook my head. "I didn't know that you can't trace a call from a phone booth."

Pogue chuckled. "Of course you can, but he didn't know that." He turned to Bagley. "Okay, Teabag, what have we got?"

The red haired man dialed a number on another phone and waited a moment.

"Hi. Did you get it?" he said. He wrote something down and grunted approval. "Thanks. Talk to you later, thanks again." He hung up. "He was at a pay phone at the corner of St. Clair Avenue and Victoria Park. I figure he'll probably use the same pay phone tomorrow morning. Let's make sure we see him there when he calls."

"We'll grab him, right? We'll question him tomorrow morning?" I asked.

"Nope," Frank said firmly. "This isn't catch and release, Ian. We'll follow him, period."

"Why?" I asked.

"Because if we do grab him, they'll know right away that the game is up, and we'll lose Patrick for good."

Lizzy Walsh gasped at that. She covered her mouth with both hands.

Frank shook his head. "Look, Lizzy, we're not going to let that happen. Patrick will be home soon, safe and sound. You have my word."

Frank turned to face me. "All right, time to take a quick recon, Ian. Let's go. Harry, Teabag, you ready to come along?"

We all went downstairs and out to the street. Frank looked around for my police car.

"Where did you park?" he asked.

"Um, my Caprice is at the station. I had to get myself put on suspension so I could do this, so I wouldn't be doing it as a cop. Karen lent me her rental car."

Pogue shook his head. "Let's take my car."

We went down the block to a nondescript gray Ford sedan. Frank and Pogue sat in the front seat, I sat in back with Bagley. Bagley and Pogue spoke in code, talking of recon, scoping, and back tracing. Frank understood some of it, but asked for explanations on other things. We drove past the corner of St. Clair and Victoria Park, looked at the phone booth as we passed, then we drove to a nearby diner for a sandwich.

We sat in a booth near the kitchen, away from the front windows. Bagley and Pogue told me that my job was to keep Kieran calm, to help Frank, do the legwork, and snoop around. They would negotiate and do whatever else was required. I couldn't help but think that they were telling me this just to keep me from getting too nervous and doing something rash.

At the other end of the diner, a big man with tattoos and a leather vest screamed at a young woman in his booth. The owner of the diner went over and asked him to keep quiet, but he pushed the owner away and slapped the woman on the back of the head, calling her names.

Pogue looked at Bagley. "You want me to take it?" he asked.

Bagley put his sandwich down. "I got it," he said. He casually shuffled out of the booth, picked up a plastic straw and walked over to the man in the vest.

"Excuse me, princess, you left your wand behind," Bagley said. He gave the man the straw.

The man looked at him, bewildered, then glared at him, furious. "What did you say?" he roared.

Bagley motioned toward the front door. "You may want to leave now, Cinderella, before your carriage turns back into a pumpkin. Get a move on."

The big man struggled to get out of the booth. Behind him, the diner's owner picked up the phone and dialed the police.

The tattooed man stood up. He was my height, burly, fat, and obviously used to fighting. He roared, then swung at Bagley, a brutal wide swipe that was intended to knock him out. Bagley ducked it casually.

"One down, one to go," Bagley said.

The man swung again, punching lower this time, aiming at chest height, and Bagley hopped back out of the way.

"Two down. My turn," Bagley said.

He swooped forward and gave a high kick like a Rockette, catching the big man under the chin. The big man sprayed spit and French fries into the air. He arched backward, landed on his back, and passed out.

"Two for two," Bagley said.

He opened out the man's curled hand and separated his middle finger. He gave a twist, and the big man howled in agony as the bone broke. He rolled onto his stomach and tried to crawl away. Bagley kicked him in the backside, and he flapped onto the floor again. Two uniforms came into the diner and looked around.

One saw me, nodded recognition, and smiled.

"Hey, Ian, what happened here?"

Bagley shuffled into our booth again. "I think he fell down."

The uniform smirked. "You wanna go with that story, then, Ian?"

"Suits me," I said. "I think he's drunk though. You may want to let him sleep it off."

The uniforms grabbed the tattooed man and dragged him out to their cruiser.

Frank grinned to himself. "You devil." He snickered. "And I thought you were such a boy scout."

I shrugged. "Shit happens, Frank. We all grow up, we all move on."

We drove back to Walsh's office. Bagley and Pogue did something with the equipment under the telephone, then settled in to sleep there in case the kidnappers called late at night. Frank suggested we should get more information about our caller.

We walked to my car. Frank walked past it, oblivious. I called him back, waved at the right door and unlocked it, clumsily. Frank got in, and I sat in the driver seat.

"This car is great," Frank sniffed. "If everything goes to shit, we can always deliver pizza with it."

I scowled. "Hey, it's a rental. The Valiant is getting fixed, so Karen got a Pinto."

He rolled his eyes. "Ooh, a Pinto. Pinch me, I must be dreaming. A Pinto."

I shook my head and sighed. "Where are we going, Frank?"

"Victoria Park and St. Clair. Let's go back and see what we can set up for tomorrow morning."

I started the engine and struggled to shift out of park. We clattered up Yonge Street, went right on St. Clair and stopped across the street from the pay phone the caller had used. There was a burger place on the north side of the intersection, a vacant lot opposite, and a gas station with a coffee counter across the street.

Frank told me to stop at the gas station and we walked in.

A portly woman in a blue shirt and jeans was behind the counter, reading a gossip magazine. She was leaning against the counter with her elbows, flipping pages of the magazine absentmindedly, mostly looking at the photographs. She saw us and closed the magazine. “Yeah?” she asked.

“Hello.” Frank smiled. “If we wanted change for the pay phone, could you give us some?”

She shook her head and sighed. “We don’t give change. Company policy, no change, I don’t open the till except for a sale.”

Frank pointed at the phone across the intersection. “Did someone else ask you that earlier?”

She seemed curious about the question. “Is this some sort of game? You guys all together?”

“So somebody did ask you for change earlier?” Frank asked.

“Another guy, an hour or two ago. Yeah,” she said. “He wanted quarters for the phone.”

“Can you describe him?” Frank asked. “This is really important.”

She leaned back, thought for a moment, and squinted her eyes. “I dunno. My memory’s kind of fuzzy.”

“Ten dollars fuzzy?” Frank said.

She sneered. “Twenty. Twenty bucks, and I can remember everything about him.”

“For twenty, it better be in Technicolor,” Frank said.

She nodded. “Yeah. Okay. He was thirty-five, maybe a little older. He had this beige golf jacket and black pants. And he had a goatee. Plus, he had this accent. Mexican, I think.”

“How tall was he?”

She held her hand out, raising it up and down in front of

Frank's face. "Maybe a bit taller than you. Yeah, just barely."

"What color was his hair?"

She thought for a moment. "He had a hat. One of those British tweedy driving hats, you know, but he had blond hair. It stuck out at the sides. The goatee was a little darker, though, brown."

"Was he fat, skinny, medium build?"

She shook her head. "Stick thin. Looked like his pants would fall off if he ran too fast." She pointed at Frank. "Ah. And he had sneakers on, tennis shoes. White tennis shoes."

Frank grinned and opened his wallet. "Here you go. So, you didn't give him any change, right?"

She took his twenty and slipped it into her back jeans pocket. "Well, yeah. But only cause he bought some gum. He pulls out a dollar bill and buys gum with it so I can give him change."

"Have you ever seen him before?" Frank asked.

"Nope. He's a new face. I been here six years. I know most of the locals, never saw him before."

"Did he have a car?" Frank asked.

"No, he walked up from the sidewalk. I saw him coming up the street."

Frank smiled. "Great. Listen, if he comes back, forget that you ever saw us, all right?"

"You guys the mob, or what?" she asked, worried. "Because I don't want trouble, you know?"

Frank shook his head. "We're investigating a serious crime. This is a tricky situation, and we do appreciate your cooperation."

He peeled off two more twenties and handed them to her. "We were never here."

She grinned and stuck the money in her back pocket with the first twenty. "Sure" she said.

We got into the Pinto. Frank rummaged through the glove box and found a map left by the car rental company. He unfolded it and looked around.

"What are we looking for?" I asked.

"Nothing, but if we're being watched, it will look like we're just lost. Good thing you have this crapmobile, too. Nobody would suspect that you're following them in this thing."

He looked over at the park, then the gas station again. "So, he knows he needs change for the pay phone, and he passes the gas station on his way to the phone. That means he was probably walking north on Victoria Park, and he didn't walk very far, either. He was on foot, like she said. Let's head south for a bit, Ian."

I drove slowly south on Victoria Park. We'd gone about two minutes, then Frank pointed to another phone booth. "Here you go," he said, satisfied. "I bet it's less distance for him to walk up to St. Clair than it is to come down here. Now we know roughly where they're hiding out."

"How do you figure?" I asked.

"It's five blocks between here and the first phone. He's probably staying about two blocks south of the gas station. Less distance to walk two blocks north than three blocks south. There's a bunch of apartments around us here, too. They could be holding Patrick in any of them."

"Yes," I said, "But can you imagine if they dragged Patrick up a flight of stairs past someone, even if he was tied up or knocked out? That would be risky, wouldn't it? What if someone saw them and called it in?"

Frank digested that for a minute. "So our guy on the phone is here, but they're holding Patrick somewhere else? Yeah, that makes sense, Ian. They may not be as dumb as we thought."

"Does that change what we do tomorrow?"

He shook his head. "Nope. Same plan, and same ending. Come on, let's get back to Walsh's."

We drove back to the building on Colborne Street, went upstairs to the fourth floor, and got out of the elevator.

Bagley and Pogue were snacking from a tray of sandwiches. Kieran Walsh sipped coffee, trying to act calm. Lizzy was in a small office to one side, curled up on a sofa. Frank grabbed a sandwich and poured himself a coffee. He took a bite and stared at the food in his hand.

"Wow, this is good. Where did these come from?" he muttered.

"We had them sent over by the hotel," Kieran said, softly.

"Hotel?" Frank asked.

"The King Edward," Kieran said, pointing out the window. "A friend of mine runs the catering."

Frank grunted and held up the sandwich for me to see. "What's in this thing?"

"Avocado and alfalfa sprouts," I said. "Very California, very west coast."

Frank nodded and turned to Pogue. "Real good. So, Harry, what next?"

Pogue looked down, thinking, and slowly nodded. "They will make us sweat tonight. They won't contact us till tomorrow morning. I'll stay here with Teabag overnight, just in case I'm wrong, but you all should go home. Get some rest. Meet back here at zero five thirty."

Kieran protested, but Lizzy, surprisingly, agreed. She asked Sam to drive them home and they left. Pogue waited till they'd gone and turned to Frank. "So, you get any intel?"

"Yup," Frank said. "Youngish guy, real skinny, my height, blond hair, goatee, Spanish accent. He got phone change at a gas station on the corner. I figure he probably walked north one, two blocks to that phone. There's another phone five blocks south, so he chose the closest one."

Pogue nodded and turned to Bagley. "Can we three-way the call?"

Bagley shook his head. "No, but we can bird-dog it."

I stepped forward. "Can I get some of that in English?"

Bagley smiled. "Harry wanted to know if we could tap that phone when he makes the call, so we could hear both sides of the conversation. I don't think we can, but I'm pretty sure we can trace any calls he makes from that phone."

"Why would he make more calls?" I asked.

"Simple. He calls us, and we agree to his terms. He then calls whoever is running the circus, and tells them what we said. We'll trace back to who he called, because they're probably sitting where Patrick is being kept," Bagley said.

I nodded. Very shrewd, very smart, very professional. The three men seemed completely at ease with each other, completely comfortable in each other's company.

"So, how do you men know each other?" I asked.

"We were in the Boy Scouts together," Bagley deadpanned.

Pogue snickered "Yeah, Scouts."

Frank chuckled. "We were in the same unit, back in sixty-five. We went through some wild shit back then, Ian. You wouldn't want to go through half of what we went through."

I turned to Pogue. "What did you do in the army?"

He smiled. "Not much, I just shuffled paper, mostly."

I raised one eyebrow, skeptical. "And you, Tom?"

"Not much, I just shuffled paper, mostly," Bagley echoed.

I wouldn't get any more out of them, I guessed. I turned to Frank. "All right, we're useless here. Do you want a ride home?"

"Sure. We going in your clown car?" Frank said.

I sighed. "If you'd rather take a cab, I understand."

"No, no. I'll put on a red nose or something. Let's head home."

We went back to our homes. Frank sniffed at the slow acceleration and noisy ride. He looked out the window for a minute, thinking, then turned to face me.

"You really put your balls on the block for Patrick there, Ian. You sure you wanted to do that?"

"I owe him a lot, Frank. He sheltered both your family and mine last year, he kept them safe. Losing my job, if it ever comes to that, would be a small price to pay."

"If you do end up looking for work, we could always use you, you know," Frank hinted.

"Doing cloak and dagger stuff?"

He shook his head. "No, doing investigative work, same as now. You'd have to learn to live on twice what the department pays, of course. Not a real hardship."

I smiled. "At least that's a possibility in case I need it. Thanks, Frank, I'll keep it in mind."

We got to Frank's house. He looked at his front door, considering something. "What are you going to tell Karen?" he asked.

"I'm not sure. I won't lie to her, but I think I'll only tell her everything after this is all over."

"After we get Patrick back, you mean?" he asked.

"Right. After we get him back," I grunted.

"You're not convinced that we're going to get him back alive?" he said.

I shrugged. "I hope we do, but the odds aren't with us, are they?"

He grinned. "With Teabag and Harry on our side, the odds are pretty damn good."

"Same question for you. What will you tell Helen?" I asked.

"Same thing as you. Confidential op, need to know, details later. See you at five a.m."

He rolled out and climbed the front steps two at a time. I waited till he opened his front door, waited till I heard him call 'hey everybody' then I drove the few blocks to my home.

Karen was in the kitchen, pacing. She heard me open the door and rushed up to meet me.

"Ian, what the hell is going on?" she snapped. "Rebecca Van Hoeke is livid. She wants to know what you're doing, and I had to tell her I didn't know. I *don't* know. Ian, what's going on?"

"Sorry, hon, I can't explain yet. As soon as I can, I'll tell you everything."

She rubbed her face. "Why did you get yourself suspended? That just doesn't make any sense."

I shook my head. "Same answer. As soon as I can I'll—"

She pushed me away, hard. "No. that doesn't wash. You have to tell me. I deserve to know."

I frowned. "Wrong. Don't do this to me, hon. It's hard enough doing what I have to do, without getting grief from you about it, too. Let it go, Karen. I will tell you, when it's time."

She rubbed her face again and inhaled deeply. "What do I tell the children? How do I explain that their father is not working, that he's off on some escapade?"

"Tell them nothing. For now, it's business as usual as far as they're concerned. Again, I will explain everything when the time is right. How often do I have to say this?"

She shook her head. "All right, so what now, Ian? What about us? Where do we go from here?"

I leaned back against the kitchen counter. "As far as you're concerned, it's life as usual. All things being equal, I'll be back at work next week."

We ate dinner as we always did, put the kids to bed as usual, and sat down to watch some TV.

Karen barely spoke to me, but thankfully the children didn't seem to notice. I looked at my watch—nine-thirty. I told Karen I had to be out very early the next morning, set the alarm for four thirty, and went to bed. I tried to sleep, but it felt like the sheets were made of burlap. I couldn't get comfortable, couldn't find a position to fall asleep.

An hour later, Karen came to bed. She wrapped her arms around me and squeezed me tight. "It'll be all right, Ian," she whispered. "We'll get through this all right."

I kissed her. "Thanks, hon. I can't tell you how much I appreciate you saying that." I fell asleep.

CHAPTER 10

I woke up with a start, the clanging sound of the alarm clock making me jump. I rolled out of bed, put on a pair of jeans, a sweatshirt and sneakers, and crept downstairs.

I made coffee, buttered some toast, and waited till it was time to get Frank. Karen came downstairs just before five, had coffee with me, but said little.

I looked at my watch. "I have to go. I'll call you later, all right? Don't worry. I'll be fine," I said.

She nodded sadly and looked up at me. "You better come back in one piece, you hear?"

"I'll be with Frank. We'll be fine. Count on it."

I drove the few blocks to Frank's house. This early in the morning, the sun was already bright enough that the darkness of night had completely left.

Frank was outside on the sidewalk, pacing. He looked at his watch as I stopped. "Four fifty-eight. Pretty good timing," he said.

We drove down to Colborne Street and walked up to the door with the buzzer. Before I could press it, the door popped open an inch, and we went in.

Sam, the big bodyguard, was in the lobby, standing in the middle of the floor like a statue. He nodded and let us walk past him to the elevator. On the fourth floor, Kieran Walsh was already waiting for us. He had changed to fresh slacks and a polo shirt, but a growth of stubble and mussed hair told me he had barely slept. Lizzy, he said, was sleeping in a back office.

Pogue and Bagley were there, too. They had slept by the phone, in case there was a call.

At five thirty, a waiter from the King Edward Hotel came by with a large tray of hot croissants and thermoses of steaming coffee. Frank collected some food, poured himself coffee, and sat at an empty desk, munching happily.

A minute or two later, he took a final swig of coffee and looked around. “Now, then, who’s on what detail?” he asked.

Pogue pointed to Bagley. “Teabag and I will work this phone. You two, head back to the payphone and wait.”

Frank nodded. “Want us to call you?”

Pogue shook his head. “You said there was a gas station across the street? Get me the number. I’ll call you there as soon as we hear from our man.”

At seven forty, Frank and I pulled up to the gas station, parked around back, where we could see the phone booth without being obvious, and went inside.

The same portly woman was at the counter, reading. She did a double take when she saw us and stood up straight. “You guys. You’re not here to get your sixty bucks back, are you?”

Frank grinned. “On the contrary. Can you let me use your phone for a moment?”

“I don’t know,” she said. “The company rules say that—” She saw Frank’s wallet open and stopped. She handed him the phone. Frank picked up the receiver, dialed a number, and waited.

“Hi, yeah,” he said. “We’re at…” He read out the phone number on the dial. “Fine. Bye,” he said and hung up. He turned to the woman again. “Here’s another twenty. We’re going to wait outside. Someone is going to call us in a while. When they do, let us speak to them. Okay?”

She nodded, took the twenty, and stuck it into her back

pocket. "You guys sure you're not with the mob or nothing?"

Frank grinned. "No, sweetheart. Nothing like that."

She smiled broadly at the "sweetheart" and went back to reading her magazine. We sat in the Pinto, glancing at our watches every few seconds. At eight am exactly, a thin man walked nervously past us, looking around. He had a shaggy beard, a beige golf jacket over a plain white shirt, and a belt cinched tight around a painfully thin waist.

He kept his head down, walked to the corner, then fumbled in his pocket for something. He pulled his hand out and counted coins, did some quick mental math, and went to the pay phone. He dialed a number and waited. He stood straight, squared his shoulders, and pointed at the air as he spoke, trying to make himself feel more imposing. He listened for a moment then relaxed. He said something else then hung up.

Frank watched him the way a cat looks at a bird across the lawn. The man fumbled in his pocket again, brought out more change, and made another call.

"Gotcha, you stupid piece of shit," Frank muttered.

This time the man slouched over the rack with the phone books, telephone to his ear, a finger in the other ear, rocking back and forth, then I could see his mouth go "Okay, okay," and he hung up. He walked away from the phone, waited on the corner for a second, then went across the street to the burger place.

Frank waited till he was out of sight before we went into the gas station. The phone rang, and the woman picked it up. "Yeah?" she said.

She handed the phone to Frank. "Here, I think it's for you."

"Yep?" Frank said. He grabbed a scribble pad from his pocket, put it on the counter and wrote something. "Nice work. We'll let you know." He hung up. "He called an address on Victoria Park. That's what, five minutes' walk from here? That would make sense. Whoever is handling this is somewhere nearby."

We thanked the woman for her help. I took two steps toward the door, but Frank grabbed my arm and pulled me back. He turned me to look at a rack where there were maps for sale. I opened my mouth to protest, but just then, the man with the golf jacket walked in.

"Hi," the woman said. "Can I help you?"

The man rummaged into his pocket and fished out a dollar bill. "Can I get some phone change?" he asked sadly.

The woman glanced quickly up at Frank. Frank shook his head, slowly. The thin man had his back to us, and he didn't see it.

"Sorry, but I told you the policy," she said. "You got to buy something."

He huffed and looked around. He picked up a large bag of potato chips. "Here," he said.

She punched some numbers on the till. "Sixty cents," she said.

He stared at the dollar bill. "Man, I gotta make two phone calls. I need another dime."

Frank walked past the man, ignoring him, put a candy bar on the counter, and put a five-dollar bill beside it.

"Just that, please," he said.

The woman muttered, "Sure, sure," and gave him change for the five. Frank grinned at the man and said, "You know, I always believe that good things happen to you if you help others."

He handed two quarters to the man. "Here you go, son. Have a good day. Jesus loves you."

The man put the potato chips back on the rack, thanked Frank, then left. Frank waited till he was halfway across the street then he leaned over the counter and grabbed the phone. He quickly dialed a number.

"Two more calls, he's making two more calls," he said. "Good." He handed the phone back.

We watched the man call someone, gesture as he spoke,

shrugging and shaking his head, then he hung up and called someone else. This time, his shoulders were drooped, his head bowed slightly, submissively. I watched him, trying to figure out what he was saying.

"He's calling his work," I said. "He's calling to say he won't be in today."

"How do you figure?" Frank asked.

"White shirt, dark pants, tennis shoes. He's a waiter. He's calling in sick."

"Then why dress for work?" Frank asked.

"The third call—they want him to go where they are, they don't want him to go to work."

Frank grinned. "Son of a bitch. Very good, kid."

The man hung up the phone, crossed the street and walked past us, heading back down Victoria Park. Frank asked the woman for her phone. She was captivated now, wondering what we were doing. She handed him the phone and looked back and forth between us.

Frank dialed a number. "Yes. The first?" He wrote something down. "And then?" He glanced at me and smiled. "You got it. We've got it from here. Talk to you later." He handed the phone back. "Guess what, Ian? You're right. He called a restaurant on Warden Avenue. But the interesting thing is the first call he made. The third call, I guess. Anyway, he called an address on Lakeshore Boulevard. Why would he do that?"

I thought for a moment. "He's getting his orders from someone who's calling the shots," I said. "He called Kieran's number, and Harry agreed to the ransom, so he called the place where his boss is hiding out, to say that things are moving along. His boss tells him to call the place where they're holding Patrick, maybe, and let them know what's happening. He calls them to say everything's okay and the big guy there says 'don't go to work today, stay home instead.'"

"Why would he say that?" Frank asked.

"Dunno. What did Harry tell him?" I asked back.

Frank asked for the phone again. The woman, fascinated, gave it to him. Frank dialed a number. "Yup, it's me. What did you tell our messenger?" He listened for a moment. "Okay, good work. Talk to you later." He handed the phone back. "Right, we're into the short strokes," he said. "Harry told him we'd have all the money by tomorrow, at ten a.m. Our messenger boy said they'd let him know where to leave it, and when they count it they'll let Patrick go. Usual bullshit, no fake bills, no marked money, no cops."

"So, what do we do now?" I asked.

"We follow the messenger and flush him out. First off, we need some bait. Harry is the voice he recognizes, so he'll be the point man on this. He should be here in twenty minutes or so."

I had no idea what we were doing. I decided to just sit tight and let these professionals work.

Frank bought a coffee and doughnut, handed the woman another twenty and told her to keep the change. He stood by the magazine rack, sipping his coffee, looking out at the road. A short while later, a plain gray Ford pulled up.

Pogue got out of it and came inside to join us. "Hey," he said.

Frank pointed to the coffee machine. "Hi, Harry. Want some coffee? It's not terrible."

Pogue shook his head. "All right, you guys know what he looks like. He most likely went to join up with the head guy. He only knows my voice, though, not yours. I need to talk to him. You two lay low."

Frank shrugged. "All right, what's the bait?"

Pogue nodded at the Ford. "Fifty thousand in a tote bag, in exchange for a photo of Patrick. I told them they'd get the rest of the money once I kill Patrick."

I gasped. "What do you mean?"

Frank smiled. "I think I see where Harry is going with this. Tell him."

Pogue nodded. "I gave him a number and told him to call it in thirty minutes. It's a phone booth at Pape and Danforth.

I'm going to tell him that I secretly hate Patrick's family, and that I want to work out a deal. When we meet, I'm going to say he can keep the fifty thou, before we get him the rest of the money, as a sign of good faith."

"Why that phone booth?" I asked.

He shrugged. "I found it and wrote the number down yesterday. I figure if he hears traffic noise in the background, it adds credibility to my story about wanting to do stuff behind Walsh's back. You two wait here. I'll call you soon. All right?"

He got back into the Ford and drove south. Twenty-five minutes later, the thin man walked past the gas station, then stopped and reached into his pocket. He sighed and came toward us.

Frank tossed his coffee into the garbage. "Hide, go into the back room, now!" He pushed me ahead of him, herding me to the storeroom. He turned to the woman at the counter. "Give him change if he wants it. I'll square it with you later."

He followed me into the back room and closed the door. We breathed softly, afraid to make noise. The store's front door opened.

I could hear the man talking. "I'm really sorry to ask, but could I get some change?" he asked.

"Sure thing, I trust you," the woman said. I heard the till open. "Here you go."

"Thanks," the man said. The front door opened, and he left.

Frank peeked into the store and came slowly out of the back room. "All clear."

We walked to the window, saw the young man as he put change in the pay phone and dialed a number. The woman at the counter leaned forward, watching us. "This is the most exciting thing that's ever happened to me," she said. "What do we do next?"

"Now we wait," Frank said.

The man spoke for a minute or two, then nodded, and

hung up. He walked back toward us, and Frank got ready to hide in the back room again. The man walked past us, south on Victoria Park.

A minute later, the phone rang. The woman picked it up, and wordlessly handed it to Frank.

"Yep," Frank said, then he said "Right." He handed the phone back.

"All right. Harry's meeting our boy's mastermind in Oakridge Park, on the Danforth, in fifteen minutes. We've got to get there first."

We drove down Victoria Park, rushing the twenty blocks or so to Danforth Avenue, then turned east toward Oakridge Park.

"Why would our kidnapper pick this spot to meet Harry?" Frank asked.

"Simple," I said. "It's a small park, surrounded by houses with back yards. Even if we had ten people watching him, there are dozens of ways for him to get away. It makes perfect sense."

Frank snickered. "All that Indian bush experience comes in handy, huh?"

"Yep, thanks to my grandfather. He took me hunting, taught me how to think like prey."

We stopped on Danforth, across the street from Pogue's Ford. He was in it, and nodded very slightly when he saw us. Five minutes later, he got out of his car, dragged a tote bag out with him, and casually walked across the street to the park.

He walked to the baseball diamond in the park, looked around and sat on one of the bleachers behind home plate. We could see him clearly, the tote bag on the seat beside him, resting one elbow casually on the back of a bleacher.

A puke brown Matador stopped in front of Pogue's Ford, and the thin man got out. He straightened his jacket, self-consciously, and walked across the street to the park. He walked past Pogue, looked around to be sure they were alone, then turned back and said something.

Pogue nodded, and the man pointed to the tote bag. Pogue opened it. The man looked in, leaned back with an amazed look, and waved at the street. The driver side door of the Matador opened, and a gray-haired man, also thin, an older version of the first one, walked carefully across the street to join the two men. He kept his hands in the pockets of a black golf jacket, his right hand twitching slightly, as though it was holding something. He said something to the first man, who walked around the park, looking for people who might be watching them. Then he motioned to Pogue, who again opened the tote. The older man leaned forward and picked up a bundle of cash with his left hand. He took his right hand out of his pocket and thumbed through the bills—making sure they were all the same denomination, I later learned. The man reached back into his pocket and pulled out a photograph. He handed it to Pogue, who nodded, satisfied.

Pogue said something and handed the tote to the man. The man took it and called over the younger man. They headed back our way, looking around, walking toward the Matador.

Frank rolled out of our car, walked far down the sidewalk on our side of the street, then crossed the road and walked casually past the Matador. He kept going to the next corner, crossed back and got into the Pinto. He scribbled something down.

"Got the license plate. Let's hope it's not bogus," he said.

We slouched down in our seat, watched the two men get into the Matador, then watched them drive off. Pogue waited in the park for about ten minutes, then slowly got up and drove away.

"Why was Harry waiting?" I asked.

"He's making sure he wasn't being followed," Frank said. "Come on, back to Walsh's office."

We went up to the fourth floor again, and met Pogue, already there, waiting for us.

"So, Harry, what happened?" Frank asked.

Pogue smiled. "They took the bait. I told them that I'm the director of one of Kieran's companies, and I was screwed out of a big bonus. More than that, I told them that Patrick got my daughter pregnant. I said I wanted to be the one to hurt him, only me, nobody else."

Kieran's eyes widened. Pogue shook his head. "As long as they believe that I'm going to hurt Patrick, they won't do anything to him. They'll leave that to me. They have already told him he's going to be beaten, but the man I just met told me they haven't harmed him yet, just in case."

Pogue took the photograph out of his pocket and handed it to Kieran. He looked at it, shook with emotion, and handed it to me. In the photograph, Patrick was sitting in a chair, somewhere in a dark room, with a copy of today's Globe and Mail in his hands. He had his eyes open, and there were cuts over one eyebrow, a red gash on his cheek, clumps of dried blood on his upper lip. I was looking at his hands in the photo. His right hand had four fingers wrapped around the front of the paper, his left hand had the thumb and index finger to the front in an L shape. I pointed to the hands.

"Look, Frank, he's telling us something, I bet."

"What?" Frank said, squinting.

Pogue looked at the photo too. "You know what I think? Right hand, four fingers. Four guys. Left hand, gun symbol. They're armed. Smart boy, Patrick."

"Do you think they figured out that he did that?" I asked.

"They wouldn't have given me the photo if they had. And it's a Polaroid, so they're not making any copies for the scrapbook."

"What about the guys in the park? Any way to tell who they were?"

Pogue shook his head. "No, I don't recognize them, they're strangers to me."

"Did you get any names—did they call each other something?" Frank asked.

"No, but the older one had an accent. Spanish, but probably not from Spain, if you understand."

Kieran Walsh rubbed his neck. "Marquez. Benicio Marquez. His family was from Chile originally, and they got cleaned out after Pinochet took power. We got out in seventy-four, and we did very well. His family stayed in the market there, however, and lost most of their money."

"Where are they now?" I asked.

"They came back to Canada, but I have no idea where they went," Kieran said.

Frank handed a slip of paper to Bagley. "Can you run this plate for me?"

Bagley dialed a phone number. "Hey, how are you?" he said. "Got a minute?" He read the license plate out and waited a few moments. "Great. Thanks."

"It belongs to one Gabriel Marquez, he lives at an apartment on Victoria Park Avenue."

"Probably near the first pay phone," Frank said. "That's the number our guy called earlier."

"But wouldn't it be risky to stash Patrick there?" I asked. "Think if he made a lot of noise."

Frank scratched his cheek. "Yeah, I suppose. What were the last two places he called?"

Bagley looked at a sheet of paper. "The third call was to a house at twenty-five ninety-nine Lakeshore Boulevard West, and the last one was to the Green Banana restaurant on Warden."

Frank nodded. "You were right, Ian. He called the people who are holding Patrick, and then I bet he called in sick for work. I think Patrick is at the Lakeshore Boulevard address. Let's go."

"Do you want to do this now, just we two by ourselves?" I asked.

"No time like the present. Let's not waste it. Harry, Teabag, wait for our call."

CHAPTER 11

We drove across town, a half hour trip southwest to Lakeshore Boulevard. This part of Toronto, to the far west side of downtown, was where old money lived, with large homes and faux Victorian mansions on both sides of the road, an old streetcar track that made the Pinto's wheels skip left and right, cobblestones in the road that bumped us around.

The address we had been given was in the middle of a long block, a red brick Edwardian home with pigeons on the corner of the roof, wide cracks in the walls and upstairs windows covered in old blankets. It was on the south side of the road, right on the lake, the more exclusive and expensive side of Lakeshore Boulevard. The house had once been a smart address in a prestigious neighborhood, a home to be proud of. Now, it looked ready to fall down, too long neglected to be beautiful, too long past its prime to be admired, too far gone to save.

I drove the Pinto past the house, parked across the street and looked over at it, curious.

Frank examined the house, looking for something that would tell him we were in the right place. He shook his head, sadly. "Maybe we're on a goose chase here, kid," he said. "How do we know we're on the right track?"

"It makes sense, Frank. This is a big enough and remote enough place to keep him hidden."

"We can't just knock on the door and ask them if they have Patrick, can we?"

I thought for a moment. "Yes, actually, we can."

"How?" Frank asked.

"Watch. If I'm wrong, we can always deliver pizza for a living, like you said."

I drove the Pinto into the long driveway, far down from the road, and parked just up from the front door. We walked down a weedy, overgrown path to the door. The house seemed even scarier, more foreboding, as I stood there. Cobwebs around the porch light said that it had been neglected for years, and dozens of dried moths, caught in the cobwebs, made a creepy lace pattern around the bare bulb.

Frank stood around the corner, tucked behind a pillar, and I knocked on the door, loudly.

I had a slip of paper in my hand, a car rental receipt that looked like a restaurant bill. A moment later, the door opened. The older man from the park, the driver of the Matador, stood in the doorway, sneering.

"Yes, what do you want?" he asked. He had an accent, slight, soft, but definitely Spanish.

"You ordered pizza?" I asked, looking at the form. "Two mediums, pepperoni and olives?"

The man waved his hand in front of him. "No, no, no. No pizza, no pizza, wrong address."

"Twenty-five ninety-nine Lakeshore Boulevard West?" I pressed. "Two mediums, pepp—"

"I told you, *no*!" the man yelled. "Now go away."

He turned to close the door, but I pressed my hand against it. "Please mister, if I mess up this delivery my boss will fire me. Can I at least use your phone to call him and explain? Maybe Jan wrote it wrong, you know? Jan's always in a rush, and she screws up a lot of orders, you know?"

He huffed and glared at me. "No, no, no, go away. Leave me alone."

He tried to close the door again. This time, I pushed the

door open and he fell back, stunned. I ran into the house, with Frank right behind me. The man looked at us, realizing what was going on. He opened his mouth to call out, but Frank put a hand over the man's mouth and shook his head. The man backed up to yell a warning. Frank punched him once, knocking him out.

We were in a foyer, with a half-glassed door opposite us that led to the main floor of the house. The main floor was empty, no furniture, no lamps, no carpets, as if the house was being stripped of any personality before it was torn down. I couldn't see anybody else here, but I figured they must be somewhere in the house. To my right, a set of marble stairs, covered in remnant carpet, curved up to a gray metal fire door at the second floor.

I opened the glass door and walked around the main floor, creeping carefully to not make noise. There was the smell of mustiness in the air, of wet carpet and old furniture. The main floor living room, which had been stripped of wood trim and furniture, had elaborate rococo wallpaper, with darker square spots on the walls where pictures had hung. The kitchen and pantry, or at least I assume that's what they'd been, had no cabinets, sinks, or cupboards. There were only blank places on the walls and holes in the plaster to remember them.

I came back to Frank, still standing over the unconscious man, and shook my head. I pointed silently up the stairs. Frank cocked his ear for a moment and nodded. He reached into his pocket and pulled out a pair of handcuffs. He cuffed the unconscious man's hands behind his back, reached into his other pocket and pulled out a large handkerchief. He gagged the man with the handkerchief and stood back, making sure the man was still unconscious.

Frank sprinted up the stairs, impossibly quietly, and waited for me to catch up. The fire door at the top landing was open a few inches. Inside, I could see a room, sparsely furnished, with two men inside. One was slight, the younger man from the phone booth, and one was tall, burly, ruddy faced. Both had golf jackets and casual pants on. They were sitting on a dingy sofa, facing two beers on a coffee table. Beside them was an old chrome and Formica table and chairs, with dirty dishes on the table. The younger man was reading a magazine, the bigger one was playing solitaire with a crumpled deck of cards. I glanced down at the bottom of the stairs. The man downstairs was still out cold. The younger man got up and walked back to a fridge.

I waited till the burly man turned to pick up something behind him, then I peeked quickly around the doorway. There was nobody else there that I could see, just these two.

I leaned back and motioned to Frank. I held up two fingers, then one finger, then I held a hand down at Frank's eye level, and then two fingers again, and held up a hand at my height. He nodded, understanding. There were two men, I'd told him, one shorter, one taller.

I waited some more. The burly man turned around again, then I opened the door. I walked up to him, no pausing, no hesitation. He saw me and stood up. He swung a large fist at me, a wild, angry punch that went right over my head. I leaned back and kicked him squarely in the chest.

He went oof and bent forward. I swung my leg back again and planted a second kick into his neck. He fell to one side, onto the coffee table, and rolled away. Frank, meanwhile, had tackled the younger man. He waited till the man swung a punch at him, then blocked it, casually turned to one side, and elbowed the man in the throat. The man fell down, gasping for breath.

Frank stood over the smaller man, watched him struggle to stay conscious, and kept him down.

I watched the larger man tumble onto his stomach and spring to his feet. He was far more agile than I'd expected. He picked up a glass ashtray and threw it at me. I moved to one side and it just missed my ear, shattering against the far wall. He flipped the coffee table over, tumbling it toward me, a desperate attempt to stop me. I took two short steps back, and the coffee table stopped at my feet.

He looked around, desperate for something to use against me. He picked up one beer bottle and threw it at me. It glanced off my left arm and tumbled along a far wall. I made a mistake then—I stayed away from him, giving him time to move away.

The big man jumped over the sofa, squatted down, and popped back up a second later, holding a baseball bat. He held the bat close to the middle, for better balance. It seemed he knew what he was doing. He would slow me down with one fast hit, then slide his hand down to the end of the bat for more leverage, and really hurt me with a power swing.

Clearly, he had been hired as muscle, and he was keen on earning his pay. I needed to stay away from him, to buy time so I could find his weak spot. He danced around the sofa, walking slowly toward me, stepping carefully so as not to trip. He swung the bat, casually, getting a feel for its weight and momentum. I had to think about what to do next.

Our defense instructor at the Police Academy was a quiet man, mild-mannered, always cheery, who looked and spoke like a librarian. He'd been in the Royal Marines, I later learned. He drilled his lessons into us, over and over. Use every advantage, find a way to get your opponent to make an error, realize that every weapon has an advantage and a disadvantage. One day he came in with a frying pan, and asked us about ways to use it as a weapon. Swung like a tennis racquet, we said, it could hit like a bat, but swung on end, it would cut like a knife. Every weapon, he often repeated, had advantages and disadvantages. The frying pan was easy to wield, and could cause a lot of hurt, but it could also be easily taken away.

This baseball bat, I thought to myself, was like that frying pan. It had advantages, but also limitations. I stepped to one side and grabbed the back of a dining chair, then planted myself in the middle of the floor. If the man lunged in close to me, I'd be able to back away. As I hoped, he moved toward me. Another of my instructor's maxims was "the first one to advance, loses." The man gripped his bat like Babe Ruth swinging for a home run, and came in for the kill. I raised the chair in front of me and jabbed at him. He took the bait, swung at me, and I stepped back, letting his bat hit the chair. The chair jerked to one side, moved by the impact, but I was still able to turn it back and jab it into the man's face. He dropped the bat, tried to cover his face and push the chair away. That was where he made his big mistake.

I pulled the chair back slightly and poked him, hard, in the chest. One leg of the chair found a sensitive spot. He growled in pain and tried to smack it away again. I pulled it back again and smacked it hard against his legs. He crumpled to the ground, moaning in pain.

I grabbed the baseball bat and held it over my shoulder, ready to swing it at him.

"Don't even think about it," I growled. I shook my head, patting the air for him to stay down.

Frank held the smaller man by the collar and dragged him to sit beside the larger one. He ran back down the stairs and came back pushing the third man, still groggy, in front of him. He placed the three men together, cross-legged on the floor, and took the bat from me.

"Stay down there or else," Frank snapped at them.

I rummaged through the other upstairs rooms, but there was nobody else up there, nothing to indicate that they had Patrick anywhere nearby. I went back to face the men.

"Where is he?" I asked.

"Who?" the one from downstairs asked.

"Patrick Walsh. Where do you have him?" I asked.

"Never heard of him. I don't know what you're talking about," the man sneered.

"Wrong answer. Tell me now," I said.

"Piss off," he answered.

"You're in very deep shit," I said. "I'll only ask you once. Where is he?"

The man stared at me, trying to decide if I was serious. He sneered. "Screw you."

I sighed, frustrated. Frank stepped back and handed me the bat. "Watch them," he said.

I stared at the men, resting the baseball bat on my shoulder, at the ready, menacing them.

Frank rummaged through the kitchen, opened a tool chest in a closet, then came back with a heavy pair of bolt cutters and a roll of strapping tape.

He pulled the downstairs man away from the other two, into the middle of the floor. He taped the man's legs together, then rolled the man onto his stomach and stepped on his back.

"Now," Frank said. "I'm going to ask you some questions. You piss me off, or you answer wrong, I cut off fingers. Where is Walsh?"

The man sneered again. "Eat shit, asshole."

Frank shrugged and placed the bolt cutters on the man's left thumb. He squeezed the handles, pinching the man's thumb joint, and the man howled in agony.

"Beach house! Beach house! He's in the beach house! Beach house!" he screamed.

The big man swore at him, angry that he'd told us.

"See, now that was smarter, wasn't it?" Frank grunted.

"Where is the beach house?" I asked.

The man, wincing in pain, poked his chin to one side. "In back of the property, on the beach."

I dragged him back to join the other two men, sat him down, and handed the bat to Frank.

"Got them?" I asked.

"Yep. They move, they die," Frank drawled.

I ran back downstairs, along a side path to an overgrown back yard. The main house had rose bushes covering the area. They had obviously once been part of an elaborate garden, but now they were just thorny weeds in a yard that had been ignored for many years.

A soft breeze off the lake blew the smell of sand and

driftwood into the air. The beach house had to be here somewhere, where the smell off the lake was stronger. I picked my way along a stone path, a zigzag of hedges and spindly maple trees that seemed to go nowhere.

I kept walking. Behind the hedges, away from the main house was the Matador, hidden from view. Beyond it was Walsh's Ford, stuck at an angle behind an old garden shed.

I found a long piece of wood, big enough to use as a weapon, if I needed one. At the very back of the yard, where it sloped down to a sandy beach, was a low picket fence. Just beyond the fence was a wooden beach house, small, with flaking paint, almost devoured by thick ivy and long grass. I peeked cautiously into a window, wondering if there was another man in there that I had to subdue.

Inside, lit by the dim sunlight that got through a small, filthy window, I saw was Patrick, sitting on a chair, with thick ropes around his ankles, his arms tied behind his back. His head was drooped, his shoulders slumped. I turned my head to look around at the rest of the house.

Across from him was a man, slim, in a dark green shirt and jeans, sitting backward on a chair. Slung over one shoulder was a holster, police-issue. The holster and the gun in it were Patrick's.

The man had a cigarette in his mouth. He took a drag of the cigarette then casually leaned forward and blew smoke into Patrick's face.

Patrick glared at the man, and struggled, trying to free his legs enough to kick him. The man laughed and sat back down.

I heard the man talking, his voice muffled through the window.

"You think you're going home, 'pajero'? You're not going home." He picked up a short riding crop and smacked Patrick across the knees. He laughed as Patrick growled with pain.

Patrick shook his head. "Why are you doing this? You must know they'll come looking for me."

The man laughed. "They know we got you. They know you're dead if they don't pay us."

Patrick shook his head. "Why me? Why did you go after me? What did I ever do to you?"

The man shrugged. "Your parents have a bodyguard. Your brother does, too. You don't. You are out there, exposed. Stupid."

Patrick looked up and saw me at the window. He froze slightly. The man across from him didn't see it. Patrick's shoulders relaxed and he smiled. "So, what happens when they pay you?"

The man laughed. "We will get your family's money, then we will kill you. The world will believe you killed the whore, and that you ran away. Nobody will believe you were taken, nobody will trust your family anymore." He clipped Patrick across the knees with the crop again.

Patrick looked up at me again. I held up one finger, questioning. He blinked his eyes. The man in the beach house was alone, just one man to worry about.

It took all of my restraint to stay where I was. I had to think. I figured these men must have some way of signaling to each other, to keep in touch. I hoped it was just a simple knock on the door. I knocked on the door and stood back. The man picked the cigarette out of his mouth and tossed it into Patrick's face. He stood up and sauntered casually toward the door.

He opened the door, still turned to look at Patrick, then he saw me. His face dropped. He took a step back and reached his right hand across his chest, rushing to get the gun out of its holster.

"Don't do it!" I yelled. He looked down, still struggling to get the revolver free of the leather.

"Screw you!" he yelled, and wrapped his hand around the butt of the gun.

I brought up the piece of wood and swung it at his arm. He raised his arm, instinctively defending himself, and the wood caught him halfway to the wrist. I heard a noise as the bone broke. The gun fell on the ground, tumbling along the dusty floor. The man didn't give up easily, though. He jumped back and tried to pick up the revolver with his left hand. I poked the wood into his stomach. He pulled his hand back, but glared at me and swung a clumsy left hook my way. I'd had enough of this game. I swung a long field goal kick into his crotch, and the man bent in half. I leaned in close and elbowed him on the back of the neck. He fell down. I thought of him hitting Patrick with his crop, gritted my teeth, and kicked him in the ribs, hard. I kicked him a few more times, until he groaned and spat blood.

"Does that hurt?" I yelled. "Huh, you stupid shit, does that hurt?"

After a half dozen more kicks, the man stopped squirming. I reached down and picked up the gun, then took the holster off his shoulder.

I turned to Patrick and squatted down to look at him.

"Hey, boss, you're not hurt or anything, right?" Walsh joked.

I undid his ropes. "How are you doing, Patrick?" I asked, checking the man on the floor.

"Yeah, I'm a little tired and hungry, but that's all. It's nice of you to drop by and visit, Ian." He looked around at the room. "Sorry I didn't get a chance to clean the place up first," he said, his voice cracking. His mouth trembled, his face contorted, and he started to cry.

He tugged at the lapel of his tuxedo, then stood gingerly, trying to straighten himself up. His bowtie was down over one shoulder, his sleeve was torn, and there were blood stains on the white of his shirt. A wide purple bruise covered most of his cheek, another bruise covered one eye, a bloody gash edged his chin, and where the crop had hit him formed a zigzag line on his pants.

He stood up straight, rubbing his legs to get the circulation back. His eyes welled up with tears. "They killed that girl, they told me. They watched us, when we were on the beach, they waited till she was talking to me, then they strangled her," he said, weeping. "They said I would be blamed for it, even if I didn't get out of here alive. Why did they kill her?"

"Do you know who she was?" I asked.

He shook his head, coughed and composed himself. "I have no idea. I was at the gala, just talking to people, and all of a sudden this gorgeous woman started talking to me. I thought it was my lucky night. She asked me to have champagne with her on the beach, so I said I would, of course. How stupid could I be? Shit, what was I thinking? Why did I get her involved?"

"It wasn't your fault, Patrick. She was a prostitute. You were set up. They lured you out there with her as bait."

He nodded sadly. "A hooker? I see. Benicio Marquez and his family—they're behind this. They got screwed in Chile. They lost their fortune, and they blame our company for their loss." He coughed and spat blood on the floor. "They said that a member of their family—an uncle—lost everything, and that he killed himself. They said they would do anything they could to me to cause my family pain." He shuddered.

"Did they tell you what they were going to do? Did they want anything from you?"

"They were asking for a pile of money. After they got it, they said, they were going to make sure I was a suspect in her death, then they were going to kill me."

His voice broke, and he started to cry again. I put my arms around him, and he wept against my shoulder. The simple act of comforting a friend made me furious at the men in the house.

"Come on, Patrick. Let's let your family know you're all right," I said.

"Are you here by yourself?" he asked.

"No, Frank's here too."

He chuckled slightly. "I pity those other three guys, then."

I holstered the gun and slung it over my left shoulder. I

grabbed the fourth man by his good arm, a kindness, and led him back to the house.

I walked Walsh up the steps to join Frank and the other men. Walsh glared at them, fury in his face, but he said nothing. I pushed the fourth man down to sit with the other three.

"Let's wrap this up," I said softly. I looked around, found the phone and called Fifty-One Division. They were closer to us than Fifty-two, and could get here sooner. I explained the situation and told them to send cruisers over right away.

Then I called Kieran Walsh's office. Pogue answered in one ring, and as soon as I said we had Patrick, safe and sound, I heard him tell it to someone in the room. In the background, I heard Kieran moan, and Lizzy scream out loud. We had done it. We had rescued him. It was over.

Pogue said they'd all be over right away to pick Patrick up. He said to just sit tight till then.

I called to Frank, to let him know what I'd been told. He turned to look over his shoulder at me, for just a moment. The big man, seeing his chance, jumped up and grabbed the baseball bat out of Frank's hands. He slammed Frank to one side, swung the bat into his gut, and plowed past him, charging toward Patrick.

He raised the bat over his head, winding up for a brutal swing.

"Stop! Stop!" I screamed.

The man rushed at Patrick, who was trying to move along the wall and stay away from him. The man cornered Patrick and pushed him in the ribs with the end of the bat, knocking him down. He took a wide stance, looming over Patrick, and raised the bat over his head again, prepared to club him.

"No!" I screamed. "No! Don't do it!"

The man sneered, went up on his toes, and moved the bat even higher behind him, winding up for a murderous hit.

I moved without thinking. The gun came out of the holster. I raised the barrel, pointed, and squeezed the trigger. A sound like thunder filled the room. The big man turned to look at me, surprised, then turned back and pursed his lips, still determined to club Patrick. Two more explosions, like the first, echoed through the house. The big man let the bat drop behind his back and staggered in my direction.

I grabbed him, rested him on one of the dining chairs, and squatted to talk to him.

"Easy, take it easy. Stay with me, all right?" I said, softly. "Just stay with me."

He looked up at me. "Screw off," he wheezed. "You can't tell me what to do. Nobody can."

Apart from the few words he said earlier, that was all I heard him say.

His breathing got more labored, slower, more painful to listen to.

"All right. Stay calm. Breathe slowly, don't panic. Just breathe slowly," I said.

A couple of moments later, a clatter of shoes up the stairs told me that the uniforms from Fifty-One had arrived.

"Here!" I called. "All clear!"

Four men raced up and peeked around the corner, then two of them came into the room.

One man, a uniform with gray temples and a push broom moustache, had sergeant's stripes on his sleeves. He turned to a uniform on the stairs and barked for him to call an ambulance. The second uniform thumped back down the stairs, headed to a cruiser.

The sergeant came over and crouched beside me. "Some bad shit went down, huh, Inspector?"

"Yeah, some really bad shit went down," I said softly.

"You want to tell me what happened?" the sergeant asked. "You don't have to, you know."

"He was going to club Patrick Walsh to death. He wouldn't stop. I had to shoot him."

The sergeant placed his hand over my wrist. I hadn't realized I was still holding the gun.

"Let me take that for you, Inspector," he said. He took the gun out of my hand, carefully, then turned to face one of the other uniforms. "Bag this. It's evidence."

I smiled sadly. "By the book, huh? You're doing this the right way, all the way?"

He nodded. "You bet, Inspector. We're going to make sure this is all by the book, sir." The other uniform put the gun in a plastic bag. The sergeant looked me in the eye. "Don't think for a minute we're trying to railroad you. But if some dipshit lawyer claims we swept anything under the rug, I want to be able to say that we dotted the Is on this case."

I sat cross-legged on the floor and sighed. I looked up at the big man. A bullet hole in his side, and two more in his chest, were oozing blood. The sergeant loosened the man's shirt buttons to help him breathe, talking to him calmly, trying to keep him awake.

"How long till the ambulance shows up? We can't lose this guy, we've got to save him," I said.

The sergeant shook his head. "Sorry, Inspector, but he's taken three shots to the chest. I don't think he's going to make it."

"I survived four in the chest," I said, hopefully. "Maybe he can hang on—"

At that point, the big man dropped off the chair and slumped to the ground, like a large rag doll, just as lifeless. I closed my eyes and said a quiet Hail Mary for his soul, then I recited the Twenty-third Psalm. Without thinking, I said it out loud. I finished with "'I shall dwell in the house of the Lord forever.' Amen," I whispered.

The two uniforms repeated it.

Frank stepped away to meet Bagley and Pogue coming up the stairs. They spoke for a minute, then Pogue walked back to the kitchen with Frank, pulled a familiar tote bag out from under a table, and handed it to Bagley. Pogue waved goodbye to us, then Bagley and Pogue left.

Frank squatted beside us. "Teabag says they're done. He just wanted me to tell you goodbye."

"They're done? What do you mean, 'done'?" I asked. "Don't they want to stick around?"

Frank shrugged. "Why should they? They achieved the mission objective. Patrick is free, with minimal collateral damage, and they got paid, so they've left. They've gone. Period."

"Paid?" I asked stupidly.

Frank shrugged. "They're going keep the teaser cash, the fifty grand. It's more than fine by Kieran, and it's certainly fine by me."

I sat there for about fifteen minutes, as the uniforms collected evidence and secured the scene. A new set of footfalls, softer, lighter, came up the stairs.

Nancy Coogan, the detective inspector for Fifty-One Division, turned the corner. She did not seem very surprised to see me.

"Hi, Ian. You got yourself in the middle of a real messy one this time, I see."

"Hi, Nancy. Yeah, I wish it had gone differently."

She spoke with Frank and Patrick then to the three men on the floor, but they said nothing.

She walked back over to me. "Do you want to talk about it? Personally, I'd suggest you say nothing, and save it all for the inquest. It's up to you, of course."

"Inquest?" I asked.

"You're a police officer, and you just killed a civilian. There will have to be an inquest, Ian."

I shrugged. "Technically, I'm on suspension, so I'm not really a cop right now."

She frowned. "Did you tell them you were a cop? Did you say you were a policeman?"

I thought back over the events of the last hour. "No, I never did, come to think of it."

She shrugged. "Well, that helps. We have Frank and Patrick here that say you were only trying to save an officer's life. The others are facing kidnapping and murder charges, but have refused to talk. I don't really see a lot for you to worry about, do you? Go home, Ian. We'll talk later."

I walked Patrick down the stairs to the road. He was unsteady, weak, walking gingerly, but he insisted on leaving on his own two feet. Kieran and Lizzy were there on the sidewalk, watching us come out to them. Kieran embraced Patrick, clutching him for dear life. Lizzy was gripping him close too, weeping uncontrollably. Sam, stood with his back to the three, watching that nobody got near.

Kieran let go and ran up to me. He shook my hand vigorously. "I can't thank you enough for what you did, Ian," he gushed. "If there's ever anything I can do for you, anything at all, please, please, just let me know."

I shook my head. "I'm just happy we were able to get Patrick back. I'm just glad he's safe."

An ambulance appeared out of nowhere, a private ambulance with a pair of burly attendants. Kieran and Patrick got into it, and it sped off. Lizzy and Sam got into their Mercedes and headed after it. Everything seemed suddenly very quiet.

I drove home and dropped the Pinto's keys on the front hall table. Karen was in the living room, pacing, waiting for me to come in.

"Rebecca called and told me what happened," she said, softly. "You rescued Patrick, she said, because he was being held hostage by someone? Do you want to talk to me about it?"

I shook my head. I was sad, elated, exhausted, alert, all at once. I felt like I could curl up and sleep for a month, or jump a high fence, both at the same time.

"I need to sleep," I said, hoarsely. "I'm sorry, Karen, I'm really tired. We'll talk in the morning."

I went upstairs, took a very long shower, and got into bed. I needed to not think for a while.

CHAPTER 12

Early the next morning, Karen made breakfast. I sat at the table eating eggs and toast, not tasting anything. I told her what had happened, that Patrick was safe, that we'd caught the kidnappers. I then said that one of them had been killed in the scuffle, and that I had killed him.

She wrapped her arms around me and cried. Then she held my face in her hands and kissed me. I cried, a deep, sobbing weeping that emptied my heart. Karen had her arms around me, wrapping me tight in her embrace. I felt, in that moment, that it would be all right, that my feelings of guilt and sadness would pass. That I would be fine again.

Later that morning, I walked Ethan to school, then called a cab and went to Fifty-two Division.

I didn't know what to expect when I walked in the door. A rush of men came up to me, shaking my hand, wishing me well, offering their congratulations at having rescued Patrick. News of what happened had come through the grapevine from Fifty-one Division. It was embarrassing, the compliments for having done something that might end my career or send me to jail.

Van Hoeke came up to me, placed his hand on my shoulder, and turned me around. "Step into my office, Ian," he said softly. I followed him, meekly, and sat across from his desk.

He closed the door behind us and sat in his chair. He

leaned back and cradled his head in his hands. "Do you know what I did in the war?" he asked.

"You were in the RAF," I answered.

"Right. I flew Spitfires, as it happens. I shot down a Heinkel bomber the first week I was with my unit. I always imagined that I'd feel like a hero when I downed an enemy bomber. I always thought I'd be pleased, that I was saving England from the Hun. Instead, I spent the next three years wondering about the families of the men who died in that plane."

"I understand. You felt remorse," I said. "But it doesn't make how I feel any easier to take."

Van Hoeke shook his head. "No, that's not what I meant," he said. "After that one, every other victory was just trash in the windscreen. After my first kill, after I drew my first blood, it didn't matter. You just drew your first blood, Ian. Very few police officers experience what you have. You have to realize that the only reason you feel bad is because you have compassion for your enemy, not because you pulled the trigger."

I grimaced. "All right, thanks for the pep talk, boss. Am I allowed to come back to work yet?"

He shook his head, reached into his desk and handed me my badge. "Not until Doctor Feldman says you can. You're on paid leave. Go home, get some rest, watch TV, bake cookies. I don't care. Later on, talk to Colleen Feldman. After she okay's it, then you can come back to work."

I got up and left his office. Reynolds and Parker were waiting for me at my desk.

Reynolds smiled weakly. "Hi, boss. Any news?" she said, being intentionally vague.

I shook my head. "I'm away from the case for now. Talk later. I'll let you know when I'm back."

Reynolds nodded, understanding what I meant. "Just to let you know, we're looking into any other connections there may have been between the victims. We'll keep you posted, okay?"

"Sounds good. Look, there's going to be an inquest, and I will be cleared, hopefully. It may not be till after I get back from Saskatchewan, though, so just keep doing what you're doing."

A pink telephone message slip on my desk caught my eye. Kieran Walsh had called, asking if I could stop by and talk to Patrick. He was at a private hospital, and had asked to speak specifically to me. I put the slip of paper in my pocket, walked through to the motor pool and retrieved my Caprice. It had been vacuumed and cleaned, which was nice of them. Just having my car back made me feel better.

I drove to the hospital, a Victorian mansion on the edge of Forest Hill, with tumbling gardens and a winding path leading to a covered entrance. Inside the entrance, there was a set of thick glass doors blocking the doorway to the main lobby. I waited politely at the doors until a woman in a nurse's uniform walked past. She strutted up to the double door and smiled at me.

"Yes, may I help you?" she asked, talking through the crack between the doors.

I held up my badge. "Detective Inspector McBriar to see Patrick Walsh."

She reached around the corner and pressed something. The door buzzed open, and I went in.

Most hospitals smell of chloroform or alcohol. This one just smelled clean and fresh, of flowers and crisp laundry. There was soft music playing in the background, something classical—Mozart, I thought. I wondered, half-serious, if it was a live orchestra.

The woman marched back to a desk around the corner and waved at an arm chair. "Please wait here."

She picked up a phone and said something. Seconds later, a man in a white orderly's uniform appeared from nowhere.

"Mister McBriar?" he asked, tentatively.

"Detective Inspector McBriar," I corrected.

"Of course, sir. Please follow me."

He led me up a wide marble staircase, with thick black wooden banisters, to the second floor.

The music grew fainter. I turned a corner, following the orderly, and stepped into a large room that reminded me more of a comfortable living room than a hospital.

Patrick Walsh was in an armchair, reading a newspaper. He was wearing crisp forest green pajamas and slippers.

He looked up at me. "Hey, boss, thanks for coming. Would you like something to drink? Tea?"

I raised one eyebrow. "Tea? Really?"

He laughed out loud. "No, it's actually very good. Hell, everything here is very good. Except for the nurses, of course."

I dragged an armchair beside his and poured tea for myself. "So, how are you feeling, Patrick?"

He shook his head, suddenly serious. "I don't know, boss. I thought I'd be fine, after you got me out, but when I close my eyes I wonder what would have happened if you hadn't found me."

"Scary, isn't it?" I asked. "They call it 'survivor guilt,' I believe."

He looked sadly up at me. "How did you do it? You got shot. You got beat up inside your own house, and your family was being threatened, yet you came back to the job. How did you do it? I have to know."

I took a sip of the tea. It was strong, hot, very good. "Do you think it was easy? Don't you think I went through months, day in and day out, wondering if it was the right decision to come back? Is that it? Are you wondering if you should come back to work, Patrick?"

He shrugged. "Yeah, but I wonder now if I'll be scared shitless every time I turn a corner, every time I answer a call, every time I see a pretty woman waving me over. I just don't know if I can handle it, that's all. I don't know if I'm too much of a coward to do the job."

I leaned back and smiled. "So, that's it? You're worried about showing fear?"

"Aren't you?" he asked.

"No. It's part of the job. It keeps you sharp, keeps you thinking. If you're not afraid, you're likely dead. But in any case, if you decide that you don't want to do the job anymore, let me know. Whatever you decide, Patrick, I won't hold it against you. I won't think any the less of you if you decide this isn't the life for you."

He looked down, nodding. "They want me to stay here for another day or so."

"You've had a traumatic ordeal. You need to rest."

"Yeah, but the way I heard it, you'd just gotten out of hospital, and a week later you were already out there, trying to arrest the guy who shot you," he said.

"Reports of my bravery have been greatly exaggerated," I quipped. "I was very pissed off at him. I went off the script as soon as he started talking, taunting him so he'd show himself." I stood up. "Thanks for the tea, Patrick. Look, let me know what you decide. We'll either have a really good 'welcome back' party, or a really good 'farewell' party. Rest up."

I drove home, parked beside a large black Mercedes in the driveway, and went inside. There was the sound of women laughing in the kitchen. That made me feel angry, upset that they were happy when I felt terrible inside. That was irrational, I knew, so I put on a smile, then rounded the corner to meet them.

Lizzy Walsh was leaning against the kitchen counter, wearing slacks and a navy blouse. She had her elbows on the counter, talking casually. Helen was sitting on the counter, kicking her legs like a child at a swimming pool. Karen poured coffee for them, setting out cake on the kitchen table.

Out of the corner of my eye, I saw Sam, the big man, sitting in the corner like a sheepdog.

Karen gave me a hug and kiss. Lizzy hugged me too, and gave me a peck on the cheek. That gave me a rush that I hoped wouldn't show on my face.

"By the way, I just went to visit Patrick," I said.

Lizzy beamed. "He said he wanted to see you. He asked that his father and I give him some space, but he especially wanted to see you. How is he?"

"Good. He's reconsidering the force, right now. I told him whatever he decides is fine by me."

Sam stood and placed a hand on my shoulder, his fingers wrapping over my collar bone, and leaned down to whisper in my ear.

"Thanks for helping Mister Patrick," he mumbled, in a low thunder of a voice. "Anything you need, you can count on me."

I nodded appreciation. "Have they fed you yet, Sam?" I asked.

He shook his head sadly.

"Let's fix that," I said.

I made him a couple of sandwiches, cut a large slab of cake, and, at his request, poured him a quart of milk. He ate quietly, occasionally watching Lizzy to be sure she was alright.

"So," Karen said. "Lizzy wants to take us all out to lunch. What do you think?"

"Sounds like lots of fun." I grinned. "You all go ahead and have a good time."

"You don't want to join us?" Lizzy asked.

I shook my head. "Sorry, I have some work stuff that can't wait," I lied.

Lizzy looked straight at me. "You know, I haven't thanked you properly for what you did for Patrick. I know that you put your career at risk to help him," she said, suddenly serious.

I shrugged, trying to act casual. "I owe Patrick a lot. Helping him was the very least I could do."

She nodded. "I realize that. In any case, as Kieran said, if there's anything we can do, just say the word."

"Do you know a good mechanic?" I joked. "Our Valiant has really crapped out."

Lizzy grinned. "We may be able to help you out with that, yes."

The three women finished their coffee and collected their purses, ready to leave. Sam placed his plates carefully in the sink and leaned down to my ear level. He placed his huge hand on my shoulder. "Real good food, mister Ian. Thanks again."

He followed the three women out to the Mercedes, looking around as he walked. The women lounged in the back seat, he got in the front and they all drove off. I was in the house alone. Ethan was at school, Charley was at a friend's birthday party for the day, and Frank was at work. There was nobody to talk to, nobody to bother me, nobody to explain my actions to, nobody to talk to. I appreciated the time to myself, time to relax, to stretch out, to not think.

I changed into a T shirt and shorts and read the newspaper. Then, I made myself an omelet for lunch, watched some ridiculous game show, and fell asleep.

Around three in the afternoon, I got up and mowed the back lawn. Ethan came home from school and immediately went back out to play at a neighbor's house. By five, I had weeded the front flower bed, washed out the bird bath and swept the sidewalk. I decided I'd make something light for dinner. Mentally, I ran through the ingredients for a salad and soup, remembering what we had in the fridge, deciding what I still had to buy.

A sound at the end of the road made me look up. A black Mercedes rolled to a stop in my driveway. Karen got out of the back seat, waved at me and smiled.

"Hey!" she called.

I walked over to her. "Hi. How was lunch?" I asked.

"Wonderful." She grinned. "We went to this hotel called The Windsor Arms. It was *glorious*."

She hugged me. "By the way, Helen and Frank are coming over for dinner. Okay by you?"

"Sure. Are they just coming to freeload, and what am I making?" I joked.

"No, Frank's bringing pizza. He said you'd appreciate the irony, whatever he means by that."

I smiled sadly. "I get it."

Just before six, Frank, Helen and their children all rolled into our front hall. The kids ran off to play with Charley, and Frank rested three large pizza boxes on the kitchen counter.

"Hey, Ian, how are we doing?" Frank asked.

"Fine, I guess."

We ate pizza in the kitchen. The children ate theirs then raced off to play with toys in the basement. Frank patted his mouth dry and wrinkled his brow.

"So, are you still in the penalty box, kid?" he asked.

"I'm on paid leave, pending the okay from Doctor Feldman," I said. Saying it out loud hurt me.

Helen watched us, studying our conversation.

I shrugged. "It should just be a matter of form, but I won't feel better till it's behind me."

Helen leaned forward. "How did you feel after that man died?" she asked.

"It was hell. I felt awful," I answered.

"How would you have felt if they'd killed Patrick instead?" she asked.

I thought about that for a moment. "Even worse."

"Was there a third option? Something else you could have done instead?"

I shook my head.

"Then this was the best possible outcome, wasn't it, Ian?" she asked.

"That may be, but it doesn't make it hurt any less," I said.

She smiled softly. "No, I don't suppose it does. That's because you're a good man."

At the end of the night, I helped carry leftover pizza to Helen's car, while she and Frank placed their sleepy children in the back seat. Helen started the engine and they drove off.

I waved at the departing car and went into the house. Karen had straightened up, put the empty pizza boxes in the garbage, and closed up the house for the night.

She looked up and smiled at me. "Hey, are you feeling any better?" she asked.

I shrugged. "Some. I'm going to call Colleen in the morning. Once she gives me the green light, I'll be back on the case. I really want to get this cleared up before I go to Esterhazy, though."

"Wouldn't seeing your dad be a good break? Won't it get your mind off work?"

I shook my head. "I know I'd be thinking about this case the whole time. I want it behind me."

We climbed into bed and Karen wrapped her arms around me. She nuzzled her head under my chin. "Good night, you," she said.

"Good night, sweetheart," I whispered. Her breathing got very slow, and very quiet. I slept.

ᏅᏅ

I run up a flight of stairs. Patrick Walsh is playing cards with four men, laughing and joking.

One of them, a large guy in a windbreaker, charges at me with a baseball bat. I pull a gun from nowhere and shoot him three times. He sits down on a dining chair. "Piss off," he says, and dies.

ᏅᏅ

I sat up, sweating. Karen was facing the other way, not stirring, asleep, it seemed. I rubbed my face and took a deep breath.

Karen rolled over. "Another bad dream?" she asked softly.

"Yeah, I had another bad dream," I said.

"Are you all right now?"

"I don't know. Go to sleep, hon. I'm just going to get something to drink," I said.

I pulled on a pair of pajama pants and walked past the kids' bedrooms. Charley was asleep, face-down in her bed, knees up to her waist, her bum in the air. Ethan was on his back, his legs shimmied up against the wall, his mouth open.

I crept downstairs and made coffee. In the kitchen, a wedge of gray light from the streetlamp lit the fridge and countertop. I sat at the table, sipped coffee and remembered the events of the last two days. I didn't think it could have ended differently, but it still didn't help how I felt.

There was a loud noise, one that filled the air downstairs. It took me a moment to realize it was the phone ringing. I looked at the wall clock—three forty-five. I picked up the phone.

"Hello?" I whispered.

"Hey, Ian," Frank's voice boomed. "Can't sleep, huh?"

"Hi, Frank," I answered. "No, I wanted to get up in case you phoned."

He laughed. "Yeah, right. Listen, do you want to grab some breakfast?"

"Now? It's not even four in the morning."

"What the hell. Live life on the wild side. How about you come pick me up?" he asked.

I chuckled. "Sure. Give me five to get dressed, and I'll be right over."

I went back upstairs and grabbed my clothes. Karen sat up and watched me, puzzled.

"Where are you going?" she asked.

"Frank wants to have breakfast with me," I whispered. "I'll be back soon."

She looked at the clock. "Now?" she mumbled.

"Yeah, I think he's doing it to help my mood. Why not? Sounds like fun."

I fumbled around, looking for my keys.

"Lose something?" Karen asked.

"My car keys. I can't find them," I said.

"Do you want to take my Pinto?" she asked.

"No, I'm—I'm just—Wait, here they are," I said. I took my keys and kissed her goodbye.

Frank was outside, on the sidewalk, waiting for me as I pulled up. He rubbed his eyes and coughed, then shook his head.

I stopped and he got in. "Where are we going?" I asked.

"The Night and Day," he answered.

"Where's that?"

"College Street at Spadina. They have these whole wheat pancakes that must be four inches thick. You'll love them."

We drove down Rogers Road, absolutely empty at this time of day, turned right on Dufferin Street, then past the subway where we'd found our second dead woman, and left on College. It took maybe ten minutes to get to the Night and Day. I parked behind a taxi and a delivery truck, put my 'police business' sign on the dashboard, and we went in. Somehow, even the small act of placing the placard on my dashboard made me feel like life was getting back to normal.

Inside, the restaurant reminded me of those diners you see in old movies. The back wall was covered in ceramic tile, the rest of the walls in dark wood paneling, and the floor was a checkerboard of black and white linoleum. Pictures of local celebrities covered one wall.

It had a half-dozen booths along the front window, in red leatherette with pale Formica tables, and a line of stools at the counter, relatively fancy, with low chrome backs and thick padding.

Frank sat at a booth against the front window, looking out at College Street. I sat opposite him, rubbed my face and smiled. "This was a good idea, Frank. I appreciate this," I said.

Our waitress came over and handed us menus, laminated sheets with pictures of food and descriptions of the dishes.

Frank waved his away, then ordered pancakes, sausages and eggs over easy. I asked for the same. The waitress, a slight, short woman with dyed black hair in a bun and thick-rimmed glasses, brought us two mugs of coffee and a pitcher of cream.

Frank looked out the window. In the distance, one of the traffic lights went from blinking red, as it did late at night, to solid red, then green. This was a clear sign that morning was on its way.

Outside, a Toronto Star truck squealed to a stop, rolled up the back door and dumped out stacks of newspapers. The driver slammed the door down again and drove off quickly.

It all seemed so surreal that we'd been looking for Walsh, were still looking for whoever killed those women, trying to make sense of it all, when at the same time here, in the cool light of early morning, people went about their lives and they never even knew what we were doing.

Frank smiled at me. "Penny for your thoughts, kid?"

I shrugged. "Do you ever wonder how much it really matters, what we do? We run around, trying to play by the rules, trying to make a difference, but out here, there are people who go to work, go home, live out their lives and never have to worry about it."

"Would they feel the same way if the criminals ran the city?" Frank asked.

"I don't know, maybe…maybe I'm just feeling like it should have ended differently, that's all."

Frank folded over one of the corners of his paper napkin, thinking.

"You met Harry and Teabag," he said. "They look like okay guys to you?"

"They looked less dangerous than they obviously are. I wouldn't want to piss them off," I said.

Frank smirked. "They were in my unit. Harry got separated from us, and had to work his way back through enemy lines. He almost died of some bug he caught. Teabag went looking for him, found him and brought him home. Teabag—do you know why they call him that?"

"Tom Bagley—T. Bag," I said.

Frank shrugged. "Not everybody gets that, you know. A couple months later he got captured by the VC. We got word they were marching him back to some shithole to parade him around as a war trophy. Harry was still kind of sick, but he volunteered to help me track Teabag down. We followed a unit of twelve VCs that were holding Teabag prisoner. We got him back."

"How did you do that?" I asked.

"We evened the odds. We cut down their numbers, knocked out their people."

"How many North Vietnamese did you kill doing it?" I asked.

"Between us, twelve." He took a sip of coffee and put his cup down. "Harry and Teabag would do what they did back there for free. These guys are closer to me than brothers. And I would kill for them again, if I had to."

He leaned forward and spoke softly. "I'd do it for Patrick, and I'd do it for you. And you know why? Because, you'd do it for me. I know, because when the shit hit the fan, you did it for him."

"I had no choice. I just did what I had to do.," I whispered.

"Bullshit. You could have wimped out, and you could have made excuses later. You didn't. You chose to save the life of a friend. Kieran will never forget it, neither will Patrick. Neither will I."

"What about Lizzy?" I asked, smiling.

He grinned. "Yeah, isn't that a tall cool drink for a thirsty man? They still make them like her?"

I chuckled. "Yup. Lots of time at the confessional over those thoughts."

Frank roared with laughter. The others in the diner stopped talking and looked at him. He put a hand over his mouth. "You know, Ian, I bet that's the first joke you've made in days."

I thought about that. "Yeah, you're right. I'm going to call Colleen Feldman tomorrow—that's today, I guess. I'll remember to mention that to her."

Frank was looking out the window, frozen, it seemed. I waited a few seconds, but he stayed in the same position. I looked at where he was looking. There was nothing unusual out there.

"What is it, Frank?" I asked. He didn't react. "Frank?" I repeated.

A few seconds later, he looked at me. "What, why are you staring at me?" he asked, puzzled.

"You were having a seizure. Where's your medication?" I asked.

He fumbled around, his hands poking into his pockets, then came out with a small pill bottle. "Here we go," he muttered, and took a pill with a sip of coffee.

He put the pills away, as if nothing had happened. We ate, talked about nothing important, about Van Hoeke's MG and his receding hairline, then around five-thirty I grabbed the check and we left. At this time of year, the sun was already up, peeking over the buildings on College Street, reflecting off northern windows and shining light on the south side of the road. People were walking to work, waiting for the streetcar, headed for the subway. The city was awake and going about its business, and it didn't pay any attention to how I felt. I drove Frank home.

After we finished breakfast, Karen said she was taking Charley to Helen's for the day. She drove off. Ethan walked to school, and suddenly I was alone in the house once again.

I waited till nine, then called Colleen Feldman. She had been expecting my call, she said, and asked me to be at her office in an hour. Just before ten in the morning, I parked in the 'Police Vehicles Only' lot in Old City Hall, walked across the street to a black metal skyscraper on Bay Street, then took the elevator up to Colleen's office.

After years of being in Toronto my claustrophobia had improved, but I still felt a tightness in my chest whenever I got into an elevator. I rode fifteen floors up, focused on taking shallow breaths to ward off the feeling of panic. I entered an office with the name *C. Feldman, PhD* on the door, and sat in the anteroom. A glass wall, floor to ceiling, looked out at Queen Street, the fountain at New City Hall, and pedestrians wandering across Nathan Phillips Square.

A couple of minutes later, I heard a woman's voice say "All right, bye," and the door to the main office opened. Colleen Feldman stepped into the doorway and waved me in.

"Hello, Ian, it's nice to see you're looking well," she said. "Please come in."

She backed into her office and waved me in. I sat in a plush swivel chair. She sat on a wooden stool, placed a notepad on her lap and rolled her pen between her fingers.

"So, I understand you've had a rather traumatic couple of days," she started.

Her voice was metered, calming, soothing. "Do you want to tell me about it?"

"Patrick Walsh was being held for ransom, we found him, and in the process of releasing him I killed one of his kidnappers. But you know that," I said simply.

She shook her head. "How scary. It seems to me that there must be more to it than that, right?"

"What else can I say? I wish I hadn't had to kill him. I wish it had gone differently. But in the end, Patrick is now safe, and nobody else was badly hurt. Am I upset that I killed a man? Damn right. Was there another alternative, any other way it could have gone? Hell, no."

She leaned forward, staring at my eyes. Her navy blouse flared open slightly, and a silver buckle on a black bra strap flashed, catching the light. I hoped she didn't see that I'd noticed it.

"You're also going back to visit Alberta at the end of the month, aren't you?"

"Saskatchewan," I corrected. "There's a service and a remembrance on the tenth anniversary of my mother's death."

"Saskatchewan. Right, sorry. Are you still bothered by thoughts of that death?"

"I wasn't until just recently. Maybe it's with the trip coming up, but I've had some dreams about her, lately, where I see her being hit by the pickup truck."

"Did they ever get the person who did it?" she asked.

"Yes. He was asleep and drunk in his truck when they found him, so we know he did it."

"Did you want to kill him back then?"

"Sure. But I figure everything happens for a reason. If her death hadn't happened, I wouldn't have joined the police force, I wouldn't have met Karen, and I wouldn't be a dad."

"How do you feel about the death that happened this week?"

"How do you mean?" I asked.

"You are a very religious person, Ian. You must have deep feelings about what happened. You probably feel guilty about what you did. Why don't you tell me about your mood since then?"

"My mood?" I asked. "I'm feeling fine."

She looked hard at me, reading my face. "I don't believe that, Ian. I don't think you're 'feeling fine,' as you say. Tell me, Ian, how have you really been feeling since the shooting?"

I felt myself getting irritated, upset at her questions. It felt like my skin was itching all over, just hearing her voice. I rolled my eyes. "Look, Colleen, I know all your psych tricks. You're saying my name frequently to build rapport, to establish trust, and you're pressing me, asking me probing questions so I'll 'open up.' It's not working, by the way."

She put the notepad on a coffee table beside her. "Would you like a drink of water?" she asked.

"No, I'm fine, thanks."

She scowled. "Again, you said 'fine.' Is that your code for 'don't ask me any more questions'?"

Something came over me. "You can be a real bitch without half trying, you know?" I snapped. I rubbed my face. "I'm sorry. I'm so, so sorry, Colleen. That was uncalled for. I don't know where that came from."

She smirked, satisfied with herself. "Very good. That was the reaction I'd hoped for, you know." She pointed her pen at me, jabbing the air as she spoke. "You've been holding your feelings in, trying to act like everything was normal. But I bet you're a coiled spring inside, aren't you?"

"Am I tense? Yeah, I suppose," I said. "Is that surprising? I just killed a man." I winced inside at just having to say those words.

"No, it's not at all surprising. So, how are you really feeling, beyond tense?"

"I'm angry, I'm goddamned angry at myself, Colleen. I *killed* a man. That's not what I expected to do when I became a cop. How am I supposed to feel right now, huh? You tell me."

She shrugged. "There are no rules for that, I'm afraid." She sighed and rubbed her eyes. "Some men can cause a fatality, even in the course of an unavoidable accident of some sort, and feel devastated for life. Others can run over a pedestrian and carry on as if it's nothing more serious than a flat tire. You're somewhere in the middle. You're feeling grief, the same grief as if a relative had died. You know intellectually that it was unavoidable. Still, you will have times when you feel fine, and other times when you'll get angry for no reason. Both emotions are perfectly normal."

I smiled sadly. "How long till I feel like me again?"

"There are no rules for that, either. It might be a week; it might be a year. I do know that you'll never forget this, but I can also promise you that the anger and sadness will fade with time."

I sat still, digesting this. I looked over at the aquarium in the corner. A lone goldfish swam up and down, occasionally moving back and forth, then examining us.

"Where's your other fish?" I asked.

"I'm afraid Sigmund went to goldfish heaven. Carl is still feeling a little depressed," she said.

"Anything you can do about that? Can't you help him get over his feelings of depression?"

She smiled. "I have no idea how I can snap him out of it, no."

"You aren't a fish therapist, then?" I joked.

She chuckled. "No, but I don't worry too much about his mood. I do worry about yours."

I nodded. "Point taken. Can I call you if I need to talk?"

"Always." She stood up.

I held out my hand. "I apologize for the comment earlier. I'm very sorry."

She took my hand. "Not at all. I was hoping for a breakthrough. That was it. I'm pleased."

I went back downstairs and walked to my car. I took my keys out, thought for a moment, then turned around and went down the street to a pet store.

I bought a goldfish, paid the man behind the counter to deliver it to Colleen's office, and walked back to my car.

I drove to Fifty-two Division and sat at my desk. Van Hoeke came up to me and sat on the corner of the desk beside mine.

"Hello, Ian. Penny for your thoughts?" he said.

"You've been talking to Colleen."

He nodded. "Part of her job is to keep me informed of my staff's mental state. When you have my job, you'll see how important that is."

"If," I said.

"If?" Van Hoeke asked.

"It's 'if' I take the job, not 'when.' I haven't said I would yet."

Van Hoeke looked at his shoes for a moment, thinking. "Even after what happened, don't you think it reflects how we feel about you, that we still want to offer you the position?"

I scratched my moustache and thought for a moment. "Yeah, true. Listen, Martin, I can't make a sensible decision right now. Give me till I come back from Saskatchewan to decide. Hopefully, I'll have my head on straight by then."

He smiled. "Fair enough. What are you doing here, then? You should be at home."

"Something's driving me nuts. Whoever did these murders, and it's probably the same person, they've tried to make both deaths look random, but they've been playing with us, more than trying to throw us off. Something just doesn't add up, boss."

He nodded. "Fine. On the same subject, the powers that be feel that the shooting is removed enough from the cases on your plate that you should still be able to work on them without it affecting the inquest. Obviously, Patrick will be off for some time so, in the meantime I assume that Reynolds will team up with Terry Parker?"

"Yes. Patrick may be off for a while, I'm told. Look, if it takes a few extra days to run this case down, I can delay leaving, as long as I'm in Esterhazy for the thirtieth. I'm sure my father won't mind that."

Van Hoeke stood up. "Very well, carry on." He went to leave and turned back. "Ah. Colleen asked me to say 'Carl the fish thanks you.' She said you'd know what she meant."

I laughed. "Tell her she's welcome."

I read through the reports again. There was something I was missing, something right there, in plain sight. But what? I looked back and forth at the photos, the reports, the maps. Nothing made sense. I looked up. Reynolds was sitting across from me, watching me.

"Hey, Alex. Been here long?" I asked.

"A couple of minutes. You were concentrating on something. I didn't want to disturb you."

I shook my head. "Ever get the sense that you're just one piece short on the jigsaw puzzle? There's something here, something we're missing. I just can't put my finger on it."

She frowned, thinking. "All right, how about this. The first victim, Brenda Grant, was killed by someone who walked up to her and poked her with a knife blade. He, or she, didn't have to worry about her being apprehensive, or screaming, or fighting back. The killer must have been somebody she knew."

"Go on," I said.

She leaned forward, resting her elbows on her knees, gesturing with her hands. "All right, so I want to kill you." She reached out and picked up a pencil. "I have a knife, and I approach you. You're not worried, because you know me. But even so, if I come at you with a knife—" She poked the pencil at me, jabbing it toward my chest.

I brushed it away. "I get it. Why didn't she fend off whoever it was? As you say, even if she knew them, she'd fight back as soon as she saw the blade."

Reynolds nodded. "Here's a twist. Suppose I kiss you?"

I raised one eyebrow. "Come again?"

She giggled. "Pretend. Watch." She raised two fingers and pressed them against my lips. "What happens to you when you get kissed?"

"Really, Alex? How old do you think I am—twelve?"

She blushed. "No, not that. I mean, do you close your eyes when you kiss?"

I sat back and thought. "Karen does. In most of the old movies I've seen, the woman does, too. Son of a bitch. I get it."

"Right," Reynolds said. "Now, try it again." She pressed two fingers against my lips, and I closed my eyes, for just a moment. I felt the sharp point of the pencil against my chest.

I opened my eyes. "I'm dead," I said. "Just like that."

Reynolds grinned, pleased with herself. "Something else, boss. She was pregnant, remember?"

"Yes, so, who killed her—the baby's father? A jealous lover? Someone totally different?" I asked.

"That's the big question, isn't it? I'd bet on the father. Imagine if she wanted to marry him, but he didn't want to marry her? Or he didn't want to become a father, and she wanted to have the baby without him anyway. Those are two possibilities," she said.

"There is a third possibility. What if he's already married?" I said.

She shook her head. "What about the other woman, though? Why kill her? She wasn't pregnant. I checked with the pathologist. The only things they had in common was they lived near each other, they knew each other, and the legal practice."

I leaned back and rubbed my eyes. Inexplicably, an image rushed in and filled my mind, the dead man tumbling off his chair, falling onto the floor. I opened my eyes quickly.

"There is another thing," I said. "Let me ask you a question, now. You have girlfriends, women you talk to, that you share secrets with, right?"

She wrinkled her mouth, sheepishly. "Yeah, so?"

"Did these women talk to each other, confide in each other, talk about the pregnancy? If the father was married, if he did bump off Brenda, then maybe he knew that the other woman would have spoken to her, and he bumped her off to shut her up."

Reynolds frowned and shook her head. "If they talked amongst themselves, then they probably would have spoken to a bunch of other women, too. Where do you draw the line? When do you stop killing women?"

I shrugged. "All right, that makes sense, let's say it wasn't that. Let's say that he killed number two to cover up the reason for killing number one."

"You mean a 'crisscross' murder?" she asked. "You want to kill B, so you kill A to muddy the water?"

"I hadn't thought that the second woman might be the target. I was focused on Brenda," I said.

Reynolds shook her head. "You like old movies. There

was the one where the two guys trade murders, remember? You know the one?"

"It was called *Strangers On a Train*. Yeah, that's another possibility, I guess. It's a lot harder to set up, though. How do you find someone who also wants to bump off a woman at the same time you do? You don't put an ad in the paper, you don't ask around at a dinner party, so what do you do?"

Reynolds sighed, thinking. "So, are we still thinking it must be something other than just two random murders? Could it be trying to cover up something else?"

I threw my arms up. "You got me, Alex. On one hand, it could be that this guy just likes killing women on the subway. Maybe he's a wacko, maybe he was frightened by a woman on the subway as a child, maybe it turns him on, who knows? On the other hand, maybe there's method to his madness. Maybe he's doing this for a reason. A crazy reason, but a reason that makes some sort of sense nonetheless. What do you think?"

Reynolds frowned and looked at her shoes, thinking. "Okay, so he chose these women for a reason. That doesn't really sound like a nut job, does it? He planned this out. He chose them before he went out that day. He didn't just sit on the subway and wait for a random victim."

I nodded. "Very good, Alex, very good. I think you're right. So that tells us we're not dealing with your regular crazy. He's probably doing what he's doing for a reason. But why?"

She grinned. "No idea. How about this? One of the girls in the law office is a friend of mine from college. She's been asked to do Brenda's job for a week or so, till they get a replacement. I could ask her to report back with any gossip."

I shook my head. "Nope. Uh-uh. No way. Not going to let her do it."

"Come on, boss. As long as she's careful, there's no real danger. This is a great way to get more information. It's a perfect chance to get an inside scoop. What do you say?"

"What would be the benefit to this, Alex? Why would I go for this cockamamie plan?"

"We get the inside scoop, find out if the killer is in the office, and it saves us days of interviews with third parties. Come on, boss, it makes sense." She grinned, expectantly.

I rolled my eyes. "And if something happens to an innocent civilian as a result, we're both washing dishes in a greasy spoon next month. We do it the right way, Alex. Period."

She threw her arms up in defeat. "All right, you win, we'll do it your way."

Parker smiled at this, came over and pulled out a black cardboard covered notebook, then opened it at a paperclip holding some pages together. He squinted and read something. "I may have something for you, boss." He flipped the pages to after the paper clip. "Our first victim, Brenda Grant, and our second one, Gwen Morgan, lived near each other. We knew that, of course. I spoke to Gwen's landlord, and he said the same thing as Brenda's landlord had said—no noise, no parties, no boyfriends."

"Right. And?" I asked.

He squirmed slightly. "Well, he says she did have some girlfriends come over on occasion."

I shook my head, not understanding. "So?"

"She was pregnant," Parker said simply. "How many of her friends knew she was pregnant?"

"Good point. Follow up with that and let's see if we can find any of her friends. Maybe they know who the father was."

Parker nodded. "True. Then again, we can't ignore the possibility of a jealous lover. Maybe he killed her because she got pregnant by someone else?"

"A pair of guys both out to kill the same woman? Sorry, I don't see it, Terry. Keep looking, but concentrate on the more likely scenarios. Let me know what you find. By the way, keep an eye on our Miss Reynolds, too. I think she may try to do something heroic."

“Yeah, I agree, boss,” he said. “She reminds me of you.”

I chuckled. “You’re the second person to tell me that. I’m not sure if I should be flattered or insulted. Anyway, don’t let her get in over her head.”

CHAPTER 13

I drove home early in the afternoon. I had my window down, letting the breeze blow through the car, the sounds and smells of the city in my face. The sun was still very high, and the weather had finally turned hot, cooking the front lawns on my street to dry brown hay. Waves of hot air rippled over the pavement, rising up and bending the light so the buildings behind looked like they were shimmying with the heat. I pulled into my driveway, opened the garage door and parked my car under the house. I came back out and slid the garage door down, just in time to hear Karen's car cruise to a stop behind me. She stepped out, pulled a thin briefcase out with her and straightened her skirt.

"Hey, you." She smiled. "How was your day?"

"Fine, so far." I nodded. "No more bodies, anyway."

She wrapped her arms around me and kissed me, passionately.

"Wow," I said. "What was that for?"

She grinned. "Just because."

I looked at the empty back seat of the Pinto. "Where are the kids?" I asked.

"Ethan is at a friend's place for dinner, and Charlotte's eating at Frank's house."

I smiled. "We're all alone for a while, then?"

Karen grinned. "Yes, we are."

"Come with me," I said.

I grabbed her hand and led her into the house. We sprinted up the stairs, shedding clothes as we went. Karen pushed me onto the bed, straddling me and undoing her bra while she unbuckled my belt. She pulled my socks and pants off in one move, tossed them on the floor and climbed on top of me again.

We made love, forcefully, almost violently, Karen on top of me, slamming my head into the wall. She grunted and groaned, her hands on my shoulders, her knees on my thighs. It was rough, animal, primitive sex. Afterward, she lay on top of me, her legs covering mine, wriggling with delight. She raised herself up on her elbows and kissed me.

"Well, that was fun, just like us in the old days," Karen purred.

I stretched my arms out wide. "Wow, no, that was even better than the old days. What got into you today?" I asked. "Not that I'm complaining, you understand."

She folded her arms on my chest. "I'm just feeling lucky to have you, that's all. I'm glad you're feeling better."

I looked out the window, the pine tree at the end of our yard rocking slightly in the mild breeze. Memories came back, random images, thoughts of people and places that were no longer here. Karen looked at me lovingly and ran her fingers through my hair.

"What are you thinking?" she asked softly.

"I was remembering something from a long time ago," I said. "I used to drive from Esterhazy to Spy Hill, Saskatchewan to pick up stuff for my dad. There was a farm there where they raised turkeys, and we'd buy them for Thanksgiving and Christmas."

"Was it a long way to go, a long drive from home?" Karen asked.

"No, fifteen minutes or so, not far at all." I shrugged. "Anyway."

Karen adjusted herself on my chest, squirming slightly. "Uh huh?" she prompted.

"There was this girl, the farmer's daughter—literally. She was sixteen. I was, I dunno, seventeen, I guess, and I was never very smooth with girls, but I desperately wanted to take her out to the school dance, you know? She was very pretty, this tall, skinny blonde Dutch girl, pigtails, plaid apron, the whole bit."

Karen smirked. "You really think it's a good idea to talk about that girl right after I've drained your tank? You're still not that smooth with women, Ian."

I laughed. "Actually, what I was remembering was the drive to their farm. Southeastern Saskatchewan is not very wooded. They had this stand of pine trees surrounding their farmhouse—most of the farmers did, it cut down on wind damage—but that family had all this turkey manure that they scattered, and their trees grew taller than most. I remember going over on blistering hot days, and just standing in the shade of those marvelous trees. I was noticing our pine just now, thinking about those trees in Spy Hill."

"Ever wonder what happened to the girl? Do you ever wish you'd kept in touch?" Karen asked.

I shook my head sadly. "Not really. She got married young, at twenty-one, twenty-two years old. Last I heard, she had a couple of kids, her husband was off driving long-distance truck and she was down at the Legion hall getting hammered every Friday night."

Karen rubbed my nose with the tip of her finger, playfully tickling the space between my eyes. She traced the outline of my lips and stroked my hair.

"So, you're not disappointed that you ended up with me instead of her?" she asked.

I caressed her spine, from the base of her neck to her butt and back down. She pressed closer, enjoying the touch. "I could never be happier with someone else than I am with you," I said.

Karen glanced over at the alarm clock. "Oops, I think we're about to get company."

We retrieved our clothes, straightened the bed and went

downstairs. I made a simple dinner for us, and Ethan walked through the front door before I placed the food on the table.

Frank and Helen showed up a few minutes later, dropped Charley off and left soon after.

We got the children ready for bed, tucked in a sleepy Charley and talked to Ethan for a few minutes. He had enjoyed dinner at his friend's, he said, but the family was Hungarian, and their food was strange to him.

He climbed into bed and reached over to grab a favorite Hot Wheels car. That's when I saw the bruise. It was across his side, wrapping around to his back, about six inches long.

I pointed to it. "Where did you get that?" I asked.

He looked guilty. "Um, I fell down in the school yard," he said, not very convincingly.

"I don't think so," I said. "That looks like you were hit with something. Who hit you?"

His expression changed, a look of guilt and sad embarrassment that was as clear as a neon sign. "Ethan, what happened there?" I asked.

He started to cry. "Dad, please, forget about it, okay?"

I shook my head. "When did you get that bruise?" I was angry now.

He sniffled. "It was this kid at school. He's really mean. All the kids hate him."

"How old is he?"

"Twelve."

"Have you talked to the teacher about him?" I asked.

"Yeah. She sent him to the principal a couple times."

"What happened then?" I asked.

"The principal talked to him, but he's still mean to us. He told me not to tell on him."

I sighed. "I'm walking you to school Monday. Good night, son."

I climbed into bed with Karen, angry, fuming, wanting to slap out a twelve-year-old. That was irrational, I knew.

"What's got you upset, Ian?" Karen asked.

I told her. She sat up, furious, and determined to talk to

Ethan. I pointed out that he was asleep, and I would walk him to school and deal with it. She was angry that Ethan had been hurt, but she agreed to let me handle it. She talked sporadically, random sentences about how she was trying to protect her children, how she loved them, how she hated bullies. Then she fell asleep.

ᏍᏍ

I am thirteen years old, in my first year of high school, eating lunch on the bench beside the football field. I am still small. In eighteen months, I'll have a growth spurt that will add almost a foot to my height, but for now, I'm only four feet ten. Two of the Rhyme boys, Merton and Reston, walk past me, talking to each other. They are fifteen and fourteen, both bigger than me, both burly farm boys. Merton pokes his brother, then points at my lunch.

"Give," he says.

I look up at him, puzzled. "What?" I ask.

"Give it over," he repeats. "Your lunch, Tonto."

He reaches down to grab at my sandwich, but I pull it away. He gets angry and kicks my lunch box, denting the metal lid. I protest, stand up to yell at him, but he punches me on the side of the head. I fall back and he laughs.

I'm aware of another figure behind them. My big brother James is sixteen, already six feet tall, he's taller than the Rhymes. He moves quickly, punching both boys in the gut, then kicking them in the back. They fall to the ground. He leans down, menacing, and says, "Leave my brother alone."

ᏍᏍ

I got up on Saturday morning and made pancakes. Ethan came down the stairs, the conversation of the night before seemingly forgotten. I didn't bring it up. I would deal with it on Monday, I decided.

Karen walked down the stairs holding Charley's hand, talking to her as they come into the kitchen. We all sat around the table and ate, talking and joking happily, but the thought of an older boy hitting Ethan burned in the back of my mind.

A little after ten in the morning, I cleaned up the dishes, then read the newspaper and did the crossword puzzle. Karen wanted to drive downtown to do some shopping, so I folded up the newspaper, ready to herd the children into the car with her. The phone rang.

"Hello?" I answered.

"Hi, boss, it's Alex," Reynolds said.

"Hey, Alex, how's it going?" I asked.

"I'm trying to interview the staff at the lawyer's, but something's strange here, boss," she said. She was speaking in a low tone, almost a whisper.

"How so?" I asked.

"Everyone here is acting kind of weird, and they don't want to tell me what's going on. I can't put my finger on it. It's just…weird, that's all."

I thought for a minute. "How late is the office open today?"

She rustled some paper. "Let me find out and call you back, okay?"

"All right. I want to talk to someone there if they can see me."

Reynolds called back to say that they were there till three, and one lawyer could see me at one.

I told Karen that I'd have to work briefly early in the afternoon, but we could all go downtown together. I pulled on a clean shirt and slacks, then loaded everyone into the Pinto. Ethan insisted on riding in front with Karen, so I sat in the back with Charley.

We headed down Yonge toward downtown. Ethan confided that when he was old enough, he wanted to drive this car, too. Karen concentrated on driving, but glanced at me through the rearview mirror every so often and smiled.

We parked at the Eaton Centre, and I spent an interminable hour and a half shopping. Karen bought clothes for the kids, a new skirt for herself, and insisted on a pair of shirts for me.

At noon, we stopped for lunch at a sandwich place, then at a quarter to one I looked at my watch and told Karen I had to leave.

"Can you manage the kids by yourself?" I asked.

"Of course. Go, do what you have to do," she said. "Will you be all right?"

"I'll be all right. I should be home before dinner, I think. I'll call you if I won't," I said.

"Be careful," she warned.

I kissed both children goodbye, hugged and kissed Karen, then walked out onto Dundas Street and caught a streetcar to University Avenue.

On one corner of University and Dundas, a flat gray concrete monolith, twelve stories of cement punctuated by geometrically placed windows, bore the address of the lawyer's office I was looking for.

I went into the lobby, a low, dark area that felt like the antechamber of a Pharaoh's tomb. My claustrophobia washed over me, making me feel like there was no air in the room.

Deep breaths, I told myself, deep breaths. I walked through to the back of the lobby, to a pair of gray-black elevator doors, and got into the elevator. More deep breaths, I told myself.

I pushed the button and went up to the eighth floor. I stepped out, relieved that I was out of the elevator, and into an expansive hallway. It was subdued, calming, with gray brown carpet, where the air smelled of roses and stale tobacco.

I reached the door of an office with a brass plaque that read *Duncan Carroll, BA, MA, LLB.*

Below that were several smaller plaques with the names of several other partners. I pulled out a small notepad and wrote the names down, then I took a deep breath and opened the door.

A young woman was at the waiting area, behind a high counter, wearing a neat blouse and a pale pink jacket. She looked up as I approached and smiled a plastic smile.

"Yes, may I help you?" she asked.

She kept her eyes on me, ignoring a couple of women in gray skirt suits walking near her.

I held out my badge. "Detective Inspector Ian McBriar. I'm here to talk to one of your staff about the case we're investigating, regarding Brenda Grant?"

"Please take a seat," she said formally.

Ten minutes later, I had read all the interesting parts of the Golf Digest magazines and I looked around, wondering what else there was to read. A face poked out from an opened door and looked at me. It was a woman, middle-aged, with a kind face, slightly angular, short blond hair poking out at angles, and gold rimmed glasses framing blue eyes. She smiled in my direction.

"Mister McBriar? Please come this way," she said.

There was an accent in her voice. English, I thought? No, possibly Irish, Scottish, I couldn't tell. She wore a very good blouse, a tasteful gold bracelet on her right wrist, and a thin gold watch on the left wrist.

I stood up and went with her. She was a small woman, perhaps a hair over five feet, and she craned her neck to look up at my face.

"Hello, I'm sorry to keep you waiting. I'm Evelyn. Please follow me. Right in here," she said, looking over her shoulder.

She waved at an open door and ushered me into a room with a leather chair facing a desk. She sat me down, leaned forward, and smiled.

"Can I get you a tea, or coffee?" she asked. I shook my head and got out my notebook.

She walked around to the other side of the desk and sat down.

"Is this a family-owned practice?" I asked.

"Yes, it is," she said simply. She twirled the ring on her finger, absentmindedly.

"Thanks for seeing me on such short notice, and on a Saturday."

"So, how can we help your investigation, Inspector?" she asked, her accent was clear now.

"You're a Scot?" I asked.

"Yes, from Edinburgh. Are you originally from Scotland too? I noticed your Scottish surname."

"No. I was born here, but my paternal grandfather was from Aberdeen, I'm told," I said. I pulled out my pen. "You're Mrs. Carroll, aren't you?" I asked.

She seemed surprised. "Why, yes. How on earth did you know that?"

I shrugged. "You played with your ring when I mentioned 'family-owned.' You thought of Mr. Carroll and marriage. It's an involuntary reaction, usually, like yawning when others yawn."

She laughed out loud and waved her hand at me. "Very good. I can see why you're a detective."

I smiled. "It's pretty instinctive at this point."

She chuckled and shook her head. A moment later, the door opened again and a man walked in. He was slightly rotund, fairly tall, with glasses that matched his wife's. He was also middle-aged, but with a bounce to his step and smooth sweeping movements as he turned.

He had short blond hair, turning gray at the temples, and a slightly bewildered expression.

"Hello, you're Inspector McBriar? I'm Duncan Carroll. You can call me Duncan, if you like."

He had a soft voice, singsong, with a subtle lisp to it that sounded like an affectation. He held a hand out, and I shook it. The hand was cool, clammy, vaguely unpleasant to the touch.

I nodded. "Hello, Duncan. Nice to meet you, but I wish it was under different circumstances."

"Well, what can we do for you today?"

His wife looked up, irritation in her face. "I've got it, Duncan. It's fine."

"Are you sure?" he asked cheerily. "You don't have any questions for me, then?"

I nodded. "I'd like to know if Brenda Grant had any enemies in this office. Was there anyone she didn't get along with?"

He shook his head. "She was a very well-liked member of the staff. She got along with everyone here."

"But she had only been working here a short time, as I understand?"

"No, why would you think that?" he asked.

"Our information is that she changed jobs about a month ago. Wasn't that when she started working here?"

"Full time, yes. Before that, I understand she was working at a bookstore, but it was only part-time. She has worked here two or three days a week for the past year. Isn't that right, Evelyn?"

The woman glared at him, now. She didn't think I'd seen it. "Yes, thanks, Duncan," she said icily.

"So, did she have any altercations, any disagreements with anyone in that time?" I pressed.

The woman shook her head. "None. She was professional, very good. Her death is a great loss."

I stood up and smiled at the woman. "I appreciate you seeing me on short notice, as I say. We'll let you know if there are any developments, of course, but we may need to ask your staff more questions at a later date."

The woman stood and held her hand out at a distance—a way of saying "now go away."

I shook it and turned to go. I scratched my nose. "Sorry, your restrooms are?"

She pointed down the hall, in the back part of the offices. I walked toward a sign on a wall, an outline of a man.

She left the office and closed the door. I threw my jacket over one arm and went back into the men's room. I stood there for a minute, then I came back and strolled toward the reception desk. I walked slowly toward the reception desk, listening at a row of a half dozen doors as I went. Most doors were open, the offices vacant, but at one closed door, marked *Private*, I heard the woman whispering, her voice hissing. Her husband, his voice lower, was saying something slowly, forcefully, trying to talk over her. She kept hissing, talking quickly. He raised his voice, loud enough that I could hear him through the door.

"It's not that serious. He's just doing his job, that's all. I don't think that's why he's here. Calm down, Evelyn, calm down," he said.

I heard the door handle turn and his voice get louder. I went silently out to the front desk and leaned at the counter. The young woman behind the counter leaned forward to talk to me, then she saw someone coming and straightened up, speaking loudly. "All right, Inspector McBriar, is there anything else we can do for you?"

As I opened my mouth to answer, Duncan Carroll came out to the front area and stood beside me. "Penny, let's not bother the good officer. I'm sure he has work to do." He patted my shoulder.

I grinned. "Thanks, thanks very much for seeing me."

The lawyer turned and went back into his office. My smile disappeared. I moved forward to speak to the young woman, but she mouthed the word "Later."

I nodded and left.

I stepped out of the building into a warm, muggy afternoon. My jacket was redundant, so I just draped it over one elbow and waved down a taxi. I sat in the back seat, rolled down the window and closed my eyes.

The cab driver, a slim young man with scraggly hair and a rumpled shirt, was silent for a few moments, then he spoke. "You all right, man?" he asked.

"Yeah, I'm just a little tired, that's all," I said.

"You look like you got troubles, mister. Everything okay?"

I opened my eyes. "You're very perceptive." I thought for a moment. "It's been a tough few days at work. Some weeks are worse than others, I guess."

He glanced at me in the rear view mirror then looked back at the road ahead. "What line of work are you in, bud?"

I smiled. "I'm a cop."

He glanced back at me again. "Yeah? What kind of cop?"

"I'm a Detective Inspector, in Homicide," I said.

He did a brief double-take in the rearview. "That a fact? You're the guys looking for the subway killer, right?"

"Yeah. Have you heard much about it?" I asked.

"Just what's on the radio. A couple of the guys at the shop got a pool going, betting on when you'll catch the guy. Got any hot tips on when that might be? I could use the cash, you know?"

I shook my head. "Sorry, we're still investigating. It wouldn't be appropriate for me to talk about it."

He reached over his head at a flap on the sun visor and pulled out a business card. "Listen, if you figure you can do me a good turn, I'd appreciate you letting me know, all right?"

He handed me the card. I read the name. "You're Gerald, then?" I asked.

"Yeah, everyone calls me Jerry, like the gas can. Like I said, I could sure use the cash in the pool. You do me a favor, and I'll get you back sometime."

I smiled to myself. "How much is in the pool?" I asked.

"Eighty-five dollars. Pretty good money, you know?"

"Yeah, good money. Tell you what, I'll let you know once we make an arrest. You have my word," I said.

I took a business card out of my wallet and handed it to him. "If you get any information you figure I can use, feel free to pass it on to me, too," I said.

He read the card, his head bobbing up and down as he read and drove along St. Clair Avenue.

"McBriar? You're the cop that stopped the bank robbery, a few years back?"

I looked out the window at children splashing in the pool at Earlscourt Park. "Yep, that's me."

He tucked the card into his shirt pocket. "Wow, what do you know, a real celebrity in my cab."

"I didn't realize that putting myself in danger made me a celebrity," I quipped.

He pulled over and turned around to face me. I wondered why he was doing this.

"My mom was in the bank when those guys held it up," he said. "She says she was scared shitless, but then you showed up with a bunch of muffins and coffee, and she felt much better. Then you punched out those three guys. She couldn't believe how brave you were, going in there all by yourself."

I shrugged. "Tell her I was terrified the whole time. And it wasn't muffins, it was donuts. Plus, I only hit two of the guys. One was smart enough to stand still."

He reached his hand back to me. "Anyway, I just wanted to say thank you for keeping her safe. I'll tell her you were in my cab. She'll love hearing about that."

I shook his hand. He grinned and went back to driving. I closed my eyes again.

Five minutes later, he pulled up to my house. "There you are, officer. Nice to have met you."

I pulled out my wallet and read the meter. I got out a ten-dollar bill, but he waved it away.

"No, man, I can't take your money, my mom would kill me. This ride's on me."

I shook my head. "Don't try to bribe me, Jerry. Besides, you have to account for the fare on the meter. Here, buy you mom lunch or something."

I handed him the ten and then a five. He smiled broadly and drove off.

I walked down my driveway to the house. The Pinto was poking out from the garage, its trunk shining in the sunlight.

The sound of Karen's voice in the house, Ethan answering her from upstairs, somehow made me feel calm, like everything would turn out fine.

CHAPTER 14

I went into the front hall, the cool relative darkness calming me, and headed for the voices, in the kitchen. Karen scooped ice cream from a large plastic tub and dunked it into glass bowls.

Charley was sitting on the counter beside her, poking her finger into the bucket, licking it when she thought Karen wasn't watching.

Karen saw me and grinned. "Hey, how did it go?" she asked.

I shrugged. "I sense they're keeping something from me. I don't know what. Anyway, Alex is on the case. I'm sure she'll dig up whatever it is."

Karen nodded, but her face showed worry. "Do you think there's something going on in that office? Something that explains why those women were hurt?"

I shook my head. "No idea. Why did you buy a tub of ice cream?"

Karen scraped out a small spoonful and offered it to me. "Taste this."

I took a bite. "Wow, that is really, really good. Where did it come from?"

"Lizzy Walsh was in New York, and thought we might like some gourmet ice cream."

"She brought that back with her on a plane?" I asked. "How did she manage that?"

"Apparently, they have a freezer on their company jet. Sucks to be poor, huh?"

I grabbed the teaspoon from Karen and scooped more ice cream out. I licked the spoon. "Man, that is very, very good. We'll have to visit New York, apparently."

Karen chuckled. "I'll tell her you approve."

She gave bowls of ice cream to the children and put the bucket in the freezer. I looked at my watch. Three o'clock. I was sure I'd hear from Reynolds if she had any more information.

I sat in the living room and turned on the radio. I leaned back, closed my eyes, and listened to the jazz station. I was relaxed, my mind blank, calm. I let the music wash over me. There I was, on stage with Miles Davis, clapping along as he belted out a sizzling horn solo. This felt good. This felt like life would all be all right again. The tune ended, and an image filled my mind, a big man with three bloody holes in his shirt, sitting on a chair. I opened my eyes.

I sat up, vaguely aware of a ringing sound. Karen yelled at me from upstairs.

"Can you get the phone, Ian?" she called.

I rolled out of the chair and picked up the phone on the third ring. "Hello?" I said.

Reynolds' voice was on the other end. "Hey, boss. Terry and I are just talking to Penny."

"Penny who?" I asked stupidly.

"The receptionist at the law office. You met her today."

"Oh, right. Sorry, I didn't pay attention to her name before," I said.

"Anyway, we wondered if you could meet us for a few minutes?" Reynolds said.

I looked at my watch. "Sure. When and where?"

"Thirty minutes, at the Edelweiss Bakery, on Parliament just south of Wellesley."

I wrote this down. "All right, I'll be there in half an hour," I said. I called up to Karen. "I have to go out for a bit. Do we need anything?"

"No. When will you be home?" she yelled back.

I looked at my watch again. "Before five."

The sound of thundering feet on the stairs made me turn around. Karen came through and poked my chest with her finger.

"You better be careful, all right? You take care of yourself, Ian," she hissed.

"I'm just meeting Alex and Terry to discuss the case," I said. "That's all."

She shook her head. "Be careful." She kissed me, smiled, and rushed back upstairs.

I got to the Edelweiss Bakery in twenty-five minutes. Terry Parker was at one of the four small tables, munching on a wedge of cake. Reynolds sat across from him, sipping coffee, and the young woman from the law office sat beside her, nibbling on a strudel.

I joined them and held out my hand. "Hi, I'm Ian. I don't think we met properly, earlier."

The young woman smiled. "Hi, I'm Penny Lewis. Nice to meet you too."

I leaned forward and knitted my fingers together in front of me on the table. "So, I understand you wanted to talk to us about our case, Penny?"

She nodded. "Yeah. Look, I don't want to talk out of turn or anything, but if there's something going on that could put me in danger, I want you to know about it, you know?"

I smiled. "A reasonable way of looking at it, I suppose. But why are you coming forward now?"

She sighed, thinking. "Well, basically the Carroll's are very nice to work for. I mean, when this all ends, I'd still like to be working there, you know? The work is fun, it's close to home, the pay is good, and they give benefits and stuff. Besides, they're nice to work for, it's a happy place."

"However," I said.

"Yeah, however. Mister Carroll and his wife had a noisy argument right after you left. I couldn't hear most of what they said, but they were talking about their son. He's one of the junior partners there."

"What's his name?" I asked.

"Bradley Carroll. He works there three days a week."

I got out my notepad and read it over. "I don't see his name on the plaques out front."

"No, he's fairly new to the practice."

"Have you spoken to him much?" I asked.

She giggled. "Yes. He drops by my desk to talk to me all the time. He's very cute. All the women in the office swoon over him."

"Swoon?"

"Yeah, you know, the women in the office get giddy around him."

"No, I know what swoon means, Penny, It's just not a term I hear very much."

She giggled again. "Yeah, I know. I'm an old fashioned girl."

"So, what did they say about him, the Carroll's?"

"He had a problem with the police, they were saying. I'm not sure of the details, only that his family was trying to keep him out of trouble," she said.

"Okay, good to know. Anything else to add?" I asked, looking around.

Parker shook his head. "This is really rich cake. Anyway, Penny, you're going to be on the front desk for the time being, right? Can you let us know if you see anything else odd? Anybody creepy in the building, or something?"

She shook her head. "Hey, I've just started this spy stuff. Give me some time."

I stood up. "Okay. Alex, see you Monday. Penny, nice meeting you, keep up the good work." I pointed to Parker. "Terry, watch the calories."

He chuckled and nodded, his mouth still full. I drove home. That night I made dinner, puttering in the kitchen by myself, not saying much. Karen watched me, also not saying much, and left me alone with my thoughts.

I was angry about Ethan's bruise, angry about the two dead women, angry about the dead man, angry at myself that I hadn't been able to find another way to end the situation. Colleen was right. I would have mood swings, and they would overwhelm me or sweep over me without warning, and I would just have to find a way to cope.

We went to bed early. I had my eyes closed, trying to get drowsy. Karen draped one arm over my chest, rubbed her hand on my stomach and lifted her head slightly.

"Hey, are you asleep?" she asked softly.

"Yes, fast asleep," I answered.

"Seriously, Ian, can I talk to you?"

I was wide awake, I realized, far too awake to sleep. I sat up. "Sure, what's on your mind?"

"The kids noticed that you're not your cheery self. Ethan wonders when you're going to be all right. I told him that it was some work stuff that had you bothered. I didn't want to say much about the kidnapping. I don't think he should hear about things like that at his age, do you?"

I shrugged. "No. I agree, let's keep the gory details to ourselves for now. He can get all that once he's older."

"When do you think you'll be back to work?"

"I don't know. Ultimately, Colleen and the Department decide when I can come back. I just hope it's soon, hon. I don't mind getting paid to do nothing, but it feels like I'm being put in a corner, being left aside, not quite a cop, not quite a civilian."

"You're still up for promotion, right? I mean, they're still offering you Martin's job, right?"

I looked over at her, puzzled. "Who told you about that? Wait—it was Rebecca, wasn't it?"

In the dark room, I could see the outline of her face, her eyes open as she looked back at me.

She giggled. "You should know better than to think you can keep that news secret, Ian."

"So, should I take the job, then?"

“Would you be happier doing that, instead of working in the field?” she asked.

“I didn’t think I would be happier doing that, until lately. I’ve been thinking about the future a lot in this last week. It would make life easier for us—more pay, less danger, less stress.”

She hugged me close. “Less danger is good. More pay is not too bad either.”

I smiled softly to myself. I fell asleep.

CHAPTER 15

Sunday morning, I went to church even earlier than usual. At six thirty, I was in a front pew, holding my prayer book open at Psalm 51, a prayer for forgiveness.

A door opened at the side of the confessional, then an old woman got out of the booth, straightened her skirt and moved to a row of pews in front of me. She knelt down, bent her head forward and began saying prayers.

I got up, genuflected as I passed the main aisle, and got into the empty booth. I knelt on the step. The priest's window became lighter and opened, and a man's voice said "Yes, my son?"

I made the sign of the cross and bowed my head. "Forgive me father, for I have sinned. It has been two weeks since my last confession."

A voice, soft, patient, answered back. "How have you sinned, my son?" the voice said.

I sat there, silent, for a few moments. The shadow I saw through the fabric window turned slightly to face me, waited patiently for me to speak, then said "Yes?"

I inhaled deeply. "I have killed a man," I said.

The man said nothing for a few seconds. I heard him sigh, then his face turned slightly away. "Was this act committed in malice or in anger?" he asked.

"No, it was done to protect the life of a police officer."

He paused a few seconds more. "Is there anyone else waiting for confession?"

I leaned back and looked out at the church. "No, there isn't," I said.

"Let's go for a walk, Ian," the man said.

I got up, crossed myself again, and opened the door of the booth. The far door opened, and the priest stepped out. He was my age, with wiry red hair and thin glasses. He looked like a cyclist, thin, supple, wearing a black ankle-length cassock, and a purple stole around his neck.

He placed a hand on my shoulder. "Come with me, my son," he said.

I followed him to the back of the church, into the sacristy. He waved at a chair by a small table and I sat down. The old woman from the front pew shuffled in, placed a foil-wrapped plate on the table, and smiled at me.

"Father Brendan, there's sponge cake and cookies here for you," she said. She nodded at me. "And for your friend, of course."

I smiled back. "Thank you very much. That's very thoughtful of you," I said.

She grinned and busied about, straightening plates and getting the coffee percolator ready.

The priest placed a hand gently on her arm. "Thank you so much, Mrs. Holton. Would you mind very much if we had a few moments alone?"

She nodded and wiped her hands on her skirt. "Oh, certainly, father. I'll be out front, just let me know when you're done."

"Bless you, Mrs. Holton. Thank you again." He smiled warmly.

The woman shuffled out, closed the door behind her, and I heard her walk toward the back of the church.

The priest watched the door for a moment then turned to shake his head at me. "She's a busybody, but she's vital to this church." He chuckled. "Still, she'll be nagging me for weeks about what we were saying in here." He peeled the foil off the plate and picked up a cookie. "Are you going to take communion?" he asked.

I shrugged. "I was hoping to, yes."

"Have some cake, Ian." He gestured at the plate.

"I can't if I'm going to take communion. I really should fast," I said.

"You haven't tasted Mrs. Holton's cooking. It counts as fasting. Have some cake." He picked up a cup from a back shelf and poured me a coffee. He placed it in front of me and sat across the table, with coffee for himself. He swirled a small spoon back and forth, mixing up the cream in his cup, forming eddies of white and brown. "I imagine you've had a very difficult time of late," he said, taking a sip of coffee and looking at me, his green eyes piercing me under his red eyebrows.

I picked up a small slice of cake, thinking of how to answer him. "Brendan, how long have we known each other?" I asked.

He smiled. "Since we were both at St. Augustine's. What is it—nine, ten years now? It's been a good long time, Ian."

"Yes, it has." I put my cup down. "In all that time, have you ever known me to be willing to cause hurt, to be glad at another's misery?"

He shook his head.

"I'm going back to Esterhazy in a couple of weeks, to attend the tenth anniversary memorial service for my mother. There is a good chance that when I'm there I'll see the man who went to jail for killing her, and I don't even feel hatred for him anymore." I was speaking softly, sadly.

"In everything that has happened, when my mom died, when I got shot, when I've encountered all manner of bad guys, I have never wanted to cause the death of another person. Yet when it came down to it, I killed a man without even pausing. What does that say about me, Brendan?"

He took the stole off from around his neck, kissed it and put it carefully folded on the table. He looked down at his coffee, thinking.

"You were always a better student than I was, you know that?" he said with a smile. "You would have been a far better priest than me, too. I think I'm lucky you got out when you did, or you'd be at a parish in Toronto, and I'd be doling out cold soup to kids in Africa somewhere now. This is a much more pleasant place to work. I thank you for that."

I shook my head. "It's not going to work, Brendan. I know what you're doing. What I need from you is a path to absolution, not praise. I want to know whether what I did was the right thing to do. What can you tell me?"

He chuckled. "All right, let's get to the meat of the issue. What exactly happened?"

I told him the sequence of events, how we'd tracked down Walsh's kidnappers, released Walsh, and how, afterward, I'd shot the man, with Walsh's gun. He listened intently, nodding and asking questions. I finished, feeling tired and slightly guilty at how it sounded, how I felt like I was acting a bit like John Wayne in the situation, not like I hoped I would in that situation.

He leaned forward and poked his finger at the table, gently. "When you went to that place where your friend was being kept, did you bring a gun with you?" he asked.

"No, I left it behind, along with my badge," I said. "I was on suspension, so I wasn't even there as a police officer."

"So you didn't go there with the intent to commit a sin, to kill someone, or not even bring along a gun in case something went wrong?"

"No, I didn't."

"Then what the hell kind of cop are you, Ian? Why wouldn't you bring your gun with you, just in case?" He was forceful, but smiling.

I felt myself getting angry. I gritted my teeth. "I didn't go there to kill a man. I went there to free one. What don't you understand about that?"

"So you went there for good reasons, not for malicious ones? That's why you were unarmed?"

"Yes, that's why I was unarmed," I snapped. I sat back, thinking. "You're right. That's why I did it. I went there wanting to do a good thing, not to commit a sin."

"And you did. You saved a man's life, an innocent man's life. The fact that an evil man tried to end that good man's life is what caused his death. You were the instrument, but the sin lies with the man who tried to kill your friend." He looked at his watch. "All right, I should get the show going. Are you staying for Mass, Ian?"

I smiled softly. "Of course, Brendan."

He placed a hand on my shoulder. "Say your prayers and go with God, my son."

I bowed my head low. "Thank you, Father."

I went back to my usual pew, near the back of the church. As the minute hand on the clock moved up to twelve, a small pipe organ at the back of the church started up, and the Mass began.

I sat through it, took communion, sat in my pew afterward, said soft prayers for forgiveness, then at eight o clock I was in my car driving home.

I opened the door, but heard nothing. "Hello?" I called.

I heard a giggle from around the corner, in the kitchen, the giggle of a three-year-old. Then I heard another sound, softer, from an older child. It went "Sshhh."

I walked into the kitchen, playing dumb. As I rounded the corner, Ethan and Charley jumped out from behind the counter at me. I hopped back, feigning fear.

"Surprise! Happy Father's Day!" Ethan cried.

"Happy Daddy Day!" Charley echoed.

I leaned down and hugged them both. "Wow, it's Father's Day? I forgot all about it. Thank you so much, guys. I really appreciate this."

Karen appeared from behind the counter, smirking. "Why don't you two give your dad his gift?"

Ethan brought out a large brown envelope and handed it to Charley. She held it in both hands and lifted it up to me.

I took the envelope and looked at the front panel. It read

'Happy Father's day to our dad' carefully printed in marker pen.

I opened the envelope, pulled out the handmade cardboard card inside, and read it. It was decorated with a Polaroid of Ethan, one of Karen propping up Charley, and a message written in glue, sprinkled with sparkles, that read *World's Best Dad.*

I sat on the floor and opened the card. There was a message that simply said *Happy Father's Day* signed *Ethan* in neat block letters, and *CharlotE* in wiggly crayon.

I sighed, deeply touched by the emotions expressed on this simple piece of cardboard. "Thank you very much, guys. I really love this. It's one for the ages," I said, hugging both children. "This is going up on the mantel." I placed the card above the fireplace, next to the photographs of Karen and the children.

"Now then," I said. "Who wants to eat breakfast?"

"We're taking you out," Karen said. "We're meeting the Burghezians for a Father's Day brunch."

I was dragged out to Karen's car, placed in the back seat, then Karen sat Charley next to me. Ethan sat in front, and we headed off. We drove south toward downtown. That was odd, where would we go into town at this time of the morning?

Karen bounced along St. Clair Avenue, turned right on Bathurst, and drove straight south again. She passed old Fort York, where Charley craned her neck to look out at the fort buildings.

Karen glanced at me through the rear-view mirror. "Remind you of anything?"

"Just like when we first met." I smiled. "I brought you to Toronto Island Airport for breakfast."

She chuckled. "You remember. Ethan suggested this. We've never been here with Charlotte."

I looked down at Charley. "Do you like airplanes, Charlotte?"

She shrugged. "I dunno."

"Do you like pancakes?" I added.

She nodded furiously. "I like cakes."

I threw an arm over her. "Good. Do you like boats, too?"

She nodded again. "We got a boat at our cottage."

I smiled. "Yes, we do, sweetheart. You like riding on the boat at our cottage, right? Well, this boat is like that, but bigger. You'll see."

Ethan turned back to look at her. "Hey, Charlotte, they got airplanes you can sit in and stuff, right, dad?"

"Right, sport."

Karen eased her Pinto into a parking spot beside a green Nova, and we got out. Frank and his family got out of the other car, we greeted each other, then we all headed for the ferry to Toronto Island.

The twins were rambunctious, giddy at this new experience, and Charley joined in, racing around with them as we waited for the ferry to come back from its five-minute trip to the other side of the narrow harbor crossing.

The ferry docked, we all piled on, and I held Charley up at the railing, as I had done with her brother, when he was four and I was dating Karen. It all felt like déjà vu, holding a young child up to see the waves go under us as we headed for the Toronto Island Airport. It felt good.

In no time, we were on the other side, walking toward the small terminal building, and steering to one side, to a door that read *The Left Seat Diner*. We went in, greeted by a man with a push broom moustache and curly hair. He remembered us from previous visits, welcomed us warmly and moved tables around so we could all sit together near a window.

We decided on pancakes and eggs, then waited, watching small planes take off outside. Charley was fascinated, seeing them line up at the end of the strip, spool up the engine and teeter clumsily down the runway, smoothing out as they built speed, then lifting off gracefully.

She was on her knees, her nose to the window, just like her brother had done five years before. She turned to look at me. “Da? What’s that?” she asked, pointing.

“An airplane,” I said. “Would you like to go on an airplane?”

She turned to face me and grinned. “Yah. Fun.”

I chuckled. “Yes, it is fun. You’re going to go on a big airplane in two weeks, you know? You’re going to visit grandpa John in Esterhazy. Do you remember meeting grandpa John?”

She shook her head. It had been over a year since my father had been able to visit us, and Charley was not quite two years old then. Of course she didn’t remember his visit.

The curly haired man brought our food and we chatted about nothing important, explaining to the younger children what an airport was, making small talk. We finished, our wives paid the bill, despite our protests that we wanted to. I later found out that Frank had slipped a five-dollar bill under a plate as a tip.

I had done the same. We spent some time wandering around the airport, poked in at a hangar where a friend of mine worked, and he cheerfully showed us the inside of a corporate jet. The kids loved it. Then we took the ferry back to our cars.

Helen invited us over to their house later for dinner, and I accepted happily.

That afternoon, I sat outside in my back yard, reading a book that I’d promised myself to read when I had the time, and fell asleep on the first chapter.

We went to Frank’s for dinner, everyone chatted and laughed, but I paid no attention to what we ate, the whole time thinking about the dead man.

After we’d put the children to sleep, I lay in bed, thinking and staring at the ceiling.

Karen climbed into bed beside me. “What are you thinking?”

“Remember when we first met, we were lying in bed, and I asked if you ever imagined walking on the ceiling when you were a child?” I asked.

She looked up and laughed. "I'd forgotten that. What made you think about it now?"

"Time is passing for me, hon. I'm getting older. I'm thirty-two years old, and in the time I've known you again, I'll be almost forty. That's kind of scary."

She propped herself up on her elbows. "What do you want to do when you grow up, then?"

I chuckled. "No idea. Can I be the first man on the moon?"

"It's been done," she said.

"Then I want to be a submarine commander."

"You don't like small dark places. You'd be miserable as a submarine commander," she joked.

"I'll be a pirate, then. Do you want to be my pirate wench?" I turned to face her and smiled.

She leaned down and kissed me. "That sounds like a plan. We already have a boat, after all." She kissed me again. "Get some sleep, Blackbeard. We both have work tomorrow."

"Aye, aye, matey." I turned out the light beside me and closed my eyes.

CHAPTER 16

At seven the next morning, I was downstairs, making breakfast and perking coffee. Twenty minutes later, Karen came down and ate her eggs. Ten minutes after that, Ethan came downstairs and had a bowl of something disgustingly sweet.

I had not forgotten about his bruise. I said nothing, had his lunch ready, and walked him to school. He peeled off to play with one of his friends, and I continued onto the school office.

The woman behind the desk looked at me and did a double-take. "Well, hello, Inspector." She smiled. "Are you here to give a talk to one of the classes?"

I shook my head. "I have a question. Ethan and some other children have been bullied by an older child, I'm told. What can you tell me about him?"

She shook her head. "Yes, the Salmo child. We have had several complaints from parents about him. I understand his father doesn't see his behavior as a problem, which of course makes it harder for us to discipline him."

"Could I speak to the boy?" I asked.

She shook her head. "No, we wouldn't be able to allow that. I'm sorry."

"How about his father? Can I try to explain to him what the problem is?"

She shrugged. "We have tried, but he doesn't seem to

want to listen. You're welcome to speak to him, though."

She pulled a card out of a long tray and wrote down an address. "Here you go."

I grunted thanks and left. The address on the card was a few blocks away, on Keith Avenue. I parked in front of the place, double-checked the number on the card to be sure I was at the right house, then knocked on the door and waited.

A minute later, the front door opened, and a big man lumbered out onto the front porch.

He had a lumberjack shirt on, dusty jeans, and work boots. He had a hairy beer gut that poked out under the shirt and hung over his belt, and a growth of stubby beard that made him look even more scraggly.

"Mister Salmo?" I said. "Can I talk to you for a minute?"

He squinted. "You here for the door?"

"Door?" I asked.

"Yeah, door. I made a front door for you, no?" he said.

"No. I'm here about your son. Apparently, he's been bullying other children."

He snorted. "Yeah, so?"

"It has to stop. He can't keep doing this," I said.

He sneered. "Your kid can't take care of himself? At's not my problem."

"Your boy is twelve. Mine is nine. Is that fair in your mind?" I asked, trying to be reasonable.

"Who you?" he asked.

"McBriar. Ian McBriar," I said.

He waved a finger at me. "Oh, yeah. You that cop."

"Right."

"Married the woman with the kid. Never married to father, not your son," he said, casually.

I felt myself getting angry. I tried to stay calm. "Did anybody ever tell you you're an asshole?"

He laughed. "All the time. So what?"

"Has anybody ever kicked the living shit out of you?" I asked.

He sneered "You won't touch me. You can't."

"Yeah, you moron? Why is that exactly?"

"I don't touch you, then you can't touch me. I not touching you."

"You are a complete imbecile. I will find a way to make this stop. You do realize that, right?"

He shrugged. "You just try. Piss off."

I shook my head. "This is not the end of this, you know? I will get to the bottom of this."

He shook his head. "Screw off." He went in and closed his door.

I got in my car and raced off, fuming. I debated taking Ethan out of this school and putting him in a different school, possibly a Catholic school. That wouldn't be fair to him, though, he had lots of friends in the school, and moving him away just because of one bully was ridiculous.

I considered going back, picking a fight, pounding the hell out of the man. That had appeal, too.

I got home and slammed to a stop in my driveway. I was still upset, still wondering what I could do. Karen was at work, Charley was with Helen, and the house was empty. I went in and checked the kitchen for groceries, mostly trying to keep my mind off wanting to beat up Salmo.

The front door bell rang. *Salmo came to apologize* I thought, then I realized that wasn't likely. I went to the door. A very large shadow filled the frosted glass, with a regular shadow beside it.

I opened the door. Sam was in the doorway, blocking it, and Patrick Walsh was in front of him.

Walsh grinned. "They let me out, boss."

"Hey, guys, come on in," I said.

Patrick came in first, a wicker picnic basket in his hand. Sam was inches behind him, looking around protectively in case someone sprang out.

Walsh had a couple of bandages over the cuts on his face, a splint on a sore arm, and a split lip, souvenirs of his confinement.

"Good to see you, Patrick. Would you both care for coffee or something?" I asked.

Walsh handed me the basket. "Sure. Here you go, my mom thought you might like this."

I took it and lifted out various jars and bottles. "Mumm's cordon rouge champagne, English marmalade, Russian caviar, Brie cheese, gourmet mustard. Jeez, Patrick, a guy could get lucky with any girl, bringing this on a date."

He smirked. "Yes. I know."

"So, do you guys want coffee with cake or something?" I repeated.

Walsh looked back at Sam. Sam raised an eyebrow slightly. "Sure, thanks," Walsh said.

I made coffee and got carrot cake out of the fridge. I remembered something. "Damn. I wanted to put some of this in Ethan's lunch," I mumbled.

Walsh smiled. "How are the kids doing? I haven't seen them in a few days."

I shrugged. "Okay, I guess. I just had a very frustrating conversation with a man whose son is roughing up Ethan."

Sam sat up at this. "Yeah?" he said, his voice a low rumble.

"Yep. He thinks children should be able to defend themselves, even against much bigger kids."

"That's not good," Sam rumbled. "I got beat up a lot in school."

"Really? You?" I asked.

"I used to be real small, then I grew fast," he said.

I looked at him, astonished. "How fast did you grow?"

Walsh pulled out a notebook. "Who is this guy?"

"A guy by the name of Salmo, on Keith Avenue. Why, do you want to beat him up?" I joked.

Walsh shook his head. "That's no fun. Give me a day or so to look into it."

We talked for a while. I told Walsh about where we were with the case, that Reynolds' friend was helping us with the investigation, and that I would be off the job for a day or two, until I could convince Colleen Feldman to let me come back to work.

Walsh said that he was going to stay home for a few days, he was but looking forward to coming back to work as well. Sam scowled at that. For the first time, I saw Sam as a very big mother hen, taking care of his charges just like a hen herding her chicks.

They thanked me for the snack. Sam had eaten more than half the cake and most of a jug of milk. They got up and left, and I waved the black Mercedes goodbye as they drove off.

I checked my watch. It was three-thirty. Ethan would be home shortly. He was still in class, but I had a sudden desire to meet him at the exit, in case the bully was there waiting for him.

I walked over to the school yard, checked my watch again, and a moment later the outside bell clanged loudly. A swarm of children, some walking slowly, some rushing, exited the door nearest me. Somehow, in the midst of them all, I saw Ethan. He was walking slowly, his head down, scowling. Then I saw the boy behind him. He was tall, gangly, with a sneer on his face, and he was smacking Ethan on the back of the head, slapping him with his fingertips. I blew up.

I waded through the sea of children, who moved aside as they noticed me, and marched straight over to the taller boy.

"You!" I barked.

He looked up at me. His face dropped, and he turned around. He ran, weaving through the crowd, back into the school. I kept going after him, into the hall, saw him turn a corner headed for the office, and followed. He ran into the office, hid behind a secretary's desk, and ducked low.

I got there a split second later. He saw me come toward him and screamed like a maniac. "Help! Help! Somebody help me!" he cried. "Call the police!"

I towered over him, my hands on my hips. "I *am* the police, you stupid piece of shit," I growled.

He tried to climb under the desk and escape out the other side. I grabbed hold of his jacket, wrapped my hands around the two sides of the zipper, and lifted him up.

"How does this feel, huh?" I said. I held him up, nose to nose with me. "Is it fun having somebody bigger scare the crap out of you, huh?"

He shrank back, terrified. "My father will kill you. Let me go," he said. His panic was passing. He was defiant, now.

"Others have tried. I wouldn't give him very goods odds on succeeding," I said.

I turned to the office staff. "Can you call the police? I want to have him arrested for assault."

One of the secretaries dialed a number and mumbled into the receiver, looking up at me and the boy as she did. By now, a small crowd had assembled outside the office. The principal shooed everybody out and locked the door behind us. I let the boy down and sat there, saying nothing, glaring at him. The secretary coughed and came up beside me.

"Should we call his father, too?" she said softly.

I nodded. "Yes, let's do that."

The boy looked nervously back and forth between her and me. I waited, unexpressive, for fifteen minutes. A pair of footsteps at the closed door caught my attention, then a knock. The principal opened up, and a uniform entered.

He nodded at me. "Inspector, what have we got, sir?"

I pointed at the boy. "Common assault. Take him in, keep him overnight. I'll handle the paperwork tomorrow."

The uniform grunted and grabbed the boy's arm. The boy squirmed, kicked, then flailed, trying to get away. The uniform sighed and bent down to stare at him. "You want the cuffs on you, kid?" he snarled. "Then shut up and calm down. Come with me."

He pulled the boy along, with less of a struggle this time, but still reluctant, out to his cruiser. He sat the boy in the back seat and drove off.

I spoke with the office staff for a minute, left them my

card, and walked back down the hall for the exit door. Another set of footsteps, loud, clunking, came my way. The big man, Salmo, was barreling down the other way, toward me.

"Where is he? Where is Ragnar?" he growled. "What did you do to him?"

I stood still. "He assaulted a younger boy. I had him arrested," I said simply.

The man just stood in front of me, livid. His face was red, radiating heat, steaming with anger. He raised a clenched fist and shook it at me. "You let him go. You bring him home right now," he snarled.

I looked at the fist. "No," I said, simply.

He pulled his fist back, threatening to punch me. I didn't react. He pursed his lips, looked around at the school staff, staring at him, and looked back at me. His face softened. "Look, I'm sorry. I talk to Ragnar, I tell him to leave your boy alone. Let him go," he pleaded.

"Screw you," I said.

The school staff snickered, enjoying this reversal of roles.

The man rubbed his hair with both hands, his plaid shirt riding up, his belly poking over his belt. "Look, you can't do this. You can't take him away like this. Please." He was begging now.

I sneered. "So, I came to you earlier, and I tried to reason with you. You insulted me, you called my wife names, and you belittled our son. But now you're asking for my help? You're pathetic."

I turned to walk away. The man grabbed my arm. "Don't turn your back. You can't turn your back," he growled.

"You did that to me," I said. "How does it feel?"

I was feeling good now, but in my heart I knew it was wrong to enjoy feeling like this. It was just another way of feeling angry. I walked away.

I got about three paces, then I heard what I thought I would hear. The man rushed at me, tried to tackle me from behind. He lunged at me, wrapped his arms around my waist, trying to pull me down.

I worked with his momentum, as I knew I would. I kept moving, pulling him along behind me, then I turned to one side and he slipped past me, tumbled onto his side and slid along the corridor, slapping noisily into a set of lockers. He tried to get up, got onto his hands and knees, but by then I was on top of him. I stretched out his right arm, kicked him onto his side, then wrapped my leg around his arm in a classic elbow lock. I twisted his wrist, pinning him into submission. The man groaned in pain.

"Let me go. Let me go. You can't do this to me. Let me go," he cried.

I twisted his wrist a little tighter. "Hurts, does it, shitface?" I sneered. "You have no idea what I can do to you, do you? I can put you in hospital and just walk away. I can maim you and go to work the next day without even thinking about you. Right now, your boy is going to be in a jail overnight. I want you to think about what I can do to you if you piss me off again." I let him go.

The school staff were no longer smiling. They were shocked now, looking at me as if I were the aggressor. I had gone too far. I felt ashamed for acting the way I had. I helped the man up.

"Your boy is being held at remand, in Old City Hall," I said, quietly. "Go get him out. Take him home. I won't press any charges."

The man stood up, brushed himself off, and muttered something that sounded like "Thanks."

I went home, called remand to let the boy go, and sat in the living room. I leaned back and closed my eyes.

I wasn't tired, but I fell asleep. It was probably just coming down from the adrenaline rush, I knew, but I slept anyway. I had a vivid dream. I dreamt of the dead man, bullet holes in his chest, tumbling off the chair and falling to the floor. Then he got up, but he was now Salmo, in a plaid shirt and dusty pants.

I woke up to the sound of footsteps in the front hall.

"Hi, where are you?" Karen called.

"Here. Napping," I answered. I rubbed my eyes.

She walked through to join me. "What did you do?" she asked. It took me a moment to understand the harshness in her tone.

"You mean at school?" I asked. "Ah, that."

"Yes, that. What in god's name did you do, Ian?"

"Ethan was being pushed around. I couldn't let that happen, so I stopped the kid who was doing it. I probably went a little overboard, I know, but—"

"A little overboard? Arresting a child, beating up his father? You call that probably going a little overboard?" She wasn't angry, just very firm, very focused, which was far more intimidating.

"I was trying to do what was best for our son. I was trying to protect him." I was feeling angry now, more forceful, less cooperative.

"My son. *My* son. You were doing this with *my* son," she snarled. "Do you want him to grow up thinking he'll never be pushed around? You can't always be there for him, you know?"

I boiled over at that, at her implying, as the big man had said, that Ethan was not my son. "Fine. You handle *your* son the way *you* want. I'm going out," I growled.

"*Out where*?" she screamed. "*Where*? *When will you be back*?"

"*Out*! *I'll be back when I'm back*!" I yelled. I stormed out and slammed the door behind me.

I drove off, not sure where I was going, not sure what I wanted to do. In the back of my mind, Colleen Feldman's voice came back to me, telling me that I would get angry for no reason, and that this was a perfectly normal part of my recovery. I drove for a good half hour, up Keele Street, down Bathurst Street, driving along side roads, not really caring where I was going. I drove till I felt stupid. It didn't take long.

After a while, the radio chatter, which I had ignored, got personal.

"Dispatch to Fifty-two zero six." said a familiar voice.

I picked up the microphone. "Go, dispatch."

The voice sounded immediately relieved at this. "Zero six, call Mr. Burghezian first possible."

Karen had called Frank. He'd called dispatch, of course. I felt like an idiot. "Roger, zero six out."

I stopped at a pay phone, got out a quarter, and called home. Karen answered in one ring.

"Hey, hon, you were looking for me?" I said contritely.

She sighed with relief. "Where are you, Ian?"

"Out driving. Do you need anything for dinner?" I tried to sound casual. It came out as "sorry."

"Just you, Ian. Your kids miss you."

I beamed at that. "On my way. You want to have dinner out?"

"Sure. Is this your way of apologizing, dumbass?"

I could hear her smirking.

I snickered. "That comes later. I'll be there in ten."

I pulled into my driveway and took a deep breath. I had to get back to normal, had to get myself back to being me. I couldn't let these mood swings ruin my life. I opened the front door and went in. Karen and the kids were in the kitchen, sharing wedges of apple, cheerily talking over each other. I joined them, and Ethan scowled at me.

"Hey, sport, what's up?" I asked.

"I got bugged at school about what you did," he said. "You chased Ragnar into the office, and everybody was talking about it."

"You said he was picking on you. I was just trying to help," I protested, weakly.

"Don't," Ethan said, simply. "Don't do it, unless I ask you to."

I smiled. From the mouths of babes, indeed. I held my hand out. "Deal."

He grinned and shook it.

ᔕᔕ

On Tuesday morning, I drove into the lot at Fifty-two Division, parked at my spot and went in.

I was feeling good. I had no idea why, but I was feeling like myself again. I hoped it wouldn't be a flash in the pan, that I wouldn't go back down to the dark feelings, the anger, that I'd felt the day before. I decided to call Colleen Feldman for some advice.

It was almost nine in the morning. The sun was beating in from the back side of the street, already shining on the buildings on the far side of Keele Street, reflecting into our front entry. I gratefully accepted the mug of coffee from our secretary, then pulled a business card out of my desk and dialed a number.

The woman at the other end answered in two rings.

"Colleen Feldman," she said, simply.

"Hi, Colleen, it's Ian McBriar," I said.

Her voice rose a half octave. "Ian, it's nice to hear from you again. What can I do for you?"

"Well, you've been spot on so far. I had a couple of really bad ups and downs, but I came in to work today feeling really good, so I wanted to know if I'm on the mend, that's all."

She sighed softly. "Has anything different happened that would have caused this change?"

I sat back. "Well, I confronted a kid who was beating up our son, then I tackled his father. I think that would qualify as 'different.'"

"When you say tackled, how do you mean that?" she asked carefully.

"He came at me and I wrestled him to the ground."

"Where did this happen?" she continued.

"Ah. At our son's school," I said guiltily.

"How did you feel after the episode was over? Were you pleased with what you'd done?"

"No. I felt like a stupid shit. I apologized to my family afterward."

She actually laughed at this. "I'm very glad that you can look back and see that objectively. It gives me a sense of security that you've come this far this quickly."

"So, you're saying this kind of outburst was normal?" I asked.

"Yes. Usually, this emotion sometime presents in different ways—like picking fights in a bar, or yelling at other drivers, or similar behavior. Most of the time, it's common for the grieving person, afterward, to say 'he started it' or something like that. In any case, it's very perceptive of you to self-analyze."

"So, am I better enough to go back to full duties?" I asked.

She laughed. "Soon, very soon. We'll talk next Monday, all right? Ten a.m.?"

"Fine. See you then. By the way, how is the new fish getting along with Carl?"

"Friedrich is doing well. That was very considerate of you. Thanks again, Ian." She hung up.

I sat back and smiled. I went through the few remaining files I had to review before I went on vacation, went outside to get a donut from the coffee truck, and wandered back in. I was not quite at the front doorway, when I caught a glimpse of a familiar car.

I turned to look at it as it cruised into the lot. A huge black Mercedes, silent and imposing, came to a stop by my car.

Sam lumbered out of the driver's seat and opened the opposite back door.

Walsh shuffled out, cradling his sore arm, and grinned when he saw me. "Hey, boss, how's work without me?"

I looked at my watch. "You're late. I'm going to dock you a donut," I joked.

I grinned. "Really, Patrick, why are you here? You should be home, taking it easy."

He raised an eyebrow. "You should talk. Anyway, remember what we were talking about?"

A picture of Lizzy Walsh went through my mind. "No idea, what?" I asked.

He reached into his tailored windbreaker and pulled out a piece of paper. "Your friend, Salmo, has made some very stupid financial decisions. He's months behind on his truck payment, and he's just barely hanging on to his house."

"I don't understand," I said.

He nodded. "His truck loan—we bought the note. Say the word, and we'll repossess it today. He loses that, and he loses the means to earn money, and he goes broke. Just say the word, boss."

I stared at the paper. With one nod of my head, I could ruin this man's life, at no cost to me. Walsh would not lose anything, nobody would lose anything, except for the man I had tackled in the school. I realized I just couldn't do it to him.

I shook my head. "How much does he owe?" I asked.

Walsh glanced at the paper. "About eighteen hundred dollars."

I reached my hand out. "Here, I'll buy his note. He can pay me back when he can afford to."

Walsh stared at me, incredulous. "You don't want to get back at him?"

I shook my head. "I want to turn the other cheek. It's the right thing to do. Give me the note."

"You know, I hoped you'd do that, boss. I'm glad you did." Walsh gave me the paper.

"What did I just do?" I asked, puzzled.

"You showed compassion. Here you go. It's all yours. Think of it as an early Christmas present. Merry Christmas. My doctor wants me to rest for a few more days, anyway. See you Monday." He got into the Mercedes. Sam grinned at me, nodded goodbye, and they drove off.

I went into the office, holding the piece of paper gingerly, wondering what I was going to do with it. I picked up the phone and dialed my house. A very girl's young voice answered.

"McBriar 'sidence," she said.

"Hey, Charlotte, it's Dad. Where's your mom?"

"Hi, da, she's here. Bye." The phone was placed on the table. Someone picked it up.

"Hey, hon, what's up?" Karen asked.

"Boy, she's growing up so fast," I said. "Are you free for lunch?"

"Um, yeah. I'm dropping Charlotte off at Helen's and I have an appointment at three, but otherwise I'm free, yeah."

"Great. Meet you at Stavro's Burgers at twelve thirty?"

"Boy, big spender, huh? Why there?"

"It's close to home, and we had one of our first lunch dates there, five years ago," I said.

There was a pause. "So we did. See you then, hon."

I finished the few pieces of paperwork left on my desk, picked up Walsh's piece of paper, and drove to the house on Keith Avenue. I knocked on the door and waited. A minute later, the front door opened gingerly and a face peered out.

The big man, looking sheepish, stepped out onto his front porch and nodded to me. "Yes, mister?" he said softly.

"Mister Salmo, I think we both said and did things we regret," I said.

He looked at his shoes. "Ya. Sorry. You got a good kid, I hear."

I took a deep breath. "I was prepared to hurt you, in a very bad way. I wanted to ruin you." He looked up at me, puzzled. I continued. "You owe eighteen hundred and twenty six dollars on your truck, and you're behind on the payments," I said.

He shrank back. The thought of someone knowing his vulnerabilities seemed to terrify him.

"A man I know bought the loan note on your truck and gave it to me. That piece of paper gives me the right to take it away from you for back payment."

His eyes widened, but he said nothing. The look in his

eyes was a terror far worse than the fear of being roughed up. I pulled the paper out of my jacket and handed it to him.

"Here. The truck loan is paid off. It's all yours," I said. I turned to leave, but he grabbed my arm.

He stared at the paper, incredulous. "Mister, why you do this?" he asked quietly.

I shrugged. "It's the right thing to do. What I did before, that's not me. This is who I am. Have a good day." I turned to leave again.

He walked up behind me, touched my arm, and waited for me to turn around. I looked at him, wondering what he'd say. His eyes were moist.

"Mister, I pay you back when I can, Okay? I pay it all back. Honest."

I thought for a moment. "Are you Catholic?" I asked.

"Nah. Lutheran. Finnish, Lutheran." He shrugged.

I smiled. "Nobody's perfect. Give it to your church, when you can afford to. Bye."

I got into my car and drove off, smiling.

ᔓᔕ

I got to the burger place just before twelve thirty. It hadn't changed at all in the years I'd been going there. It was still just a take-out counter, with one table for two in the corner, facing a main window, and some of the best French fries in the city. I sat at the table and rolled my glass of water between my hands, watching the ice reflect the light as it rotated.

A couple of minutes later, a Pinto stopped behind my car, and Karen got out. She grinned, seeing me through the window, and came in to join me. She plunked herself firmly down on the seat across from me and stared at me, a faint smile on her lips. "So, why the reason for this lunch?"

I inhaled deeply. "I wanted to apologize for being such a…" I searched for a word.

"A dick. A complete moron. An asshole. A shmuck?" she suggested.

"Yeah, all of those." I laughed. "Anyway, I just wanted to say sorry with a very special, very expensive meal."

She looked at me, waiting for me to say something else. "And?" she said.

"Ah. And, I visited the man I pushed around at Ethan's school. Patrick bought the note on his truck loan, and offered to repossess it for me to punish him. I gave it to the man instead. He's got his truck free and clear, now. I just thought you'd want to know." I took a sip of my water.

Karen was still looking at me, still smiling slightly. I couldn't read her.

"What?" I asked.

"That's the Ian I know. That's the man I married," she said softly. "Thanks for coming back."

"Want to go home for an hour?" I asked. "We're all alone."

She laughed out loud. "Sorry, I have an appointment, as I told you."

We ordered lunch. Karen said she wasn't too hungry, and she settled on a milkshake and water. I had my burger, then I walked her to her car.

"Want me to check on how soon we can get the Valiant back?" I asked.

"Yes, please. I'm not thrilled with the Pinto, but it runs, at least."

I nodded. "Good enough. I'm going to speak with Colleen Feldman. Talk to you later?"

She pulled my face down and kissed me. "I do love you, you know," she whispered.

"Love you too, hon."

She drove off, and I drove home. I called the coroner, cleared up some procedural details about our dead women, and then I called Colleen Feldman. She answered in three rings.

"Hi, Colleen, it's Ian," I said.

"Yes, Ian?" She sounded pleased to hear from me.

"Can I quickly talk to you about something?" I asked.

"Um, yes, I have ten minutes free now. Will that do it?"

"Sure." I told her about the incident with Salmo, talking to him, then roughing him up, talking to Walsh, getting the loan note, giving it back to the man. She listened, only saying 'uh-huh' every so often.

I finished telling her my story, took a deep breath, and waited.

"So, Ian," she began. "How do you feel now?"

"I feel like my old self," I said honestly. "I had a chance to do something cruel, and I chose not to do it. I feel much better about that choice. What do you think?"

"I think you need to keep busy," she said. "You're acting reasonably, Ian. I'm cancelling our next meeting. Go back to work."

I almost jumped up and down with joy. The memory of the dead man was now in the past. The details no longer invaded all my thoughts. I was back, and I felt whole again.

"You know, I could hug you, Colleen," I said.

She laughed. "Tell Martin hello from me, and that I've signed off on you returning to work."

I hung up the phone and leaned back, smiling. Tomorrow, I would be back at my desk, doing my job. Tomorrow, I would be myself again, not constantly wondering about whether I was acting the way I should or not.

I made a coffee and sat in the living room, listening to jazz. I sat there for over an hour, feeling like I was embraced by contentment. The coffee was good, the jazz was good, life was good.

The front door opened, and a familiar voice yelled out "Dad? Hi?"

"In here, Ethan," I called back. I was aware of two sets of footsteps, so I got up to investigate.

Ethan was in the front hall with Ragnar, the boy I had chased in school. He saw me and shrank back. Ethan pulled on the older boy's sleeve and grinned.

"Guess what, Dad?" he said cheerily. "Ragnar likes trains, and he wants to see my train set. Cool, huh?"

"Yeah, cool," I muttered. "You guys want cake or cookies and milk?"

The boy's face lit up. "Yes, please."

I led them into the kitchen, cut some carrot cake and poured milk, and watched them eat and talk like old friends. They finished, then both raced upstairs to play with Ethan's train set.

The older boy turned back on the stairs and looked at me. "Thanks, sir," he said, and continued up the stairs.

I grinned. Colleen had been right, again. After an hour, the two boys thundered down the stairs again, and the older boy picked up his backpack, ready to walk home.

"Thanks for the food, sir," he said. "It was very delicious." There was a crispness to his speech, a tentative tone, that made me curious about him.

"So, Ragnar, were you born in Finland?" I asked.

"Yes," he said.

"When did you come here?"

He shrugged. "Three years. Not a long time."

"You speak English very well, though," I commented.

He grinned. "Thank you."

"*Ole hyva.* I'm afraid that's all the Finnish I know."

Ethan frowned. "What did you say?"

Ragnar laughed. "He said 'you're welcome.'"

The boy slung the backpack over his shoulder and walked home.

Ethan raced back upstairs and went back to playing with his trains. I checked my watch—five-thirty. Karen would be coming home shortly with Charley, and I wanted to start on dinner.

I had a couple of casseroles in the fridge, so I put one in the oven. It would be ready within an hour, which gave me time to read the paper and do the crossword.

I got most of the way through the crossword, was stuck on a nine letter word for seafood, and decided to give up for the day. The door opened and Karen came in, with Charley running ahead of her. I crouched down to be at her eye level.

"Hi, Dad," Charley said, "We went to the park."

"Wow, you did? That sounds like lots of fun. What did you do there?" I asked.

She giggled. "I played on the swing, and I jumped on the monkey bars."

"Boy, I wish I was with you," I teased. "I would have jumped high, too."

Charley laughed at the statement. "Silly Daddy," she said, and totted off to watch TV.

Karen had a faraway look, distracted. "Hey, you," she said. "How are you?"

"Fine, actually." I grinned. "Ethan brought that boy over, the one who bullied him, to play with his trains. He looks like a good kid at heart. And, by the way, Colleen gave me the okay to go back to work, so that's really good news, too."

She smiled warmly. "I'm so pleased for you, Ian. I know how hard this has been for you. When do you go back to work?"

"Tomorrow. Tomorrow I'll be back at the job, and happy to be there."

We ate dinner, with life seeming as normal as it had felt a week ago, before I had shot a man dead. No matter how normal the mood of the evening was, though, no matter how we all smiled, ate and laughed, a fleeting image of the dead man came to mind every few minutes.

∞∞

Wednesday morning, I was up at six, dressed and making coffee before seven. Karen came downstairs in her robe, wrapped tight around her, and opened cupboard doors, looking for something.

"Can I help you, hon?" I asked.

She sighed. "Where is that cereal of Ethan's? You know, the Cap'n Crunch?"

I frowned. "You want that for breakfast? I can make you some scrambled eggs, if you'd rather."

She shook her head. "No, thanks. Just the cereal."

She poured herself a bowl of cereal and a glass of milk. She sat across from me and scooped cereal into her mouth, crunching contentedly.

I watched her eat, fascinated. "You're actually enjoying that stuff?" I asked.

"Sure. Some days, you just feel like comfort food, you know?"

I stood up and turned toward the counter. "Let me pour you a coffee, hon," I said.

"No, I'll just drink this milk, thanks."

I shrugged. "Okay. Whatever." I sat back down and drank my coffee.

Ethan and Charley came downstairs, had breakfast and then Ethan ran upstairs to get ready for school.

I turned to Karen. "So, what's on for today?" I asked.

"I'm watching Helen's kids. She's working today, I'm not." She grinned at Charley. "It looks like we're going to the park with Theo and Melina, Charlotte."

Charley smiled and munched her toast. "I like the park," she said. "Can we go on the swings?"

Karen nodded. "Yes, we can go on the swings. And the slides."

I put my holster on, slid the revolver into place, self-conscious as I held the grip, and clipped my breakaway tie onto my shirt. I pulled my jacket on, looked in the mirror, and headed back downstairs to say goodbye.

Ethan was in his room, and Karen was still in the kitchen, talking to Charley. I yelled goodbye to Ethan, and he yelled, "See you, Dad," through his door.

I kissed Charley on the forehead then wrapped an arm around Karen. "Goodbye, hon. I'll call you around lunchtime, okay?"

She gazed up at me with a look I couldn't quite read. "I'll talk to you later, then."

I got into my Caprice and backed onto the street. I waited for a lull in radio traffic then picked up the microphone.

"Fifty-two zero six to dispatch," I said.

"Go, zero six," came the response.

"Any messages, Nadine?" I asked.

There was a pause in the chatter.

"Roger, zero six. DC Reynolds on scene, code ten-fifty-four. Aylmer Avenue, East of Yonge."

I grimaced. Ten fifty-four. That meant another dead body—great. "Roger, zero six out."

It took me a few minutes to work my way through the morning rush-hour traffic, driving along St. Clair Avenue, then north onto Yonge, blipping my siren to make an illegal left turn.

Traffic was heavier on Yonge, even heading away from downtown, and I had to plod through blocks of stop-and-go before I found could weave around slower cars and get to Aylmer.

Aylmer Avenue is a street that seems like it was built as an afterthought—it crosses Yonge Street and flows east on an overpass reaching over the subway track, before turning southbound and running parallel to the tracks. I turned off Yonge Street, pulled over immediately and stopped behind a yellow cruiser.

I go out and showed my badge to the nearest uniform. Just being able to do that made me feel like myself again. Ahead, on the sidewalk beside the overpass, I saw Reynolds, her Moleskine in one hand, directing uniforms by pointing her pen in the other hand. I walked casually toward her, letting her do her job. She spoke to one uniform, patted him on the shoulder, and he went to his car.

Reynolds headed my way. "Morning, boss. I hear you're back in the field again," she said.

"Hi, Alex. Yeah, it's good to be back. What do we have this morning?"

She pointed past the overpass, down on the tracks. A hundred yards north, Rosedale subway station stuck out from one side, seeming to almost block the path of the trains.

"We have a dead body. According to the train driver, this woman went off the overpass just as his train was approaching. He had no chance to stop—she landed on the rails, then she actually got up on her feet just as he hit her."

"Messy," I said. "Do we have an ID on her yet?"

She shook her head. "I just got here. I haven't had a chance to look her over, but the uniforms on the ground have her covered up, so I'm just about to see what we've got."

"Good enough. I'm going to talk to the driver, then I'll meet you at the body," I said.

I walked the hundred yards along Yonge Street to the subway station. It was odd, but I felt very good to be doing this, even though I was going to investigate another death. I was doing what I was meant to do, trying to find the guilty, and helping to speak for the victims.

On the sidewalk outside the subway station, a familiar man in a jacket with *TTC Supervisor* sewn on it was waving commuters away with a clipboard. He shook his head.

"This is not good, Inspector," he growled. "I don't enjoy the heat we're getting here. This looks bad for the transit system, you know."

"Hello again," I said. "Sorry we have to meet like this again. This is not fun for us, either."

He held his clipboard out to block me. "Look, before we get going, I just want you to know it was not our driver's fault. He's been working this job for fifteen years, he never had a complaint about him, he never had an accident, nothing."

"I know. I was told there was no way for him to stop in time. We know it's not his fault," I said.

The man grunted and let me past him. I walked down a set of steps to the platform. At the end of the platform, a group of people huddled around a man in a blue-gray uniform, squatted on the ground. I walked up to him and crouched beside him.

“Hey there. I’m Detective Inspector McBriar. You’re the driver of the train that had the accident, right?” I said. I didn’t use words like ‘hit’ or ‘kill.’ I thought it would put his guard up.

He looked up at me and nodded. “Yeah. Horrible accident. I couldn’t stop. I couldn’t stop, man.”

I patted his shoulder. “I know. It wasn’t your fault,” I said. “What’s your name, sir?”

“Bert.” He thought for a moment. “Bert Podowski.” He coughed and retched, then got on all fours, crawled to the edge of the platform and vomited. I looked over to the track bed, and saw that he had vomited a few feet up from there earlier, apparently.

He uncapped a thermos bottle beside him and took a swig of tea, then spat it out onto the track. He wiped his mouth and coughed again.

“Shit, this is horrible,” he moaned. “You have no idea how bad it feels to kill someone.”

“Actually, I do,” I said. Everyone on the platform stared at me. “But I can tell you, the feelings go away when it was not your fault.”

He looked up at me, trying to read something in my face. He nodded slowly.

“Listen, Bert,” I said. “What can you tell me about the incident? What do you remember, exactly?”

He pointed down the track, toward the overpass. “I pulled away from the station, and I was going maybe twenty-five, thirty. All of a sudden, I see this thing go off the bridge. Sometimes we get kids tossing rags, or newspapers, or water balloons, you know, but I never thought—” He rubbed his face and shook his head. “Anyway, so I’m headed for the bridge,”

“You mean the overpass, right?” I clarified.

“Yeah, I guess it’s an overpass, right. Anyway, I’m just

about to go under the bridge, and this thing flies down onto the track. I thought it was a pile of rags, but then she got up." He scrunched up his face and winced. "She stood up, and she stared at me. She looked me right in the eyes and stared at me. Then I hit her. Christ, I'll never forget that moment."

I looked down the track at the overpass. "Listen, Bert, do you remember if she was on the near side or the far side when she went over? It's important."

He looked down the track too, remembering. "The other side. Yeah, I'm sure of it, cause I never saw her falling till she cleared the bottom of the bridge. Maybe if she'd jumped from this side, I could have stopped in time, you know, cause I would have seen her climb over the railing, but no, she jumped from the other side."

I frowned. "Are you sure she jumped? Could she have been pushed or thrown by someone?"

He shrugged. "Maybe, I don't know. I was just watching her. I never looked to see if there was someone else on the bridge."

I stood up. "All right, listen, if you remember anything, or if you have any questions, here's my card. Give me a call, and talk to me, okay?"

He took the card and nodded, read the card then looked up at me. "You the cop that stopped the bank robbery?"

"It was a team effort. I'm just the idiot that went into the bank."

He snickered softly. He put the card in his shirt pocket, leaned back and closed his eyes.

I went down to the end of the platform, climbed the short ladder down to the track, and walked along to a cluster of uniforms at the base of the overpass. There was a blue canvas painter's tarp over a lump on the tracks, men talking in hushed voices around it.

One of the uniforms nodded to me. "Hey, boss, good to see you back in the field. We got another messy one here."

"Any word on who she is?" I asked.

"We're not going through her purse or anything till the coroner shows. I don't want to get in any shit for disturbing a crime scene," he said, matter-of-factly.

I lifted one corner of the tarp and looked at the body underneath. She was pretty, young, with an expression on her face somewhere between anger and horror. The bumper of the subway train had struck her in the ribcage and caved in her chest. A pool of blood had soaked into her sweater, making the light blue wool completely red. Her face had been gouged deeply as she was dragged along before the train stopped, imbedding gravel into her eye socket. I put the tarp gently down, dropped to one knee and said a quick prayer for her soul. I got up again.

"Her name is Penny Lewis," I said. "She works at a law firm downtown. Worked, sorry."

I brushed the dirt off my pant leg, keeping my eyes away from the tarp.

"You knew her? Any idea why she would have jumped, then?" the uniform asked.

"She didn't jump. She was pushed, or thrown. When we spoke to her on Saturday, she was afraid someone might go after her for speaking with us. I guess she was right."

A figure walked along the track, tracing my steps, headed toward me. It was Reynolds, walking purposefully, gripping her Moleskine as she stumbled over rough rocks on the track bed. I walked to head her off before she could reach the tarp. She nodded at me and smiled, then looked past my shoulder and saw the looks on the faces of the uniforms. Her face dropped.

"What is it?" she asked, warily.

"Come on, Alex, let's go back to the platform," I said.

"Why?" she said. She tried to pivot and go around me, to head back to the body under the tarp.

"It's not a pretty sight, Alex. You don't need to see it," I said.

"It's my job, boss." She stared up at me. "Are you doing this to me just because I'm a girl?"

I shook my head. "It's Penny Lewis."

She stopped, covered her mouth with her hands, and let out a soft whimper. For a brief second, her eyes registered horror and grief, then she took her hands down again and straightened up.

"I'm sorry about that, sir," she said formally. "Let's see what we can find out, okay?"

She marched over to the tarp and lifted a corner, gently. She squatted down, pointed with her pen, and made comments. Penny's fingernails were long and painted a bright red. They were not so long that she couldn't type, but long enough to be glamorous. The ends of her middle fingers had scrapes, where she had likely clawed the railing of the overpass, trying to stop from being thrown over. I had missed that on my first look at her.

Penny had pantyhose on, and the knees were scraped and torn, also most likely from trying to stay on the overpass. Reynolds wrote all this down, made notes about her injuries, then closed her Moleskine, and stood up.

"All right, I'm done here, boss," she said.

She walked briskly back to the platform. I asked a uniform to wrap up after the coroner arrived, and I followed her.

She climbed the access ladder to the platform and found an office door. She walked in, threw herself against a wall and began to wail. She cried pitifully, moaning and weeping, for a couple of minutes. Then she straightened herself up, wiped her face with a handkerchief, and came out of the office.

"Are you okay now?" I asked.

"No," she answered.

"Want to talk about it?"

She shook her head, thought for a second, then shrugged. "How do you do it, sir? How do you stand it?"

"Is it because of the way she looks, or because you met her before she was killed?" I asked.

She sighed. "I was talking to her after you left the bakery. She sounded like a nice woman, a good person, like she was trying to help us out. I never thought that she was putting herself in danger by talking to us. If I had, I would have told her not to do it."

"Look, Alex, we don't know why this happened. It might not have had anything at all to do with her talking to us. It might have been that whoever did this was going to kill her anyway. We don't know. Listen, do you want to take the rest of the day off? I understand if you need to."

She shook her head and straightened her shoulders. "No, no way. I have to talk to the people at her office. I have to contact her next of kin and tell them she's dead, sir. That's my job."

I nodded. "Fine, go to it, then. I'll catch up to you at the shop later. Call Terry and ask him for backup if you need to, all right?"

She sighed. "Yeah, good idea. I'll talk to Terry, sir. Catch up with you later."

She walked out of the station, and I watched her march the hundred yards back to her car. She was a thoughtful person, a good cop, and she would probably be a good Inspector in the future. It must have been hard for her to see Penny's body lying there like that. I decided to give her a lesson in being a cop, and this was the perfect time to do it.

I wanted to get to the bottom of this case. I had been distracted by Patrick's disappearance, and I had to clear up this mess fast, before I went back to Saskatchewan. I walked back to my car. Reynolds was in her car, flipping through notes on her Moleskine. I tapped on her window, and she jumped at the sound. She rolled the glass down.

"Hi?" she said tentatively.

"Where are you going now?" I asked.

"I'm, um, going to interview the staff at—" she started.

"Wrong. We're going to talk to the staff at the law firm. I want you there, but I want to do all the talking, is that clear?"

"Yes, sir."

"Good. Follow me, don't go into the building before I do, I'll meet you in the lobby downstairs."

"Um, okay," she said.

I got into my car and drove downtown. I found a meter across the street from the law firm, put my '*police business*' sign on the dashboard, and waited for Reynolds to show up.

She arrived a minute later, shuffled up to me, and straightened her jacket. She looked scared, like I was a drill sergeant that was going to ream her out. That was the look I was trying to give, actually. It snapped her back to reality, back to doing her job.

"Ready?" I asked.

She squared her shoulders and nodded. We walked to the elevators and went up to the eighth floor, not speaking. We were about to get out of the elevator, and she turned to look at me.

"You or me?" she asked.

"You," I snapped.

She nodded, strode ahead and opened the door to the law office. She stood just inside the entry, waited for me to saunter in behind her, and walked quickly to the reception desk. The receptionist, a young woman with a puzzled expression, was trying to transfer a phone call.

Reynolds reached into her jacket and retrieved her wallet.

"I need to speak with Duncan Carroll," she said.

The receptionist glanced up at her, distracted. "Just a minute, please," she muttered.

Reynolds opened out her badge and showed it to the woman. "I need to speak with Duncan Carroll," she repeated. "Now."

The woman stared at the badge then looked helplessly up at Reynolds. "I'm sorry, we're short-staffed today, and Mister Carroll has a meeting in five minutes. Can you come back in a couple of hours, and—"

Reynolds shook her head. "No. Call him. Now," she said forcefully.

The receptionist shrank visibly and picked up a telephone. She stared at the buttons for a minute, figuring out what to press, then dialed three digits.

"Mister Carroll, there's a policewoman here who—"

"Homicide detective," Reynolds corrected.

The woman cringed. "A homicide detective who says she needs to talk to you, right now."

She nodded at the air and put the phone down. She looked down the hall, expectantly.

Reynolds sighed. "Can I take it from your expression that he's on his way?" she asked.

The woman looked up. "Yes, sorry, he's just coming."

Reynolds looked down the hall, and Duncan Carroll walked around a corner and toward us. I had still said nothing.

"Hello, Detective. Inspector. This sounds urgent."

"We have found a body on the subway tracks, near Rosedale subway station," Reynolds said.

"Oh, dear. That is bad news. How does this involve our firm, though?" he asked.

"The body was that of Penny Lewis," Reynolds said. "She was thrown onto the tracks from an overpass, and dragged by a subway train."

Carroll gasped. "Penny? We wondered why she wasn't in this morning. We thought she was just feeling sick. When did this happen?"

"Today. Did she have any relatives nearby that you know of? Someone we should contact?"

He shook his head. "I believe her parents passed away some time ago, and she once said she was an only child. I don't think there's anyone that needs to be notified."

"Did she have a boyfriend, someone she was close to?" Reynolds was writing his answers down.

"Nobody she ever mentioned, no. She seemed to be quite self-content."

"Where were you between seven thirty and eight thirty this morning?" Reynolds asked.

"Me? I was here, in this office. I had a seven am conference call with a client in Paris." He shrugged. "Why would you think I'd have anything to do with her death?"

"We're going to ask the same questions of everyone," Reynolds said. "I just asked you first."

Carroll waved at the office area in general. "Ask away, then. I have to inform our staff of what happened."

Reynolds turned back to the receptionist. "Do you have an office we could take over for today? We will need to talk to everybody here, of course."

The woman stood up hurriedly, tugged her skirt straight and shuffled across the room to a closed door. She opened the door, turned on the light and waved her hand at the opening.

"You can use this room, if you like," the woman said, almost apologetically.

"Fine. I need a list of all your employees. Now," Reynolds snapped.

She put her Moleskine on the desk inside the office and took off her coat. She put the coat on a corner rack and sat in a large chair. The holstered revolver on her belt gave her a menacing appearance.

The receptionist scurried off to get the list, and Reynolds watched her go, staring at her.

I grinned, leaned forward, and whispered, "Good work. Call me later."

Reynolds smirked at me then looked behind me at the receptionist coming back with a sheet of paper, and frowned again, putting on a serious face.

I went back down the elevator and got in my car, smiling to myself. Reynolds would be fine.

Chapter 17

The latest dead girl, Penny Lewis, should have been picked up by now. I checked my watch and radioed the dispatcher. She patched me in to a uniform at the scene. The radio crackled as he stood outside his cruiser, talking to me.

"Fifty-two eight three, go," said the voice.

"Fifty-two zero six," I answered. "Do we have the scene wrapped up yet?"

"Roger. The coroner has it, and we've got photos of the scene. Okay to reopen the subway line?"

I went through a mental checklist. "Yeah, let's open it. All evidence has been collected along the site, hasn't it? No forensics at the scene?"

There was a slight pause, then he came back. "No, sir. We did a shoulder-to-shoulder check, no other clues. Do you have ten to meet me, Inspector?"

"Yeah, the McDonalds at Yonge and St. Clair?" I said.

"Sure. See you there in ten," he said.

I parked in a laneway behind the corner of St. Clair and Yonge, walked around to the front and went up a short flight of steps to the McDonalds restaurant.

In the back, at one corner, was the senior uniform I'd spoken to earlier. He looked like a Marine, wide-shouldered, with a look that scared most people into behaving. His sleeve had three broad gold stripes, and his shirt pocket had a neat cluster of pens, that told me he was meticulous about details. He saw me, waved, and I sat across from him.

"Inspector? John Lowe," he said. He reached out his hand, and I shook it. He slid a paper cup my way. "I bought us coffee, sir. Do you want one?"

I took a sip. "Not bad. Ian, call me Ian," I said. "So, how can I help you, Sergeant?"

His eyes closed for a moment as he thought. "The dead girl. We were interviewing possible witnesses, on the street, but nobody saw anything. Then one of my constables said we should check with the people in the office building down the street. There was a chance that someone was in early, he said, and maybe they saw something."

I nodded. "Very good. We would have canvassed the building later, by the way, but good to see he has initiative."

He waved his hand, casually. "Right. Anyway, he said that most of the staff on the northeast corner of that building, the corner that would have seen anything, doesn't usually get in till almost nine. It's an insurance office, he said, and they keep banker's hours, you know?"

"I hear a 'but' coming."

He grinned. "But. The top two floors are a customs brokerage firm. They get in real early, because they deal with truck shipments from the States, and the East Coast docks, and the like, so they start around five. It turns out that one of the ladies that works there thinks she 'may have seen something.' I figured we'd leave it to you to pop the lid on that one. If we ask her too many questions, it will change her story by the time you talk to her."

My eyes widened. "Wow, I'm impressed. Who's this rookie detective? I'd like to talk to him."

The sergeant chuckled. "He went to the can. Here he comes now." He pointed over my shoulder.

A slim young man, a younger version of Walsh, walked into the restaurant, a notebook in his hand. He looked about twelve years old, with a uniform shirt that was a size too large, his belt done up to the last hole, and his pant cuffs scuffing the tops of his polished dress shoes.

He stood stiffly by our table, waiting to be invited to sit.

"Hey there, I'm Ian McBriar," I said. "You are?"

"Constable Brian Webb," he said, his voice slightly squeaky. "It's a pleasure to meet you, sir."

"Sit down, Constable. Do you want coffee or anything?" I asked.

He looked at the serving counter and glanced at his watch. "I could really use a snack. I'll go get it for you, sir." he said. He went to get up.

"No, I got it. John, want anything?" I asked.

The sergeant leaned back and looked at the menu board. "Yeah, an egg muffin thingy, if you could. Thanks. And you, Brian?"

"A couple of those, yeah," he said.

I went to the counter and ordered some food for the two men. I brought it back on a tray, and the younger one, Webb, had his notebook out, flipping through notes he'd made.

I handed two plastic boxes of food to Webb, and one to Sergeant Lowe. They nodded thanks and started eating immediately.

Lowe finished his food and patted his mouth on a paper napkin. "You still getting comments about the King Street bank job, boss?" he asked.

I chuckled. "I've been asked about that a couple of times this week, actually. It's amazing what people think they remember."

The younger uniform frowned, puzzled. Lowe pointed a finger at me. "The inspector, when he was just a detective sergeant, walked into a bank during a robbery. Three guys, with a shotgun and crowbar, held a dozen people hostage. He left his gun outside, so they could see he was unarmed, and he went in with a tray of coffees and a bag of bagels."

"Donuts," I corrected.

"Donuts. Anyway, he calms them down long enough to

get them to let down their guard, grabs the crowbar away from this guy and uses it to cream another one, so he drops the shotgun. Got all the hostages home safe and sound, got a hero's welcome in the press."

I squirmed. *I never felt like a hero at the time,* I thought. *I was just doing my job.*

The younger man looked at me with awe. That made me feel even more self-conscious.

"Is that the way it happened, Inspector?" he asked.

"Well, yeah, except for the laser beams and the bikini bimbos," I joked. "How do you remember it so well?"

Lowe nodded. "I was about the second man in the door after you gave the 'all clear' sign. I still remember someone asking Inspector Burghezian what to do, and he said 'don't ask me, Sergeant McBriar is running this show,' or words to that effect."

I smiled. "Yeah, believe it or not, I got shit at home for putting myself at risk. Still, we do what we do, because we have to, right?"

Lowe nodded. "How's Mr. Burghezian doing? I haven't spoken to him in a month or so."

I thought back to Patrick being kidnapped, the dead man, and eating breakfast with Frank at four in the morning. "He's good. I'll pass on your regards," I said simply.

I thought about the latest dead girl, and the comment that Lowe had made as we sat down.

"Constable Webb, you said you spoke to some people in the building across the street from where our victim was pushed onto the tracks?"

He sat up, alert, and smiled. "Yes, sir. I figured that they might have seen something, so I canvassed that side of the building. A lady on the top floor office says she may have seen something. I asked her to wait till you could talk to her. I didn't want to say anything that might bias her answers, you know?"

"Wow, very well done, Brian. Good work," I said. I thought for a moment. "That building is on the southwest corner of the intersection. There's another building kitty-corner, on the northeast corner of the street. Did you go there too?"

He nodded. "Yeah, of course, sir. But with the sun's angle at that time of morning, all those offices on that side had their venetian blinds closed to keep the heat out. I checked."

I sat back, impressed. "So, Constable, have you ever considered dropping the uniform and going into plain clothes?" I asked.

He grinned. "I'd have to think about that, sir."

Lowe chuckled. "I keep telling him he's slumming here. Good for you telling him so too."

I pulled out a business card. "Here, Brian. When you get a chance, come talk to me."

He pocketed the card. "You want to interview the lady I spoke to, sir?" he asked.

"Yeah," I said. "Sergeant, can you spare him for a half hour or so?"

Lowe waved his hand across the table. "Take him. Show him the great big world."

We finished our coffee, and I walked Webb out to my car.

He touched his shirt pocket, where my business card was, and coughed. "Uh, sir, were you serious about calling you later?"

I looked straight at him. "Absolutely. You don't get it yet, do you, Brian?"

"What?" he asked, puzzled.

"You think two steps ahead. You had the idea to go to the first building, and later you realized that hot morning sun in the second would mean that they would close the blinds. Do you have any idea how rare it is to think that way?"

"No, I guess not, sir. I just always think that way, you know?"

We drove back to the overpass where Penny Lewis had died, Webb staring out the passenger window at passersby. I parked behind a cruiser and we walked up to the building where Webb had spoken to the witness. He pulled out his notebook and flipped to the last written page.

He read his notes. "Okay, her name is Mavis Owens, and she works for Blue Planet Customs Brokers, on the fourteenth floor. She said she'll be in till noon, but then she has to go uptown to pay off some brokerage or other."

I snickered. "Very good. Now, I'll ask her questions, but if you think of anything, or if I've missed anything, just jump in, okay?"

"Sure," he said.

We rode the elevator to the fourteenth floor. The building had a hallway that went around the perimeter of the floor, and the office we were looking for was in one corner.

There was a pale wood door with a plastic sign on it that read '*Blue Planet Customs—Everywhere, Anytime*. It had a logo of a world with an old-style airplane circling it, like in the old movie opening scenes.

The door was locked, so I knocked and waited politely. A minute later, I heard drawers being slammed shut, and the clop, clop, clop of heavy shoes. The door opened, and a woman who looked like a retired librarian opened up.

"Yes?" she said. She had jet black hair in a beehive style, a thick wool skirt, despite the warm day, and a matching cardigan and sweater. She wore heavy black Oxford shoes, the clopping sound I'd heard earlier, and her expression said she had just eaten something very bitter.

I held out my badge. "Hello, you're Mavis?" I smiled. "I'm Detective Inspector McBriar."

She looked at me, then Webb, then me. "Come in," she snapped and turned on her heel.

We went in with her, maneuvering between tall filing cabinets, then followed her to a thick wooden desk in one corner. She sat at the desk and pointed out the window.

"I was looking out here for my partner. He usually gets in around eight, and he was late, so I was looking to see if he was walking over from the subway," she said.

"Is he often late?" I asked.

She looked at me with small dark eyes, reminding me of a raccoon. "No, never."

"And what did you see?" I asked.

She poked her bony finger at the glass, as though willing it to replay what had happened.

"This girl was on the walkway, headed for Yonge, when a man walked up to her. She stopped, and they talked, then he pointed at the track. She turned around, real fast, like she saw a ghost or something, and they struggled, and he finally flipped her onto the tracks. Just like that."

I wrote this down. "Can you describe him?" I asked.

"No, they were too far away," the woman said.

"How was he dressed?" I asked.

"He had a track suit. It was silver or gray, I think."

"What did he do next?" I asked.

"He walked away, like nothing happened."

"Was anyone else on the overpass? Did anyone else see him do it?"

She reached across the desk and dragged an ashtray toward her. She opened a large brown purse beside her and pulled out an open pack of cigarettes. She lit one with a paper match and tossed the match into the ashtray. It went out, leaving a curly trail of smoke lingering in the air.

She sucked on the cigarette and stared at the ceiling, thinking. "No, nobody," she said. "It was deserted, nobody else on the walkway, no."

"Why was your co-worker late?" I smiled.

"His two-year-old puked all over the kitchen. Kids, huh?"

Webb leaned forward. "Do you often look out and observe people on the walkway, you know, people-watching?"

She scowled at him, then shrugged. "Work can be slow, you know. Sometimes you just got to amuse yourself."

"So, had you ever seen her walking over that way before?" he continued.

She looked at the yellow tape and sawhorses blocking

the sidewalk, thinking. "Yeah, a couple of times, I think. I remember her handbag."

"Handbag?" Webb asked.

"Yeah, you know. She had this big red plastic handbag. I remember it because we sold handbags at the place I used to work, and it reminded me of those."

"How about mister track suit? Did you recognize him?" he asked.

"Nope. I'd never seen him before."

Webb looked out her window, running his tongue along the inside of his lip. He turned to face her. "Which way did he walk away? Toward Yonge, or down Aylmer? "

She nodded. "He went down Aylmer, then I lost track of him. I didn't see if he got into a car or anything. I figure that's where your question was going?"

He smiled. "Yeah, you're right, ma'am. Listen, if you think of anything, can you give us a call?" He gave her a business card and turned to me. "Sorry, Inspector, did you have any questions?"

I shook my head. "You got it covered. Good work."

I thanked the woman for her time, and we headed back down in the elevator.

"So, what would you do next, Constable?" I asked.

We walked out to the street, and he looked over at the yellow crime tape, his hands on his hips.

He pointed down Aylmer Avenue. "I think I should knock on doors down the street, and see if anyone remembers seeing a guy in a gray track suit go by."

"I agree. Take a couple of men with you and knock on doors, okay? Tell them I said to."

He nodded and walked toward the uniforms behind the yellow crime tape.

"Hey!" I called out. He turned to look at me. "Call me. Seriously, call me." I grinned.

He smiled broadly, nodded, and joined the other men.

Chapter 18

I drove to Fifty-two Division and parked at my spot. A familiar LTD was parked in the general staff area. I walked into the detectives' room to see a cluster of men around Patrick Walsh. He was smiling and answering questions from everyone in the room. He turned when someone saw me and said something, then like a diva brushing away annoying fans he dismissed them and walked up to me. "Hey, boss, good to see you. What are you up to today?"

"I thought I'd catch up on my stamp collecting. How about you?"

"I'm just about to pick up Frank. Do you want to come with us?"

"Pick him up?" I asked. "Come where with you?"

He grinned a movie-star grin. "You'll see."

I told our secretary that I'd be out for a few hours and got into Walsh's Ford. He chirped the tires getting out of the parking lot, zipped between slower cars heading down Keele Street, and in far too short a time pulled up to Frank's house. Frank kissed Helen goodbye, hopped down his steps and sat in the back seat. "Okay, where are we going?" he asked, excited. "Are we going to egg the chief's house, or cover his shrubs with toilet paper, what?"

I rolled my eyes. Walsh chuckled. "Something just as much fun, I hope."

He drove downtown, veered east onto the Gardiner Expressway, and turned south toward the waterfront. We went down a small road that said *Private Property—Members Only* and parked at a numbered spot a few feet from the lake.

Walsh got out, opened the trunk and pulled out a large picnic basket. "Follow me," he said.

Frank looked at me, shrugged, and walked behind Walsh. I tagged along, too.

Walsh walked to a chain link fence, with a locked chain link door, and pulled a key out of his pocket. He unlocked the door, we went through, and headed toward a marina.

We were now on a long dock, zigzagging along between the bows of pleasure boats that poked out, blocking our way, but Walsh seemed to know where he was going. He turned a corner, and the dock became wider, the boats bigger. He stopped at a boat and climbed up onto the deck.

He put the basket down and helped me aboard, then pulled Frank up onto the deck. Hanging on the wheelhouse, above the deck, was a life preserver—mostly an ornament, I guessed—painted with the name *Santiago* across the top, and Nassau, Bahamas across the bottom.

"Okay, let me give you the grand tour."

He opened a door near the bow, and we followed. Inside, the boat looked like a very comfortable living room. A wicker coffee table and chairs were interspersed with a couple of wing chairs. A small galley kitchen by the steering wheel had a wraparound bar, with champagne glasses hanging in a rack. Fresh flowers on the coffee table and flower-patterned throw pillows on the chairs gave a tropical look to the arrangement.

Walsh waved his hand at the space in general. "This, of course, is the lounge," he said. "Come." He went into the galley, turned a hidden corner and disappeared down a flight of stairs. Frank barreled down the stairs, curious, and I followed. Walsh pointed at a door, explaining. "There's a half bathroom here, and a full one in each of the staterooms."

"Room-Z?" asked Frank.

"Yeah, three of them," Walsh said, matter-of-factly.

He opened a door to one side. "I've been staying here since I broke out of the hospital. It's peaceful."

The door opened to a small stateroom with a queen size bed, teak dressers built into the walls, and a bathroom to one side. It was more luxurious than any hotel I'd ever been to.

Frank shook his head. "How big is this ship?"

"I think she's about sixty-three, sixty-five feet?" Walsh shrugged. "I never asked."

"Yeah, why would you?" Frank muttered.

Walsh showed us the other two staterooms. They were equally impressive, with pale wood furnishings and elegant arrangements in both.

Walsh took us back up the flight of stairs to the main deck, then went forward to another door, stepped out onto the outside walkway, and went up another flight of stairs. This took us to an upper bridge, an open area with a large vinyl sofa and a pair of swivel chairs, one of which was at the steering station.

"On hot days, it's more fun to sail from up here," he said. "You guys ready to get underway?"

I grunted approval, and Frank nodded sheepishly. Walsh jogged down the stairway and released the mooring ropes.

Frank shook his head. "Jesus, Ian, what did Patrick do in a previous life to deserve this kind of luck?"

Walsh came back up the stairs, started the engines, and eased us out of the dock, then as we cleared the tip of Toronto Island, he pushed the throttles forward and we picked up speed. The boat rocked slightly, then nosed down and raced through the water, giving a very slight bob as it went over larger waves, smoothing out again after a moment.

Frank was sitting in the swivel seat beside Walsh, enjoying the rush of air. I stretched out on the sofa seat behind them, feeling the wind in my face and the smell of the lake on this warm summery afternoon.

Walsh skimmed along the lakeshore, heading east, then he slowed to a crawl, stopping at a small cove, shielded from the wind. He flipped a switch on the instrument panel and an anchor winched out, mooring the boat in place.

He headed back down the stairs, wordlessly, and came back up with the picnic basket. He opened it out and handed out sandwiches.

"What, no waiter to serve us?" Frank joked.

Walsh smiled. "This is an informal picnic, sorry. Coffee, Frank?"

He poured coffee from a thermos into three Styrofoam cups and handed a cup each to Frank and me. He raised his in the air. "To true friends."

I raised mine. "True friends," I said. Frank repeated it.

We ate our sandwiches in silence, listening to the splashing of soft waves on the hull, being lulled by the gentle rocking of the boat.

"To what do we owe this delightful interlude?" I asked.

"I just wanted to take you guys out and give you some R & R as a thank you for helping me. Now, who wants to drive?" Patrick grinned.

We took turns steering as we raced around the lake, then after a couple of hours I looked at my watch, and suggested we head back.

We eased the boat back into its slip at the marina, and tied it up. Walsh drove me to the station so I could pick up my car, then he stopped behind it and turned around to face us.

"Listen, you two." He said seriously. "I just wanted to let you know how much my family appreciates you both risking yourselves for me. We can't thank you enough."

Frank shrugged. "No problem, kid. You'd do the same for us."

"Anyway, thank you both. See you tomorrow morning, boss. Frank, I'll drop you home."

He let me off in the parking lot and drove off. He seemed to be smiling to himself, enjoying a private joke.

I got into my car, humming a silly tune. When I got home, there was a Pontiac Parisienne parked in my driveway. It seemed we had company. “Hello, Karen I’m home,” I called.

Karen raced out of the kitchen and met me at the front entry. “Did you see it?” she asked.

“See what?” I answered.

She pointed at the Parisienne. I didn’t see anything, just the car in our driveway.

“What? Who’s here?” I asked.

She pointed to the Parisienne again and grinned. “That car. It’s mine.”

“You upgraded the Pinto rental. You got a Parisienne instead?” I asked.

“No, it’s *mine*. All mine, to keep.”

“I don’t understand.”

“Remember you asked Lizzy Walsh if she could help us out with the crappy Valiant? She did. She gave me that car.”

I looked at the car more closely. It was a deep navy blue, brand new, shiny, with chrome and paint that gleamed in the sun. It seemed to be speeding down the highway just sitting there.

I shook my head, firmly. “No, no, no. We can’t keep it. Sorry hon, but I can’t accept this gift.”

Karen frowned. “You don’t have to. It wasn’t given to you. It’s *mine*.”

I sighed, frustrated. “What about Helen? Won’t she be upset that you just got a new car?”

“No, her Parisienne is maroon. She preferred that color.”

I scratched my head, trying to think of ways I could convince Karen to give it back. She read my mind, apparently.

“Here, come with me,” she ordered. She dragged me to the passenger side and opened the back door. “Sit.”

Politely, I sat in the back seat. It was very comfortable. She closed the door.

She walked around and sat in the driver’s seat, started the engine, and rolled down the road.

She looked at me through the rear-view mirror. "How does it feel back there?"

I relaxed against the armrest in the middle of the velour seat. It was luxurious. "It's fine."

She reached down for something. "It has electric windows. I can open your window from here." She powered my window down then back up. "But the piece de resistance is the climate control." She turned a control on the dashboard and a blast of frigid air blew over me. "Can you imagine what it will feel like to drive it on a sweltering hot day? Heaven."

We drove around for another few minutes, Karen talking nonstop, giddy with delight. I wasn't listening to her. I was only thinking that I couldn't accept this gift, no matter how nice it was, no matter how much it might have cost me personally to help Patrick. Another part of me, though, said that Karen had to cope with a lot, between worrying about my safety and raising the children, and that this indulgence, even if I thought it was extravagant, was small compensation. Besides, I really didn't want to upset Lizzy Walsh. I conceded defeat.

She rolled to a stop in our driveway. I got out and looked the car over. It was as big as my Caprice, and would keep my children safe. I walked completely around it, shaking my head.

Karen got out and leaned against the driver's door, hugging the roof, a clear sign of ownership. She bit her lip and wrinkled her brow.

"Well, what do you think?" she asked, hesitantly.

I shook my head. "All I can say is, you better not expect me to wash it for you."

She squealed with joy and threw her arms around me. She kissed me passionately. "Thank you." She smiled. "I hoped you'd change your mind."

"Hey, in your business you need to make an impressive entrance. This will sure do it," I said.

She hugged me again.

I went inside and dialed the number for Durham & Walsh. I gave my name to the woman who answered, and she transferred me right away. Lizzy Walsh answered the phone.

"Hello, Ian, how are you doing?"

"Great, Lizzy. Listen, I just wanted to say that I wasn't expecting something like that car. It's an awfully extravagant gift."

"Are you saying Karen doesn't like it?" she asked.

"No, it's not that at all. She loves it. I just wanted to say that I was overwhelmed by your generosity, that's all."

She chuckled, her voice warm and smooth even over the phone. "Nonsense. You've put yourselves in peril for Patrick, and we'll always be grateful to you and Frank for what you did. This is just a small way of saying thank you to you both."

I sighed, resolved that it was all right for us to accept the gift. It was just a trifle for her.

"Well, thanks again, Lizzy. We all appreciate your generosity. Good evening."

"Ian, you saved our son. I'll never forget that. Bye, now." She hung up.

CHAPTER 19

Thursday morning, I was dressed for work, sitting at my breakfast table. I got out my Moleskine and wrote on the top corner of a new page: *Thursday, June 22, 1978.*

I wanted to get to the bottom of why these women were killed. They all knew each other, in some way. We knew that. There was a witness who saw a man killing the third victim, Penny Lewis. It seemed reasonable that the same man likely killed the other two women, too.

So, we were looking for one man, one killer. What had made him kill all three women?

Brenda Grant had been stabbed. Gwen Morgan had been pushed onto the tracks, and Penny Lewis had been thrown off an overpass. The last two had been brutally killed, but Brenda had been killed mercifully, more or less.

Was it a stretch to think that the killer had a closer relationship with her than with the other two? Also, the first death happened late at night, while the other two happened in the morning. Was that significant in some way, or was I clutching at straws?

I wrote a couple of these ideas down as notes, with lines connecting the women. That much, at least, I realized was just a way for me to put the crimes together in my mind.

Since the first death, however, I had been distracted by everything that had happened with Walsh. Now that he was free, and now that I had cleared the haunting fog from having killed one of his captors, I was thinking clearly. There was a knock at the door, then two more knocks.

I knew immediately who it was. "Come," I called.

Walsh walked into my kitchen and sat at a bar stool. "Morning, boss."

"Patrick, it's nice to see you again," I said. "Karen said to thank you to your mom, by the way."

"She likes the car?" he asked.

"'Likes' is too subtle a word. She loves it. Thank you again."

He swiveled on the stool, playfully rolling back and forth. "So, where are we with the case, boss?"

"We have three dead women, in addition to the girl the Marquez people killed. Have you had a chance to read the latest report?"

He nodded. "I read it last night—it's a real pity about the latest victim, Penny? It sounded like she was trying to help our investigation."

"Yeah, that was a rough scene. It hit Alex very hard, seeing her on the tracks like that."

Walsh shrugged. "That's part of the job, though, isn't it, boss? We get to see the worst of people, and yet we need to keep our distance between them and ourselves."

"Yeah, that's a good way of looking at it, I suppose."

He poked his chin at me. "So, boss, how did you get over it?"

"Get over what?" I asked, puzzled.

"Armando, the guy you shot. How did you get over it?"

"I never even knew his name before, you know?" I snickered, amused at the irony. "As a matter of fact, Patrick, you helped that. The altercation I had with the Salmo fellow, and the reconciliation after, is what got me over it. Thank you."

He looked over the counter at my sink, a silent question.

"Anything I can get you, Patrick?" I asked.

"Um, yeah, boss. Could I get some scrambled eggs?"

"Coming right up," I said. "I'm getting a distinct sense of déjà vu, by the way."

Karen came downstairs, in jeans and a sweat top. "Morning, Patrick. How are you?"

"Hello, Karen. I'm good. You're looking lovely today."

"Thanks. Ian, where's the cereal?" She opened cupboard doors, looking.

"Top left. Don't you want eggs?" I asked. "And there's hot coffee, too."

She shook her head. "No, just Cheerio's and a glass of milk, thanks."

"You don't want some coffee?" I repeated.

"No, just milk, thanks," she said again.

I looked at her outfit. "Not going to work today, hon?"

"Nope. Helen is handling the meetings today. I'm watching the kids."

She poured herself a bowl of cereal and sat at the counter, munching contentedly.

Walsh sat at the other end of the counter, scooping scrambled eggs onto toast and nibbling the end of the bread. He slurped coffee, then scooped more egg onto the toast. "So, boss, what are we doing today?"

I took a sip of coffee and sat back. "We need to find out what the common link was between the three women. There has to be something they all did, or knew, or had, that got them killed. Also, Constable Brian Webb, a uniform with Fifty-two, is a sharp young cop. He took it upon himself to canvas the building near the third girl's death. He's the one who found a witness, the woman that saw a guy in a track suit throw her over the overpass. I asked him to do a house-to-house for other witnesses. Let's touch base with him today."

"I can do that with Alex, boss. That's okay. Anything else you want me to do?"

I sighed. "Patrick, you're not firing on all cylinders yet. I want to keep an eye on you till I'm convinced you're fine. Tell you what—Alex and Terry Parker can run down the eye witnesses, and we can talk to the people where our three victims lived. Fair enough?"

"Sure, that works for me, boss," he said. "Do we want to go in my car, or yours?"

"Yours," I said. "Karen, do you need anything while I'm out?"

She wiped her mouth and nodded. "We're out of Cheerios. Can you pick up a couple of boxes while you're out?"

I nodded. "Sure. Anything else?"

"Milk. We need milk. And bananas."

"Milk and bananas," I repeated. "Fine, see you at dinner." I kissed her goodbye.

She looked at me with an odd expression, but it didn't register at the time.

We got into Walsh's car, and he chirped the tires heading out of my street, as he usually did.

We drove down to Bloor Street, west to High Park, then stopped at the corner of Bloor and Quebec. Walsh got out and flipped open a flat gold case, then extracted a cigarette, with 'PW' printed on the filter. He placed it in his mouth, reached into his pants pocket and came out with a gray metal lighter. He lit his cigarette and inhaled, deeply.

"Replacement lighter?" I asked.

"Yeah, my regular one is in evidence for now," he said. "Funny, the things you miss, huh?"

On the sidewalk, looking north, there was a broad, older four-story building facing the park. It had a covered entryway, and glass doors leading to a wood-floored lobby. The doors had faded lettering stenciled on the glass, that read *Bloorview Apartments*. A paper *For Rent* sign was taped up under the letters.

I walked forty feet east, to the corner, and looked north on Quebec Avenue. Sticking out over the sidewalk was a TTC subway sign. The sign was for High Park subway station. We walked north on Quebec, and under a minute later it met Gothic Avenue.

We followed Gothic for another minute, at a casual

stroll, and came to the apartment where Gwen Morgan had lived.

Walsh pulled out his Moleskine and started making notes.

"So, even if the first two victims didn't know each other in the beginning, they would probably have crossed paths at the subway station, eventually," Walsh said. "Gwen is coming home from work, Brenda is heading to work, they say hi, they chat, 'nice day, what do you do for a living,' and so on. They could have become friends that way, don't you think?"

"Maybe. But what was Gwen doing at the lawyer's office? Was it a rental dispute, a divorce thing, what?" I said. "Besides, you don't say 'nice day, how are you, I need a lawyer.' They probably knew each other from somewhere else, don't you think?"

Walsh thought for a moment and nodded. "Yeah, probably. Let's talk to the building super."

We walked up the steps of Gwen Morgan's apartment building, a wide, flat building about twenty stories tall, with skinny balconies overlooking a curved front driveway. The front door was three steps up from the street, behind a broad canopy. To one side of the door was an intercom system, the names of tenants in blue plastic labels on the panel beside black buttons. One of the labels was in red, and it read Office. Walsh pushed the button and waited. There was no answer, so he pushed it again.

From inside the entry lobby, a sliver of light appeared for a moment as a side door opened and closed, then a slightly disheveled-looking older man in a dark green shirt and pants came toward us. He had heavy work shoes on, a massive clump of keys on his hip, and wire-rimmed glasses near the end of his nose. He looked suspiciously at Walsh then at me, and he shuffled to a stop on the other side of the door. He glared at Walsh and puffed out his chest, trying to look intimidating.

"Yes?" he snapped.

Walsh held out his badge and said nothing. The man read the name on the badge and sighed. He opened the door and let us into the lobby. It smelled of pine cleaner and deodorizer.

"Look," he said, apologetically. "We got a nice building here, a quiet building with good tenants, nice people, you know? Can we keep this low-key?"

Walsh smiled at him. "Sure, we're not here to rattle your cage, you know, we just want to ask you some questions, okay?"

"It's about Gwen Morgan, right?" the man asked.

"Is there anyone else we should be asking you about?" Walsh said.

The man shook his head. "Nope, just Gwen. Terrible thing—nice girl, hard worker, always paid her rent on time, no noise issues, nothing."

"Well, as long as you have your priorities straight," I said.

He shot me an irritated look. "Listen, just one bad tenant can give you a case of ulcers, you know? We only got good tenants in this building right now, bar a couple of night owls. That makes my life a whole lot easier, you know? If her apartment goes to another noisy tenant, then I can kiss goodbye to sleeping through a weekend night. That's all I meant, I didn't mean to make it sound like I didn't care about her."

Walsh placed a hand on the man's arm. "Hey, look, we're just here to help if we can, all right, mister…Say, what *is* your name?"

The man seemed touched by this gesture. "Trevor. Trevor Dunphy." He smiled a little.

Walsh nodded and wrote that down. "Trevor. Dunphy," he said, writing slowly. "It's good for you to know, Trevor, that you can be helpful to our investigation."

"Really?" the man asked, curious now.

Walsh gestured with his hands. "Oh, yeah. We figure you have the pulse of the building, since you're the manager and all, so you must know the comings and goings of everyone, the lay of the land, as it were."

The man stood up on his toes for a second and tugged at his belt, like a gunslinger, then hooked his thumbs over his waistband. "Yeah, well I keep a pretty close eye on what goes on. Course, you have to, you know? Otherwise, lord knows what stuff these people would get up to." He sneered the last words.

"Right," Walsh said solemnly. "So, Trevor, can I call you Trevor?" The man nodded. "Okay, Trevor, so, what can you tell us about Gwen?"

The man sniffed and looked around, as if to make sure nobody was listening to him. "Yeah, nice girl. Cute, too. Come summer time, when it got real hot out, she would go sun tanning on the top floor patio, you know? Very pretty girl, I tell you. But she was never noisy, never late with the rent, like I said. Good person to have living here."

Walsh nodded. "Any problem with visitors? Boyfriends, relatives, stuff like that?"

The man shook his head. "Nah. This one guy came over a couple times, but that's none of my business, you know, she's an adult, after all. Still, they had a fight in the hall one morning while he was leaving. That's the only time I ever had to talk to her about noise. She apologized, said it would never happen again, and it didn't."

Walsh wrote this down. "Could you describe the man? What did he look like?"

The man swung his arms casually back and forth, thinking. He huffed, looked at the ceiling and wrinkled his nose. "Okay, yeah. One time, he showed up in a suit. Real sharp dresser, this guy. He had the shiniest shoes I ever seen. That was when he was leaving one morning. I said 'hello' to him, but he didn't say nothing, just walked past me. Some people, huh?"

Walsh shook his head. "Yeah, those rich buggers are real asses, huh?"

The man nodded. "You said it. Anyway, other time he

was dropping in after work, evening time. That's funny, though, cause Gwen worked nights at Bell? So she left around eight every night for work, and he got here around six."

"You're fairly certain of the time?" Walsh asked.

"Oh, yeah. I get off at six, and I remember he walked in just as I was closing up the office."

"Did she buzz him in, then?" Walsh asked, curious.

The man thought for a moment, then his eyes opened wide and he wagged his finger at Walsh. "No, no, she didn't. He had a key. I remember now, he opened the door with a key. She must have given him one."

Walsh wrote this down. "Can you describe the man? Young, old, short, tall?"

The man nodded. "Yeah, okay." He looked down. "You know the movie, the disco one?"

Walsh frowned. "Saturday Night Fever?"

"Yeah, that one. He looked like the greaser from that movie. Skinny guy, slick black hair."

"So I'm looking for John Travolta?" Walsh asked.

"I suppose. Anyhow, that's what he looked like."

Walsh wrote this down and tapped his pen against his notebook, thinking. He had run out of questions to ask.

I stepped forward. "Do you know if he had a car? Did you see him get into one?" I asked.

Walsh made a prune face. He realized he should have thought of that.

The man nodded. "Yeah, big-ass Lincoln."

"Can you describe it?" Walsh asked.

"Black, two-door, with them 'opera windows' in the back like on TV." He nodded for emphasis.

"Was it fairly new, then?" Walsh asked.

"Yeah, looked like it was right out of the showroom, you know?"

"Yeah, I know," I said.

Walsh smirked. "Great, Trevor. Listen, if you think of anything else, give me a call, okay? Here's my card."

The man read it carefully. "You're a sergeant?"

"Yes, I am," Walsh said. "A detective sergeant."

"How do you like working for the Police department?" the man asked.

"It keeps me off the streets and out of the pool halls," Walsh joked.

"Just, cause, I got a nephew, and he's wondering if he should become a cop. I told him the money's good, and the work is good, too. You don't work too many long hours though, right?"

Walsh scowled. "Nothing in life is free. We work as long as it takes to solve the case. We deal with killers, muggers, thieves and drug dealers. If your nephew is looking for an easy job, tell him to become a librarian. I do what I do to catch criminals, not because of the pay check."

The man shrank back slightly. "No, I didn't mean, you know—Still, you do get paid pretty good, right?"

Walsh ground his teeth slightly. It was the first time I'd really seen him angry. "I wouldn't know. You see, I'm one of those rich buggers you bitched about. I give my police salary to charity." He closed up his Moleskine. "Thank you for your assistance, Mister Dunphy. Let us know if you remember anything else."

I put my hand on Walsh's arm. "Sorry, Trevor, but we've had kind of a rough week. Could we go up and look at Gwen's apartment?"

Walsh looked at me for a moment. His face softened and he mouthed "Sorry." The other man didn't see it. I rolled my eyes and smiled.

We went up the elevator, the man looking back and forth between us. The door opened on the eleventh floor, and Dunphy picked through a thick set of keys, looking for a specific key.

He opened the door to an apartment halfway down the hall, stepped back and let us in.

"You guys need me with you?" he asked.

"No, we're fine here. We'll let you know when we're finished," Walsh said.

Dunphy nodded and went out to the elevator. Walsh wandered into the center of the living room and looked around.

"Feeling dumb, are you?" I asked.

"I shouldn't have let him get to me. I have no idea why I blew up at him. Sorry, boss." He said.

I chuckled. "You're going through what I just went through, Patrick. Don't feel so bad. I'm told what you're feeling is normal."

"Well, it sucks, normal or not. Still, thanks for the back-stop, boss."

He walked through the apartment. It had a worn sofa, a second-hand coffee table and a small dining table, two chairs, and a dried flower arrangement in the middle of the table. There was a wide picture window leading to a shallow balcony, and a telescope on a tall tripod off to one side. Toronto skies were not friendly to stargazing, so it was just for show, I thought.

"I'd say her style was early Salvation Army," Walsh joked.

"Certainly not Swedish modern, by any means," I said.

We opened all the kitchen cupboards. There was some canned food, jars of pasta sauce, regular things like bread and peanut butter, milk in the fridge and a half bottle of chilled orange juice.

There was a mismatched set of dishes on the shelf, some glasses and four champagne flutes, for special occasions. Overall, it looked perfectly average, perfectly normal.

The bathroom had an oval mirror opposite the vanity mirror, so she could see herself front and back, I guessed. There were a number of bottles of shampoo, lotion, conditioner and so on, again, completely normal.

In the bedroom, the double bed was made neatly, with two large pillows fluffed up against a quilted headboard. A pair of wicker night tables flanked the bed, with an alarm clock on one, and a telephone and a small bottle of perfume on the other.

I pulled open a drawer in one of the night tables. There was a telephone book and a notepad in it, along with a book of matches. In the other night table, there was a box of birth control pills and a bottle of aspirin.

Walsh looked over my shoulder and wrote down what I found. "Okay, so she wasn't a nun," Walsh said. "But it sounds like she wasn't a total party girl, either."

"Yeah, Patrick, nothing here that tells me anything."

Walsh walked to the picture window in the living room. It had a wide glass door that led to the balcony. He slid the door open and stepped out, breathing deeply. "It's nice up here, huh, boss?"

I stood beside him. "Yeah, nice view. Pretty nice apartment. You can see half of High Park from here." I pointed out to the south.

Walsh froze. He pointed down. "That's Brenda Grant's apartment."

I looked down, following his finger. "Where?"

"You weren't with Alex and me. We spoke to Brenda's landlord, and we went through her apartment. She has this big fancy rug hanging on her wall. That's it, right there." He pointed.

I turned the telescope to face the rug. "You know, with this thing, I could see the faces of anyone who was in that apartment," I said. "Take a look."

Walsh looked through the eyepiece. "Son of a bitch. The penny drops." He stood back, amazed. "If Brenda was home with someone, maybe Gwen saw them there. That person killed them both. How did that person know Gwen saw them? Why did he kill them both?"

"He, or she," I said.

"Yeah, or she," he agreed.

"So, what would you do next, if you were a cop?" I prodded.

He looked at me sideways and grinned. "Let's ask Brenda's super if he saw someone like Mister Travolta hanging around."

We headed down to the lobby, told Trevor to lock up the apartment, but said that a forensics crew might be over soon, and that he should not disturb anything.

It was a two-minute walk down Gothic Avenue, past the subway station on Quebec, then a left onto Bloor Street to Brenda's apartment building.

Seventy years ago, this area had been out in the boonies, far away from downtown. A doctor had built a health spa here, complete with mineral springs and a heated pool. I read about it once in a book about old Toronto. Now, the land was the site of some old apartment buildings. Brenda's apartment was just a block east of there, in a three-story brick building that looked like something out of 1930s Chicago.

The building was in a big U shape, with a central pavement leading to the covered front door. Just like Gwen's apartment, we saw a buzzer on a panel that said *Office*, and Walsh pressed it.

A minute later, a voice came over the speaker. "Yes?" it said, a man's voice, firm and crisp.

"Toronto Police department," Walsh said.

There was a brief pause. "One minute, please," the voice said.

I tucked my hands behind my back and looked around, curious. I leaned forward and said to Walsh "This one's all yours." He grinned, then saw someone coming and frowned.

The man who had spoken to us walked up to the front doors. Through the beveled glass panes, we could see him in pieces, separate body parts moving toward us.

He peered through a pane, recognized Walsh and opened up. "Oh, hello, come in." He said.

Walsh smiled and introduced me. "This is Mr. Marks. Mr. Marks, can we take another look at Brenda's apartment?"

He looked at us, nodded, and fumbled for a set of keys. He flipped through a bunch of them till he found the one he wanted, and walked us to the back of the building and up a flight of stairs.

"Did she live here for long?" I asked.

The man nodded. "Five years. She was a good person, Brenda. My wife can't walk very far, and she used to pick up groceries for her when she was shopping. She was very considerate."

Walsh was silent, followed the man up the stairs and waited as he opened the door to Brenda Grant's apartment.

"Are there any nicer apartments in this building?" Walsh asked.

The man seemed surprised by the question. "Yeah. This was one of the darker ones, at the back, facing north. I asked her a few times, when some front units came up, if she wanted to move, but she always said she wanted to stay right here. I don't know, maybe she didn't want to hear the noise from the road."

Walsh stepped back from the door and looked around. "Is there another way out from here?"

The man waved his arm. "Yeah, there's the back stairwell right here. Some tenants use it if they park their car in the back lot."

"Brenda parked her car there, didn't she?" Walsh asked.

"Yeah, she did. She would bring in groceries through that door. It saved her walking around."

Walsh nodded. "All right, Mr. Marks. We'll let you know when we're done. Thanks very much."

The man shrugged and went back downstairs.

Walsh watched him leave and we went into the apartment. "I didn't want a chaperone, boss," he muttered.

I followed him into the apartment and looked around. My first apartment, when I moved to Toronto, was like this one. The windows were single-pane glass, the hallway had arches between the living room and the kitchen, and the bedroom had a tiny closet, barely enough for an armful of clothes. The kitchen had a flat, two burner stove flush against one wall, a small fridge and a small single sink. It was what was called a 'galley' kitchen, a space-saver for singles in small apartments.

The living room was comfortably furnished, with a bean bag sofa and a hand-me-down easy chair, parked around a glass-covered wagon-wheel coffee table.

Walsh walked around, sniffing. "Apparently, she shops the finer dumpsters and alleys." He said.

"Hey, maybe she was saving up for something?" I said.

"Baby stuff?" Walsh reminded me.

"Maybe," I said. "Maybe she just wasn't a big spender. She was nice to the magazine vendor, remember? She used to make sandwiches for him."

Walsh nodded and opened the fridge. "Sandwich loaf, sliced ham, cheese singles, mayo, yeah, she had more stuff here to make sandwiches." He squatted down. "And a bottle of Veuve Clicquot." He pulled it out of the fridge.

"What in the world is that?" I asked.

Walsh grinned. "In 1805, the husband of Barb-Nicole Ponsardin Clicquot died, and she was left to run their champagne business on her own. The French for widow is—"

"Veuve," I said. "So she was the 'Veuve Clicquot'?"

"Yeah. More to the point, this is pricey bubbly. If Brenda was buying cheap stuff, second-hand furniture and the like, do you think she'd be buying Veuve Clicquot to drink?"

"You think mister Saturday Night Fever brought it over?" I asked.

"Sure. Why didn't they drink it, though?"

"Easy," I said. "Hey, I can't drink, I'm pregnant."

Walsh nodded. "Jeez, it all falls into place, doesn't it?"

He walked around the sofa to the picture window in the living room. He turned around to face the sofa, and a multi-colored shag rug on the wall behind it. This was what he had seen from Gwen Morgan's apartment. He walked to the window and looked up, squinting.

"I can't see squat," he said. He put his hands beside his face and looked again. "No, nothing."

"So," I said. "Gwen could see down, but Brenda couldn't look up. What does that tell us?"

Walsh looked up and down, figuring something out. "Gwen saw something. Either Brenda had a fight, or something, and she saw the other person. She confronted them, and they killed her."

"Why not just talk to Brenda about it first?" I asked.

"Okay, how about this?" he said. He got out his Moleskine and started making notes. "Gwen looks down and sees someone she knows, Brenda. Then she sees who Brenda is with, someone she also knows. A man. He kills Brenda, don't know why yet. The day after Brenda dies, she asks the man what happened to Brenda, cause she hasn't read the news yet, and she thinks Brenda's just gone somewhere. The guy thinks she's found out what he did, and kills her."

"Two out of three," I said. "What about Penny Lewis?"

Walsh sighed. "Shit. Penny Lewis. Okay, never mind, it was just an idea."

"Pretty good idea, though. Tell you what, want lunch?" I said.

"Yeah. My treat," he said. "I've got just the place for you."

"The Windsor Arms Hotel?" I joked.

"No, but if you want to eat there?" he asked.

I shook my head. "I was joking, Patrick."

He drove us to a diner a few blocks away, with a big sign proclaiming their love for the Maple Leafs and a painted window that advertised *Home Style Burgers and Fries*.

Walsh accepted the waitress's menu and smiled politely. She seemed to linger for a second, then wiped her hands on her hips as she walked away. She was very cute, a coke-bottle shaped brunette with a pretty smile. Walsh was oblivious, talking to me as she came by a second time, offering us coffee and water.

I smiled at her, and glanced at him, but he was looking

down, not noticing her at all. She left.

"Patrick, I think she's giving you the eye," I said.

"Yeah?" he said, casually. "I'm not really interested right now. You can understand that, right?"

I smiled. "I figure you're probably a little shell-shocked, but don't become a hermit—come on."

He shrugged. "Okay, we'll see."

The waitress came back with my burger and Walsh's club sandwich. She put down my plate, then turned to face Walsh slightly and squatted as she placed his plate in front of him.

"There you go, Patrick," she said.

He looked up quickly at that, then he leaned back and smiled. "Kelly? Kelly Dawson?"

"I didn't think you remembered me." She grinned. "How are you?"

We were the only people in the diner. "Did you want to sit for a minute?" I asked.

She looked around quickly and sat beside me, then she leaned over and touched Walsh's arm. "So, what did you do after school? My mom said you were in the civil service?"

He put his hand over hers. "I'm a cop. A detective sergeant, actually. How about you?"

She waved at the kitchen. "I'm doing this to work my way through grad school. I told my folks I wanted to do it on my own. They've been very good about letting me do it."

Walsh leaned his face on his hand and looked deeply at her. "Kelly Dawson. Wow, you look good. So, you married, or engaged, or what?"

With every word, I could see the old Patrick come out of his shell.

She shook her head. "No, I'm sharing with a girlfriend of mine, but after this summer I want to get my own place. They're giving me a scholarship for next year, so I'll be able to afford my own apartment."

"Scholarship in what?" he asked, focused on her eyes.

"Microbiology and immunology. That's what my doctoral is on. It's pretty boring for someone like you, I guess."

"No, not at all. I'd like to hear about it, over dinner or something." His voice turned to honey.

"You're not married, or anything?" she asked tentatively.

He smiled. "Not anything. When can I call you?"

She wrote her phone number on a blank bill and handed it to him. "I'm off at six, if you're free. I should be home before seven."

"I'll call you at seven," Walsh said and carefully folded the paper into his wallet.

The woman got up and waved bye, then she disappeared into the kitchen. I smirked and looked at my watch.

"And the duration of Patrick's celibacy comes to an end right—now," I said.

Walsh rolled his eyes. "Come on, boss, she's a great girl. We went to university together."

"And she wiggles very nicely when she walks," I added.

He glanced toward the kitchen. "Well, yeah, there is that, too."

Chapter 20

Walsh radioed Constable Webb, and he suggested we meet on Aylmer Avenue, just east of the overpass where Penny had been killed. I got Walsh up to speed as we drove, talking fairly quickly, since Walsh got us there sooner than I had thought he would.

We parked in a laneway just off Yonge Street, and walked over the train tracks to meet Webb.

Walsh unbuttoned his jacket and brushed his tie down, pressing it against his shirt with his hand.

"That doesn't look like a clip-on tie, Patrick," I said. "You know the regulations."

He lifted up the tail of the tie and looked at it. "No, I had it made specially, boss. Watch."

He tugged on the tie, imitating someone trying to pull him close to punch him. The tie came apart, as a snap at the back of the neck popped open. He undid its Windsor knot, snapped the two pieces of tie together, and re-knotted it as we walked.

"Cool. Can you chew gum and juggle at the same time, too?" I joked.

On the far side of the bridge, Brian Webb was looking over the railing, down at the subway tracks. He seemed to be looking for something, then he saw us coming and walked toward us.

He took off his cap, tucked it under his left arm, then stood stiffly, waiting for me to talk.

"Brian Webb, this is DS Patrick Walsh," I said.

Webb stuck his hand out. "Sergeant, good to meet you, sir."

Walsh grinned. "Patrick, please. Only my mother calls me sergeant."

Webb nodded at me. "Inspector, nice to see you again, sir."

I nodded back. "Likewise, Brian. So, what have you got for us?"

He put his cap back on and leaned over the railing. "Scuff marks. There are scuff marks on the outside of the railing, where she was trying to get a foothold as she was being pushed over the bridge."

I looked over at the narrow concrete edge on the outside of the railing. There was a series of thin black lines, scuffs left by a shoe, just at the spot where Penny Lewis had been thrown over the bridge.

Webb pointed at them. "So, I figure she was talking to the guy, and he lobbed her over, but she struggled for a few seconds, trying to get back up, before he pushed her down."

Walsh shot me a look and shook his head. "You figured this out on your own, man?"

Webb nodded. "Yes, sir. I was thinking about it earlier this morning, and I figure from our witness's description, she probably didn't go without a struggle."

Walsh looked over at the scuff marks and grunted. "You ever want to work in plain clothes?"

Webb glanced back and forth between Walsh and me. "Um, Inspector McBriar asked me the same thing. He said I should call him."

I shook my head. "Now I'm saying you *have* to call me. We need people like you in our office."

Webb grinned broadly. "All right, you also asked me to look for other witnesses, right?"

"Yeah. Any word on that?" I asked.

He pulled out a small notebook and gestured with his hand, pointing down Aylmer Avenue. “Yeah, I walked down this way for a bit. Now, there’s no parking on this road for about a hundred yards. It’s one narrow lane in each direction, so he must have parked at one of a couple of apartment buildings down the way. We talked this morning to people who left the building about the same time yesterday, but nobody saw anything.”

“No guy in a track suit stood out then?” I asked.

Webb shook his head. “No, sir, but I got to thinking that he was wearing a track suit, so maybe he jogged back to his car. If he was jogging, nobody would pay any attention to a guy jogging in a track suit, right? And the best place he could park his car, then, would be on Collier Street.”

“Why Collier Street?” Walsh asked.

Webb pointed to the south east with his pen. “Most of the streets here, you can’t park in the morning. Collier, at the east, is a dead end street, but heading west it joins up with Yonge Street. The dead end has parking spaces, so if he parked his car there it wouldn’t be noticed, maybe, except for people that lived there. They might notice an unusual car parked there.”

Walsh rolled his eyes and looked at me. “You want to hire him, or should I?” he joked. Webb grinned.

I nodded. “How far is it from here to Collier?”

“It’s just under half a mile. I drove it twice, in both directions. It also has several roads out, so he’d have a choice of escape routes if he was being chased,” Webb said.

I looked up and down the street. “Ok, so I’ve just thrown a woman off the overpass. I jog down to my car, half a mile away. That would take what—ten minutes?” I asked.

“Maybe less,” Webb said.

“Maybe. So I head down to my car and drive away. Let’s get a door-to-door and see if anyone noticed a strange car yesterday morning,” I said.

Webb nodded. “If people saw the car at eight in the morning, then they were probably heading to work, right? If they're coming home at the end of the day, then they'd probably be walking or driving home between five and six tonight, I figure."

Walsh patted him on the shoulder. "Do you mind helping us out on this, Constable? You and I can canvass the neighborhood this evening."

Webb shrugged. "Sure, glad to help."

"But we won't be working very late," Walsh said. "I have a dinner date."

Walsh drove me to Fifty-two Division, and I read the coroner's report on Penny Lewis. She had been killed by the train hitting her, of course. Before then, the drop off the overpass had shattered her ankle, and cracked several ribs. It must have been excruciatingly painful for her to stand up.

I imagined her walking over the subway track, stopping to talk to this man, having him push her over the railing. She had clung to the railing for dear life, the coroner said. Webb was right—there were scuff marks on her shoes and scrapes in her fingers that indicated she had fought to stay alive. Paint under her nails, scraped from the railing, confirmed it.

That meant that whoever did it, the mystery man, had pushed her over the side of the overpass, but Penny had tried to pull herself back up. I imagined her, clinging to the railing, and thought of the man in the track suit peeling her fingers away, pushing her off and into the path of the subway train.

Walsh wandered over to my desk and sat across from me. "Any news, boss?"

I handed him the report. "The coroner confirms what our witness said. She was tossed over the railing, then she struggled, fought hard to get back, but the guy pushed her off into space."

Walsh grimaced. "Messy. I hear Alex was really upset by this one."

"Yeah, she had met the victim a while before the death, so she sees her as a real person, not just a corpse. Do you want to talk to her and see how she's doing?" I asked.

"Sure. Tell you what, do you want to make it a short day? I'll drop you home, then I'm going to do the door-knocking with Brian, see what we can dig up."

"Are you still going to keep the date with Kelly?"

"Certainly. I always liked her—never kept in touch much, but I should have, you know?"

I tossed my pencil down. "Yep, let's call it a day. I've done all the damage I can here."

Walsh drove me toward my house. I remembered that I'd promised to buy some groceries, so I asked him to drop me a block from home, at the corner store on Silverthorn Avenue.

I walked down the aisles, past cans of tomato sauce, gallon cans of olive oil, and jars of olives, to the back of the store, where the fresh produce was stacked. I picked up a handful of bananas, stuck them in the basket, then turned the corner to the cooler for a jug of milk. I continued toward the cash register, stopping to pick up two boxes of cereal.

I paid for the food, said the pleasantries to the lady at the counter, and exchanged greetings with her in Portuguese. She always seemed happy that I tried to speak her language. I could never tell if she was pleased or amused, but it was a familiar banter that we both engaged in.

I walked toward my house, cresting the hill at the top of my street, seeing the top of my house roof, then the front windows, then the two Parisiennes in the driveway.

I glanced down at my paper bag of groceries, casually reading the label on the Cheerio's box. The last time I had bought Cheerio's for Karen, I remembered, was when she was pregnant with Charley. She was eating lots of bananas then, too, and she also got nauseous if she drank coffee. It hit me like a lightning bolt—I had missed the signals. Oh my god.

I walked faster, speeding up to a run by the time I got to my front door. I raced into the kitchen, my mouth open. Helen was sitting on the edge of the dining table, swinging her legs, laughing at something Karen had said. Karen was leaning against the sink, her ankles crossed, wearing shorts and a tee shirt. Both women looked up as I walked in.

Helen stood and said, abruptly. "Well, I have to go. Call me later." She gave me a kiss on the cheek, giggled, and left.

I reached into the paper bag and pulled out a box of Cheerio's. "Remember this?" I asked.

Karen wrinkled her mouth, amused. "Finally figured it out, did you?"

"The appointment you had the other day, when you had the milkshake. It wasn't work, was it?"

She flipped up her tee shirt, exposing her navel. "I'm around eleven weeks pregnant. That means a New Year's baby. Happy?"

I wrapped my arms carefully around her and kissed her sweetly. "Delirious," I cooed.

Chapter 21

At six in the morning, I was wide awake. I let Karen sleep, went downstairs and made a small pot of coffee, just enough for one, then I crept out to the patio, picked a handful of flowers from the back yard, and put them in a skinny vase. I assembled a bowl of cereal with slices of banana, and carried it upstairs on a bed tray, with the flowers as a decoration.

I nudged open the door to our room as Karen rolled over. She opened her eyes.

"Hey, you," she said. "Good morning."

"Good morning, Mommy. Would you like breakfast?" I asked.

"Ooh. What's on the menu this morning?" She sat up and looked at the tray. "Cereal? What a lovely surprise, my favorite. Thank you."

"I thought you might like to have breakfast in bed for a change." I smiled. "How's this, okay?"

I propped her up against a pillow and tucked the sheets under her armpits. She smirked at the attention, then watched me fold down the legs on the bed tray and position it on her lap.

"Will I get this kind of attention every morning?" she asked.

"If you want, my love. Your wish is my command," I said.

She shook her head. "Once the novelty wears off, I'm sure you'll go back to normal."

"Then enjoy it while it lasts, hon." I grinned. I sat on the edge of the bed and kissed her. She wrapped her arms around my neck and held me close, kissing me back with a passion that felt like she would never see me again. "Hey, are you feeling all right?" I asked.

"Yeah, just…what do we tell the kids?" she said. "They're going to notice, you know."

"Let's say nothing till we get back from Esterhazy. Then we'll decide how to tell them."

Karen spooned some cereal into her mouth. "Okay. What are you up to today?"

"Patrick and I are getting some help from a young constable. He's a smart kid, he came up with a witness to our latest crime, he figured out how a suspect may have escaped, and I've asked him to do a door-to-door to get a description. I've also asked him if he wants to go into plainclothes. He's far too smart to spend his career ticketing left-turning cars."

"How's Patrick doing?" she asked, concern in her voice.

I chuckled. "He bumped into an old girlfriend of his. She pretty well asked him out, and I understand they had dinner last night. I'll find out this morning how it went."

Karen crunched her cereal loudly, scooping rogue Cheerio's away from the rim of her bowl and into a clump. "This is good, you really should try it."

I grinned. "I'll pass, thanks. What about you, though. How are you going to pass the time?"

She pointed at the door. "Helen and I worked it out. I'll watch the kids during the day, she'll handle appointments and show the units, and I'll do all the paperwork while the little ones nap. It works well for us both."

"How does she feel about your pregnancy?"

"Auntie Helen is thrilled. Wait for Frank to rush over and congratulate us, by the way. He might drop by before work today."

I kissed her nose. “Fair enough. I’m going downstairs to eat. Anything I can get you?”

She shook her head. “Go. I’ll be down soon.”

I jogged cheerfully down the stairs and made myself toast. I munched toast and drank my coffee, but I didn’t taste anything. I was on autopilot, just doing the things I did every morning.

There was a knock at the door, a fervent, hurried knock. “Come,” I called.

Before I’d uttered the first letter, the door swung open and Frank raced in, wide-eyed.

“Helen just told me. Why didn’t you tell me?” he gasped.

“Did you run here, Frank?” I asked.

“Yeah, had to get over quick. Why didn’t you let me know?”

“I just found out last night, man. You’re out of breath. Do you want to sit down, or what?”

He sat and sighed, composing himself. “Okay, thanks. Is that toast?”

“Yeah, would you like some?”

“Sure. Is there fresh coffee too?”

“Coming up.” I replaced the filter in the coffeemaker and poured in water.

Karen padded down the stairs, carefully holding the banister and stepping gingerly. Frank’s eyes widened.

“Are you feeling all right, Karen? Do you want to sit?” he asked.

She shook her head and tucked her hands into her bathrobe. “I’m feeling okay, Frank. Good morning, by the way.”

“Frank,” I said. “It’s all right. She’ll be fine. Calm down.”

He sighed deeply and gave Karen a gentle hug, then kissed her cheek. “You have our love and best wishes, Karen,” he said. “Anything you need, you know you can count on me.”

She smiled warmly. “I know. Thank you for that.”

He settled down, sitting casually on a stool, sniffing the air for fresh coffee. I poured him a cup, then slid toast in front of him. He buttered it and chewed on his bread, talking casually with me, glancing every so often to see that Karen was comfortable.

"So, did you want me to drop you at work, Frank?" I asked.

He glanced at Karen again. "Sure. If you don't mind, I mean, Helen was going to drive me, but if it's on your way?"

"Yeah, we can gab as we drive, talk about women or sports or something," I quipped.

Frank called home, told Helen he was getting a ride, and waited patiently as I collected my things for work.

I kissed Karen goodbye, told her I'd phone her a few times during the day, and walked Frank out to my car. We drove off, cruising down St. Clair Avenue toward Avenue Road.

Frank looked out his window, grinning silently, watching the scenery roll by.

He turned to look at me. "So, are you hoping for a boy or girl?" he asked. "And where would the baby sleep?"

"It doesn't matter whether it's a boy or girl, Frank. We talked about that last night. The baby will sleep in our room for the first year, then the kids all play musical chairs. Charlotte will get Ethan's room, he gets the basement, the baby gets Charlotte's old room. It's a good solution."

"Smart thinking. Smart thinking, right," he said.

"It was Karen's idea. I thought it was a good idea, too," I said.

He chuckled. "Trust her to figure it out. Is there anything at all I can do for you guys?"

"Just be yourself, Frank. That's all I can ask."

He stared at his shoes for a minute. "Um, Ian, you know that I would never let anyone hurt your family, right?"

"Uh-huh?" I said, puzzled.

"If anyone ever did hurt you guys, you know I'd take care of them, right?"

I chuckled. "If it ever came to that, I'm certain you would."

"Just so you know." He looked out again. "So what do you want as a baby gift from us?"

I laughed. "Interesting segue. Nothing, Frank. Your friendship is more than enough."

"Helen was beside herself when she told me this morning, you know. Karen asked her to not tell me till this morning. I thought she was going to explode when she gave me the news."

"Don't feel so bad. Karen was leaving hints for the last few days, but I only clued in when I remembered how she craved cereal and bananas with Charlotte," I said.

He grinned and looked out the window again. "So, you think you'll wrap this case up before you go back home?"

"I sure hope so. We may cut the trip a bit short though, considering our news about the baby."

I slowed to a stop outside Frank's office, the concrete and glass box on Avenue Road, and he stepped out casually. He turned and leaned back into the car. "If you need anything, anything at all? You know?" he said.

"Got it. Thanks, Frank."

He smiled, then walked to the steps at the edge of the building plaza, skipped up them and stuck his hands in his pockets, bouncing cheerily into the building.

I picked up the microphone and waited for a pause in the chatter. "Fifty-two zero six to dispatch," I said cheerfully.

"Go, zero six," came the answer.

"And how are you this fine morning, Nadine?" I asked.

"Exciting news, huh, Ian?" she said.

"Sorry?" I asked.

"You hoping for a boy or a girl, Inspector?"

I rubbed my forehead. "So, should I bother telling you anything, or just send all my messages directly to Rebecca Van Hoeke?"

There was a cackle of laughter on the other end. "All our love, Ian, pass it on."

"Shall do. Any work messages then?" I said.

The voice became firm and businesslike. "Roger, zero six. Please meet Sergeant Walsh at the station, first possible."

That meant he had something for me. "Roger, zero six out."

I made a U turn and drove up Avenue Road, joined the Allen Expressway, and got onto the sixteen lanes of the 401 to Fifty-two Division. It took me less than ten minutes to get there. I pulled into my spot, glanced over at the unreserved lot, and saw Walsh's Ford beside a cruiser I recognized, Webb's car.

Webb was sitting in a chair across from Walsh, leaning forward, tossing his cap casually in his hands, talking, and nodding as they discussed something.

I sat on the edge of a desk across from him. "Morning, Patrick, how are we doing?"

"Great, boss. Exciting news for you guys, huh?"

"Yes. Thanks. So where are we in the case?"

"Brian and I were just going over some details. We canvassed the houses at the end of Collier last night, and we think we got a handle on our track suit guy. Tell him, Brian."

Webb nodded. "Well, sir,"

"Ian," I said.

"Okay. Well, we found a couple of people that saw an unfamiliar car on their street. They said it was black, either a Cadillac or a Lincoln, probably a two-door. One of the women we talked to said her husband is an airline pilot, but he's on a layover flight to Germany, she said. He should be back this afternoon. The thing is, she says he called her from the airport before he left on Wednesday morning, like he always does, and complained that there was a guy in a car blocking his driveway. I figure it's a good chance that's our track suit guy, don't you think?" Webb said.

"Good call. So, have you thought more about going into plain-clothes?" I asked.

Webb grinned at Walsh. "Patrick tells me you date prettier girls in your unit. Is that true?"

"It is in my case. I married one," I said. "Speaking of which, how was your date, Patrick?"

Walsh shrugged. "Good. We hit it off pretty well. She wants to take me to the summer concerts at Ontario Place, and I promised to have dinner with her at her parents' house this weekend."

"Sounds serious," I joked.

He tilted his head sideways slightly. "She's a very smart woman. She's nothing like the girls I've been dating so far. It's a whole different ball game with her."

I chuckled. "Gosh, our little boy is growing up. Okay, anything else from you two?"

Webb sat up. "Yeah, sir. Ian. A black Lincoln, or a black Cadillac, doesn't sound like your ordinary everyday car. I bet it belongs to someone pretty special."

"Makes sense, but how to we find out, of all the Caddies in this town, whose it was?" I asked.

"I figure it's someone connected to the case, the dead subway girls?" Webb said. "What are the odds that two different people killed three women, on and around the subway?"

"Way ahead of you on that one, Brian," I said. "But where would you investigate next, then?"

"Was there something all three women had in common, besides a law office?" he asked.

Walsh looked at me and smirked. "Brian and I discussed the three deaths earlier. I think we're all on the same page that the law firm is the hinge point here."

"Good," I said. "Where's Alex?"

"She said she was running down some leads on her own, but she'd be in shortly," Walsh said.

"Okay. Keep me posted," I said. I sat at my desk, went through some telephone messages, and tried to concentrate on work. All I could think of was Karen, imagining her pregnant again.

Last time, when she was expecting Charley, Ethan was five, and not very aware of the changes she was going through. Now that he was nine, he would be keenly aware of how this would affect him. Charley would probably be thrilled, seeing a new baby in the house as a big toy, but she might still feel upset that she was no longer the center of attention.

A shadow across my desk made me look up. Reynolds sat on the edge of the desk across from me and beamed. "Good morning, boss. Guess where I've been?"

"Ok, where?" I said.

"Our second victim, Gwen Morgan? She hit a rough spell back in January. She'd been put on suspension at work. I couldn't find out why—it was hard enough to get her supervisor to tell me that she'd been in trouble. Anyway, she was off the payroll for sixty days, and her landlord says she was barely able to pay her rent. She sold off all her nice furniture, and used that money to pay the rent. He said that you visited her place? It was then that she picked up the bunch of hand-me-down stuff you saw. She was still two months in arrears, though, and he was on the verge of having her evicted. Anyway, a couple of weeks ago, he said, she came into a bunch of money. She paid her back rent, plus another month's rent in advance, all in cash. He didn't ask her where the money came from, but he said she was feeling very pleased with herself."

I smiled. "Very well done, Alex, very well done. Have you met Brian Webb yet?"

"Yeah, Patrick introduced us." She giggled. "He's kind of cute."

"If you say so. Anyway, he's also very smart. I've been trying to coax him over to our team. Would you mind finding out if we can have his services for the day? He can go with you."

"Sure. I'll talk to his desk sergeant," she said. "You think he has potential, huh, boss?"

"Yes, I do. He has come up with a couple of really good ideas so far. I want him to run with this case, see how he does in the long stretch."

She nodded. "Sure thing. By the way, how's Karen feeling?"

"Why do you ask?"

"Really? The news is all over the office, boss." She linked her fingers together to make a cradle, then she rocked an imaginary baby in front of her.

I threw my hands in the air. "Guilty. Yes, we're all thrilled. I'll give Karen your best."

"I already called her. She's expecting to hear from you, too." She skipped off to her desk.

I picked up the phone and called home. A small voice answered. "McBriar 'sidence," she said.

"Hi, Charlotte, is your mom busy?" I asked.

She put the phone down on the table. I heard "Mom, Dad on the phone."

A minute later, Karen picked it up. "Hey, how are you?"

"I'm happy. More to the point, how are you doing, sweetheart?" I asked.

She laughed. "I've gotten a dozen calls already this morning. Who all did you tell, Ian?"

"Nobody. Everyone knew when I got in. I think Helen told Rebecca, and the rest is history."

"Well, thank everybody for the good wishes. Tell them I'm feeling fine. Talk to you later?"

"You bet. Bye, hon." I hung up.

Walsh came over and sat across from me, clutching a piece of paper. "Want to come with me?"

"Where?" I said.

"Gwen Morgan's place. Her landlord called me. He said they were packing up her personal belongings, and they found a box with some photos and a camera, hidden under the sofa. He didn't want to touch anything, just in case it was connected to her death, so he called me."

"Good man. Let's go pay him a visit." I grinned. "You drive."

Walsh parked outside Gwen Morgan's apartment, jogged up the steps to the intercom and buzzed the landlord. I followed him, waiting a step below him as he looked through the door. A few seconds later, the same thin, older man from our last visit came out to greet us.

Walsh waved at him. "It's Trevor, right? Trevor Dunphy?"

The man nodded. "Yeah. Look, we was clearing some things up, 'cause your people said we could have the apartment back, so we could clean it, you know? And we found some stuff you probably want to look at."

Walsh put a hand on the man's shoulder. "Good thinking, Trevor. Lead on."

We rode the elevator to the eleventh floor, walked down the hall to Gwen Morgan's apartment, and waited patiently as the man fumbled through a set of keys to find the right one.

He opened the door and pointed to an object on the carpet. "There, we found that stuff under the sofa."

Walsh turned to look at him. "Trevor, would you mind giving us a few minutes?"

The man grunted and walked back to the elevator. Walsh closed the door behind us and squatted down, looking at the box. It was a boot box, flatter but bigger than a shoe box, and Walsh used his pen to lift open the hinged lid. There was a Nikon camera, a very long lens, and a small box of photographs inside it.

Walsh picked up the small box and flipped through the photographs, holding them gingerly by the edges.

"Look at this, boss," he said, holding one out.

It was a photo, one that appeared to have been taken from high above Gwen's balcony, looking down to Brenda's living room. The photo was black and white, but the rug on her wall was clearly visible, and showed Brenda sitting on her sofa, talking to someone. I could only see part of the person, a man, sitting, facing her.

Walsh picked up another photo. This one showed the same scene, but now the man was standing in the window, looking out, his hands on his hips. It was Duncan Carroll.

I shook my head. "Jesus, Patrick, what does this mean? Does this link him to the deaths?"

Walsh sighed. "All right, so he was over at her place, but was it just innocent? Are we jumping to conclusions here?"

He flipped through more photos. Most were the same as the first two, Duncan standing, walking around, gesturing with his hands. Brenda was on the sofa for all the pictures, talking to him, pointing and gesturing as well.

"They might have been talking about work," I said.

Walsh looked at the photo under that one. Brenda was in a robe, laughing at something, her hair in a towel. Duncan was naked, standing behind her, his hands around her waist.

"Jackpot," Walsh said. "We got him."

"So now we know who the father probably is," I said.

Walsh flipped to the next photo. Brenda had her head tilted to one side, smiling. Duncan was kissing her neck. "He doesn't look very upset, if he does know about the baby."

"No, he doesn't, does he?" I agreed.

Walsh turned to the next photo. Brenda was stretched out on her sofa, again in her robe. Duncan was still naked, now kneeling beside her, hugging her.

It reminded me of when Karen was pregnant, and I would hug her. "Yeah, he knows," I said.

Walsh frowned and looked at the telescope. He unscrewed it from its tripod mount, then he put the camera on the telescope tripod. It screwed into the bracket, and held securely. Walsh mounted the long telephoto lens onto the camera and pointed it down at Brenda's apartment. "Here, take a look at this."

I looked through the viewfinder. It was exactly the same angle of view as in the photos.

"Well, now we know *how* she took the pictures," I said. "But *why* did she do it?"

Walsh flipped through more photos, all of them showing Brenda, most with Duncan in them as well, in what looked like just ordinary intimate images of two people, a happy couple.

I flipped over one of the pictures. "Where did she get these developed? I don't see a stamp on the back. It should say 'Kodak' or 'Black's Cameras' or something on the back, right?"

"Unless she did it herself," Walsh said. "Look, they're uneven, like they were cut by hand."

He walked toward the bedroom, stopped at a linen closet, and opened the door. There was a cardboard box on the floor, loosely covered with a white bed sheet. Walsh pulled the sheet away and opened the box. There were black plastic bottles, flat boxes of paper, and what looked like paint trays, all stacked inside it. On a shelf above the box was a device that looked like a bellows on a metal rod. Walsh turned it around.

"I thought so. Here's an enlarger, and some chemicals." He picked up a yellow light bulb. "It's a safelight. She was developing her own film. She didn't want to risk letting someone else see the pictures, so she developed her own film, and printed her own photos. Wow, industrious girl. Was she blackmailing Mister Carroll, I wonder?"

I shook my head. "It would explain where she got the money to pay her back rent. Maybe she's stashed more photos somewhere?"

Walsh nodded agreement, and we opened doors, looked under and through everything, looking for more photos. We looked under the kitchen sink, behind the fridge, and even dragged out the stove. We found nothing. Finally, in the bedroom, he opened a drawer on the dresser, and looked at everything in it. There wasn't much—a scribble pad, a telephone book, and a box of cough drops. He slid the drawer back in, paused, then pulled it out slightly and slid it in again.

"Something's wrong here." He pulled the drawer completely out and looked in the gap. "It's sticking," he said. "What's making it stick?" He reached in and felt around then smiled.

He pulled out a manila envelope, its contents bulging the folds. He opened the envelope, and pulled out wads of cash.

Turning the cash over and over in his hands, he then thumbed through the money. "Random bills, fifties and twenties, all different series, some new, some old. At a rough guess, there's around ten grand here, maybe more. Where did she get this from?"

"I think your blackmail idea might be right, Patrick," I said.

"Yeah, boss," Walsh said. "So what, she sold photos to Duncan Carroll in exchange for silence?"

"That would explain the cash, certainly," I said. "But why kill her *after* he paid her? Wouldn't it make more sense to kill her here, then just take the photos? It doesn't make sense to pay her off, kill her, but leave the photos here."

"Maybe she wasn't paid off here. Maybe she was given the cash somewhere else," Walsh said.

"Good thought. That would explain her being killed on the subway instead of here—she was bumped off rather than being paid a second, or third, or fourth time? Maybe she was milking the victim for all she could get, and he got tired of paying her."

Walsh nodded in agreement. "So, should we talk to Duncan about his girlfriend?"

"Yeah, but," I said. "Your friend Trevor here said the guy he saw looked like a skinny greaser. Duncan certainly doesn't look like that, does he?"

He sighed. "No, you're right. So was she blackmailing someone else, besides Duncan?"

"Maybe. Have we found pictures of anyone besides Duncan and Brenda?" I asked.

He shook his head. "Nope. Tell you what, let's let the forensics guys go on a scavenger hunt. I want to team up with Brian, once our airline pilot gets home, and find out what he can tell us."

"Fair enough. Look, do you want to grab lunch? After that, meet up with Webb and let me know what you two find out," I said.

"Sure. Where will you be, boss?"

"I want to take Alex with me, and speak to the people at the law firm again. I think somebody there knows what happened, and they're just not telling us."

"Okay, boss. Let's see where she is. She can join us now," Walsh said.

We called forensics and told them what we'd found, then we went down to the lobby to let the super know there was another police team coming over. We got into Walsh's car, and he picked up the radio.

"Fifty-two ten to Fifty-two four-four," he said.

A moment later Reynolds came on. "Go, ten."

"Hey, Alex, want to meet us for lunch then take DI McBriar with you?" Walsh said, leaving as much detail as possible unsaid.

"Sure, where are you?" she asked.

"On Bloor Street. We'll be at the Bloor-Jane Diner in ten. Where are you?" Walsh said.

"Brian and I were talking to the people on Collier Street. Want to discuss it at lunch?"

"Perfect. See you there." Walsh hung up the mike. "Let's eat."

Walsh parked outside the same diner he had taken me to earlier, bounded up the steps and found an empty booth. He looked around, expectantly, then saw the waitress who had spoken to him before and his face brightened. He waved to her, and she blinked recognition, grinning as she served someone on the other side of the room.

She picked up two menus and handed them to us. “Hey, Patrick,” she cooed.

“Kelly, it’s good to see you,” he said smoothly. “How’s it going?”

She grinned. “Fine. I was hoping to see you again soon. Want to go to a concert tomorrow?”

“Who’s playing?” he asked.

She rested her elbows on our table and leaned forward, staring into Walsh’s face. “The Beach Boys. They’re going to be performing at the CNE. Want to come?”

He nodded. “Wouldn’t miss it for the world. I’ll call you in the morning—we’ll make it a whole day thing, all right?”

She glanced around furtively, leaned forward and gave him a quick kiss. “Okay. See you then.” She smoothed her hips and headed back to the kitchen. Walsh watched her go, focused on her swaying hips, his mouth slightly open.

“Do you need a moment here to decompress?” I asked.

His head snapped my way. “No, no, I’ll be fine. Just a little taken aback, that’s all.”

“Taken aback by the invitation or by the kiss?” I asked.

Walsh turned to look toward the kitchen. “She is a good kisser, a really, really good kisser.”

He sat up straight and opened his menu, then looked over to see Reynolds and Webb stepping through the door. Webb was in a corduroy jacket, dark shirt and black slacks. He looked more like a male fashion model than a cop. Reynolds was talking pleasantly to him, smiling broadly and touching his arm as they walked. I waved at the empty seats across from me.

He waited for Reynolds to sit, then he sat close beside her. “Hey, boss, afternoon.”

“Alex, Brian, good afternoon,” I said. “Anything from you two?”

Webb nodded, sitting stiffly upright. “Yes, sir, we think we found something.”

“Good, Brian. And it’s Ian. Or ‘boss,’ if you’re feeling formal.”

Our waitress came back with two more menus, and Webb leaned even closer to Reynolds, discussing the food choices with her.

I could almost smell the chemistry between them, but I said nothing. Webb waved at an item on the menu, suggested they split it, and Reynolds looked up at him, agreeing with a smile.

"So, what's the good word?" I asked.

Reynolds looked up from her menu, remembering Webb's comment. "Oh, right." She pulled out her Moleskine and flipped to the page after the last one with a corner cut off. "Brian figured that Penny Lewis must live nearby, if she was walking toward the subway, so we looked up her home address. She lived just off Aylmer, on Rosedale Valley Road. We figure that, in the morning, she would walk a hundred yards from her apartment, take the overpass to Yonge Street, and get on the subway at the station near where we found her. It makes sense that our mystery man was walking with Penny Lewis, from her apartment."

"Did anyone see him walking with her, then?" I asked.

"Yeah," she said. "A janitor from a building on the route saw her walking with a guy in a track suit. He remembers because she was dressed for work, and he looked so casual. He said they were talking, and it looked like they were friendly, not like he was harassing her or anything."

Walsh scratched his head, thinking. "Okay, so, he parks his car on Collier Street, meets Penny at her apartment, walks and talks with her to the overpass, then throws her over?"

Reynolds shrugged. "Yeah, so what's the deal there? Why would he do that?"

I nodded. "The bigger question is, who is he? If we find that out, we can ask him why he did it."

"Patrick and I found something else," I said. I reached into my jacket and pulled out a small stack of photos.

"There were a whole lot of these hidden in Gwen's apartment. We also found several thousand dollars in small bills. What does that smell like to you guys?"

Webb snickered. "The bank of Kodak? Sounds like blackmail to me."

I nodded. "The forensics team is there now, doing a complete search. So, how does Penny's death fit into this?"

Our waitress brought our food out. Reynolds and Webb shared a club sandwich, picking fries off the same plate. Walsh watched them, silently, then glanced at me with a raised eyebrow.

I was reminded of the scene in 'Lady and the Tramp' where the two dogs eat the same piece of spaghetti and their noses meet. I hoped they wouldn't order one milkshake with two straws.

"So, do you think our mystery man works at the law firm?" Webb asked.

"That's the most likely scenario, don't you think?" I said. "Also, our pilot said he saw someone in a Lincoln on their street. Assuming that's our guy in a track suit, if he WAS driving a Lincoln, my guess is he's not the mail room boy. He's got to be one of the lawyers."

Over coffee, we discussed the plan for the rest of the day. I thought Walsh should work with me instead, so I told Reynolds and Webb to visit the law firm and ask if there was any office gossip that might help identify our mystery man. I also asked them to not let on that we knew about Brenda and Duncan.

Walsh and I would talk to the pilot once he got home. Until then, we would check with forensics about what they had found at Gwen Morgan's apartment.

Reynolds pushed back from the table and smiled at Webb. "Ready, Brian?"

He smiled warmly back. "Any time you are."

"I got the tab. My treat," Walsh said. He grabbed the bill and watched Webb hold the door open as Reynolds walked out. Webb held her elbow, steadying her. Walsh turned to face me.

"Could they be any more blatant?" he joked. "I mean, really."

Our waitress took Walsh's cash, then she smoothed the uniform over her hips again. "See you tomorrow, then?"

He smiled a disarming smile. "Absolutely. How about if I pick you up around nine for breakfast?"

She grinned, her cheeks dimpling. "Sure. Or if you come over earlier, I can make us breakfast."

His smile got wider. "Done. Eight thirty it is, then."

She touched his shoulder and went back to the kitchen.

We drove back to Gwen Morgan's building, parked behind two white forensics vans, and buzzed the intercom for Gwen's apartment. A moment later, a man's voice came over the speaker. "Yes?" he barked.

"DI McBriar. Okay if we come up?"

"Come on up, Ian," the voice said.

Walsh and I walked down the hall on the eleventh floor, stopped at the open door, and knocked on the door jamb. A man in a lab coat came out to meet us. "Hello, Ian, good to see you again. Congratulations to you and Karen, by the way."

"Thanks, I'll pass on your best wishes. So, what have you found?" I said.

He waved me into the apartment. "Come, I'll show you. This was hidden under some books, but not very well. I don't think she expected anyone to look for it."

He picked up a plastic sheet, a page of photo negatives, strips of film in sleeves. He handed me the sheet, then he gave me a small metal magnifying lens. "We've dusted for prints already, don't worry," he said.

I looked at the negatives on the sheet. Some were pictures of Brenda's apartment, with Brenda wandering around by herself, or Brenda talking to Duncan Carroll. Others were of Brenda on the sidewalk, taken from the park across the street. In some photos, she was walking on her own. In others, she was walking with Duncan, but on the street she stayed farther away from him, not touching him, trying to hide the fact that they were intimate. Then there were three photos that made me stop. Brenda was on the street, walking beside a man in a track suit. The photo was black and white, and it was a negative, but the suit could have been gray or silver. In one photo, she was talking pleasantly to him, walking toward the subway with him. His face was turned away from the camera, facing her. In the next photo, she was facing the camera, wagging her finger at the man, but he still had his back to the camera, his hands on his hips. In the last photo, he again had his back to the camera, but now he gripped Brenda's arm, and she was scowling, upset with him. They were pictures of an argument in progress.

I called Walsh over. "Here, Patrick, look at this."

He looked them over, going back and forth between them, peering at the negatives for any clue about the man's identity.

"How tall do you think he is?" Walsh asked.

I thought for a moment. "I saw Brenda's autopsy report. She looked to be about five feet three, five four, so I'd guess that the guy in the track suit is five eleven, five ten."

Walsh grunted. "Okay, so what do we do now, boss?"

"Let's see if our pilot is back from overseas. I want to get some traction on this case."

We parked on Collier Street, walked up to a townhouse in the middle of a row of townhouses, knocked on a gloss black door, and waited. The door opened, and a pretty woman in her late thirties opened it. She looked at Walsh and her face brightened. "Hello, Sergeant. Nice to see you again. How can I help you?"

"Mrs. Hart, hello again. Could we come in and ask you some more questions?" Walsh said.

She glanced at me. "I'm sorry, are you Sergeant Walsh's assistant?"

I grinned. "Sort of," I said. "I'm his boss, but don't tell him that."

She laughed. "I see. Please, come in, by all means."

We followed her through a narrow hallway to a back

kitchen, and she waved at some barstools. "Make yourselves comfortable. Would you like some coffee?" she asked us. It seemed an almost mechanical statement.

"Were you ever a stewardess?" I asked.

She chuckled. "It shows, does it? That's how we met. Steven was flying the Toronto to Montreal route, and we ended up in the same crew a bunch of times. The rest is history."

"I would love coffee, thanks," I said. She turned to the stove and put a kettle on an element.

There was a noise at the front door, and Walsh and I turned in unison to look. It was a man in his early forties, wearing a blue-black pilot's uniform and dragging a folding cart with a suitcase strapped to it. We both stood, and he looked up at us, surprised.

"Hello, who are you?" he asked.

"Captain Hart? We're with the police department," Walsh said.

He nodded. "This is about that Lincoln? I assume you're not here from parking enforcement."

Walsh nodded at me. "This is Inspector McBriar, and I'm Detective Sergeant Walsh. Your wife said that you mentioned seeing an unfamiliar car on your street. What can you tell us about it?"

He rolled his suitcase into the corner of the hall, hung his hat on a hook above it, and walked through to join us. "First things first."

He wrapped an arm around his wife and gave her a quick kiss. "Hello, sweets."

She blushed slightly. He turned to face us, then held out his hand. "Hi, Steve Hart."

We shook his hand. "So, Captain, what do you remember about that car?" Walsh asked.

The man reached into his inside jacket pocket and pulled out a small notebook. "Sorry, what's this about, again? My wife told me about the dead girl on the subway."

"We're trying to find out who the car belongs to. It may

be a person of interest in our ongoing investigation. What can you tell us?" Walsh asked.

The man looked at his notebook. "It was a black, two-door Lincoln, and it was blocking my garage. I loaded my luggage into my car, but by the time I opened the garage door, he was gone. That's about it, I guess."

"Do you remember what time that was?" I asked.

"Sure. Eight twenty-five. I had to be at the airport by nine thirty, so I was glad that he was gone. I didn't want to call a tow truck. The last time I had to, they took over an hour to get here, and it kept me late."

"You've had this happen before, then?" I asked.

"Yeah, once, years ago, and once last month. It was the same Lincoln last month, too."

"You're sure of that?" I asked.

"Sure. I wrote down the license plate number," he said.

Walsh smiled broadly. "Could I have that plate number, Captain?"

The man read his note. "NBY 826. I double checked. It's the same car that I called about, to get towed a month ago. He was here for over an hour that time."

The pilot's wife brought out four coffees on a tray, and we sat in the small living room. She poured cream into her husband's cup and her own then handed him his.

"Thanks, sweetheart."

"Have you lived here long?" I asked.

She nodded. "Yeah, what's it been—seven, eight years, Steve? It's a nice area, quiet, and I often volunteer at the museum, so it's easy to get to on the subway."

Walsh sipped his coffee. "Is it just the two of you, then, that live in this house?"

The woman nodded. "Very tactfully asked, Sergeant. No, we don't have children. Neither of us wanted them. What about you?"

Walsh shook his head. "I'm just getting out of a situation where I was feeling rather…confined, so no, I don't ether. Inspector McBriar is the family man here."

She put her cup down and glanced at me. "How many children do you have, Inspector?"

I chuckled. "Two and a half. I just found out about the latest addition."

She rested her clasped hands between her knees, her slacks tight around them. "What does your inquiry have to do with the poor girl who was found on the tracks?"

"I'm afraid I can't tell you much more about that. It's an ongoing investigation," I said.

The pilot leaned forward. "Can you tell us anything else? Is my wife in any danger?"

I shook my head. "We believe the deaths are connected to each other. I can't say any more than that, but I can tell you that we don't think they're random attacks, and she's not at risk."

Walsh sipped his coffee, then his head jerked up. "You said 'he.'"

The pilot frowned. "Excuse me?"

"You said that, by the time you opened your garage door, 'he was gone.' How did you know it was a 'he'?"

The pilot looked back and forth between Walsh and me, slightly puzzled. "Because I saw him, of course."

"Can you describe him?" Walsh said.

"Sure. About your height, slightly taller, maybe. He had black hair, slim build."

Walsh wrote furiously. "What was he wearing?"

"This time, he had a gray track suit. Last time, when I called the tow truck, he was in a blue three-piece suit."

"So, it was the same guy both times?" Walsh said.

"Yes, I'm sure it was."

"Was he upset with you when his car was towed? Did he talk to you, yell at you?" Walsh asked.

The pilot shook his head. "No, as I say, it took the tow truck more than an hour to get here. As a matter of fact, I was writing a nasty note to put on the man's windshield when he showed up and drove off. I had to call the tow truck back to cancel the call."

"Did you talk to him at all before he drove off?" Walsh pressed.

"Nope. I was in the front room, I saw him walk up to the car, and by the time I got to the door he had started the engine and he drove away. That's when I took down his license number."

Walsh tapped his pen against the Moleskine, thinking. "Okay. Do you have any questions, boss?"

"Yeah, did you see the car both times at the same time of day? In the morning as well?" I asked.

The pilot nodded. "I was on morning flights to Amsterdam that month. I wanted to be out of the house by eight fifteen, and it was almost a quarter to nine by the time he drove off."

I wrote everything down and pulled out a business card. "Very well, Captain. Thanks very much. If you have any questions, or if you happen to see that car again, can you call me?"

He nodded, reading the card. "Hey, are you the officer who was shot a few years back?"

"Yes, I am. I'm surprised you remember. It was five years ago, after all."

He smiled. "My cousin was your doctor. You came in to see him one day, some weeks after you'd been shot, he said. He couldn't elaborate, of course—patient confidentiality."

I chuckled. "I had brachial neuritis—nerve pain. I overrotated my shoulder, and it hurt like hell."

He tapped my business card. "I'll let you know if I hear anything."

We all shook hands, thanked the couple for coffee, and left. Walsh looked around, checking that there was nobody nearby. "So, why was he here a month ago?"

"Was he someone Penny Lewis was dating? Why else would he be there?" I said.

Walsh shook his head. "He'd park at her place overnight, or take a subway or a taxi to her place. But, he was just here for a short visit. I bet he only parked on Collier so nobody would recognize his car at her apartment."

"And he didn't know he almost got towed, so he parked there again the next time," I said.

"Yeah, that makes perfect sense, then," Walsh agreed.

"Why would he park right at Gwen Morgan's place then, assuming it's the same guy?" I asked. "Why wouldn't he park down the street from there?"

"He's getting desperate, making mistakes, taking chances because he's desperate," Walsh said.

I nodded. "Yeah, I agree. Tell you what, let's talk to Alex and Brian, and see what they've come up with."

Walsh got into his car and waited for a break in radio chatter. "Fifty-two ten to Fifty-two forty-four."

Reynolds came on a moment later. "Go, ten."

"Hey, Alex, anything to report?" Walsh asked.

"Some, Sergeant. We're going to do some more digging. Will you be around tomorrow?"

Walsh looked at me and shrugged, helpless. "I've got a date, boss."

I nodded and picked up the microphone. "Hey, Alex, it's Ian. Are you two free on Sunday?"

"Yeah, boss. Anytime you like," she said.

"Good. You and Brian can drop by my cottage, around lunch time."

There was a minute of silence. I guessed she was explaining to Webb where our cottage was. The radio crackled again. "Got it, sir. We'll be there." She almost laughed the words.

CHAPTER 22

Early Saturday morning, I made toast for me, took a bowl of cereal upstairs for Karen, and gave her breakfast in bed. She sat up and waited as I set up the bed tray on her lap.

"Here you go. Cheerio's, bananas, milk, and a small bowl of strawberries," I said. "Anything else you'd like, hon?"

She picked up a berry and put it in her mouth. "Mm. they're good. Where did you get them?"

"From a local fruit stand. I thought you might like some variety in your diet. How are they?"

She picked up more berries and put them in her mouth. "Good. I could get hooked on these."

She crooked her finger and motioned me over. "Come here, you."

I leaned in close and she pulled me toward her. She kissed me, slowly. "Hey, you. Good morning, Ian."

I smiled. "Good morning, Mommy."

Walsh was off with his all-day date. Reynolds and Webb would meet up with us tomorrow. I wanted to forget about work for the day. I suspected that Frank and Helen would drop by before lunch, to check on Karen if nothing else, so I decided to play in the kitchen.

Before I'd met Karen, just before, actually, I would make carrot cake for Frank and Helen. Karen still asked me make it for special occasions. I figured this counted as a special day, so I spent an hour shredding carrots, mixing batter and pouring the mixture into a number of cake pans.

I got all the cream cheese and butter we had together to make frosting, then I waited for the cake to cool so I could ice it.

Ethan and Charley came downstairs for breakfast. Ethan pressed his nose against the glass of the oven, watching with glee at the cakes rising in the pans. He made himself a bowl of cereal and ran down to the basement to watch cartoons.

Charley asked me for eggs with toast, specifically, and munched her breakfast, eyeing the glow of the oven light with curiosity.

"Dad?" she asked.

"Yeah, sweetheart?"

"What's that?" She pointed.

"I'm making carrot cake. You've never had it, have you?" I said.

"No. Carrots cake?" she asked, puzzled. "Yuck."

I chuckled. "No, it doesn't taste like carrots. It tastes like cake. It's yummy."

She shook her head. "Yummy cake?"

"Yes, yummy cake," I repeated.

I took a small dab of frosting and put it on a spoon for her. "Here, taste this."

She licked it onto the roof of her mouth and chewed it, uncertain. "Mmm. Yummy."

"There you go. You can have some for dessert tonight, all right?"

She nodded, finished her eggs and ran downstairs to watch cartoons with her brother.

I loaded the dishwasher, poured myself a second coffee, then flipped through the newspaper, mindlessly, not really absorbing anything. I was bothered by thoughts of the dead women. Had Gwen been killed because she was blackmailing someone? Why kill her, but still give her money? Why was Brenda killed? Did she threaten to say or do something? She was killed inside a subway car, the other two were pushed onto the tracks. That seemed to be an angry act, but Brenda's death seemed almost apologetic by comparison. Then, why kill Penny? She wasn't pregnant, and she wasn't blackmailing anyone, was she? Wait, was she?

I picked up the phone and dialed a number. The desk Sergeant answered "Fifty-two division"

"Hey, it's DI McBriar. Is DC Reynolds in the office?"

"Yeah, Ian. She's at her desk. One sec," he said.

The phone clicked and I heard it ring again. "Constable Reynolds."

"Hi, Alex. You're in early this morning," I said.

"Hey, boss. Good to hear from you. What's up?"

"Penny Lewis. Do we have any ideas on why she was killed?"

I heard paper shuffle. "Uh, no. I was looking through her apartment last night, wondering if there was anything that would give us a clue. No photos, no stacks of cash, nothing like what you and Sergeant Walsh found."

I chuckled. "You're reading my mind, Alex. I was wondering if she'd been blackmailing someone, the way we thought Gwen might be. Any money trouble, or a sudden influx of cash, nothing like that?"

"Nope. I found her bank book in her apartment. She earned thirteen thousand five hundred per year, and she paid her rent by check every month, on time. She bought groceries at the same market, twice a week, according to the receipts I found, and she didn't splurge on clothes or booze. There were only three bottles of liquor in her kitchen, mostly full."

"Very thorough. What did you and Brian find out at the law firm?" I asked.

"Does this mean no barbecue at the cottage?" she asked cautiously.

"Of course it doesn't. I'm just asking," I said.

"Okay, well, in that case, I'll tell you," she joked.

I heard more paper shuffle. "Bradley Carroll has been out of the country for the last week. He's in Michigan, working on some case or other. They weren't very forthcoming about the specifics, but it looks like he's out of the running as our bad guy."

"Did they describe him? Does he sound like our slim dark-haired guy?" I asked.

She sighed. "Yeah, but it also sounds like two of the other guys in the office. They're a stepping-stone for young lawyers, apparently. They work them hard and push them out the door."

I sighed. "So, Bradley's not our guy? Crap, and I thought we were on the right track with him."

"Yeah. Also, Sergeant Walsh told me about the car you were looking for, the Lincoln? I checked the plate number. No luck there, it's registered to some holding company, and their address is a post office box downtown. I'll do some more digging, then talk to you tomorrow, Ok, boss?"

"Fine. Don't go anywhere on your own, though. Take care, Alex."

"Got it. See you then, boss." She hung up.

Karen came downstairs, tugging on the sleeve of a sweat shirt, and went straight to the fridge for more milk. "Everything all right?"

"Yeah, Alex is a real keener, but she's also a very determined cop."

"Nice girl," Karen said. "Cute, too." She glanced quickly at me, checking my reaction.

"Yeah, she really thinks I'm cute, too," I said.

Karen's eyes burned through me, glaring at me with venom.

I laughed out loud. "Sorry, hon. I couldn't resist that. No, I don't have a 'thing' for her. I do think that Brian Webb does, though. He as much as said so."

She smirked and sipped her milk. "Sending out signals, is he?"

"Yeah, they go both ways, actually. He seems like a

smart guy. She likes him a lot. You'll meet him tomorrow, by the way."

"Tomorrow? What's tomorrow?" she asked.

"I thought I'd surprise you with a day at the cottage. We can barbecue on the back lawn, take the boat out for a spin, roast some marshmallows. What do you think?"

She thought for a moment. "All right. Sounds like fun. Does Helen know about this plan?"

"No, but she will shortly. I suspect she'll be over soon?" I said.

"Yes. She's going to drop by right after breakfast," Karen said.

She sat at the table and picked up the sections of newspaper I'd finished. "Eaton's is having a sale," she muttered. "The baby department."

I leaned forward on my elbows and kissed her softly.

"What was that for?"

"The baby department," I said. I sipped my coffee and read the paper.

I never started the paper from the front page. I started at the back and worked forward, a habit I got from my father. He always said you should read the comics and sports before the news, because it gave you a more realistic view of the world. The news always made him sad and angry, while the back of the paper would make him forget the bad news at the front.

I eventually got to the front page, and read the piece on the dead women we'd found. It was accurate, but the reporter managed to make it seem that we had not arrested someone, because we didn't know what we were doing. I was used to this, in my work. I ignored it.

CHAPTER 23

A knock at the door made me look up. Karen unfolded her leg from under her and went to answer. I heard Helen's voice, Frank's voice, and the chatter of three-year-old twins. The cacophony made its way into the kitchen, and I folded the paper up. Helen, Frank and their children streamed in. The twins headed downstairs to watch cartoons and we adults settled onto seats around the table.

"Hey, Frank, would you like something for breakfast?" I asked.

He looked at Helen. Helen scowled at him. "You're on a diet."

Frank looked sadly at me and sighed.. "I'm on a diet."

I shrugged. "Coffee, then?"

He nodded and took the mug from me.

"By the way," I said. "I was going to have a barbecue tomorrow at the cottage. Could you break your diet long enough to join us?"

Frank looked straight at me. "Believe it. We'll be there."

Karen and Helen went off into the living room, talking about work, the baby, and children in general. Frank sipped his coffee and looked out our kitchen window at the back yard.

"So, how's Karen doing?" he asked.

"Pretty good, apart from not drinking coffee. I guess she

may have different cravings and stuff later on, but so far nothing too radical."

"Have you spoken to Patrick this morning?" he asked carefully.

"No, was there something he told you that I don't know?"

He squirmed slightly. "You didn't get a call this morning, then?"

"Tell me, Frank."

"I heard from a source of mine. Those guys we put away, the ones that kidnapped Patrick? They're dead."

I went rigid. "What? How?"

"No details. I just heard that those three Marquez guys died last night in a prison fight. I thought for sure you'd have heard."

I gritted my teeth and picked up the phone. I called Walsh's pager, left my home number, and waited.

After three minutes, Walsh called me back. He sounded winded, bubbly, the old Patrick. "Hey, boss. What's up?"

"You don't know?" I said.

There was a pause. "Know? Know what?" He sounded sincere.

"The three Marquez men are dead in prison. Do you know anything about that?"

I heard fabric rustle, bed linen. Walsh's voice said, "One sec, Kelly. When did this happen, boss?" he growled.

"I just got the news from Frank. I'm going to the office and check it out. You're saying you don't know anything about this?"

"Jesus, Ian. That's not like me, you know that. I'd never be party to something like that."

I rubbed my face, frustrated. "Look, I'll be at the shop in an hour. Call me then."

"No, I'll be right over there too, boss," he said.

I told Karen I had to go in to work, threw on a clean shirt and drove to Fifty-two Division.

On this Saturday morning, the traffic was still light, and I made good time racing up Keele Street. I pulled up to my parking spot, stormed into the building, and hunted down the duty Sergeant.

He was a slim man, near the end of his career, with thin gray hair and a tired look on his face. He was walking away from me, a manila folder in one hand, a mug of coffee in the other.

"Hey!" I called out. "What do you have on my three guys from the fifty-one case?"

He stopped and turned slowly to face me, shuffling his feet carefully, protecting his injured back. "Inspector, is there a problem?" he drawled.

"My three guys that fifty-one picked up. They went to the Don Jail. What happened to them?"

He nodded. "Ah. The Marquez boys. Yeah, we just heard about that. Tough shit, huh?"

I shook my head. "I only heard about it twenty minutes ago. What happened, exactly?"

He took a sip of his coffee and opened the flap on the manila folder with one finger.

"Here you go. We just got this information sent to us." He tilted the folder, and a sheet of paper slid out into my hands. "Anything else?"

I took the paper and shook my head. He sipped his coffee again, grunted and walked away.

The message said that there had been a riot in the jail last night. A half dozen cells had been unlocked, somehow, and in the commotion, somebody had smashed the overhead lights. After that, they had gone into the three cells where the Marquez family members were being held, and all three were found dead. There were no suspects, nobody was talking.

About the time I finished reading the report, Walsh raced into the building, tucking his shirt into his jeans, pressing his hair flat with the palm of his hand.

I scowled and handed him the sheet of paper. "Well, Patrick, at the very least, I guess this saves us court time, right?" I sneered. "Any idea who could orchestrate something like this?"

He read it over, quickly, and shook his head. "Look, boss, you don't think I knew anything about this, look, you know me. I would never, ever." His voice trailed off.

"No, but what about your family? Could they set this up? Huh?"

Walsh ran his fingers through his hair, thinking desperate thoughts. "I don't know. I don't know. Look, do I think our family are a bunch of angels? No. Could I imagine them doing something like this?" He sighed. "I don't know."

I sat on the edge of a desk and drummed my fingers on the metal trim. "Okay, come with me. We're going to pay your parents a visit."

He shook his head. "No, don't ask me to do that, Ian. I *swear* to you, I had no part in this whatsoever, but please don't ask me to give my parents the third degree. I won't. I'll quit."

I stared at him for a long minute, thinking. "Fine. I believe you. All I ask is, whatever shit hits the fan, don't get in the way, all right?"

He nodded, slowly. "I'm staying completely out of the loop on this, you do realize that, right?"

I grunted assent. "Yeah, I get it, Patrick. Just keep out of the line of fire, whatever happens."

ꕥ

I drove downtown, stopped outside a familiar building on Colborne Street, and pressed the discreet buzzer on the aluminum door frame. A minute later, a voice like low thunder came through the speaker. "Yes."

"It's D I McBriar. I need to talk to Kieran Walsh."

There was a pause of almost a minute. Then the voice came back. "Come in."

The door popped open an inch, and I went through to the

elevator and up to the fourth floor. The big man, Sam, was sitting in an easy chair, reading a magazine. Kieran Walsh was at his desk, reading a thick, stapled report, writing on the margins with a glossy black fountain pen.

He looked up to see me and casually placed the cap back on the pen.

"Hello, Ian, it's good to see you again." He smiled. "To what do we owe the pleasure?"

I sat down, facing Kieran, trying to stay calm. "I just found out that the three members of the Marquez family we arrested were killed in a jailhouse riot last night."

He seemed amused. "Really? Well, I must say I'm not terribly upset by this news."

I gritted my teeth. "So you had no idea that they were going to be killed?"

He shrugged. "How could I? They were criminals, who died at the hands of other criminals. I can't say that I'm surprised, given their violent actions toward us. Did you think that I had something to do with this riot? I'm not quite that resourceful."

I was angrier now. "What could you do to those guys in jail, then?" I asked. "What did you do?"

He smiled a coy smile, one that said he knew exactly what I meant. "Sorry?"

I stood up. Sam moved silently to stand beside me, a foot behind me. I ignored him. I burned with anger. "I believe you were involved in the deaths of those men."

Sam put his hand in front of me, a rock-hard palm pressing my chest back away from Kieran.

I turned to glare at him. "Don't get in my way, Sam. I mean it, don't get in my way here."

Sam gritted his teeth, glanced at Kieran and looked at me, pleading. "Please, Mister Ian, back away. Please."

Kieran leaned forward. "Sam, I'm sure Inspector McBriar is feeling upset, but he's only doing his job. It's quite all right, Sam."

Sam pulled his hand away and took a step back, but he

stayed close enough that if I did anything to threaten Kieran he could stop me.

"Do you deny that you were aware of those deaths before I told you?" I said.

He glanced behind him and smiled. Lizzy Walsh came out of a back office. She smiled at me and touched Sam's elbow. "It's fine, Sam, I'll speak with Ian."

I could feel myself calming down, just from the sound of her voice. She took my arm and led me to the office she'd come from. She waved at a chair across from a desk. "We were just going out for brunch, but I'd like to take some time to speak with you first. Please, sit down."

I sat, mostly to be polite. She sat across from me and placed a ledger book in the desk.

"How is Karen doing? She must be excited," she said. "And you must be feeling happy, too."

"Yes, she's fine, thanks. I'll pass on your good wishes," I said, gritting my teeth. I leaned forward. "Look, I'm a cop. I need to know if you had anything to do with the death of those men in custody. Whatever I may feel for your family, whatever has gone between us personally, I still have to do my job."

She smiled softly, but there was a very subtle edge there I was unfamiliar with. "Are you asking if we were involved in this event? That is what you're asking, isn't it?"

"Were you?"

Her smile disappeared. Her face turned cold and hard, and she glared at me, an expression that I'd never seen before. "Your family was in danger last year. Patrick helped you keep them safe," she said, in a staccato tone.

I nodded. "Yes, and I will always be grateful to him for that."

She leaned forward. "Imagine if those people had gotten to your family. Imagine that they had taken Karen or Charlotte away from you. What would you have done?"

"Patrick is safe. We got him back."

She shook her head very slowly. "No, he was taken. He

was hurt, and he will never feel as safe again. Do you know what they took from him? His security. That's what they gave up. Security."

I felt a cold chill on my neck, looking at Lizzy. The warm, sweet woman I thought I knew was now a cold, hard matriarch.

"How does Karen like the car?" she asked.

"She likes it very much. I will send you a check for it tomorrow. I can't accept it as a gift."

She shook her head slowly again. "I won't cash it. If you want to, give it to the church."

I sighed, frustrated. "You can't just go around doing this to people, Lizzy. There are rules."

She picked up a slim silver letter opener and twirled it slowly in her hands, thinking. "Yes, that's true. There are rules." She pointed the letter opener at me, casually. "You have insurance against your house burning down, or your car window being broken," she said. "In a comparable way, we have insurance too. We don't need to call a broker, or have to let anyone know what happened. All we have to do…is nothing."

"What kind of insurance do you mean?" I asked, feeling very worried.

She shook her head. "In our stratum, having a family member placed in jeopardy is more than a personal crisis, it also puts everyone else like us in danger. We represent a goal which some people think is unattainable, and others think they can achieve through theft. Neither is true, of course, but for a very few people we also represent an easy target. Once Patrick went missing, certain actions were set in motion, actions *over which we had no control*, and which may have ended with the demise of those men in prison. I have no idea who or what was involved, but I know that it was for the best, for all concerned."

"That's brutal. I could never go along with something like that," I said.

"Really?" She sneered. "You and Frank constructed a

fictional version of an event five years ago, one where two people died."

I was stunned. How could she know that? How could she find out? I was suddenly feeling defensive. She looked hard at me, reading my mind.

"You also personally helped orchestrate the incarceration of Ethan's biological father, so you could adopt him. Was that ethical?"

I said nothing. Her shoulders slumped slightly, a sign of concession, and she leaned forward. "Look, Patrick is a very good detective. You've said so. He is also quite removed from our business, by the way."

I leaned back and rubbed my face. "So, you're telling me that you have no idea what happened to those men?"

She smiled slightly and raised her palms up toward the ceiling. "Can't help you, sorry."

I shook my head and stood up. "Fine. Thank you for your time. We'll let you know if there are any developments."

"You're flying to Saskatchewan on Thursday, Karen said?" she asked.

"Yes, for a memorial service," I said.

"We have a ranch in northern Alberta. I'm going out there for a week. We have room on the plane. We could drop you off in Regina. It's no trouble—it's on the way, and it's a lot more comfortable than flying coach, especially for someone in Karen's condition."

I gritted my teeth. It was a tempting offer. "I thank you, but no."

She blinked slowly. "I understand. Give Karen my best nonetheless."

I turned to leave. "I will."

"Ian?"

I turned back.

"There is a big difference between accepting a ride, and accepting a bribe. I was only offering you a ride. I hope you realize that."

Her voice was still hard, firm, but now had a hint of regret.

I smiled slightly. "Ever stand at the edge of a swimming pool?"

She nodded.

"Trouble is, if you stand at the edge long enough, you always want to jump in. I can't let myself jump in. please understand that."

She smiled, a wide, understanding smile. "You're a good man, Ian. Don't ever let go of that."

I walked back to the main part of the office. Kieran Walsh was still writing on the edges of a sheet of paper. He looked up at me. "Did you get everything you needed?"

I shrugged. "Everything I could. Thank you again for your time."

I drove home. I was angry, upset at nothing in particular, but everything in general. I carved some carrot cake for Ethan and the younger kids, then I sat in the back yard and stared at the trees for a few minutes. Frank sauntered out and sat beside me, coffee in hand, stretching out to catch the late morning sun. "Rough day?" he asked.

"Yep. Rough day," I said. "Lizzy Walsh knows about our little play with Palumbo at the furniture store. She basically told me that if I could turn a blind eye to that, I could turn a blind eye to what happened to the Marquez boys."

Frank snickered. "Hmm. Go figure." He took a sip of coffee. "Still, could be worse. If we'd gotten to Patrick too late, then we'd be in deeper shit." He leaned his head back. "So, the barbecue still on for tomorrow?"

"Sure, why not?" I said, cynically. "People die, life goes on."

Frank sat up and leaned my way. "Ian, it happens. It's not your fault. Hell, it may not even be the Walshes' fault. In the end it was the fault of those men who killed the girl and took Patrick, and they're the only ones dead. Karma."

ꞩꞩ

I wake up in an unfamiliar room. The walls, all flaking gray paint, are hard and cold. The window is a postage stamp sized piece of wired glass, and the door is metal, with bars. All at once, alarms go off, lights flash, and men in striped denim run past me, yelling and waving clubs. I hide in the bed, pressed back against the wall, hoping nobody sees me. The door to the room opens, and Sam walks in. He looms over me, a knife in his hand. "Sorry about this," he booms.

ઙઙ

I woke up, sweating. The room was cool, the open window letting in the breeze from the back yard, but I was soaked in sweat. I sat up and rubbed my face.

"Are you all right?" Karen asked softly.

"Yeah, bad dream, that's all," I said.

I looked at the alarm clock. Six thirty—time to get moving. I got to Immaculate Conception Church by seven, and sat through the early mass, thinking about the dead men in jail. I said a prayer for them.

By nine o clock, I was back home, out of my suit and loading the trunk of the Parisienne with food for the cottage. Karen insisted on going in her car. I didn't relate the discussion I'd had with Lizzy Walsh. She didn't need the grief.

She drove north, Ethan beside her, Charley sitting beside me, and I forced myself to relax and not think about work for a day.

It was a glorious day, warm, with only a hint of breeze, and soft puffy clouds dotting the sky, like only Southern Ontario could produce. By ten thirty, Ethan had set up a pup tent on the back lawn, Charley was playing with a doll on the back porch, and our speedboat was out and set up to take us on an after-lunch tour of the scattered islands off the shore. I had, for a precious few hours, put work out of my mind. Frank and Helen showed up around eleven, their twins merging with Charley as one mass of squeals, chatter, and flying toys.

I had soaked corn cobs for the barbecue, burger patties were in a cooler, and all the other things I needed were at the ready. Frank mooched some fries when Helen pretended to not see, and we talked about kids, babies, and nothing in particular.

Patrick showed up with his friend Kelly, looking unsure of herself, but within minutes we were all talking and joking like we always did.

Just before noon, Reynolds and Webb showed up in a red convertible, dressed casually, and looking like a couple. We set up folding tables and draped them with cloths, then had a semi-formal barbecue on the back grass. A few passing boaters waved and gawked, curious at what the special occasion must be.

We waved back and kept eating.

Webb was sitting beside Reynolds. He leaned forward, past her, and commented on the food. His hand went onto her thigh, rubbing it as he spoke. I'm sure he didn't know I'd seen it. Reynolds turned to ask him something, her breast rubbing against his arm. She didn't think I'd seen that, either.

Walsh stopped partway through a bite of burger as Kelly asked him a question. He looked into her eyes, nodded, and answered. It was the same look I gave Karen sometimes. I felt warm inside, just seeing that. It made the events of the past week seem far away.

Webb said something, and Walsh asked him to repeat it. That got my attention.

"What was that?" I asked.

Webb nodded. "I was just saying, we were in Bradley Carroll's office, but he wasn't there. He'll be back tomorrow, though. He's been in Flint, Michigan for the last two weeks."

"Right. And?" I said.

Webb patted his mouth dry. "Oh, he has an airplane

model on his desk. It's like the one I just saw going overhead." He pointed up.

I only saw a white blur, streaking away to the north. "I see. He likes airplanes, then?"

"Yeah, boss," Reynolds said. "He flies them, too. That's why he's in Michigan, doing some deal with an aircraft distributor."

I grunted. "Hmm. I thought it had something to do with the pilot we interviewed, my mistake."

After lunch, we took turns weaving along the edge of the lake in the speedboat, or just sitting on the dock and dangling our feet in the water.

Reynolds and Webb stayed close to each other, and by the end of the day they didn't seem to mind if I caught them being familiar. She sat on the edge of the dock, bumping his shoulder with hers as they talked. He put his hand on her back, stroking it softly as they spoke. They smiled a lot.

The sun went down over the roof of the cottage, the shadows longer and the warm afternoon getting cool. I took a deep breath. *Remember this feeling*, I told myself. *Remember how this moment feels*. The shadow of the cottage crept higher, the lawn got darker, and at the point where the sun's light still shone, dragonflies darted in and out of the light, appearing and disappearing as if by magic.

We all packed up, closed up the cottage, stored the boat in its shed, and formed a convoy that left the lake again, back to our lives in the city. Karen tucked the children into bed, turned out all the lights upstairs and slid under the sheets beside me. She gave me a long kiss and looked at my face. In the light from the outside streetlamp, I could see her eyes, reading my expression.

"What?" I asked.

"You don't want me anymore?" she asked me.

"What do you mean?"

She slid a hand into my boxers. "It's Sunday night. Tomorrow you go back to work, so let's start the week with a bang."

I pulled my head back. “But you’re pregnant.”

“So? I’m not made of porcelain, Ian. It’s all right.”

She slid her hands under my tee shirt and peeled it up. She sat up on all fours and slung one leg over me. “There. Does that make you feel better? I’ll be on top.”

I grinned broadly, tucked my hands under her armpits, and held her up. “I’ll help.”

ଓଓ

A half hour later, I crept downstairs, poured two glasses of ginger ale and came back up. Both children were fast asleep, snoring quietly.

Karen was on her stomach, her head on her hands, waiting patiently for me to get back. She sat up, her nude top sweaty, glistening in the pale light, and sat cross-legged as she sipped the ginger ale.

She rolled the glass back and forth between her hands, clearly thinking. “So, do you think it will be a boy or another girl?”

I shook my head. “I don’t care, as long as it’s healthy. Either is fine by me.”

She took a sip of her drink. “Do you think it will have black hair, like you, or lighter hair, like Ethan and Charlotte?”

I chuckled. “Either is fine. In any case, I’m sure he or she will have brown eyes, just like us.”

She put the glass down and slid under the sheets. “Do you have any names in mind?”

“Stuart for a boy, Margaret for a girl, after our middle names, how’s that?” I said.

I slid down beside her. She put her arm over my chest. “Sounds good,” she said. She fell asleep.

Chapter 24

Monday morning, I was dressed for work at seven in the morning. I made a small pot of coffee, brought a bowl of cereal up to Karen, and went back downstairs to drink my coffee.

Karen came downstairs a few minutes later, gave me a 'good morning' kiss and poured herself a glass of milk. "So, what do you have on for today?"

"Usual Monday," I said. "We have Captain Hook's rah-rah meeting, then I'm going to see what we have on the subway case. We've been getting hammered in the papers, and our receptionist has spent hours blocking reporters on the phone."

I strapped my holster on, clipped my tie to my shirt, and got in my car. I drove to Fifty-two Division, listened to the radio chatter, and parked at my spot.

I got to my desk, accepted the cup of coffee offered, and read through the telephone message slips from the weekend. I looked at my watch—eight thirty-five. The usual Monday meeting would start in twenty-five minutes. Out of the corner of my eye, I saw Martin Van Hoeke wave at me. He crooked a finger and went into his office. I followed him in.

"Hi, Captain, what's up?" I asked.

He sat on the edge on his desk. "So, it looks like the inquest may be just a formality, now that the other men are dead."

"Really?" I said. "Not that I'm complaining, but we still have to clear that up, don't we?"

He shook his head. "It was 'you said, they said,' but now it's 'you, Frank, and Patrick said.' They're dead. There's no point in wasting court time, after all."

I grinned. "That's the second-best news I've heard this week. Thanks, Captain."

"You're welcome. Rebecca wants to know if Karen is feeling well. I've been asked to report back."

"She's fine. Rebecca can call her. I'm sure she'd appreciate the call."

Van Hoeke stood and picked up a piece of paper from his desk. "You know, I think I'll take it easy this morning. Why don't you take the meeting for a change?" He handed me the paper.

I read it over. "All right. Trial by fire, I get it."

At nine, I stood in the middle of the room and bellowed out "Can I have your attention?"

The rumble of voices and shuffling paper stopped suddenly.

"I'm giving the meeting details this morning," I said. I ran through the open cases, the ongoing investigations, and stopped for comments and questions. I held off on the subway murders, waited till everyone had made notes about their work, then I put the piece of paper down.

"As you all know, we're getting hammered on the transit killings. The press is going after us, the TV stations have been slamming the TTC, and we're getting crank calls left and right," I started.

"That said, here's what we know for sure so far. The first victim, Brenda Grant, was two months pregnant. Whether that was the reason she was killed, we can only guess. The second victim, Gwen Morgan, lived near Brenda, and they knew each other. Gwen had taken photos of Brenda at home with her boss, a married lawyer called Duncan Carroll. She also had several thousand dollars in small bills stashed in her apartment. Now, Gwen also took photos of Brenda on the street, in the company of a man matching the description of a man seen at Gwen's apartment. That's another point they have in common.

"That brings us to the third victim, Penny Lewis. She worked at the same law firm as Brenda and Duncan, and she called us, offering to keep us informed. She was thrown off the Aylmer Avenue overpass shortly after that. The man seen throwing her over fits the same description as the man seen with Gwen Morgan, and talking to Brenda on the street. That's common point number three connecting the victims. We think he drove a black Continental, license number NBY 826. I'll have case notes copied for you all, feel free to ask. So, boys and girls, we need to find this man. If he isn't guilty of all three murders, he certainly must know who is. That's all. Any questions?"

A low rumble came over the room as they talked amongst themselves. A hand went up.

"Hey, do we have a better description of this guy?"

"Five ten, skinny, black hair. A witness said we're looking for John Travolta," I said. There was a smattering of laughter. Another hand went up.

"Did he wear a white suit?" one man asked.

I grinned. "Gray or silver track suit, we think."

"What about eye color, moustache, other features?" he continued.

I shook my head. "No other information known. Let's see what you can come up with."

A different hand went up. "How's Karen doing?" he asked.

The men and women in the room whooped and catcalled. I bowed, ceremonially, and pointed to the man. "She's well, thanks. I will pass on all your best wishes."

"Boy or girl?" the man asked.

I thought for a moment. "Yes. Now, get to work." I waved my arms and they dispersed, off to their desks and cars. Van Hoeke appeared from nowhere and sat on a desk beside me.

"How did that feel?" he asked. "Could you get used to doing that?"

"Yeah, it felt natural," I said. "Still, I won't decide till I get back from Saskatchewan."

"You're leaving Wednesday, right?" he asked.

"Thursday morning. I changed my flight. I'd like as much time on this case as possible."

"I understand the Walsh's offered to fly you out to Regina. You were wise to not accept, it could be seen as a bribe."

"That's what I said. It's tempting, though, to catch a ride whenever you feel like it."

He smiled. "I agree. Still, there is no such thing as a free flight."

I sat back. Something clicked for me, that hadn't made sense before. "My daughter has dark hair. Karen has dark hair, same as I do. We both have brown eyes. So does Charlotte."

Van Hoeke shook his head. "I don't understand."

"I think I know why the women were killed," I said.

I called Walsh, Webb and Reynolds together. We drove in two cars to the Carroll's law office, then Webb and Reynolds sat in the lobby, and Walsh and I went through into the main office.

A door marked 'Bradley Carroll' was open. Bradley was inside. I assumed it was Bradley, I'd never seen him in person, but he looked like the man in the photos Gwen took.

I walked in as he was telling a funny story to a secretary. He was leaning back in his chair, waving a pen in one hand and watching her legs as he spoke. He saw me come in with Walsh and sat up. His face went hard, his lip curled and he pointed the pen at me.

"How *dare* you walk in here without an appointment? Get out right now."

I didn't blink. "You're Bradley Carroll? We have a number of questions for you."

He shook his head. "If you're not here to arrest me, go

away. There's no law that says I have to talk to you."

"Yes, you would know that. You're a *lawyer.*" I sneered the last word. "You also know that I can arrest you if I feel you're hindering an investigation. What's it going to be, Mister Carroll?"

He slapped the pen on the desk, linked his hands behind his back and leaned back. He blinked, slowly, a sign that he was showing disrespect. "Shelley, could you leave us, please?" he said. The secretary left. His brown eyes looked bored, disinterested. "All right, what do you want?"

"You were in Michigan for the last two weeks?" I asked.

"Yes."

"Where, exactly?"

"Flint. Flint, Michigan." He said it as though it was unlikely for me to know where Flint was.

"You specialize in corporate aircraft law, I understand?"

"No, I just like airplanes," he said. He tapped the aircraft model Webb had mentioned.

"That's very pretty. What kind of plane is it?" I asked.

His shoulders softened slightly as he relaxed. He clearly was going to talk about a favorite subject now. "This is a Mooney 201. It's a real rocket. It takes a lot of skill to fly it, though."

"Wow, so it's fast, is it?" I asked.

He grinned. "Yes. Over two hundred miles an hour at cruise, hence the name."

My smile disappeared. "So, it would get from Flint to here in what, just over an hour?"

His grin faded, and he slowly sat up straight. "That's it. This conversation just ended."

I shook my head. "Nope, it doesn't work that way. Your mother has blue eyes. Your father has blue eyes. Blue eyes are a recessive trait, but you have brown eyes. Why is that?"

He smirked and wagged a finger at me. "Very good. My real father died when I was two. My mother married Duncan, and he adopted me. That's not a crime now, is it?"

"No, it's not. Did you know that Brenda Grant was pregnant?"

His expression didn't change, but his jaw tightened. "No, I had no idea."

"No? Does it surprise you that she was pregnant?"

He paused for a moment. "Yes, I suppose it does."

"Anything you want to ask me about that?"

He looked down at the desk and shook his head. "No, not that I can think of."

"Funny. Most people would ask if we knew who the father was. That is, most people would want to know, unless they already knew." I stared at him.

A set of footsteps, heavy despite the thick carpeting, came around the corner and into the office. I kept my eyes on Bradley, but Walsh turned to look.

"You're Mrs. Carroll? Evelyn Carroll?" Walsh said.

She walked behind Bradley's chair and swung it around. She grabbed his arm and tried to pull him up. "Come, we're leaving. You don't have to sit here and listen to this." She turned to me, her face angry and terrified. "He hasn't done anything. You can't do this to him, he hasn't done anything."

I shook my head. I didn't feel pity, or remorse. I just wanted to talk. "We have photos of him with Brenda Grant. We also have a witness that saw him with Gwen Morgan. If we find his fingerprints in Gwen's apartment, we'll have enough to tear his life apart. All we need is to prove that he flew one of his client's planes back from Michigan last week, and we can connect the dots. We can charge him with the deaths of both women. After that, getting him for the murder of Penny Lewis will be easy."

I was holding back some details. I didn't want to show my hand yet. Evelyn looked up at the ceiling and ran her fingers through her short hair, desperately trying to find a way out.

"Look, it was me," she said. "I'm sorry, it was me. Brad had nothing to do with it. I was guilty of it, all of it."

I opened my notebook. "June seventh, where were you, Bradley?"

He glanced at his mother. She smiled softly and nodded, giving him permission to say something. "I was in Tennessee all that week," he said, with certainty. "You can check with the Mooney dealer outside Nashville. I was with them all week—I never left Tennessee. I couldn't have killed Brenda."

"No, you didn't. Someone else did," I said.

Another set of footsteps came up, louder, heavier. Duncan Carroll stormed into the room. He stood at the doorway, his mouth open, looking at all of us, disbelieving. He shook his head and growled. "What the hell is going on here?"

"I'm about to charge Bradley with murder," I said. "He killed Gwen Morgan, and we believe he killed Brenda Grant, or he had her killed."

Duncan's mouth opened and closed silently, as he took this all in. He turned to look at his wife. His face went red. "But Brenda was killed by a mugger, you said. You told me that she was *mugged*."

His wife's face wrinkled up in pain. She gulped, her eyes filling with tears. "You were going to leave me! You were going to run off with that little tramp, you fool! I spent my life building this firm, and you were going to throw it all away on that little tart! I had to do it!"

His mouth stayed open, incredulous. "She was going to have my child," he whispered. "I was going to be a father. Finally, after all these years, I was going to be a *father*." His expression changed to rage. "You stupid bitch! You stupid, stupid, bitch! I wasn't going to leave you, Evelyn. I was going to send her away, that's all. I was going to send her away and take care of the child," he moaned, despondent. "I was going to send her away."

His wife cleared her throat, smoothed her skirt and turned to look at me, all business. "Well, there you have it, Inspector. Take me away. I'll get my jacket."

I shook my head. “Sorry, but Bradley will have to come with us too.”

She glanced down at him then looked at me. “But why? I’ve confessed. I killed both of those girls. I did it. Take me.”

“Nope. He was seen throwing Penny Lewis off the Aylmer Avenue overpass. He wore a track suit, and I know we’ll find fibers from that track suit on Penny’s body, and in Bradley’s Lincoln. Beyond that, he was seen running back to his car after he killed her. We have you both.”

Bradley shook his head. “You can’t prove any of this. You’re bluffing. You’re just trying to railroad me.”

I spread out my arms. “Try this. Gwen Morgan knew Brenda. She could see into Brenda’s apartment from her place. She had a camera with a long lens that took photos of your father with Brenda—I’ve seen them, by the way—and she blackmailed you, cash in exchange for them.”

He shrank back and shot a quick look at his mother.

“So you and your mother decided to clean up the mess once and for all, I continued. “She got rid of Brenda when you were out of town, giving you an alibi, and you got rid of Gwen when you thought she’d given you all the photos and negatives. The building super saw you fighting with her in the hall. He assumed it was a lover’s quarrel, but it was a business negotiation, wasn’t it? What you didn’t know was that she had copies of all the photos, *and other negatives*, hidden in her apartment. So you paid her off, three, four times, and when you thought she’d turned over everything she had on you, you pushed her onto the tracks as she was heading home one morning. How am I doing so far?”

Bradley and his mother said nothing. That told me I was right. Walsh leaned forward.

“Boss, what about Penny?”

“Bradley’s car was seen in the same area a month ago. I thought he was having an affair with Penny, but when I remembered how she talked about him, I realized that probably wasn’t the case. She was smitten with him, but she wasn't sleeping with him. If I had to guess, I'd say that you went to see her a month ago, stopped by her apartment in the morning, and said something like 'I was in the area, do you want a ride to work'? You had left your car on Collier Street, and when she agreed to the ride, you went back for it. Then you talked to her on the drive, and you realized she didn't know anything. Last week, something she said or did made you think that she knew what you'd done. You dropped by her place again and said something like 'my car broke down, let's walk to the subway together.' Then you threw her over the railing."

He gulped and stayed perfectly still. I nodded. "I'm right, aren't I? We found spots on the railing where she clawed at the metal, and where she tried to get a footing to climb back up. I get the impression that if we check your arms for scratches, we'll find her fingernails left some marks."

He looked at his sleeves, unconsciously. "You don't understand, I had to do it."

His mother gritted her teeth. "Shut *up,* Brad. Say nothing."

"It's too late. We've got you both," I said. "You know the biggest laugh in this whole mess? If you'd done nothing, it would have all gone away. Now, you're both going to jail, and your office will have to close anyway."

Duncan stepped forward. "Listen, isn't there something we can do here? We don't have to go through a whole sordid trial, do we? We can come to some sort of understanding?"

"What?" I asked. "Look the other way, let them disappear to Brazil, what? Now that you've lost your girlfriend and your wife, you're just trying to save the practice as a last resort?"

He glared at me. I shook my head. "Sorry, I've given out all my 'look the other way' tickets for this week. Let's go."

Webb and Reynolds took Evelyn Carroll in their car, and Walsh sat in the back of our car with Bradley. We processed them, had them sign statements, and put them in holding cells.

I went back to Fifty-two and collected the papers to hand the case over while I went to Saskatchewan. Van Hoeke walked out of his office and sat on the chair across from me.

"You can be really psychic sometimes, Ian, you know that?" he said. "How did you know why they did it?"

I smiled. "Charlotte's eyes. I remembered that both Carroll and his wife are blond, but their son is dark-haired. For Charlotte both Karen and I have brown eyes, so she has brown eyes. Bradley has two blue-eyed parents, but he was described as dark-featured, so the rest fell into place."

He shook his head. "And you did it with three days to spare. Go home, Ian. Rest up, pack, whatever. You earned it."

I leaned back and sighed. I was exhausted. "Yeah, Martin, you're right. I need the time to relax."

"Will Karen and the kids join you in Manitoba?" he asked.

"Saskatchewan."

"Sorry, Saskatchewan," he said.

"Yeah, in a couple of weeks. Karen has a couple of doctor's appointments she doesn't want to miss, and it gives me time to touch base with the old place before she gets there."

He nodded. "Good. By the way, the radio stations have already spread the news that the subway is safe again. Well done, Ian."

I grinned and handed him my case files. "Want anything from Esterhazy?"

"I dunno, what's it famous for?"

"Potash and a fake Hungarian Count," I said.

He threw his arms up. "Bring me back a cowboy hat."

I drove home, listening to the police radio. I pulled into my driveway beside the Parisienne, and waited a moment before I shut down. The last three weeks had been draining, exhausting. There had been seven deaths, and the waste of life saddened me.

From the house I heard Karen calling to Ethan and Charley. That, and the thought of our new child, lifted my spirit. There was a pause in the radio chatter, so I picked up the microphone.

"Fifty-two zero six to dispatch," I said.

"Go, zero six," came the answer.

"Zero six, any messages?"

There was a short pause. "Yeah, Ian. Bon voyage."

I chuckled. "Thanks, Nadine. Zero six out."

The End.

About the Author

Mauro Azzano was born in Italy, north of Venice. He grew up in Italy, Australia and finally Canada, settling on the west coast outside Vancouver, Canada. He has a broad experience to call on as a writer, having worked as a college instructor, commercial pilot and a number of other unusual occupations. Currently, he is working on the Ian McBriar Murder Mystery series and training as a distance runner.